Little Red Riding Hood

TJ Rose

Proofreading by SJ Buckley

Cover art by Lina Ganef

Map by Amanda Meuwissen

CONTENTS

FOREWORD

Welcome! Little Red Riding Hood is an MM fairytale retelling, set in the world of the GriMM Tales. Please heed the following content warnings:

- explicit adult content

- main character with poor self-esteem, brief references to suicidal thoughts

- giant spiders (present for two pages)

- mild gore, including hunting of animals

- mild fantasy racism/classism

- set during a time of famine (background context rather than plot driver)

I hope you enjoy the book—I adore twisted fairytales, and I had such a fantastic time crafting Red and Wim's adventure! **Note: this book is written in British English.**

— TJ Rose

Varinien
Hallin
Hallin Castle
Cinder's Estate
Frog Prince's Lair
N
W
E
S
The GriMM Tales

Falchovari
Evil Queen's Castle
(Rumpelstilzchen's Haunting Grounds)
Shoemaker's Shop
Pied Pipers Music Shop
Sorcerer's Tower
Dark Forest
The Candy House
Miners' House
Mines
Old Oma's House

- "The wolf thought to himself, 'What a tender young creature! What a nice plump mouthful...'"
—Brothers Grimm, Little Red Riding Hood

One

Once upon a time, in a kingdom where shadows danced beneath ancient trees, a young man named Red ventured through the forest. On this moonless eve, he travelled deep into the woods, his tread hushed by the dense blanket of autumn's castoffs.

Red pulled his crimson riding hood tighter around his slender frame, seeking warmth against the biting chill. The worn fabric, soft from decades of wear, was his most treasured possession—a constant reminder of the mother he'd never known.

He trudged onwards, his eyes darting between the gnarled trunks. The forest seemed to close in, branches reaching out like grasping fingers. He shivered, not entirely from the cold.

A twig snapped.

Red froze, his breath catching in his throat. He peered into the inky darkness, straining to see beyond the veil of night.

Nothing.

He shook his head, chuckling nervously. "You're a fool, Red. A damned fool," he muttered, resuming his journey with quickened steps.

But the feeling of being watched persisted, prickling the back of his neck. Red's fingers twitched, seeking the familiar weight of his bow, presently strapped to his back in its quiver.

Another sound—a rustle of leaves, too deliberate to be the wind.

Red's heart thundered in his chest. He spun, searching for the source. "Who's there?" he demanded, his voice sharp with false bravado.

Silence answered, heavy and oppressive.

He turned back, only to halt abruptly. There, in the gloom ahead, two pinpricks of amber light gleamed. They blinked, and Red's blood ran cold.

Eyes. Watching him.

Red's breath caught in his throat as he stared into those magnificent eyes. They seemed to glow with an otherworldly light, drawing him in despite his terror. He couldn't look away, couldn't move, couldn't even blink.

Golden irises vanished behind dark lids, reappearing with predatory intent. Red's breath hitched, gooseflesh prickling along his arms beneath his cloak.

"W-who's there?" he called out, cursing the tremble in his voice. He cleared his throat, trying to summon the haughty tone usually so naturally deployed. "Show yourself, you coward!"

A low rumble answered him. Not quite a growl, but something deeper, more primal. The sound vibrated through the air, sending leaves quivering on their branches.

Red's heart hammered against his ribs. He took a step back, foliage crunching beneath his feet. The eyes followed his movement, never wavering.

"I'm warning you," Red said, steadier now, fuelled by desperation. "I'm armed and I know how to use my weapon."

The eyes narrowed, and Red could have sworn he saw amusement in their depths. Another rumble, this one almost like a chuckle, echoed through the trees.

Red's fear gave way to indignation. How dare this... whatever it was... laugh at him? He was Red, the Queen's second-best archer, feared and respected throughout the Kingdom of Falchovari. Well, throughout *some* of the kingdom, at least. Maybe. Regardless, he wouldn't be mocked by some beast in the woods.

"Right, that's it," he snapped, reaching for his bow. "You asked for this, you mangy—"

But before he could nock an arrow, the eyes moved. They rose higher, then higher still, until they towered above him. Red's mouth went dry as he realised just how massive the creature before him was.

A shape formed around those burning eyes. Broad shoulders, powerful limbs, a muzzle filled with gleaming teeth. The beast stepped forward, moonlight filtering through the canopy to reveal dark grey fur and gigantic paws.

Red's fingers went slack on his bow. He'd heard tales of the great wolves that roamed these woods, but he'd always dismissed them as fairy tales. As he stood there, heart racing, he realised just how unprepared he truly was.

His prowess as a hunter extended no further than wild swine, though such prizes had become as elusive as mythical beasts of late. Panic clawed at him—what was he even doing out here? He'd fancied himself as a fearsome adventurer, yet here he was, a child playing at being brave in a world far too dangerous for him.

The wolf tilted its head, regarding Red with those deep orange pools that seemed to see right through him, stripping away his defences and leaving him bare.

In them, Red saw something. Something unsettling. Something... hungry. Something... human?

Red's hand trembled as he reached for his bow, but before he could grasp it, the beast burst from the shadows, lunging towards him, its jaws snapping mere inches from Red's face. He stumbled backwards, tripping over a gnarled root and crashing to the forest floor. The impact knocked the breath from his lungs, leaving him gasping. Even more tragically, it knocked his bow from his hands, sending it flying across the forest floor to be devoured by the shadows.

The beast loomed over him, its hot breath ghosting across Red's skin. He scrambled backwards, leaves and twigs catching in his long hair and cloak.

"Stay back, monster!" Red shouted. He fumbled for a rock, anything to defend himself.

The wolf growled, low and menacing. It stalked forward, muscles rippling beneath its thick grey coat. Blood rushed through Red's ears as the predator's bulk eclipsed the moonlight. He shrank back, the rough bark scoring his palms as he flattened himself against the ancient oak. *Fuck.* He was trapped. Those smouldering golden eyes bored into him, stripping away his confidence until all that remained was a trembling husk of a boy.

The wolf tensed to spring. Then a deep, gravelly voice cut through the night.

"Well now. Don't you smell delicious?"

Red blinked. Had he gone mad with fright? But the wolf had paused, its amber eyes now filled with an unsettling intelligence.

"Did you... speak?" Red whispered, scarcely believing his own words.

"Aye, I did," the wolf rumbled, as rough as tree bark. "Name's Wilhelm. Though most call me Wim."

A wolf is talking to me. A wolf that wants to eat me is talking to me, and telling me his name.

Red gaped for a moment before clamping his mouth shut, his mind reeling. He stared at the wolf. "You're... you're a..."

"A wildling. A shapeshifter," Wim the wolf finished, a hint of amusement in his tone. "And you, little one, smell delicious."

The beast's hot breath washed over Red's face, carrying the scent of earth and something primal.

"D-delicious?" Red stammered, in barely a whisper. "Me? I'm not... I mean, you surely don't mean to..."

The wolf's lips curled back, revealing rows of razor-sharp teeth. His eyes seemed to glow brighter, filled with a vicious hunger that sent chills down Red's spine.

"Oh, but I can," he growled, tone deepening to a guttural rumble. "And I will."

The wolf lunged forward, jaws snapping inches from Red's throat. Red yelped and tried to scramble away, but his back was pressed firmly against the tree. There was nowhere to run.

The creature's massive paw pinned Red's shoulder, claws digging into his flesh through the fabric of his cloak. Red whimpered, terror coursing through his veins as the wolf's muzzle pressed against his neck, inhaling deeply.

"Aye, you'll make quite the tasty snack."

This was how he was to die? Alone in the woods, mutilated by an animal? Would anyone mourn him, back at the palace? Would they even bother to send a search party?

"Tasty snack? I am but skin and bones! Please!" Red begged, tears stinging his eyes. "Don't—"

But the wolf wasn't listening. His eyes had taken on a feral gleam, all traces of humanity vanishing. He snarled, saliva dripping from his jaws as he pressed closer, teeth grazing Red's skin.

Red squeezed his eyes shut, waiting for the inevitable pain of those fangs tearing into his flesh.

Suddenly he had one of his flashes of brilliance.

"Wait!"

The wolf paused, his breath hot against Red's face.

"How about instead of one tasty snack, I offer you two?"

A low rumble in reply. The beast stepped backwards, creating an inch of space between them.

"Go on."

"Earlier this eve, I spied two idiots following the river. The bumbling fools have clearly never ventured through the forest before." Neither had Red, but he was pulling off the feat quite nicely. For the most part.

The beast did not look convinced.

"Two young men. They would make for a far more delicious meal than me! Their flesh looked supple and... juicy! And they're... as fat as pigs!" he invented. "Rolls and rolls of meat, ready for the munching!"

It was partially true; the two men had been attractive. The gloriously tall redhead with the gorgeous scruff of beard—who his companion had called Hansel—had looked particularly scrumptious to Red.

"The tall one... his thighs looked especially biteable. You wouldn't want to miss out on him." Red wouldn't have minded a taste of them himself, come to think of it.

The wolf leaned forward to graze his muzzle against Red's cheek. "Aye, might be I'll feast three times tonight."

Red swallowed, his throat dry as parchment. He desperately searched for a reason that might save his skin. "You don't know which direction they went! West or east. I never said."

"Their trail will be strong. I'll find it easily enough."

"But... why risk it? Oh, and did I mention one of them was carrying a rabbit?"

At the mention of the word 'rabbit,' the wolf's ears perked up. His orb-like eyes gleamed with interest, and a fragile spark of hope ignited in Red's chest.

"A rabbit, eh?" he rumbled, low and considering. "Fresh kill, not rotted by the forest?"

Red nodded eagerly, seizing upon this thread of possibility. "Yes, freshly caught. Plump and tender, I'd wager. Far more appetising than my scrawny frame, wouldn't you agree?"

The wolf's gaze roved over Red's body, as if reassessing his potential as a meal. Red held his breath.

"Aye, have it your way," the beast snarled. "But mark me well... if my belly isn't full after, I'm coming for you next. It won't matter if you walk one mile or ten. Make no mistake. I'll hunt you down." The terrifying creature leaned in, his toothy mouth pressing directly into Red's ear. "Because you, boy, have the most uniquely delicious scent I've ever smelled."

"You won't be hungry," Red promised, with as much conviction as he could muster.

"Aye, you've no idea how deep my hunger runs. 'Specially when there's such sweet prey before me."

Then, the beast *winked*.

He raked his wolfish eyes over the length of Red's body. "By the way. You should know that I *always* play with my food."

Red's heart pounded like a drum as the creature's words echoed in his ears. The wolf's hot breath lingered on his skin, sending a shiver down his spine. A shiver of... terror? Partially maybe, but also... something else.

For a moment, neither moved.

Then, with a low growl, the wolf stepped back. His eyes never left Red's face as he retreated into the shadows. The massive grey form melted into the darkness, leaving only the fading sound of rustling leaves in his wake.

Red remained frozen against the tree, scarcely daring to breathe. He strained his ears, listening for any sign of the wolf's return. But the forest had fallen silent, as if holding its breath along with him.

"Well, great job, Red," he muttered. "Three days into the journey and you've run out of rations, gotten lost twice, and now you've attracted the attention of a wolf that wants to tear you apart, possibly in more ways than one. Really, Red, you may as well lie down here and wait to die."

The forest around him seemed to mock his predicament, the rustling leaves sounding suspiciously like laughter.

When Queen Schön had called him into the throne room to announce his royal quest, he couldn't believe his luck. Finally, a chance to prove himself, to escape his mundane life locked in the palace, to have an *adventure*, just like the storybooks. But now, rationless and likely to become wolf food, he was rather missing the safe comfort of his attic bedroom.

Adventuring was not what he'd imagined, so far.

But there was no choice but to press on. He had to complete the Queen's instructions.

Like everything else in his life, the choice had been made for him.

For one mad moment, Red pictured himself refusing the Queen—telling her that he wasn't going. Though he supposed it would be hard to appreciate her expression once his head had parted ways with his shoulders.

The wind picked up, roaring a howl, and Red shivered.

Who knew the forest could get so damned cold at night? Not Red.

He pushed himself off the tree, wincing as his muscles protested. The encounter with 'Wim' had left him shaken, but he couldn't afford to linger. He needed to move, to put as much distance between himself and the wolf as possible.

Red took a tentative step forward, then another. His legs felt like jelly, but he forced himself to keep going. He scanned the forest floor, searching for his bow. It had to be here somewhere...

A glint of moonlight caught his eye. There, half hidden beneath a pile of leaves, was his precious weapon. Red snatched it up and clutched it to his chest like a lifeline. A small measure of his confidence returned.

He set off through the trees, his steps quick and light. Every shadow seemed to hide a threat, every rustle of leaves a potential predator. Red's eyes darted from side to side, his body tense and ready to flee at the slightest provocation.

Red's mind whirred, replaying the conversation he'd had with the wolf. Thank goodness he'd seen those two young men earlier. However, he'd certainly embellished a fair bit. The pair of them looked even skinnier than he did—which made sense, as they looked to be commoners, and Red at least had access to the palace kitchen scraps.

Would the wolf come back, angrier and hungrier than before?

And what had he meant by 'playing with his food?' Reading people was one of Red's strengths, and he wielded it like a weapon. But his powers of intuition didn't quite reach to deducing the words of wolves, apparently.

Regardless, the memory of those amber eyes raking over his body wasn't entirely unpleasant...

This is the starvation talking.

Red shook his head, trying to clear it of such dangerous thoughts. He needed to focus on survival, not... whatever that was.

He pushed on through the night, determined to lose the predator in the depths of the forest. But no matter how far he walked, he couldn't shake the feeling that those eyes were still watching him, waiting for the perfect moment to strike.

Two

Red's hands shook, slivers of ice digging into his skin as he fruitlessly struck stone against flint. The gnawing cold consumed him, seeping beneath his thin cloak and settling in his bones. He cursed the insubordinate sparks, his breath misting in the glacial air. Even the trees jeered at him, their bare branches shivering in mockery.

Was it folly, after the wolf's unsettling words, to journey even deeper into the forest, away from any semblance of warmth or civilisation? Yet some part of him remained stubborn, refusing to be bested by the biting cold or the fear that whispered through the shadows.

Red struck stone and flint once more. A pale ember danced to life, but a sudden gust snuffed it out like a cruel joke. He cried aloud, hunching over the feeble collection of twigs. When had his life become such a wretched tale?

His feet had long since lost all feeling, the ragged holes in his boots inviting the bitter cold to feast upon his toes. He'd walked for what felt like a thousand eternities before making camp for the night, though 'camp' was a generous term for his set-up, which consisted of a simple bedroll, the cooking pot Auntie Anne gave him, and the fire that would not start.

A loud snap of a twig, just to Red's left, made him jump out of his skin. He scanned the darkness, heart thundering in his chest, fingers tightening around the flint.

A massive grey form emerged from the shadows. The wolf. *Wim.* Back again.

Back to eat him.

Within a heartbeat, Red's fingers closed around his bow, nocking an arrow with practised precision as he aimed at the approaching beast.

The wolf stared at Red.

The feral glint in Wim's eyes had vanished. Once wild and hungry, now they held a calm intensity that made Red's skin prickle. His posture, before predatory and tense, now seemed more relaxed, although cautious.

Red blinked, uncertain whether his eyes were playing tricks on him in the dim light—the wolf's entire demeanour had shifted.

"You're... different," Red managed to croak out.

"I've sated the beast inside me, for now," rumbled Wim.

"So you... ate those two men?" Red whispered. It seemed an awful waste of that very handsome man to become a meal, but at least it wasn't Red who'd been eaten.

Wim snarled, revealing those ever-so-sharp teeth. "Wildlings don't feast on human flesh. Goes against our sacred code."

"Well, you seemed awfully keen on eating me earlier!"

"I wasn't myself back there."

"What do you mean, not yourself?"

There was no reply, and the silence lingered between them. Red lowered his bow, then glanced behind Wim to the dark trees, as if he could will him away. "And if you're not going to eat me, why are you standing in my camp?"

A wolfish laugh. "Been keeping an eye on you for a bit. Great entertainment, watching you struggle with that fire." Wim's furry grey head nodded towards Red's feeble attempt at a firepit. "Reckon a hot bowl of broth might help me sleep soundly tonight."

"Go and make your own broth elsewhere, wolf. I have no desire for company." *Particularly not from a beast who threatened to eat me.*

"I have no cooking pot, and you've got no fire. Trust me, the last thing I want is to break bread with one of Queen Schön's supporters."

Red flinched. "How did you know I'm from the palace?" How could this creature possibly know that? He'd been careful to blend in with the common folk scattered around the forest.

Wim's eyes gleamed in the darkness, a hint of amusement dancing in their depths. "That smell on you," he growled. "All those fancy perfumes. Only palace folk wear scents like that."

Red's cheeks burned. He'd bathed in the river that morning using the tiny bar of lavender-scented soap Auntie Anne had procured for him. "Is it so bad to smell nice?"

The wolf took a large step closer, then sniffed the air. "Not a bit. But where I'm from, standing with that cruel witch who wears the crown... now that's a crime. She had members of my pack slaughtered until my alpha bent to her will, and her tithes are crippling the kingdom, not that she gives a damn."

Red couldn't argue with that, but the wolf's attitude towards him, as if *he* were equally responsible, made him bristle.

"The Queen does what needs to be done," Red retorted. "In fact, right now she has sent me on this very quest to rid Falchovari of the Great Famine." Probably, he was revealing too much, but he couldn't help but brag, allowing pride to seep through him and warm his bones.

Wim sneered, and those horribly sharp teeth of his appeared even sharper. "What *quest*?"

"Look, if you're going to hover in my camp, I insist you return to your man-shape." Red also found he'd grown rather curious to see what this strange man looked like when he wasn't a mangy mutt.

"Fine by me."

Red watched, transfixed, as Wim's form began to shift. The wolf's massive body contorted and twisted, fur receding into skin like waves retreating from the shore. Bones cracked and reshaped themselves, the sound echoing through the silent forest. It was both terrifying and mesmerising, a dance of nature defying all logic. It was magical. The palace staff were not going to believe their ears when Red recounted this tale upon his return.

The transformation neared its end, and Red found himself holding his breath. The last vestiges of fur melted away, revealing a man kneeling where the wolf had stood moments before. Wim raised his head, meeting Red's gaze with those same intense amber eyes.

Red's heart skipped a beat. Gone was the flea-infested beast, replaced with something far more... magnificent. Wim's hair was the colour of the chestnuts they roasted every Yuletide, tousled and wild, framing a strong, chiselled face. His beard, thick and well-groomed, accentuated his masculine features, giving him an aura of ruggedness that made Red's breath hitch.

Because there was no doubt about it; this was the manliest of men on his knees before Red.

He was older than Red for sure—a good handful of winters older. His broad shoulders and muscular chest spoke of raw power, and made Red feel like a feeble twig in comparison. Wim stood and stretched his arms behind his back. A thick dusting of dark hair covered his chest, trailing down to...

Red jerked his gaze away, heat rising to his cheeks. He cleared his throat, willing away the sudden dryness in his mouth. "Do you often wander about stark naked?" he asked, aiming for a haughty tone but falling short.

Wim chuckled—a deep, rumbling sound that sent an involuntary shiver down Red's spine. "Not when it's this cold, no." He disappeared into the tree line, returning with a large pack, bulging at the seams. He pulled out a pair of breeches, fur-lined boots, a layered tunic and a thick wool cloak.

As Wim dressed, Red found his eyes drawn back to the man's form. He couldn't help but fixate on the way Wim's muscles flexed as he moved, the grace with which he carried himself. Wim had implied earlier that he was starving—like most of Falchovari was—but his muscular body suggested otherwise.

There was no denying it. This stranger was effortlessly attractive for a commoner. It was infuriating.

Red shook his head, banishing such thoughts. This was ridiculous. Wim was a beast, a 'wildling,' someone who had threatened to eat him mere hours ago. He needed to banish these absurd, preposterous thoughts. He was on a grand quest, a mission from the Queen herself.

Yet he heard himself saying, "You have the same colour eyes. You and your wolf."

"That I do." Wim kneeled, reaching for Red's firepit.

Without hesitation, Red surged forward. "I don't need help from the likes of you!" He gathered up his fragile bundle of kindling, only to have Wim yank the wood out of his hand.

"Well, you're charming," Wim said. "Anyone ever tell you that?"

"Plenty, actually."

An icy gust of wind blew through the small clearing, and Red sighed, moving away to perch on a large log. If this dog wanted to build a fire, Red would be a fool to stop him.

Wim pulled a small metal contraption from his pack. With a few deft movements, the man struck sparks onto the kindling. Flames licked upwards, catching quickly. Heat bloomed outwards, and Red couldn't help but lean closer, savouring the warmth that chased away the chill that had made its home in his bones.

When Wim helped himself to Red's cooking pot, Red didn't stop him.

"That rabbit of Hansel's hit the spot." There was an odd smirk on Wim's face. "Kept some of the bigger bones." Wim brought out a handful of grisly animal bones from his bag, and tossed them into the pot, then tipped in the contents of a leather waterskin.

Red watched as Wim tended to the fire, his fingers itching to take over. He'd always prided himself on his survival skills, honed under the tutelage of the Queen's huntsman. Yet here he was, relying on a wildling to keep him warm.

The aroma of simmering broth filled the air, making Red's stomach growl traitorously. He hadn't realised how famished he was until that moment. Wim stirred the pot with a wooden spoon he'd produced from his pack, humming a low tune that Red didn't recognise.

"Got any vegetables?" Wim asked hopefully.

Red blinked, caught off-guard by the mundane question. It seemed absurd, discussing vegetables with a man like Wim. "No. I... ran out of rations this morning."

Wim sighed, then perused his pack again, leafing through packets of herbs before sprinkling some into the pot. Soon the broth bubbled and steamed, filling the air with a tantalising scent that made Red's mouth water.

"Won't be long now," Wim said, stirring the pot. "Best get some food in you. You look like you're about to keel over."

Red bristled at the comment, drawing himself up straighter. "I'm perfectly fine, thank you very much. I don't need your concern."

Wim raised an eyebrow, a hint of amusement dancing on his lips. "Suit yourself. But don't be surprised if you faint from hunger in the middle of your grand quest, sweetheart."

Red's cheeks burnt at the sarcastic endearment. He opened his mouth to retort, but his stomach chose that moment to growl loudly, betraying him.

Wim chuckled, the sound deep and rich. His pupils were like molten gold, gleaming in the firelight. "Sounds like your belly's telling a different tale."

Red scowled, crossing his arms over his chest. "Fine. But how much energy do you think I'll get from a ladle of bone broth?"

There was no reply. The wolf must have known Red had a solid point. If he didn't find food somehow in the morning, he wouldn't survive much longer out here. Red should have demanded more rations, but the kitchen master had insisted Red would be able to hunt small game along the route. So far, the only rabbit he'd seen had been the one those handsome men had.

Wim ladled the steaming broth into a wooden bowl and passed it to Red. The warmth seeped through, warming his cold fingers. He hesitated for a moment, eyeing the liquid suspiciously, but the enticing aroma proved too tempting to resist.

Red took a cautious sip. The rich, savoury flavour exploded on his tongue, a symphony of herbs and a hint of meat that made his taste buds sing. Before he could stop himself, a small moan of pleasure escaped his lips.

"This is... actually quite good," Red admitted, then immediately regretted his words. He shouldn't be complimenting this wildling's cooking, no matter how delicious it was.

Wim gave him a smug smile. "Well now, I'm glad it meets your royal standards, sweetheart."

Red's cheeks burnt even hotter. "Stop calling me that!"

After a chuckle, Wim said, "Go on, then. What's this grand errand Her Majesty's got you running? One that will magically solve the famine?" He seemed to repress a laugh.

"It's hardly a laughing matter," Red snapped, his grip tightening on the wooden bowl. "People are starving across the kingdom. Children go to bed with empty bellies, and the elderly waste away in their homes."

Wim's smirk faded, replaced by a more solemn expression. "Aye, I know plenty about this famine's bite. My pack... we've buried our share."

Red's brow furrowed. "The crops have failed for three seasons now. Even the palace stores are running low. Residents outside of the Queen's close court, like myself, haven't had enough to eat in months. The Queen fears riots if we can't find a solution soon."

"And you reckon this quest will solve everything?" Wim's tone was skeptical, but not mocking.

Red nodded. "The Queen's advisors discovered an ancient prophecy. They believe the Great Famine is a curse that can only be broken by..." He trailed off, suddenly unsure if he should reveal the *exact* details of his mission to this stranger.

Wim leaned forward, the flicks of gold in his eyes intensifying in the firelight. "By what?"

"By the death of a powerful witch," Red finished. "Old Oma, they call her. The Queen believes she's the source of the famine."

Wim's reaction to the witch's name was subtle, but Red caught it nonetheless. The man's shoulders tensed, eyes widening for a fraction of a second before he schooled his features back into a mask of indifference.

"Old Oma, you say?" Wim's voice was carefully neutral, but there was an undercurrent of... something Red couldn't quite place. "And you believe killing her will end the famine?"

Red nodded, watching Wim closely. "The Queen's advisors are certain of it. They've studied the ancient texts for months."

Wim's jaw clenched, a muscle twitching beneath his skin. He turned away, pretending to stir the pot of broth, but Red could see the way his knuckles whitened around the wooden spoon.

"And you?" Wim asked. "Do you believe it?"

Red hesitated. Did he? The Queen had given him a mission, and who was he to question her wisdom? But something in Wim's reaction made him pause.

"I... I'm not sure," Red admitted, surprising himself with his honesty. "But I have to try. For the kingdom. It would bring me the highest honour."

Saving Falchovari from starvation would surely escalate Red from his current social standing—a touch above the servants, on a good day—to one of the Queen's court. He might even become a celebrated hero of sorts. Maybe a statue or two of him would be erected. He wouldn't say no.

Wim nodded slowly, his eyes fixed on the fire. "For the kingdom," he echoed, his voice barely above a whisper.

"What is it?" Red snapped, because he was obviously holding something back.

Wim visibly flinched. "Finish your broth."

A few minutes of silence passed, the only sound the crackling of the fire and the soft slurping of broth. Red continued to sneak glances at the wolf, who broodily sat on his own log, staring into the flames. Then he finally looked at Red again.

"So, as it happens," the man started, hesitant-like. "I'm heading that way myself."

"But I haven't told you which way I'm travelling," Red shot back, sharp as an arrow. He studied Wim's face for any sign of deception. The man's gaze remained steady, but there was a flicker of *something* in its depths.

"Your pack," Wim said, nodding towards Red's gear. "Spotted that map of yours poking out before. Got a path marked right up to the Dark Forest."

Red's hand instinctively moved to his pack. He'd been careless, again. He'd been taught better than to leave such vital information exposed. Queen Schön would be furious if she knew.

"And you just happen to also be going into the Dark Forest?" Red asked, trying to keep his tone light despite the sudden tension coiling in his gut. "That's a coincidence, isn't it?"

Wim's lips quirked into a half-smile. "Fancy that, eh? Could be fate talking. This forest is dangerous. Might be we could help each other out. Travelling companions, just for a few days."

Red gaped at Wim, shock and indignation warring within him. The *audacity*! Suggesting they travel together, as if Red needed his help.

"Absolutely not," Red snapped, drawing himself up to his full height. "I don't need you, dog. I'm perfectly capable of surviving in this forest. I was trained by the Queen's huntsman himself."

Wim only laughed. "That so? I can't imagine the Queen's huntsman walking about with his toes poking through his boots."

Red quickly covered his well-worn leather boots with his cloak, glaring at the wolf.

Wim's lips twitched. "You'll starve before sundown tomorrow, sweetheart."

The words stung. They held a grain of truth, but Red would be damned if he'd admit it. "I've survived this long, haven't I?" *Three whole days.* "I also fail to see what you'd get out of the arrangement."

As he met Wim's fiery gaze, Red's blood ran cold as realisation seeped through him. Red raked his eyes over the man's muscular form. He dropped his voice low to ask, "Unless... unless what you want in return is... is me?"

Wim's eyebrows shot up, and for a moment he looked genuinely taken aback. Then he burst out laughing. "You?" Wim chuckled, shaking his head. "Settle down. I have no interest in scrawny little waifs like you. I prefer my men sturdy enough for rough handling, not breakable as a twig."

Surprise and irritation warred for dominance, quickly replaced by a healthy twinge of offence. "Waif?" Red sputtered indignantly. "I'll have you know I'm considered quite desirable at court!" A bit of a stretch, but Red wasn't completely without his charms.

Wim's laughter subsided, but his eyes still sparkled with mirth. "Of course you are, sweetheart. But that's not why I offered to walk with you."

"Then why?" Red demanded, crossing his arms over his chest. "What could you possibly gain?"

Wim's expression sobered, the amusement fading from his eyes. "Like I said before, these forests aren't safe. Two sets of eyes are better than one, even if it's just us. And..." He hesitated, seeming to choose his words carefully. "Since I've got my own business that way, makes sense to stick together for a bit. The forest can be a scary place, especially for a little thing like you."

"Fine!" Red jumped up, busying himself with rearranging his meager pile of possessions. "I suppose you might come in useful, the next time my fire is being fickle." The dog might come in handy for other things as well, like scaring off any more lurking predators and chasing away annoying bandits who might dare to attempt to rob him.

Wim laughed, then rumbled in agreement. "Aye, that."

"I'm going to sleep," Red pointedly announced. "I will sleep on this side." He laid out his bedroll on his side of the fire. "And you will sleep over there."

"Oh, will I now?" Wim laughed again, the sound booming through the trees, a deep, rich rumble that felt as though it vibrated through the very ground beneath them. It was a mix of amusement and challenge. "You think you're in charge here, sweetheart?"

Something very peculiar twinged through Red's stomach. Likely it was the broth settling in.

But thankfully, the wolf conceded, laying out his own—remarkably thicker—bedroll on the opposite side.

Red turned over so that his back was being warmed by the fire, and so that he wasn't faced with Wim's burning eyes for a second longer. He curled into a tight ball, rubbing his freezing feet. It was the coldest night yet. He hated to admit it, but he might have been in trouble if the wolf hadn't found him again.

Though, even *with* the fire, he was still bitterly cold. He clamped his teeth together so Wim wouldn't hear them chatter.

"Hey," Wim said, after an age of silence.

"What?" Red snapped. "I'm sleeping."

"I just realised I never got your name."

Why was that simple statement making Red's heart pound? And should he tell the stranger his name, or invent one? But there was no harm in it, he supposed. After all, he'd need someone to recount the brave tales of his adventures when this was all over. Spread the word from inn to inn.

Without turning to face Wim, Red replied, "My name's Red. You know... because of my riding hood."

"Red. Right, then. Sweet dreams, Little Red. Mind the wolves don't bite."

There was a long stretch of silence, and then Red's mouth betrayed him by saying, "Thank you," through gritted teeth. "For the fire. And... the broth."

A low chuckle reverberated through the camp.

"My pleasure, Red."

Three

A cool wisp of wind brushed against Red's cheek, dragging him from the depths of his dreams.

Stretching out his aching limbs, Red's eyes peeled open, ready to be greeted by the rafters of the palace attic.

Instead, his eyes met rough bark, branches creaking overhead. The usual dusty smell of his bedroom had been replaced by woodsmoke and damp earth.

Red sat up, disoriented, still bleary-eyed. A clattering sound pierced the morning stillness. Then, metal on stone. Footsteps. Heavy breathing.

His hand flew to his side, searching for his bow. Gone. Panic clawed at his throat.

A low growl rumbled nearby. "Good morning, sweetheart."

Reality crashed over him like a cold wave, seeping into his bones and chilling him to his very core. The familiar comfort of the palace attic seemed a distant memory now, replaced by the wild, untamed forest that surrounded him. He blinked rapidly, willing the scene before him to dissolve, to reveal itself as nothing more than a vivid nightmare. But the stony ground beneath his fingers and the damp earth's scent lingering in his nostrils refused to fade away.

Red's eyes snapped to the source of the noise. Wim crouched by a small fire, fiddling with something in his hands. Steam rose from his cooking pot, balanced precariously over the flames.

"Good morrow to you too, dog."

"I've found three goose eggs. I *was* going to share. Careful I don't change my mind."

Red rubbed at his eyes before staring over at his pot, presumably boiling Wim's impressive find. Red had been scouring the landscape high and low since he'd left the palace, and hadn't found even a common goldfinch egg.

"Well," Red said slowly, then yawned. He hadn't had nearly enough sleep the previous night, with the biting cold refusing to let him rest deeply. "As you're using *my* cooking pot, it seems as if you owe me an egg. That would only be fair." His stomach rumbled in agreement.

Wim chuckled, then nodded to the log next to the fire. "Come here, then."

Red joined the wolf, perching on the log opposite him. Wim fished out the three eggs with a stick, leaving them to cool on a slab of stone. How Red longed to devour his there and then; his stomach was eating itself from the inside out. A small moan escaped him—the hunger pains getting the better of him—and Wim's gaze shot to his.

An uncomfortable prickle coursed through Red.

If Wim hadn't noticed Red's mismatched eyes in the darkness of the night before, he'd surely detect them now. *"One iris of beautiful ocean blue and the other a dirty mud puddle."* The Queen had said it often enough, in those rare moments she'd acknowledged him.

Red stared at his boots, removing his eyes from Wim's sight. It's not as if Red wanted Wim to find his face pleasing—definitely *not*, in fact—but he'd rather get the inevitable question over with.

Wim frowned at him. "What is it?"

"You haven't remarked on my eyes. People usually do, when they meet me."

A bark of a laugh. "I've had slightly more important things to think about. What of your eyes?" Wim cleared the distance between them to kneel by Red's log, capturing his chin and lifting it up. His large hand was warm, his touch gentle, and for a moment Red forgot to be angry about the sudden violation of his body.

"As you can see, I have one good eye and one bad eye," Red replied, stating the matter factually.

"That's not ideal for an archer."

"I can see perfectly fine out of it!" Red snapped, jerking his chin away. "It's only that it's the wrong colour." Wim's own bewitching golden eyes only blinked, and so Red added, pointing at the offending eye, "Instead of matching its twin, this one is an ugly brown colour."

A complicated expression Red couldn't decipher passed over Wim's face. This wasn't the first time the man had been surprisingly hard to read. It was infuriating—now was the time Red needed his people-reading skills the most.

Wim opened his mouth, then clamped it shut again.

"The eggs are probably ready," Red said pointedly.

Wim tentatively chose one, then blew on it a few times before passing it to Red. When Red held the warm egg, his hands started to tremble, the anticipation of food all too much. *Praise the heavens!* He lightly tapped it against his log to crack it, then peeled the shell off with gentle fingers, lest he waste a single morsel of egg white.

The second the egg entered his mouth, a loud groan of appreciation slipped out of him. Would he even have been able to continue walking today, without this sustenance?

Red had somehow devoured his egg before Wim even finished deshelling his. His gaze settled on the third egg, sitting between them on the slab.

"Go on," Wim said with a disgruntled huff. "Take it."

What? "But you're twice the size of me," Red whispered, his mind scrambling to understand Wim's reasoning.

"It won't do if you keel over on our journey. Plus, I can't stand that waifish look in your eyes."

Red opened his mouth to spit out a retort, then closed it, snatching the third egg up before Wim could change his mind.

"Would've thought the palace kept their people fed better than this. You're nothing but bones in a sack."

"The Queen's inner court has enough. The rest of us get the scraps." Was Auntie Anne getting enough to eat, now that Red wasn't there to slide some of his own portion onto her plate before he brought it to her?

Wim grunted. "More food than some, still."

Swallowing the last bite of egg, Red nodded. It was true—he was thankful he didn't live in any of the nearby villages, where reports of starvation were frequent. But hopefully, not for much longer. He jumped up, brushing some shell from his cloak. "We'd best get moving."

A frown etched itself between Red's brows, the stupid map crinkling between his fingers. He squinted at the spidery lines, twisting it this way and that. Then he sighed. As if *that* would magically reveal some hidden path. He puffed air through pursed lips.

Forest. More forest. Trees.

Bloody useless.

"Lost your way, sweetheart?" Wim's deep voice rumbled. Red whipped around. The wolf rested against a thick oak, leaning some distance away, arms crossed over his broad chest. Amusement danced in his eyes.

The situation was far from funny.

"Certainly not! Simply... strategising." Red refolded the map with a sharp snap, tucking it away.

"Right. Strategising." Wim chuckled, a low sound that vibrated through the air. "Because wandering aimlessly in circles is the finest art of navigation."

"I wasn't wandering in *circles*."

"Course you weren't." Wim pushed himself off the tree. "Hand over the map. I'll take point."

Red clutched the map tighter, glaring. "Absolutely not. The Queen has entrusted me with this task, and this map! I am perfectly capable—"

"Of getting us both killed?" Wim raised a brow. The challenge hung in the air, thick and heavy as wood smoke.

Red's grip loosened. Wim's hand, large and calloused, reached out.

"Fine!" he all but shouted. "You may assist, until I get my bearings again." Red wasn't particularly convinced he'd ever had his bearings in the first place.

Wim pored over the map, mouth twitching into a smirk. "You've gone a very funny way so far. You've added at least two days onto your journey."

Red groaned, smacking his forehead. He knew it. He should have turned left at that forked path with the gnarled oak. Instead, he'd stubbornly insisted on taking the right fork, certain it would be quicker. Now he'd wasted precious time.

The Queen's words echoed in his mind. *"Get it done, Red. Show me your worth, after all this time."* He'd been so determined to prove himself, to show he could navigate this cursed forest without help. Fat lot of good that had done. Red's cheeks burned with embarrassment and frustration. He'd have to swallow his pride and admit his mistake.

"Well?"

Red's jaw clenched. He'd rather eat dirt than confess his error to the insufferable wolf. But what choice did he have?

"I... may have made a slight miscalculation," Red muttered, refusing to meet Wim's gaze.

"A *slight* miscalculation?"

Red bristled. "Oh, do shut up. As if you could do any better!"

Wim's lips quirked again. "Actually, sweetheart, I could. These woods? They're almost as familiar to me as my own home. I know every stream, every hidden path."

Red's eyes narrowed. "Then why in blazes didn't you say something earlier?"

"You seemed so confident." Wim shrugged, his eyes twinkling with mischief. "Who was I to argue with the Queen's chosen one?"

Red's fists clenched at his sides. He wanted nothing more than to wipe that smug look off Wim's face. But the sands of time slipped further away.

Wim pointed in a direction that Red thought could be northeast, the complete opposite direction from what Red would have chosen. "Got a wider trail this way. Help us pick up the pace. But listen—traders of the shadier sort use it regularly. They're not fond of company they don't know."

"Fine," Red spat. "Lead on, then, Oh Great Navigator of the Forest. But I'm watching you. One wrong turn and I'll—"

"You'll what?" A growl rumbled deep in Wim's chest, primal and raw. He stepped closer, looming over Red with his considerable height. The morning light caught on the sharp edges of his canines as his lips curled back—not quite a snarl, but a clear reminder of what lurked beneath his human facade.

Red's mouth snapped shut. He'd forgotten, for a moment, just what Wim was capable of. The wolf's eyes darkened, pupils dilating until only a thin ring of colour remained, reminding Red of their first encounter in the forest. Those were not a man's eyes, they were a predator's, sizing up their prey.

Wim's broad shoulders seemed to expand as he drew himself to his full height, his presence suddenly overwhelming. Everything about him seemed magnified in that moment—how very large his hands were, how very sharp his teeth gleamed, how very wild his eyes had become. This was no ordinary man standing before Red, but something from the old stories, something that devoured unwary travellers who strayed from their paths.

Wim's tongue shot out to moisten his lip, and a shiver ran down Red's spine, settling low in his belly—fear, certainly, but something else too, something he refused to acknowledge as their gazes remained locked in a silent challenge.

In the space of a blink, Wim abruptly broke the intense moment to turn and walk, weaving around a fallen log.

Red let out the breath he was holding in, clutching his red hood closer around his shoulders.

He jogged to catch up, falling into step with Wim. "I'm not scared of you."

"You should be." Wim growled it like a threat. "I've... hurt people."

The hairs on the back of Red's neck prickled, but he scoffed.

"You laugh, but I've claimed three humans as my meals."

A chill shot through Red that had nothing to do with the frigid air. "I thought that was against your wildling code?"

"Aye, it is. It's the reason I'm here in these distant woods, rather than running with my pack back home." Wim's voice wavered ever so slightly. "Many moons ago now, I developed this... condition." He slowed his steps to glance at Red. "One that takes over inside of me. A beast that demands to be sated. My pack has banished me until I can cure myself of it."

"This sounds... dangerous for me," Red pointed out, because he really didn't want to get eaten. "What if you try and eat me again?"

"First hint I'm slipping, I'll put distance between us. Come find you when I'm myself."

This plan didn't sound particularly foolproof to Red. He eyed the wolf warily. "And how often does this... sickness of yours strike?"

"It's unpredictable," Wim admitted, his brow furrowing. "But I can usually feel it coming on."

"That's not exactly reassuring," Red muttered, kicking at a pebble on the path.

Wim's vivid eyes flashed. "Rather I walk away and leave you to the forest's mercies?"

The word 'yes' was on the tip of Red's tongue, but didn't quite make it out of his mouth. This short time with Wim had been far more pleasant than the start of his journey, despite the man's infuriating nature.

"Hmmph," he eventually replied. "If you turn into your beast form again, I will simply construct another cunning plan. Or I shall shoot you with my bow."

Wim's laugh was so loud it startled a small flock of birds, sending them scattering.

"You seem to find everything I say awfully amusing," Red remarked.

The wolf shot him a bright smile that made his stomach do that strange, fluttery thing again. "Can't deny it. You're the best fun I've had in these dreary woods."

The foliage on the path grew thicker, and Wim brushed up against Red as they walked. The man was a full head taller and often had to duck. Red's riding hood snagged on a low-hanging branch, and he was momentarily jerked backwards. Wim freed the garment before running the velvety, deep-crimson fabric through his large, callused fingers. "What's the story of this, anyway? This cloak you say you're named after."

Red tugged the material out of Wim's grip. He sighed, exhaling a long breath. "I was found wrapped in it as a babe, abandoned by my mother on the staircase to the palace's grand entrance. It is all I have of her. Not a name, only a cloak." Before Red could stop himself, he clucked his tongue.

"You're an orphan? An orphan, allowed to live in the palace?"

"I was raised by one of the Queen's maids. Auntie Anne. She's the one who found me on the staircase." A pang of homesickness, his first since he'd left the palace, shot through Red at the mention of the kindly old woman's name. "When the Queen saw my irregular eyes, she raised her sceptre. Auntie Anne risked the Queen's wrath by begging her not to kill me. She insisted the servants would keep me out of her way, and that I'd grow up to make myself useful. And so, I went to live in the attic."

Red's gaze drifted to the forest canopy, his very first memories flooding back like pages in a book. The attic. Cramped, musty. Slanted ceilings pressing down. Dust motes dancing in shafts of sunlight that slipped through cracks in the roof. He'd spend hours perched by the tiny window, watching the comings and goings of the palace below. The clatter of hooves on cobblestones. Shouts of guards. Laughter of noble children at play.

At night, he'd curl up on his threadbare mattress, listening to the scurrying of mice in the walls. The creaks and groans of the old building would lull him to sleep. Sometimes, Auntie Anne would sneak up after her duties, bringing scraps from the kitchen. Warm bread. Bits of cheese. Very occasionally, even a slice of cake from a royal banquet.

But mostly, it was loneliness. Isolation. The ache of not belonging. Of being different. Hidden away like a shameful secret. Red's fingers tightened on his cloak: the only connection to a mother he'd never known.

A twig snapped underfoot. Red blinked, dragged back to the present. Wim's eyes were on him, curious, almost... sympathetic?

"I don't need your pity." Red glowered at Wim, pulling his face into a scowl. "It wasn't a bad childhood. Once I was seven, I started training with the Queen's huntsman." For as long as Red could remember, rumours had flown around, alleging that the huntsman was, in fact, Red's father, and this was why his mother left him on the palace staircase. Though Red and the huntsman had never openly discussed this hearsay.

"So tell me, what—"

"You ask a lot of questions, wolf."

Wim snorted. "What, you prefer to walk in silence? Sounds dull."

"Some people are perfectly happy in their own company."

"Right, so you've got no one to talk to."

Red stumbled, tripping over a gnarly root. He twisted to glare at the dog. "That's rich, coming from a lone wolf."

Wim's orange eyes flashed, a predatory glint catching the dappled sunlight filtering through the forest canopy. Red flinched involuntarily, his heart skipping a beat as he instinctively took a small step backwards.

Red resumed walking with a brisk stride. "We're going too slowly. Let's pick up the pace. I want to reach the Dark Forest before I turn twenty-five winters, if that pleases you."

Wim snorted before staring at Red's face. "Twenty-four winters? I thought you more like nineteen!"

"And why is that?" Red retorted, indignant. He was not an infantile youth, and nor did he act like one.

Right?!

The wolf-man shrugged before making a show of scrutinising Red, eyeing him up, then down. "Besides that baby face of yours? Your stature, perhaps. And that fiery temper of yours."

"I'll have you know, I'm perfectly mature," Red huffed, crossing his arms.

Wim chuckled, scratching his thick beard. "Aye, as mature as a babe with a wooden sword."

Red's cheeks burned. "And how old are you, then, you great lout?"

"Thirty-two winters, give or take."

"Practically ancient," Red muttered under his breath.

"We need to hunt something for supper," Wim said.

The two eggs from earlier had long since been digested, and Red's stomach gave a hopeful squeeze at the idea of actual meat for dinner, rather than bone broth. "I was about to suggest that."

"Were you now? Go on, then. What's your brilliant plan?"

Red stiffened. He ran his fingers across his leather quiver, embossed with delicate leaves. "I will hunt us some meat. I'm an excellent shot." He couldn't restrain his proud tone.

"Well, let's see what you can do with that bow, then."

In case an opportunity presented itself, Red readied his bow, holding it down low. As they walked on silently, he scanned the forest floor for any sign of life. A rabbit was their best chance for a filling meal, though they were growing as rare as gold dust nowadays. More likely would be a sparrow or a woodpecker.

The thought of biting into a piping-hot, juicy bird wing sent acid roiling through Red's gut, and a wave of dizziness hit him. He didn't realise he'd stumbled over a large rock until Wim caught him.

"You alright, sweetheart?"

"Perfectly!" Red wrenched his arm from the man's strong grip. It took several moments for the vertigo to pass, the fuzziness at the edge of his vision receding only after several deep breaths. He couldn't possibly faint in front of this man. The thought was mortifying.

As they trudged on, the forest grew denser, the air thick with the scent of pine and damp earth. Red's legs ached. Several times he opened his mouth to beg for a break, before snapping it shut again. He took sparing sips from his waterskin. It was almost empty already.

Mouth dry as sandpaper, Red urged himself forward each time he thought about stopping, matching Wim's pace step for step. He wasn't going to lag behind and give Wim the satisfaction, or see his face twist in scorn for slowing them down.

Wim's hand shot out, gripping Red's arm. Red flinched in alarm, and the man quickly unhanded him, after an incredulous look.

"There," Wim whispered, pointing to a nearby oak.

Red's gaze followed the gesture, landing on a plump grey squirrel perched on a low branch. His heart leapt. It wasn't much, but it would make a decent meal.

With practised ease, Red reached for an arrow, nocking it to his bowstring. The familiar weight settled against his fingers as he drew back, the feathered fletching brushing his cheek. He inhaled deeply, steadying his aim. The world narrowed to a pinpoint—just him, the bow, and his target.

The squirrel twitched, unaware of its impending doom. *Got you.* Red was already salivating at the thought of the roasted meat. His muscles tensed, ready to release. Then, as he began to loose the arrow, that horrible wave of dizziness returned, crashing over him like a sudden tide sweeping the shore, dragging him down into its depths. His vision swam, the forest tilting sideways. In a moment of pure instinct, he released the bowstring, losing all control as his fingers betrayed him. The arrow flew wide, embedding itself in the tree trunk with a dull thunk.

Startled, the squirrel darted up the tree and out of sight.

"Bollocks!" Red swore. For a moment, the horror rooted him to the spot. He'd missed. He never missed. Heat crept up his neck, shame and anger warring for dominance. He refused to look at Wim, certain he'd find mockery in those amber eyes. "I... I don't know what happened," he muttered, glaring at the ground. "The sun must have been in my eyes." His fingers trembled as he lowered the bow.

"Are you alright?" Wim asked, surprisingly gentle.

Red didn't trust himself to reply. His cheeks burned with humiliation as he stared at the arrow lodged in the tree trunk. He'd never missed a shot like that before.

"Red?"

Red whirled to face him, anger flaring before he could tamp it. "I'm fine! It was just the sun!" He pointed upwards, where a cloudy sky blocked all sunlight.

Wim frowned, moving closer. "You're white as milk. Been a while since you had a proper meal, hasn't it?"

"That's none of your concern," Red tried to snap, but his voice sounded weak and distant. The forest gave another sudden lurch around him, and he stumbled.

Firm hands gripped his shoulders, holding him upright. "Steady now. Need to get you sat down somewhere, alright?"

Red wanted to protest, to insist he was fine, but his legs felt like jelly. He allowed Wim to guide him to a fallen log, sinking onto it gratefully.

"Here." Wim pressed something into his hand. A chunk of dried meat. "Eat this. It's not much, but it'll help."

Red's pride warred with his hunger for a moment before he gave in, tearing into the jerky with his teeth. The salt and smoke exploded across his tongue, and he had to fight not to moan in relief.

"I would offer more, but that's all I've got left of my backup supplies."

Why are you being so kind to me? It was baffling. Red had been nothing but rude to this wolf, yet here Wim was, giving Red food for the second time today.

As the meat hit his stomach, the dizziness began to recede. He'd been so incredibly close to fainting. His determination not to show weakness in front of Wim had been his folly.

"Thank you," Red muttered, not meeting Wim's gaze.

"Don't mention it, sweetheart," Wim's said, with a hint of laughter, but it wasn't unkind. "Can't have you swooning in my arms, now, can we?"

Red rolled his eyes, feeling some of his familiar fire returning. "As if I'd ever swoon for the likes of you!"

Wim chuckled, the sound rumbling deep in his chest. "Keep telling yourself that, Little Red." Wim reached for Red's waterskin, strapped to the side of his pack. Finding it empty, he sighed, tossing Red his own.

Red guzzled it down gratefully, though the precious liquid came with a guilt-ridden aftertaste. "We're still no closer to finding our evening meal."

"Are we not?" Wim nodded at the oak tree, bearded chin pointing at Red's failure of an arrow. Then Red saw it—the squirrel was back, perched atop a branch, gnawing at a nut.

Red slowly reached for his bow. How humiliating would it be to fail twice in a row? He may be about to find out...

Wim's hand shot out, pushing it away. "My turn," he said, a mischievous glint in his bright eyes.

Before Red could protest, Wim began shedding his clothing at the speed of a startled deer bolting from danger. What the devil was he playing at? The man stripped down completely, his muscular form bare to the forest air.

"What in the blazes are you doing?" Red hissed, averting his gaze, then affixing it to a nearby patch of moss.

Wim didn't answer. Instead, he bent down, scooping up a smooth stone. With a swift, fluid motion, he hurled it at the squirrel. The rock struck true, and the creature let out a startled squeak before scampering down the trunk.

In that instant, Wim's form began to blur and shift. His skin rippled, sprouting thick grey fur. His face elongated into a muzzle, teeth sharpening to deadly points. Within moments, where a man had stood, a massive wolf now crouched, muscles coiled and ready to spring.

Red's breath caught in his throat. He'd seen Wim's wolf form yesterday, of course, but the transformation in broad daylight was a sight to behold. It was both terrifying and oddly beautiful, like watching a storm roll in over the mountains.

The wolf bounded after the fleeing squirrel with astonishing speed. His powerful legs carried him in great leaps, closing the distance in heartbeats. The massive creature's lupine form vanished into the dense undergrowth, the silver-grey blur of his fur melting into the shadows of the forest. The rustling of leaves and snapping of twigs faded, leaving an eerie silence in its wake.

Alone once more, with only the pounding of his heart for company. The forest seemed to close in around Red, the trees looming taller, their branches reaching out like witches' fingers. He gripped his bow tighter, eyes darting from shadow to shadow.

What if the wolf didn't come back? The thought ambushed Red, stealing the air from his lungs. It had been barely a handful of hours, really, but he'd already grown accustomed to his companion's presence, irritating as he was. Without the wildling, he'd be truly alone again in this vast, hungry forest.

Red shook his head. What foolish thoughts! Why should he care if the mangy mutt abandoned him? He was better off alone, wasn't he? He didn't need anyone, least of all a sarcastic, exasperating wolf-man.

Yet, as the silence stretched on, a knot of anxiety tightened in Red's chest. He strained his ears for any sound of Wim's return, hating himself for hoping.

Just as Red was about to call out—against his better judgement—a rustle in the undergrowth caught his attention. The wolf emerged from the foliage, padding silently towards Red. In his massive jaws, he carried the limp form of the squirrel.

Relief flooded through Red, quickly followed by a wave of displeasure at his own reaction. He schooled his features into a mask of indifference as Wim approached.

The wolf's muzzle was stained with blood, crimson droplets matting the grey fur of his jaw. His eyes gleamed with triumph as he deposited the squirrel at Red's feet.

Red found his words at last. "I suppose that's one way to catch dinner," he said, trying to sound unimpressed despite his racing heart. "Though I daresay my method would have been far less... dramatic."

Wim sat back on his haunches, his large eyes fixed on the squirrel. His tongue lolled out in what Red could only interpret as a wolfish grin. "Careful. I could happily swallow this prize right here, rather than share it with you this eve."

It would only be fair. Red wouldn't have blamed him at all. But with a shake of his massive body, Wim padded over to where his discarded clothing lay, and began his miraculous transformation back into man.

This time, Red didn't turn his head when presented with Wim's bare form. Instead, Red's gaze traced the contours of Wim's naked body. His admittedly glorious naked body. Broad shoulders tapered to a narrow waist, a canvas of lean muscle and coarse, dark hair. Scars criss-crossed his chest and abdomen—from the teeth and claws of other wolves?—telling tales of battles fought and won.

Red couldn't deny it—the sheer size of him was... appealing.

Wim's thighs, thick as tree trunks, flexed as he moved. Red's eyes followed the trail of dark hair down his stomach, lower and lower until—

Fuck, that was one large cock.

Wim was a towering bear of a man, so it wasn't completely unexpected, but Red was certain it was at least slightly disproportionate, being so absolutely massive. The longer Red looked at it, swinging around in the air as Wim dressed his torso, the bigger it seemed.

Blood ran south, and Red's own member began to thicken, the poor thing clearly as confused as Red was. Heat flooded Red's cheeks. He jerked his gaze back up, meeting Wim's knowing smirk.

A low chuckle rumbled in his chest. "See something you like, sweetheart?"

Red's mouth went dry. His pulse rabbited against his ribs, blood rushing in his ears. How did one respond to such a question? And why did the sight of this infuriating man affect him so? He'd never been attracted to anyone so... brutish before.

"Would you put... that *thing* away!"

Wim unleashed a booming laugh. "A prude, are you?" He grinned, finally tugging on some well-worn drawers. "Saving yourself for your wedding night?"

"No! As I said, I've had many the suitor. And many, many... romps in the hay as well! Too many to count!" Could wolves smell lies? Red could only pray not.

"You're as red as your cloak again."

Red turned his face away. Oh, how he regretted this alliance. He'd go mad spending another day with this fool.

"I think you were named after the colour your face favours, not your cloak, after all."

"Can you just... *stop!*" Red's foot may have performed a tiny stamp of its own accord. "Please!"

Wim laughed as he reached down to pick up Red's quiver that he hadn't even realised was on the ground. As he did so, the flap at the top came loose, spilling several arrows onto the forest floor. Among them, a single shaft caught the filtered sunlight, gleaming with an otherworldly radiance.

Red's heart seized in his chest. The golden arrow.

Of course, it did not escape Wim's notice. His large hand closed around it, lifting it high for inspection. The arrow seemed to glow even brighter in his grasp, its shaft adorned with intricate engravings that spiralled from nock to tip. The arrowhead itself was a work of art, impossibly sharp and glinting like a fallen star.

"Well, well," Wim murmured, turning the arrow this way and that. "What have we here?"

Panic clawed at Red's throat. He lunged forward, snatching the arrow from Wim's grasp with such force that he nearly toppled over.

"Don't touch that!" Red clutched the golden arrow to his chest, his heart pounding so fiercely he was certain Wim could hear it. "It's not to be played with!"

Wim's eyebrows shot up, surprise etched across his rugged features. "Easy there. I meant no harm."

Red took a step back, his fingers tightening around the precious arrow. How could he have been so careless? The Queen would have his head if anything happened to it.

"It's..." Red trailed off. Should he reveal the entire plan to Wim? But he already knew half of it. Surely there was no extra harm in telling him about the arrow? "For Old Oma. I'm to shoot her through the heart with it."

Wim's expression darkened, amber eyes narrowing to dangerous slits. For a moment, Red could have sworn he saw a flash of something primal, almost feral, in those depths. But as quickly as it appeared, it vanished, replaced by nonchalance.

"A golden arrow, eh?" Wim's manner was deceptively casual, but there was an undercurrent of tension that set Red's nerves on edge. "Bit fancy for hunting, no?"

Red clutched the arrow tighter, suddenly aware of how exposed he felt. "It's not just any arrow. It's... enchanted, I suppose you could say."

Wim's eyebrows shot up, interest clearly piqued. "Enchanted? How so? What will happen to her?"

Red hesitated. This was now a lot of questions. But he'd already revealed this much... Besides, a small—well, rather large—part of him wanted to impress Wim with the importance of his quest.

"When it pierces Old Oma's heart, it will turn her to dust," Red explained, unable to stop himself from adding a dramatic edge to the statement.

Wim's face went through a series of rapid transformations—shock, and something that looked almost like... panic? But in the blink of an eye, his features smoothed out, that standard smirk back in place.

Confusion had Red's breath catching in his throat. Wim was certainly hiding something. But why the devil would Wim care what happened to Old Oma? Could he actually be an ally of Oma's? No... that was plain silly. But what other reason would explain his reaction?

"Dust, you say?" Wim's tone was light, yet strained. "That's quite the trick. And you're absolutely certain it will work?"

Red nodded, though a flicker of doubt crept into his mind. "The Queen says it's the only way to lift Old Oma's curse on our land." He eyed Wim. "Why all these questions?"

Wim shrugged, his massive shoulders rising and falling like mountain peaks. "Just curious. It's not every day you hear about magical arrows turning witches to dust."

Red wasn't fooled by Wim's attempt at nonchalance, and anxiety burrowed into his almost-empty gut.

"Hmm."

"Look, the road is just up ahead." Wim jerked his head forward.

Red followed Wim. Indeed, it wasn't long before the path widened, deep-rutted wagon tracks carved into the packed earth—they'd reached the road Wim had spoken about. The well-worn path would be a welcome change from stumbling over roots and rocks.

Red took a step forward, but Wim caught his arm, cocking his head to one side. "Hear that?"

Red strained his hearing. A light breeze, the tweeting of birds... "No?"

"Course not. Too distant for human ears. But there are horse carts coming. With *bells*." Wim's mouth set in a grim line.

"And?"

"Know what those bells mean?"

Red scowled at him. He'd never been this far from the palace before, so of course he didn't know. "*What?*"

"Slave traders. Slavers are heading this way."

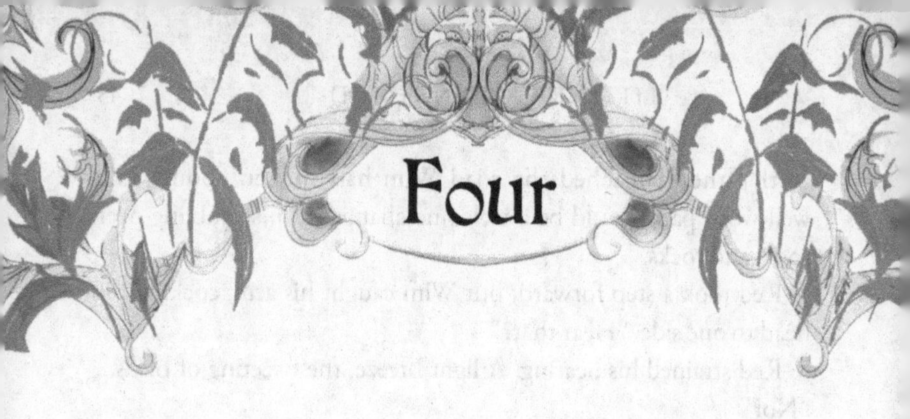

Four

"*S* lave traders?!"

Startled, Red gaped at the wolf as though he were spouting nonsense, despite having heard numerous accounts of the savage custom. Although officially prohibited, Her Majesty had of course turned a blind eye to the escalating practice of capturing elves from the northern kingdom of Varinien to sell on the black market. Red had seen a few of them himself, working in The Royal City, their delicate frames crumbling under iron shackles until they were nothing but hollow-eyed ghosts.

"Slavers? Here? In this forest?"

"How else do you expect them to get past the border?"

Red would have glared at Wim, but then he heard it—the subtle clink of bells in the near distance. "Why do they announce themselves with that sound?"

"Makes folk scatter. Tells everyone to clear off unless they fancy getting skewered. They're counting on us running scared."

Well, we better get going then.

"But we won't be." Wim took a step away from Red, surveying both edges of the path.

"We... won't?"

Wim's piercing gaze locked onto Red, the wolf's eyes narrowing with a challenge that made the hairs on the back of Red's neck prickle. "Up for a spot of mischief, sweetheart?"

Surely he can't mean...

No. Absolutely not. What a terrible idea, surely ending in our untimely demise.

Red opened his mouth to assure Wim he would be taking part in no such hijinks with *slave traders* of all people, then the challenge in the wolf's eyes deepened, outright daring Red to refuse.

But Red *was* on a royal quest, and the adventurers in Auntie Anne's stolen library books wouldn't have shied away from danger. Plus, if he could shoot a few of the traders with his bow, he could prove to Wim he wasn't a useless idiot who needed constant support.

"Of course," Red said smoothly. "I live for mischief."

Wim's brows shot up as a surprised cough spluttered from his throat. He smiled—and could Red see a hint of... admiration in his eyes? The thought warmed his belly more than he'd like to admit.

Deep voice laced with sarcasm, Wim said, "Well, colour me surprised, sweetheart. Follow me, then."

Glancing behind him, likely to confirm Red was indeed trailing him rather than frozen in place with trepidation, Wim guided them off the broad track, slipping between a pair of overgrown blackberry bushes.

The dense foliage closed in around them, filtering out what little sunlight managed to penetrate the forest canopy. The scent of damp earth and decaying leaves filled the air, enveloping them in a secluded pocket of wilderness.

"Keep close," Wim whispered, his breath warm against Red's ear. "They'll be passing by any moment now."

Red nodded, trying to focus on the approaching danger rather than the proximity of the wolf. The jangling of bells grew louder, accompanied by the creak of wagon wheels and the occasional snap of a whip.

"What's the plan?" Red whispered, attempting to sound confident despite his racing heart.

"We watch first. Count their numbers." Wim's voice was all business now, his eyes fixed on the path beyond their hiding spot. "If there's only a few, we might be able to free whoever they've captured."

Red swallowed hard. This was real. They were about to confront actual slave traders. His fingers instinctively reached for his bow.

Suddenly, Wim pulled Red deeper into the bush as the sounds grew louder. Their bodies pressed together in the cramped space, and Red found himself pinned between the dense foliage and Wim's solid chest.

"Don't move," Wim murmured, his voice a low rumble that Red could feel vibrating through his own body.

The closeness was... unexpected. Red could feel the steady rise and fall of Wim's chest against his back, the wolf's heartbeat surprisingly calm compared to his own frantic pulse. The heat radiating from Wim's body seemed to engulf him, making it difficult to concentrate on anything else.

As they waited in tense silence, Red became acutely aware of every point of contact between them—Wim's broad chest against his, the firm grip of Wim's hand on his waist steadying him, their legs pressed together in the confined space. With each breath, the air between them grew thick with tension, Red's stomach coiling tighter and tighter.

Wim shifted slightly, adjusting his position, and his breath ghosted across the nape of Red's neck, sending an involuntary shiver down his spine.

"Cold?" Wim whispered, his lips so close to Red's ear that he could feel them moving.

"N-no," Red managed, grateful that Wim couldn't see his face flushing.

The wolf reached over Red's head, plucking something from the bush. "Well, would you look at that," he rumbled, rough and husky. "Two lone blackberries left." He shuffled back slightly, his eyes locking onto Red's as he brought his hand down, a mischievous glint sparking in his gaze. "Sweet, ripe, and just begging to be... devoured."

Red stared at Wim. *What in the ever-loving fuck?*

Was he only talking about the berries? What was going on? Shouldn't they be focused on their ambushing plan presently? Red schooled his expression while he racked his brain for a witty response that was appropriately neutral. The wolf was simply joking with him, and Red would think nothing of—

Wim pressed a berry to Red's closed lips.

The tiny, dark purple fruit's juice spilled as Wim's calloused thumb gently squeezed it. The tart scent of the berry mingled with the earthy musk of Wim's skin, creating an intoxicating aroma that made Red's head spin.

Don't react. Don't you dare react, Red scolded himself, even as his traitorous heart raced.

The warmth of Wim's finger radiated against his lips, sending a shiver down his spine that he desperately hoped the wolf couldn't detect with his keen senses.

He's just offering you food again, you fool. So you don't faint on him, remember? Red's rational mind insisted. But another part of him, a part he usually kept locked away, whispered dangerous possibilities. What if he parted his lips? What if he allowed himself to taste not just the berry, but the salt of Wim's skin?

Red swallowed hard, his throat suddenly dry. He was acutely aware of how close they stood, of the heat emanating from the larger man's body, of those intense eyes watching every miniscule detail of his expression.

The moment stretched, taut as a bowstring, waiting for Red to make his move.

But Red wasn't going to move a single inch. Because he wasn't about to make a fool of himself. Not after his previous attempts to flirt with others, which had all failed, each more spectacularly than the last.

"Halt! Ten-minute break!"

The shout, deep and coarse, jolted Red. He'd managed to tune the slave traders' carts out, so focused on that damned berry, and now the slavers were right next to them, by the sound of things.

With a wink, Wim removed the fruit—and that lovely warm hand—popping the tiny berry into his own mouth.

"But... How did you know they were going to stop?" Red whispered.

"Heard them say it. But it's fine luck that they've stopped right beside our bush, aye, sweetheart?"

Why was the way Wim said 'our' doing funny things to Red's heart? More to the point, why did Red agree to this ridiculous plan he hadn't even heard the details of yet?

"Look." Wim lightly pushed him forward, to a slight gap between the leaves.

Red peered through, his heart plummeting at the sight before him. Eight humans stood around two horse-drawn carts, their appearances as vile as their trade. Matted hair hung in greasy clumps around their unwashed faces, and their clothes were stained with sweat and grime. When they spoke, their voices were harsh and guttural, thick with unfamiliar accents.

But it was the carts that truly made Red's stomach churn. Each one held a large metal cage, and within those cages... Red had to stifle a gasp. Elves. Dozens of them, crammed together like animals. They were a touch smaller than your average human, with delicate pointed ears and round faces that should have been full of life. Instead, their cheeks were hollow with hunger, their eyes wide with fear.

As Red watched, one of the traders rattled the bars of a cage, laughing cruelly as the elves inside whimpered and huddled closer together. Their thin arms wrapped around each other, seeking comfort where there was none to be found.

Red felt bile rise in his throat. He'd heard rumours of such cruelty, but to see it with his own eyes...

But what exactly did Wim have in mind when he'd said, 'mischief?' The wolf could certainly hold his own, but there were eight of them, and they had numerous sharp weapons strapped around them...

"You look terrified," Wim hissed in his ear.

"I'm certainly not!" Red retorted. "But... what are we... Surely you don't mean to kill them all? You might get one down, but the others will be on you!"

"Aww, didn't know you cared so much, sweetheart."

"I'm concerned for *my* safety!" Red had whispered it too loudly—Wim slapped his large hand over Red's mouth to silence him. Wrenching the offending limb off his face lest he get distracted again, Red spat, "That's all!"

On the road, the slavers chatted loudly, going about their business with merry tunes. One man, gangly with a patchy blond beard, marched towards the bush. Red flinched, taking a step back, but Wim caught him, softly laughing in his ear. The slaver shuffled down his breeches, then his drawers, before relieving himself.

Right outside their bush.

Lovely.

Red stared at the earthy ground, ready to jump out of the way of any trickle of urine that coursed their way.

"Right then, sweetheart. Listen closely, and I'll tell you the plan..."

Red's heart raced like a startled hare as he crouched in the bough of a large gnarled oak, fingers curled around the rough bark, with ridges digging painfully into his skin. He held his breath, waiting for the signal.

Perched on top of the first horse, the slave driver watched the other seven men wrap up their break.

A wave of acid made its home in Red's gut. *Not long now.* Red had plenty of experience shooting animals. How different could shooting a human possibly be?

The driver's gravelly voice cut through the forest air. "One minute, folks! Get ready to move out!"

A low growl rumbled from the foliage down the track. Red's muscles tensed. Wim burst from the undergrowth, a massive grey blur of fur and fangs. His howl pierced the air, sending birds scattering from nearby trees. The sound stirred a primal fear within Red, but there was no time to calm his stuttering heart.

Chaos erupted—the horses reared up as the slavers shouted in panic, scrambling for weapons. Cages rattled as the captured elves stirred, fear flickering in their eyes. One of the elves, a young girl, screamed as she was thrown against the bars, her head cracking against the metal with a sickening thud.

"Bloody hell! Is that a wolf or a wildling?" One of the men stumbled backwards, nearly dropping his heavy crossbow.

Red's fingers twitched, itching to nock an arrow. But he held back, remembering Wim's instructions. *"Wait for my signal."*

The slave driver's face drained of colour as he fumbled with his whip. "Don't just stand there, you idiots! Kill it!"

Red's stomach twisted into knots. Knots of fear. If Wim was hurt or killed for these random elves...

A high-pitched howl pierced the air. Wim's signal. Red's heart hammered a frantic rhythm as he nocked an arrow, his fingers trembling. Wim lunged at the nearest trader, jaws snapping around his neck. The man's scream was cut short as Wim's teeth crushed his windpipe, blood spraying everywhere. Red's stomach churned with a mix of revulsion and gratitude, the brutal display making his skin crawl. Wim, still in his wolf form, stood tall, his chest heaving with exertion, as if daring anyone else to make a move. Red's gaze lingered on the carnage, his mind struggling to reconcile the violent beast before him with the man he'd eaten broth with last night.

Red's gaze locked onto the slave driver. The man's whip glinted in the dappled sunlight. Red's stomach churned, his fingers trembling, shaking the bow. He'd never killed a man before. There would be no coming back from this. But then the image of that whip tearing into Wim's flesh flashed through his mind.

He loosed the arrow.

It whistled through the air, finding its mark with a sickening thud. The slaver's eyes widened in shock as the shaft protruded from his throat, blood spurting in a crimson arc. He stumbled backwards, clawing at the arrow, his eyes bulging as he choked on his own blood. As he toppled from his horse, a horrible gurgling sound came out of him. His body hit the forest floor with a dull thump, twitching as his life drained away.

Red's breath caught in his throat. He'd done it. Killed a man. A slave driver carrying around a dozen captured prisoners, but still. What would Auntie Anne say if she could see him right now? *"Life is complicated and filled with choices, Red,"* most likely.

Another slaver stumbled away from the body, a splatter of blood on his dirty shirt. "Show yourself, coward," he screamed in Red's general direction. His eyes scanned the trees, and for a moment, they locked onto Red's hiding spot. A cruel grin spread across his face as he raised his crossbow, taking aim.

Red ducked to the side, avoiding the crossbow bolt by mere inches.

Fuck! Fuck! Fuck!

Red didn't sign up to be shot at!

The bolt struck the tree trunk with a deafening thud, sending splinters flying everywhere.

Red forced himself to breathe, peeking back out through the leaves.

Two slavers were advancing on Wim, their daggers glinting wickedly in the dappled light. Red's hands shook as he nocked another arrow, gaze darting between the men before he loosed it to slice through the air and into one slaver's back. The man crumpled with a strangled cry as Wim's jaws clamped around the other slaver's arm, yanking him to the ground.

Red tore his eyes away, focusing on the cages. He aimed at the rope binding the first cart, his arrow severing it cleanly. *Yes!* He'd done it, and with only one arrow too. A thrill of satisfaction burst through Red, almost dizzying him.

The elves inside surged against the bars, tipping the cage. It crashed to the forest floor, splintering apart. The small, dirty mare that was dragging it bolted with a loud neigh, charging past Wim with the speed of five horses.

Six elves scrambled free, their chains clanking as they bolted for the trees. *Run little elves, run!* A slaver sprinted after them, whip raised. Red's bow was ready in a heartbeat, and his next arrow found its mark in the man's thigh, sending him sprawling. His screams reverberated through the forest as he clutched at his leg, blood pooling on the forest floor.

Around them, the mayhem intensified, the acrid stench of blood and sweat reaching Red's nostrils. Screams and shouts filled the air as the elves scattered.

One last slaver staggered around, his expression frozen in dismay, palms clamped to his temples.

Hold on.

Red scanned the ground, littered with mutilated bodies. Five dead or fallen slavers, one cowering in terror...

Where were the other two?

Red's vision was partially obscured by the branches. He shuffled to the left—

Fuck!

The second cart had turned itself around and was now careening back up the track, its wheels kicking up dirt and leaves. A slaver atop the driver's seat cracked his whip, urging the horse faster. He was clearly happy to leave his friend behind—the man on the ground bellowed curses, his face contorted with rage.

Four elven faces pressed against the bars of their cage, eyes wide with terror. They gazed in Red's direction, as if they could see right through his leafy cover. Their fear-stricken expressions pierced him, stirring a deep ache in his chest.

No! Red wouldn't let them get away. They would save them all.

Why wasn't Wim chasing after them? Red's gaze darted about, searching for his wildling companion. Then he found Wim limping towards the final slaver, favouring his left hind leg. A patch of blood matted the wolf's fur around his neck, a stark contrast to his grey coat. Was he injured? How badly?

It was all falling apart.

The slavers were getting away with innocent lives, and Wim was hurt, possibly fatally wounded.

The inside of Red's cheek stung—he'd been biting it.

Though there was no time to panic. The man was raising his crossbow, and Wim was clearly preparing to strike—muscles tensed, ears angled. But he was going too slowly for Red's liking. Red loosed another of his arrows, and just like its previous comrades, it found its mark, burying itself deep within the slaver's neck.

Red smiled to himself. How many times in a row had his arrow struck true? If only the huntsman could see him now! All of those long, long months of training had finally been put to proper use—and he'd certainly proven his ability to Wim. There could be no further questioning of his skills.

The second cart disappeared around a bend, into the dense foliage, the sound of creaking wheels and panicked elven cries fading into the distance.

Red's fingers tightened around his bow, an arrow already nocked. He could shoot the horse—bring the whole cart down. The angle would be difficult through the trees, but he'd made harder shots today. More elves could be saved...

But Wim was hurt. Blood matted his grey fur, and he was favouring that leg. What if the injury was worse than it looked? What if that last armed slaver—

Red's jaw clenched. *Damn it all.*

Shaking off his dismay, Red scrambled down the tree, his boots hitting the forest floor with a soft thud. He sprinted towards Wim, leaves and twigs crunching beneath his feet. The wolf's massive form came into focus, and Red's breath caught in his throat.

He dropped to his knees before Wim, suddenly overwhelmed by the sheer size of the creature whose teeth had torn through human flesh like paper. The wolf's head alone was nearly as large as Red's entire torso. Wim's piercing eyes met his, and Red swallowed hard. His entire body could fit within Wim's powerful jaws.

Red's eyes travelled to the matted fur on Wim's neck, where crimson stained the grey. His hands hovered hesitantly, wanting to help but unsure how. The enormity of Wim's presence made Red acutely aware of his own fragility.

"Wim," he whispered, barely audible. "You're hurt."

The wolf was silent for a long moment before bursting into raucous laughter. "Don't worry, sweetheart. It's only a scratch—it'll be gone in a minute. Though if you're offering to kiss it better..."

Red smacked the side of Wim's neck, though his blow was cushioned by the dense, thick fur. He couldn't resist tangling his fingers in the soft strands before dragging his hand away.

Red stared up the road. The second cart was now long gone, and a pang of guilt twisted in his gut. Would he have been able to save them if he'd tried? Now they'd be sold at market to cruel masters.

A faint whimper rang through the air, drawing their attention to the injured slaver. He lay on the ground, clutching at his thigh, his eyes wide with pain and fear. *One left.*

Wim's ears folded back, and his tail twitched. He padded over to the injured slaver, his massive paws silent on the forest floor. The slaver's whimper turned to a panicked cry as Wim loomed over him. Red turned away, but not before he heard the sickening crunch of bone as Wim's paw came down on the slaver's head, ending his suffering.

The sudden silence weighed heavy on Red's shoulders. He swallowed hard, trying not to think about the ease with which Wim had dispatched the man. He forced himself to look at the mangled corpse—the skull was crushed, the bone splintered and fragmented, with a sickening amount of brain matter spilling out onto the forest floor. The slaver's eyes were frozen in a permanent stare, the pupils blown, and the irises cloudy with death. A bloody halo surrounded the head, with splatters of grey and pink brain tissue radiating out from the impact site like a gruesome sunburst.

Red retched, bile burning his tongue.

"Keep those eggs down, would you?" Wim growled.

Surveying the sea of bodies, Red said, "You could eat them, you know. It's meat that will go to waste." Fuck, what had the famine reduced him to?

Wim growled. "Wildlings don't eat humans. Not even scum of the earth." His large amber eyes snagged on the cart behind Red. "But we can eat *those*."

Red jumped up so quickly, a wave of vertigo washed over him, causing the world to tilt precariously on its axis. As he steadied himself, Wim trotted over to a small sack, carrots and potatoes spilling out of it.

Gasping, Red took stumbling steps towards it, before snatching up a carrot, shoving it into his mouth. Dirt and sweetness mingled on his tongue, followed by the most satisfying crunch. Red eyed Wim guiltily. It should be him devouring all these vegetables, after the extra food he'd given Red.

Another rumbled laugh. "It's alright, sweetheart. It's only a carrot. You've earned it."

Red gathered his arrows, grimacing at the sticky crimson coating the shafts. He yanked off a strip from a dead trader's tunic—cleaner than expected—and methodically wiped each one before sliding them back into his quiver. He didn't want his pristine golden arrow getting blood on it.

Wim's tail swished as he nosed through the scattered supplies. "Take that waterskin—and grab those onions."

Red stuffed everything useful into his pack—the vegetables, a length of rope, flint, and even a small knife with an elaborately carved handle.

"Now let's get out of here before anyone else comes along." Wim's eyes scanned the surrounding area, his expression grim. "Here, have another carrot. You still look pale."

As they vanished into the trees, the only sound was the soft crunch of Red's carrot. The forest was quiet once more, but the silence was oppressive, heavy with the weight of death and violence.

The blood on Red's hands might wash away, but the knowledge that he'd killed would stain his soul forever. Slave traders or not, he was a murderer now. There was no going back from that.

Red swallowed a large mouthful of carrot.

The strangest thing of all?

The vegetable had never tasted so sweet.

Five

"And did you see when I hit the rope? Bang in the middle! It split instantly, cleaved it in two!"

"Mhmm." Wim took a large slurp from his bowl. Squirrel, potato, and carrot stew, seasoned with the sweet taste of success. "I sure did."

"And then with that driver on the horse... I thought I'd have to use two arrows, at least, but I got him first try!"

The hearty stew he'd devoured coursed through Red like a warm embrace, the rich flavours igniting a spark of confidence he hadn't felt in ages. It was as if the meal had breathed life into him, energising his thoughts and pushing back the ghost of self-doubt.

Wim set his bowl down next to their fire. Earlier, with Wim's help, Red had lit the fire himself, coaxing the tiny flickering embers to life as they danced beneath the kindling, growing the flame into a warm, inviting glow. Wim wiped his mouth and beard, then grinned at Red. "I saw it all, Red. It was brilliant. You were brilliant."

Red's chest swelled with pride at Wim's words. *Brilliant.* He'd never been called that before. The huntsman had taught him skills with the bow and arrow, but praise had always been sparse, more of a grunt of approval than a cheer of encouragement.

A warm flush crept up Red's neck, and he ducked his head, pretending to focus on his stew. The praise felt foreign, yet intoxicating. He wanted more of it.

His mind raced back to the moment he'd loosed that arrow. The surge of power, the rush of adrenaline. For once, he'd felt... useful. Important. Not just some cast-off orphan with ugly, mismatched eyes, knocking around the palace like an extra cog in a machine that didn't need him.

Red snuck a glance at Wim, studying the way the firelight danced across his rugged features. How could someone so fierce, so powerful, think *he* was brilliant? It didn't make sense. And yet...

A niggling doubt wormed its way into his thoughts. What if this was all an act? What if Wim was just buttering him up, waiting for the right moment to—

"Gone all silent on me, sweetheart. First time taking a life, I'm guessing?"

"Yes," Red admitted. "I know I shouldn't give a flying fuck about killing those monsters. But..." He sighed, rubbing a hand over his face.

"I've lost track of how many I've killed now," Wim said, almost absently.

"You mean... the ones you accidentally ate? That wasn't really your fault, though, if your sickness or whatever made you do it."

Wim fell silent, his gaze fixed on the dancing flames. The firelight cast strange shadows across his face, deepening the lines around his eyes, making him look older, more haunted. His neck wound hadn't fully healed when he shifted back, and some blood had leaked onto his shirt, leaving a dark stain.

Red shifted on his log, uncomfortable with the sudden change in mood—the victory of their earlier triumph had melted away like frost in sunlight.

"They visit me every night when I try to sleep," Wim whispered, his voice barely audible above the crackling fire.

Red's chest tightened. He couldn't bear to see this powerful man look so... broken. "But you shouldn't feel guilty, surely? It wasn't *you*."

Wim's eyes snapped up to meet his, and Red flinched at their intensity. "It's not only guilt I feel. It's *desire*." His fingers curled into fists. "When the beast takes hold, I crave the taste of blood, the feeling of ripping flesh between my teeth while they scream."

Ice slithered down Red's spine. His hand instinctively moved towards his bow, though he forced it back down. The way Wim spoke those words—with such raw hunger—made Red's stomach churn. This hardly seemed the same man who'd just praised him moments ago, who'd helped him light the fire and made them both stew.

Red pulled his red cloak tighter around himself. "I keep thinking about the elves," he said, mournful. A subject change was more than necessary. "The ones that we didn't save. They looked so desolate when they pressed their faces to the bars. It was like they were looking straight at me. And what about the ones we did save? They just ran off into the woods!"

"Elves are survivors." Wim's tone had softened, losing that terrible edge of hunger. He rubbed his palms against his thighs, shaking his head, and Red's shoulders loosened a fraction. When Wim leaned over to place a large hand over Red's, he didn't flinch. "Red. We did a good thing today. You can't save everyone. That isn't how the world works."

Red wasn't completely convinced they'd saved *anyone* today. Surely the runaway elves would starve to death in the forest, still chained together, but he forced himself to smile at Wim.

Draining the last of his bowl, Red sighed in contentment. It tasted delicious, with the extra herbs Wim added from his pack. He had to admit, this man could *cook*. He could probably give the palace kitchen staff a run for their gold.

The moment Red placed his bowl down, Wim reached for the cooking pot, pouring the last of the stew into it.

"What? Stop!" Red protested. "You have it."

"I gave myself more when I dished up."

It was an outright lie, but Red accepted the refilled bowl. His heart pounded in his chest, and he kept his eyes firmly on the stew. "Why do you keep feeding me?"

Wim chuckled. "Maybe I'm fattening you up to eat, aye?"

Red flinched so violently, the bowl almost slipped out of his fingertips.

Wim's face dropped. "Shit, that was stupid of me. Bad joke. Suppose that's still a bit raw after I did almost eat you the other day."

Red quickly changed the subject. "Speaking of eating, you're a great cook, I have to say. I could eat this until I burst."

Humming, Wim ran his finger along the insides of the cooking pot, scraping the very last remnants out. "Always liked cooking. I used to cook for my pack most nights, before..."

The fire crackled and popped.

"Before your... sickness?"

Wim nodded. "Been too long since I've had anyone to cook for. Good to see someone appreciate my food again. Even if you do chew with your mouth open."

"I do not!" Red said, through his final mouthful of potato, then slapped his hand over his mouth. As he swallowed, he imagined Wim cooking on a much larger flame, dozens of others sitting around in a circle each evening, sharing food and stories. The thought both warmed his heart while simultaneously making him feel very alone.

"Do you miss them terribly?"

"Yes," Wim answered, as soft as a whisper. "Terribly."

Wim's entire body sagged. What was it like, being away from the people who made you whole? Red wouldn't be able to say. Wim was missing a piece of himself, but it was a piece that didn't even exist for Red. At least you couldn't miss what you'd never had. Yet Red's heart ached, a painful gnawing sensation like a phantom limb, one he could feel but had never known, leaving him with an emptiness that felt as vast as the night sky.

"Does your pack... all live together?"

For a brief moment, Wim appeared startled by the question. Then he grinned. "Not all squeezed under one roof, if that's what you're thinking."

"I obviously didn't mean that." Was the wolf determined to remain infuriating for their entire journey together?

"Most live near the heart of our land—there's a big clearing there, with a well. Got a proper stone kitchen where I used to cook. The pups play in the grass. My place is just a small cottage, out on the edge."

"Oh?" Red pretended there was still food left in his bowl to scrape with his spoon. "You live there alone?" he asked, in an extremely casual manner.

Not casual enough—Wim left a beat of silence before replying, "Aye, I do. Why do you ask?"

"Just making conversation!" Red forced himself to look at the wolf, where a small smirk was waiting for him on Wim's lips. "I suppose I wondered if you had a... partner. A... wolf-mate, perhaps."

"No mate. Got the cottage all to myself. There's space, though, for two... should I need it."

Red's gaze lingered on Wim across the fire, conscious of his brow furrowing. Wim's expression remained inscrutable, offering no hints of what lay behind his words.

"Umm... Well, that's good. It's good to be prepared for these things, I guess."

Wim's large chest shook, and his lips pressed together tightly. "Aye."

The wind picked up, rustling the leaves above them and flickering the fire, casting dancing shadows around them. A chill ran through the air, wrapping around Red like an icy blanket.

He hasn't asked me if I have anyone special waiting for me back at the palace. For a moment, Red pictured himself through Wim's eyes—a pathetic nobody, disposable, friendless.

"I do have friends, by the way," Red said, more to his empty bowl than Wim's face. "You know, earlier. You said I didn't have any friends."

Red caught Wim's gaze, and for a fleeting moment, he saw a flicker of understanding in those deep, steady eyes. Wim's posture softened slightly, and he leaned forward.

"I'm sure you do, sweetheart."

Red blinked at the softness to the endearment. Wim must have caught it too, as he coughed, busying himself by poking their fire. "Tell me about them, then. Your friends."

"Well..." Red cycled through his very short list. "There's Auntie Anne. Not my real auntie, obviously." He stared into the crackling orange flames, memories of Anne warming him more than the flames ever could. "She's been in the Queen's service for over thirty years now."

Wim snorted. "And she doesn't wish to leave?"

"You can't just *leave* the palace." Red schooled his face lest he shoot Wim a scornful glare. "Of course she'd *like* to leave. But anyway, she's the closest thing I've got to family." A fond smile tugged at his lips. "When I was a child, many winters before the famine, she'd always sneak extra treats onto my plate when she thought I wasn't looking. A honey cake or a bit of candied fruit." These days, their roles had reversed, with Red ensuring the aging woman didn't starve. "And the stories she tells! She knows every bit of gossip in the castle, I swear. She'd whisper them to me at night, like we were sharing great secrets."

Now that Red had begun talking about her, the words wouldn't stop gushing out of him. "There was this one time, when I was about eight winters old. I'd overheard some nasty comments about my eyes from the noble children. Auntie Anne found me crying in the kitchen pantry." He gave an exaggerated roll of his eyes to show Wim how pathetic he was, but the memory tugged at something deep within him, stirring an all-too-familiar sense of inadequacy. Then he softened his tone to continue. "She didn't try to tell me it wasn't true, or that they were wrong. Instead, she told me a story about a prince with eyes like mine who could see magic that others couldn't. Said it was a gift, not a curse."

Red shook his head, feeling the tug of a smile stretch his lips. "Utter nonsense, of course. But it made me feel special, instead of... different."

Silence enveloped them, and Red's skin prickled. He'd over-shared, for certain. *He doesn't want to know all this, you fool!*

After shifting his gaze to the ground, Red had to force himself to meet Wim's eye—for he was surely smirking at the silly tale. But Wim's face held no judgement, only a quiet attentiveness that encouraged Red to continue. The way his deep, steady eyes were fixed on him, absorbing his words, made Red's heart race in a curious way.

"She taught me to read, you know. The Queen would have sneered, but Auntie Anne would sneak books from the library. We'd huddle by candlelight, sounding out words together."

"She sounds like a treasure, that one. World could do with more folk like her." Wim piled the empty bowls into the cooking pot, then tossed some more of their gathered wood onto the fire. He leaned back, inhaling deeply as he inspected the starless sky. "A wind's coming. Can smell it in the air."

As if the air could hear him, a sudden gust whipped through the trees, rustling the leaves before picking up fiercely, howling a warning. Their warm flames struggled against the onslaught of the rising wind, flickering precariously.

"Should get some sleep while we can," said Wim. "Won't be pleasant if this fire dies in the night."

R ed's eyes snapped open, his body racked with violent shivers. The wind roared through the trees, a bitter, relentless assault that penetrated his threadbare bedroll. He curled into himself, desperate for warmth, but found none.

Why was he so cold?

Bloody hell. The fire. What had happened to it? He squinted through the darkness to where embers should have glowed. Nothing but ash remained.

His fingers, numb and clumsy, fumbled with the edge of his blanket, trying to tuck it tighter. A futile effort. The biting cold seeped through every fibre, stealing his breath and clouding his thoughts.

You idiot. You should've known better. Should've brought a bedroll that didn't resemble holey cheese. You'll freeze to death by daybreak. The self-recrimination burned, but did nothing to warm him.

Red's jaw clenched, fighting against the tremors, but it was no use. His teeth began to chatter, an incessant, maddening rhythm that echoed in his skull. A whimper escaped his lips, unbidden and raw.

The wind shrieked, mocking his misery. Red squeezed his eyes shut, willing the cold away, but it only seemed to intensify.

His toes curled painfully, as if trying to retreat from the icy assault. Red flexed them, desperate for any scrap of sensation beyond the numbing cold. Nothing. Panic fluttered in his chest. Was this frostbite? Would he even have feet to walk with come morning?

Or perhaps the wolf would simply find an icy corpse when he awoke.

Hopefully Wim would relent on his 'wildling code' and eat Red's body. At least he'd be of some use, then.

The wind's relentless howl intensified, hurling icy needles that pricked at his exposed skin. Red burrowed deeper into his pathetic excuse for a bedroll, but the cold pursued him mercilessly. It seeped into his bones, turning his marrow to ice. His breath came in ragged gasps, visible in the frigid air.

Stupid, stupid, stupid. Should've stayed awake to guard the fire. Should've gathered more wood. Should've done a thousand things differently.

A particularly vicious gust tore through the campsite, ripping away what little warmth he'd managed to trap. Red's body convulsed, teeth chattering so violently he feared they might shatter.

Oh, what a way to die!

Something warm and solid pressed against his back.

Hot breath ghosted across Red's neck.

What in the seven hells...?

His mind reeled, struggling to process this sudden intrusion. Confusion gave way to realisation as soft fur pressed against his skin. *Wim.* The wolf had somehow wedged himself into Red's bedroll.

Red's teeth chattered violently, his whole body quaking.

"Shh," Wim rumbled, pressing closer. The wolf's massive form enveloped Red, radiating heat.

"W-w-what are y-you d-doing?" Red stammered, his words barely intelligible through his trembling.

"Couldn't bear to hear your teeth knocking together anymore," Wim grumbled. "But if you'd rather freeze to death, I can go back over there."

Red's limbs tingled as warmth slowly seeped back into them. The numbness in his toes receded, replaced by pins and needles. He flexed his fingers experimentally, relief flooding through him as sensation returned.

Wim's fur tickled Red's nose, and he fought the urge to sneeze. The wolf's scent filled his nostrils—earthy and wild, with a hint of pine and something musky that Red couldn't quite place. He burrowed deeper into Wim's thick coat, seeking more of that blessed warmth.

The wolf's body curled around him protectively, a living, fluffy shield against the biting wind. One by one, Red's muscles gradually unclenched, tension melting away as heat seeped into his bones. He pressed his frozen nose into Wim's fur, inhaling deeply.

Drowsiness crept over Red, his eyelids growing heavy. The wind's fury seemed distant now, muffled by Wim's solid presence.

Red's thoughts drifted, losing their sharp edges, the comforting sensation of Wim pressed up against him lulling him to sleep. His consciousness soon teetered on the edge of oblivion. Just before darkness reclaimed him, Red murmured into the soft fur. "Thank you."

Wim's only response was a low rumble that vibrated through Red's entire body. The sound reverberated in his chest, soothing and familiar.

Familiar?

Red almost laughed at himself. How had he become *familiar* with a wolf?

But as he buried himself even deeper in the wildling's warm embrace, he couldn't help but laugh at himself—for he was now very glad Wim had wanted to eat him the night they met.

Six

Red was enveloped in the most delicious warmth. He was perhaps the warmest he'd ever been. He snuggled deeper into the cocoon of heat, savouring the comfort, then peeled his eyes open. The first rays of sunlight streamed through the trees, casting a golden glow that kissed their camp and chased away the remnants of the night's chill.

Red's gaze drifted lazily across the extinguished fire, to where Wim would be—

Wim's bedroll was empty.

Memory crashed over him like ice water. The wolf. Wim had climbed in with him last night.

His eyes flew open. His pulse quickened to a jubilant dance. He lay frozen, hardly daring to breathe. Slowly, cautiously, he reached behind him, bracing for the brush of coarse fur.

His fingers met warm skin. Smooth. Soft. A light dusting of downy hair.

Red's breath caught in his throat. Human skin. Not fur at all.

Wim's chest rose and fell in a steady rhythm against Red's back. Still fast asleep.

When had Wim shifted back? It was one thing cuddling with a wolf for warmth, it was very much another with a naked man. How long had they lain like this, with Wim's human body pressed up against him so snugly? And why did the thought send a shiver down Red's spine that had nothing to do with fear?

Red squirmed against the bedroll's constraints, heart lodged in his throat as he tried to put distance between them. Yet Wim's slumbering form mumbled an incoherent protest and clutched Red closer, hot breath tickling his ear.

It was no good. Red was a prisoner in the wolf's arms. The wolf's strong, muscular arms, that were wrapped securely around him as if Red were a precious treasure needing to be protected at all costs.

Wim shifted, the barest movement, and the unmistakable press of an arousal nudged against Red's thigh. Shock coursed through him like liquid fire, but something else simmered beneath it—his own excitement.

A groan threatened to escape Red's trembling lips when Wim's solid length grazed against him where his leg met his buttock. He swallowed hard, unable to tear his thoughts from the intimate contact. The sensation sent tingly jolts through his limbs, his own cock happily swelling.

How could he, Red, who'd scorned and scoffed at the infuriating wolf-man, now find himself consumed by desire for him?

His cock mocked him, becoming as stiff as Wim's, a needy ache throbbing through it.

Oh, how easy it would be to touch himself, to relieve himself of this awful torture.

But the image of Wim's eyes pinging open the moment he did so froze his eager fingers in their tracks.

Again, Wim shifted, his very large member nestling even further into the thin material that covered Red's ass.

There was no other option. Red couldn't take it anymore. He was going to have to shuffle around so that Wim's bare cock would at least be poking a less compromising place.

At a snail's pace, Red turned to lie on his other side. *What a view.* His gaze traced the path of a sunbeam illuminating the golden flecks in Wim's stubble. Wim looked so different up close—a dusting of freckles not previously noticed peppered his sun-kissed cheeks.

If Red wanted to, he could lean over and kiss those cheeks. Wim would never know.

Traitorous want coiled in the pit of his stomach.

Then a sudden bolt of pure madness struck Red. What would happen if he climbed on top of Wim right now? What would the wolf do if he awoke to such a sight? The feel of Red's body against his surely aching erection?

Would he growl with need? Dig his large, strong fingers into the flesh of Red's thighs? Pull Red against his length to offer himself relief?

Would Wim become so wanton with desire that he'd beg Red to use his hands—or even his mouth—on him?

And would he cry out Red's name when he reached his peak, with the same reverence that lovers used when lost in each other's embrace?

All of this imagining had not helped Red's situation.

He brought his hand to his mouth and bit down hard, using the pain to bring him back to reality.

Red needed to stop this nonsense. Because this man, this attractive, surprisingly kind-hearted wolf, did not *care* for him, and Red needed to get these dangerous notions out of his head before Wim woke up.

He already told you he had no interest in fucking someone like you.

A tightness clawed at Red's throat as he stared at Wim's rather lovely face.

As if someone like him would want someone like you! Pah!

Besides, even if Wim *did* somehow want him, he'd likely be quickly put off by Red's lack of experience, the sum total of which consisted of letting the stable master fuck him a handful of times. Quick, mechanical experiences in dark corners that left him feeling hollow.

Melancholy seeped through him as he stared at the handsome man he shouldn't be dreaming of having.

This suffering had gone on long enough. He'd simply carefully remove himself from the bedroll before—

Wim's eyes fluttered open, and Red forgot the rest of the world existed outside their gorgeous golden depths. He heard himself take a large gulp of air, then held his breath, waiting for Wim's expression to harden in regret at waking up so close to Red.

It didn't. Wim's face remained pleasantly soft, gazing over at Red with a languid, peaceful smile, as though they woke up together like this every day.

"You changed back." Red's voice, raspy from sleep, wavered.

"It wasn't deliberate. Though by how you're clinging to me like a vine, I'd say you're not complaining."

Red opened his mouth to protest that yes, he did mind, thank you very much, but nothing came out.

"Didn't have a single dream," Wim said, brows furrowing. He stretched one arm out before scratching his beard, then slid it behind his head to act as a pillow. "Been weeks of the same nightmare haunting me. Always starts the same—I'm cured, heading back to my pack, but I can't find them. I keep walking in circles through the forest. Lost. Never finding my way home. Just me, alone, forever."

Wim stared at the trees above them, where a light breeze knocked many leaves from the branches, sending them drifting down to the forest floor.

Red cleared his throat. "That does sound awful."

Wim shuffled so that he was facing Red, propping his head on his arm. "Nice change, not being plagued by it for once."

The way Wim was staring at Red had his heart hammering in his chest. He looked like he expected Red to say something in response, but Red was completely out of words, what with Wim's face so close to his own. He could count every freckle if he wanted.

Why were the two of them still lying here, even? There were pots to wash, water to fetch, forests to be journeyed through, quests to be completed. Yet they were lazing about as if they were on a leisurely camping trip!

Wim's tongue darted out, moistening his lips, and Red's gaze locked onto the movement, his mind conjuring unbidden images of how those lips might feel against his own. Soft? Rough? Would they taste of the forest, of wild things?

A tremor rippled through Red's body, starting at his core and radiating outward. His fingers twitched, his toes curled, and his breath caught in his throat. He couldn't tear his eyes away from Wim's face, drinking in every detail as if seeing him for the first time. The faint scar that arched over his left eyebrow. The slight crookedness of Wim's nose that only served to enhance his rugged handsomeness.

Because, *fuck*, was he handsome! More handsome even than that nobleman from the Spring Ball that Red had plucked up the courage to talk to after several cups of ale.

And how did that end, Red?

Wim's hand reached out, slow and deliberate. Red's pulse thrummed like plucked strings as calloused fingertips brushed against his cheek, gently tucking a stray lock of hair behind his ear. His tender touch lingered, warm and intoxicating, sending sparks dancing across Red's skin. It was too much and not enough, all at once.

Red's lips parted, a shaky exhale escaping. He wanted to lean into that touch, to chase the warmth of Wim's hand. But he remained frozen, caught between desire and disbelief that Wim wanted him.

Oh, how Red would trade all the gold in the kingdom for just one kiss from Wim. But there was no way Red could initiate it, not after what Wim had said, not after the awful encounter with the handsome nobleman, the one who'd laughed in Red's face.

If only Red were strong enough that the sting of rejection would wash off him like water, instead of needling ever deeper into his bruised heart.

Wim's warm hand was still on his cheek.

Keeping impossibly still, Red only blinked, waiting to see what happened next.

Wim, voice low and husky, finally broke the silence. "Red, I—"

"Wilhelm!"

The unknown shout pierced the air, shattering the moment and making Red nearly jump out of his skin. Red scrambled upright lightning quick, fingers dashing madly for his bow.

"Who...?" Red searched for the intruder, pulling the bedroll up around him as if he were the naked one, not Wim. He saw nobody.

Then a wolf stepped out of the shadows of the foliage into their small camp.

"Astrid!"

Red's breath caught in his throat as Wim leapt up, evidently utterly unabashed by his nakedness. The wolf-man strode towards the newcomer, muscles rippling beneath his skin. He placed a large hand on her neck, fingers sinking into jet-black fur.

Astrid. She was smaller than Wim's wolf form, lithe and sleek. Her dark eyes darted between Wim and Red, intelligence glimmering within their depths.

Red's stomach twisted. The familiarity between Wim and this wolf—Astrid—was unmistakable. A hot, ugly feeling clawed at his insides. Who was she? Why was she here?

Astrid jerked away from Wim's touch, hackles rising. Her lips curled back, revealing sharp white teeth. A low growl rumbled from her chest as she backed away, gaze fixed on Red.

Wim held up his hands. "Easy now, Astrid. Let me explain this—"

She snapped her jaws, cutting him off. The accusation in her eyes was clear.

Red's fingers tightened around his bow. Just who was she to Wim? Had Wim lied about not having a mate? *No,* Red decided, looking between them. Not mates—but close, nevertheless.

"Who is *this?* You left the pack to cure your sickness, with promises of getting back to us as soon as possible. And now..." The black wolf glowered at Red.

"I'm travelling with him, that's all."

That's all.

Wim seemed to have caught the phrase too—he winced and glanced at Red, who forced his face to remain impassive.

"I mean, Red is a new friend. We're travelling the same way."

The wolf snorted. "I'm not sure how much *travelling* can be done wrapped up in a bedroll together. Besides, surely he's only slowing you down!"

Red opened his mouth to protest, then shut it. Because yes, he likely was slowing Wim down. The wolf could run at least four times as fast as him.

A horrible coldness washed over Red, all of Wim's gifted warmth vanishing. He couldn't help but glare at the new wolf, who'd appeared from nowhere, ruining everything.

"He's not," Wim said firmly, an edge of warning to his voice, and Red inwardly smiled.

See! Fuck off, lady!

"We're travelling as quickly as we can," Red said, because he hadn't said anything yet. "I'm on an official royal quest, which requires the utmost haste."

Wim spun, eyes wide, shaking his head subtly.

What? Was Astrid not to be trusted?

"I don't have time for you," the wolf spat at him, before turning back to Wim. "The reason I'm here—not that you've asked me yet—is because Tobias is missing."

Wim's face drained of colour, his eyes widening in horror. "Tobias? Missing?" His voice cracked, raw with emotion. "How? When?"

Red watched as Wim's strong frame seemed to crumple, his earlier confidence evaporating like morning mist. The name Tobias stirred something in Red's memory—hadn't Wim mentioned this young pack member yesterday, while they were exchanging numerous tales?

Astrid's tail drooped, her ears flattening against her head. "Five nights ago. He overheard us discussing your departure. My little fool of a son got it into his head that he could help you somehow."

A child, lost in these treacherous woods? The slave traders were simply one of many, many dangers that lurked in the shadows.

"Fuck!" Wim's anguished cry cut through the air. "Seven winters old! Wherever he is, he's probably shit scared."

Seven winters. Red's heart clenched. So young, so vulnerable. He remembered being that age, lost and alone in the palace, desperately seeking a place to belong. The thought of a child braving the forest's perils made his stomach churn. A surge of protectiveness washed over him with surprising intensity.

Astrid growled, frustration evident in her stance. "Don't you think I know that? I've been searching non-stop, following his scent. Then I picked up yours a couple of hours ago. He can't be too far from here!" Her voice broke, a whine escaping her throat.

Red's gaze darted between Wim and Astrid, noting the shared pain in their eyes.

Wim scratched his arm, his fingers travelling upwards to a wound on his biceps that Red hadn't noticed before. He seemed to pick at it, digging his fingers into it until he winced. "If only I'd tried to see Toby myself before I left, and explained everything properly."

Astrid's tone softened. "Don't blame yourself, Wilhelm. Everyone makes choices. Tobias chose to try to help you. And now I've chosen to follow his trail alone, because what else can a mother do?"

The words struck Red like an arrow to the chest. *Choices.* How many times had Auntie Anne said those exact words to him? *"Everyone makes choices, my dear Red. Even choosing to do nothing is still a choice."*

He remembered her weathered hands on his shoulders the day he'd chosen to train as an archer. Remembered how she'd smiled and told him she was proud, even though it meant seeing less of him.

"Some choices define us," she'd said.

"I'll help," Red blurted out, surprising even himself. Both Wim and Astrid turned to stare at him. "I mean, I'll try. I might not have wolf senses, but I have a pair of eyes."

Wim's expression softened, a flicker of gratitude passing over his features. "Red, you don't have to—"

"I want to," Red insisted, meeting Wim's gaze. "No child should be alone in this forest." If Red, a grown man, had found it challenging enough, goodness knows how frightened this boy was.

Astrid's hackles lowered slightly, her eyes studying Red with new-found interest. "I wouldn't say no to an extra pair of eyes. I separated from the rest of the search party yesterday to cover more ground."

Wim kneeled to press his head against Astrid's snout, rubbing his face into her fur.

Looking between them, a lump formed in Red's throat. The way they communicated without words, the shared understanding in their eyes... it spoke of a bond forged through season after season of companionship.

The pang of loneliness that struck Red was sharp, but familiar. He turned away, busying himself with adjusting his cloak. The fabric felt rough beneath his fingers. Red had never truly belonged anywhere. Not in the palace, and not out here.

A gust of wind rustled through the trees, and Red shivered. He glanced back at Wim and Astrid, still lost in their silent communication. The ache in his chest intensified. Would anyone ever look at him with such concern, such devotion?

Red squared his shoulders, pushing the melancholy aside. There was no time for dilly-dally daydreams, as Auntie Anne would say. There was a child to find.

Seven

R ed's legs burned with exhaustion as he stumbled over yet another tree root. The sun hung low in the sky, casting long shadows through the dense forest. He'd lost track of how many hours they'd been searching, his feet aching with each step.

Ahead, Wim and Astrid loped along in their wolf forms, noses to the ground. Every so often, Wim would glance back, slowing his pace to ensure Red was keeping up. Astrid, however, seemed single-minded in her pursuit, her black fur a blur as she darted between trees.

"Astrid!" Wim's gruff bark echoed through the woods. "Slow down. We need to stay together."

The wolf growled but complied, allowing Red to catch up. He leaned against a tree, chest heaving as he gulped down grateful breaths. One thing was now for certain—Red *was* far slower than a wolf.

"Any sign?" Red asked, voice hoarse from hours of calling Tobias's name.

Wim shook his massive head, concern evident in his amber eyes. Astrid whined, pacing impatiently.

They pressed on, the forest growing denser. Red's foot caught on a bramble, and he stumbled, barely catching himself. Wim was at his side in an instant, steadying him with his bulk.

"Thanks," Red muttered, flushing at his clumsiness.

Suddenly, Astrid's ears perked up. She let out a series of excited yips, bounding forward with renewed energy. Wim and Red exchanged a look before hurrying after her.

They broke through the treeline to find a small, gurgling stream. Astrid paced along the bank, sniffing frantically.

"She's found something," Wim explained. "Tobias's scent. It's stronger here."

Oh, please let us find him. Red's tired legs wouldn't handle many more miles. His heart raced with a mixture of hope and apprehension as they followed the stream uphill. The terrain grew rockier, the incline steeper. His calves screamed in protest, but he pushed on, determined not to slow them down.

As they rounded a bend, Astrid let out a triumphant howl. There, nestled in a steep, vertical cliff, was a narrow opening in the rock face. The cliff rose abruptly from the flat terrain, a fortress of stone that seemed to scrape the very sky. A few stubborn wildflowers found purchase in the crevices, adding pops of colour to the grey stone.

The two wolves wasted no time approaching the crack.

"Tobias?" Wim called, the name echoing off the stone. "Are you in there, friend?"

They all waited, breaths held, straining to hear any response from within the cave.

Nothing.

"He's in there!" Astrid pawed at the pup-sized crack. "I can feel it in my bones." She pressed her furry head into the gap, managing to burrow it a fair way in before she met resistance.

After a pitiful growl of frustration, Astrid shifted. Red averted his gaze as her fur melted away, revealing dark skin and toned muscles. Shooting Red a strange look, she huffed and snatched up her pack from where it had tumbled from her back to the ground. She yanked out a simple tunic, pulling it over her head.

"I'll be able to squeeze through now," she said, dropping to her knees.

Red glanced at Wim. He ought to stop his friend—the tall, broad woman was well-built, and was surely going to get stuck.

But Wim only watched as Astrid's short coils brushed the top of the crevice while she attempted to pass through. Despite her twisting this way and that, her shoulders caught on the rough stone. "Blast it all!"

Red chewed his bottom lip, studying the gap. His shoulders were narrower than Astrid's, his frame more slight. The space looked tight, but... He touched his red riding hood, drawing comfort from the familiar fabric. If Tobias was trapped in there, scared and alone...

"I could fit through," Red said, stepping forward.

Wim's growl rumbled through the clearing. "No." He stepped between Red and the cave entrance. "Too risky. Those rocks could give way at any moment, trapping you in there—"

"Then what's your alternative?" Red snapped. Frustration simmered within him. Clearly, Wim didn't think he was capable. "Leave him in there? I'm smaller than both of you. Let me try."

"It's too dangerous." Wim shifted back to human form, helping himself to a shawl from Astrid's pack and hastily wrapping it around his waist. His jaw clenched as he said, "We don't know what's in there, Red."

"*Toby* is in there, Wim!" Astrid practically snarled the words, looking between Wim and Red. "If he wants to try, let him!"

Red crossed his arms, meeting Wim's worried gaze. "What's the worst that could happen?"

You get permanently stuck between the rock slabs and die a slow, painful death.

Wim's shoulders slumped. He stepped away from the cave. "Fine. If you want to try, I won't stop you." His voice wavered, brown eyes wide.

Just what was his problem?

Red's pulse jumped skittishly, like a startled hare, and as he shrugged off his pack and quiver, he hesitated over the golden arrow inside. The Queen's words echoed in his mind... *"Guard it with your life, or forfeit that life instead."* He tucked it carefully beneath his other supplies.

Red stepped towards the crack.

"Your hood needs to come off, Red," Wim said softly. "It'll catch and tear."

Red's fingers tightened around the red fabric. Take it off? He never took it off, apart from when he needed to bathe. It was his mother's only gift to him, and his shield from the world. It had protected him through every nightmare, every cruel word from the Queen, every lonely night.

"It doesn't tear. It never has, not in all these winters."

"Do you really want to test that theory?"

Wim stared at him, concern spreading across his face as Red fisted his cloak.

It's just a riding hood, Red.

With trembling hands, Red unclasped the hood.

When Wim took it reverently, folding it with careful movements, a strange warmth flooded Red's system, combating the chill from removing the garment.

Red approached the narrow gap between the rocks. The darkness within seemed to pulse, to breathe. His skin prickled.

Don't think about being trapped. Don't think about being crushed. Don't think about the fact you're meant to be saving Falchovari from the Great Famine, not saving a cub from a cave to impress a handsome wolf.

That wasn't true, he was doing this to help a lost little boy. Mostly.

Red pressed his body against the crack, angling it sideways. One step, then another.

A jolt of joy rocketed through him as he slid straight through. *Success!*

He resisted shooting Wim a victorious grin and pressed on, inching his body through the gap.

Though the further he went, the more the space constricted around him, as if the cave itself was a living thing intent on holding him captive. He could feel the weight of the stone pressing in from all sides.

Each breath became a struggle as panic clawed at his throat, tightening like the very walls around him.

The jagged rock walls bit into Red's flesh as he forced his body through. His shirt and breeches were surely tearing, and pain blazed across his shoulders, his ribs, his hips. Blood trickled down his arm where stone had gouged deep. Each forward movement brought fresh agony as the rough surface scraped away more skin.

Thank goodness Wim made him take off his hood.

"Red?" Wim's shout came from behind. "You've stopped. Are you stuck?"

"I'm fine," Red ground out, pressing onwards despite the burning sensation across his torso. He wouldn't fail at this. Wouldn't prove himself weak.

The passage narrowed further. Red's chest compressed as he inched sideways, fighting for each breath. The darkness pressed in, absolute and suffocating.

Was this how he would die—crushed between two slabs of unforgiving stone, all because he needed to prove himself to a wolf who'd probably forget him by tomorrow?

He'd never complete his quest.

And then what of the kingdom? What of the children with hollowed cheeks and the elders too weak to leave their beds? The golden fields that once flourished now lay barren, and the marketplace that once bustled with life now echoed with desperate pleas for scraps. Red had seen it all—had witnessed the queen's indifference as her people starved. This mission wasn't just about proving his worth; it was about saving lives. If he failed here, trapped in this unforgiving darkness, what would happen? There would be nothing Wim and Astrid could do to free him. Though maybe Wim would take the golden arrow to Oma himself, complete the quest in Red's honour. That would be nice.

With one final surge of energy, Red gritted his teeth and pushed forward. The crack widened, stone walls falling away from his bleeding shoulders. He rushed forward, desperate to escape the crushing pressure. Three more steps and the passage opened into blessed space. His lungs expanded and sweet relief flooded his aching muscles.

Wim and Astrid's voices drifted to him as if through water, muffled and distant. Their words blurred together, meaningless save for the concern in their tone.

"I'm through!" Red's shout bounced off unseen walls, multiplying until it died away into nothing. He squinted into the darkness, willing his eyes to adjust. Shadows took shape—not a cavern at all, but a tunnel stretching endlessly ahead. The air hung thick and stale, untouched by sunlight or wind.

Loose pebbles crunched under Red's feet as he took his first tentative steps forward. The ground was damp, and wetness soon seeped through the holes in his boots. The tunnel curved slightly to the left, promising secrets in its depths. Something skittered in the darkness ahead, and Red flinched backwards.

What waited for him in these forgotten passages?

You are Red, brave royal adventurer, he told himself, but as he reached for his riding hood and found nothing, every morsel of bravery bled away.

He pressed on.

Something scampered over his feet.

His heart raced as he peered down. He could just make out a rat-shaped thing darting away from him. A shiver ran down his spine, but not before his brain cried out at him to catch it. The palace servants had roasted many a rat over the last few months.

Out of nowhere, his foot caught on an unseen object. He stumbled, flailing as he fell forward, hands outstretched. He hit the ground, his fingers brushing against something cold and smooth. Panic washed over him as his mind raced—could it be a bone?

His mind was assaulted with awful images of the rocky floor heaving with skeletons. Was that tiny crunch the sound of Red grinding a long-forgotten hand into dust? What if the shadows held the remnants of lost souls, their hollowed eye sockets staring into his, accusing him of trespassing in their dark domain?

Red pressed a shaky hand to his mouth. He was going to die here, in this filthy cave, with only skeletons for friends.

Then he heard it—the quietest cry. The whimper echoed through the tunnel, soft and frightened. Red's heart leapt—it had to be Tobias.

He leapt to his feet.

"Tobias?" His voice bounced off the stone walls. "Toby, is that you?"

Another whimper, louder this time, followed by a choked sob. Red pressed forward, ignoring the sting of his wounds as he half ran, half stumbled through the darkness. The tunnel curved sharply, opening into a small chamber. A tiny sliver of light illuminated the space from a gap in the ceiling.

"Toby?"

The boy huddled against the far wall, naked and shivering. Dirt and grime covered his dark skin, and tears had carved clean tracks down his cheeks. His left leg stretched out at an awkward angle, caught in the cruel teeth of a rusty rabbit snare. The metal contraption had bitten deep into his flesh, and dried blood crusted around the wound.

Red's stomach turned at the sight.

He'd seen these devices thousands of times, when out training with the Queen's Huntsman. Sharp metal teeth designed to snap shut on anything that triggered the pressure plate, anchored to the ground by a heavy chain. The length of chain attached to the trap trailed upwards to where it disappeared through the narrow crack in the ceiling. Someone from above—desperate villagers hunting for food, perhaps—had lowered the device into the cave system, likely hoping to catch whatever creatures might dwell in the darkness. Instead, they'd ensnared a child.

"It hurts," Toby whimpered, his small frame shaking. "I c-can't get it off."

"I know, little one." Red crouched beside him, careful not to touch the snare. "I'm going to help you, alright? Your mother's just outside. We've been looking everywhere for you."

Fresh tears spilled down Toby's face. "Mama's here?"

"She is. And Wim too."

"She found Wim?!" For some reason, this made Toby explode into a fresh torrent of tears. "I couldn't find him! I tried so hard!"

"Now, I'm going to need you to be very brave. Can you do that for me?"

Toby nodded, his bottom lip trembling. "I've been trying to shift, but every time I start, the pain gets worse, and I can't go through with it."

Red's fingers trembled as he examined the rusted trap. His heart ached at each of Toby's quiet whimpers. The scrapes to his skin were nothing compared to what the boy must be experiencing right now. The mechanism looked simple enough—all he needed to do was press down on the springs at either side to release the pressure.

"Now, this *will* hurt," Red warned, positioning his hands. "Ready?"

Toby squeezed his eyes shut and nodded.

Red pressed down hard on both springs. The metal teeth retreated with a harsh screech, and Toby yanked his leg free with a strangled cry. Blood welled fresh from the puncture wounds.

"Can you stand?" Red offered his hand.

Toby gripped it tight and pulled himself up. The moment he put weight on his injured leg, he crumpled with a yelp.

Red steadied him. "You need to shift. Your wolf form will heal faster."

"But it hurts so much—"

"I know, little friend. But the sooner you shift, the sooner the pain will stop."

Toby's face scrunched up in concentration. His small frame trembled, then blurred. Soon, where the boy had stood, a black wolf pup now balanced on three legs, his fourth held carefully off the ground.

"Good job." Red smiled. "Think you can make it back through the tunnel?"

The pup limped forward, determination evident in every step. Red followed close behind, ready to catch him if he stumbled.

"Is my mum really mad? I bet she is. But I bet she isn't as angry as I was, when I heard they were making Wim leave our pack."

"Is that why you tried to follow him?"

"Yeah! It wasn't his fault he ate those people. His sickness made him do it. It's not fair he had to leave all by himself!"

Red hummed in agreement.

"And before that, he was hiding away in his cottage for months, all by himself! Alpha wouldn't let him out even to continue to train me to hunt. It's so stupid. Like he would hurt *me?* I'm his best friend!"

Red snorted, quickly turning it into a cough. "Best friends? How... nice!"

Tobias stopped his three-legged hop. "I'm not joking." His black ears twitched. "He's been my best friend since I was five, when a storm came while we were out playing. I was a stupid scaredy-cat and started crying like a baby, but he made a shelter with his own body, keeping me warm until the rain stopped. He always puts others before himself, just like a brave knight does."

"I believe you," Red replied. Hadn't Wim acted similarly towards Red? Taking care of him, at the expense of himself? *Did you think you were special, Red?* A cruel voice whispered in his mind. *Wim sees you like a child—weak, helpless, needing protection.*

"He sounds like the perfect best friend," Red forced himself to say.

"He is!" Toby said forcefully.

Red's chest tightened at Tobias's earnest defence of Wim. The child's unwavering loyalty struck a raw nerve—memories of his own desperate attempts to gain Queen Schön's approval bubbled to the surface. He'd spent countless hours practising perfect posture, memorising etiquette, trying to hide his mismatched eyes by styling his long hair just so. All for nothing.

Yet here was Wim, who'd earned such devoted friendship simply by being kind. By sheltering a frightened child from the rain, by teaching him to hunt.

How different would his life have been if someone had wrapped him in their arms during storms, instead of leaving him wrapped in wool on cold palace steps?

Red untangled the strange knot of envy that had formed inside him before pushing the vile feeling deep down. How pathetic to be jealous of a child.

"Are you alright?" Tobias asked, his wolf head tilted to one side. "You look sad."

Red strode briskly ahead. "Let's focus on getting out of here."

"Who even are you, anyway?" said Tobias, curious.

"I'm Red. I'm from the palace."

"The palace? Do you know the Queen?" The pup whispered the question, as if even uttering the phrase might summon Queen Schön to strike him down. "Is it true she's ruled for over two hundred winters? That's what Ma said!"

"It's true," said Red. Two hundred winters, and no sign of weakening, not a single wrinkle on her brow.

"So are you a prince?"

"Definitely not! Do I look like one?"

"Not really."

Ouch.

"You look like you have too many adventures to be a boring prince!"

Red snorted. "Is that so?"

"But, but, I saw the frog prince once!" Toby almost stumbled over something, and let out a moan of pain. "Nobody in my pack believes me, but I really did!"

"The legendary frog prince? I believe you."

"No you don't," Toby said crossly. "You're just pretending. But it's really true! I accidentally got separated from everyone on a hunt, and I found a small frog friend. I followed him for ages, and he led me to the frog prince."

Red side-eyed the pup. Could the tale be true? Only a very small number of people knew the true identity of the frog prince, and Red happened to be one of them. "Oh?"

"He lives in these super cool ruins!"

"And what did the frog prince do?"

"He said if I gave him my favourite stick, he'd help me find my pack!"

"And did you?"

"Yeah! He led me all the way back to the part of the forest that I know well. But then, when I saw my mum's pawprints, I turned around, and he was gone!"

"Huh," said Red, smiling to himself. "He sounds like a very nice frog prince."

They fell silent after that. Slowed by the limping pup, the journey back felt endless, each of Toby's occasional pained whines cutting straight to Red's heart.

Finally, blessed daylight filtered through the narrow crack. Red helped guide Toby through first, wincing as the jagged stone scraped his own wounds anew.

"Toby!" Astrid's cry of relief echoed off the rocks.

Red squeezed through after the pup, emerging into sunlight just in time to see Astrid gathering her son into her arms, peppering his furry face with kisses.

Red's chest tightened as Astrid shook her son by the scruff. "What were you thinking? You could have died!" Her words shook. Then, in the next breath, she crushed the pup to her chest, burying her face in his fur. "My stupid idiot. My baby, my precious boy."

The raw emotion in her words pierced straight through Red's defences. His throat constricted. This... this wild swing between fury and fierce protection... Was it what having a mother felt like? The question ached in his chest.

The familiar weight of his red cloak settled on his shoulders. Red turned to find Wim studying his face with concern. The pad of Wim's thumb brushed across his cheekbone, coming away red.

"You're bleeding all over, sweet—" Wim cut himself off with a cough. "*Red*. These cuts need cleaning."

Red lifted his chin. "What's one more battle scar to a true adventurer?" he said brightly, though the thought of angry red lines rendering his face even uglier made him want to cry.

"Is that what we're calling your graceless tumble through that tunnel? An adventure?"

Before Red knew what was happening, Wim's fingers tangled in his hair, ruffling his mess of strawberry-blond strands. The gentle touch sent sparks dancing across Red's scalp, down his spine. His breath caught in his throat as Wim pulled him into a tight embrace.

Red's face pressed against Wim's broad chest. The wolf's scent—pine needles, earth, and *wildness*—wrapped around him like a blanket. His head spun, thoughts scattering like autumn leaves in a storm. The steady thump of Wim's heart echoed through Red's body, and heat bloomed across his cheeks.

What was happening to him? His legs felt like jelly, his stomach doing strange flips. Perhaps he'd lost more blood than he'd realised from the tunnel scrapes.

Before Red could process these bewildering sensations, a black blur launched itself at Wim. Toby crashed into them with an excited yip, breaking the embrace.

Wim dropped to the ground with an exaggerated "Oof!" as the wolf pup pounced on his chest. His deep laugh rang through the clearing as he scratched behind Toby's ears. The pup's tail wagged frantically, his injured leg forgotten in his joy at finding his missing pack member.

"Miss me that much, did you?" Wim's voice held such warmth as he ruffled the pup's fur. Toby responded by licking Wim's face enthusiastically, drawing another rich laugh from the man.

Red pressed a hand to his still-racing heart, willing it to slow. The dizziness lingered, even though Wim no longer held him. He couldn't tear his eyes away from the sight of Wim sprawled in the dirt, playing with the pup as if he hadn't a care in the world.

"These two are like peas in a pod," Astrid said, appearing beside him. "They have the same mental age, apparently."

Red laughed. It certainly seemed that way, currently.

"Tobias used to follow Wim everywhere. We'd call him Wim's shadow. Before he left, Wim was confined to his cottage for several months, and Toby tried to sneak there every single fucking day."

Red liked this kid more and more by the second.

Panting, Wim stopped rolling around with Tobias, leaning backwards on one arm. "Stay the night," he said to Astrid. "Go back tomorrow. That's if you..." His face twisted. "Feel safe enough. Round me."

"Can you still feel the onset of your condition? Do you still get that warning period?"

Wim nodded. "Aye, but I'd understand if—"

"Then of course we'll stay, Wim. We'd love that."

A sharp unpleasantness suddenly coiled in Red's stomach—he'd presumed that he'd get Wim to himself again, as soon as the pup was found. But it appeared he'd be sharing Wim a little longer.

That's perfectly fine, Red. There's no reason to care.

A soft bump against his leg scattered his brooding thoughts. Tobias gazed up at him with dark, pleading eyes, his small wolf form pressing closer.

"Will you play with me later?" he asked, so sweet and so hopeful.

Red's breath caught. He dropped to one knee, bringing himself level with those earnest eyes. His fingers sank into impossibly soft fur as he scratched behind Tobias's ears.

"I'd love to," Red whispered, any earlier negativity melting away as Tobias's tail wagged with unbridled joy. The pup butted his head against Red's chest with such enthusiasm that Red toppled backwards onto his bottom.

"Careful there, sweetheart," Wim called out, eyes dancing with amusement. "He'll have you wrapped around his little paw in no time."

Red swept his riding hood around his shoulders with a flourish, nose pointed towards the stars. He minced across the forest floor, each step a perfect imitation of the Queen's affected gait.

"Mirror, mirror, on the wall..." He pitched his voice into her nasal drawl. "Who is the most *perfect* of them all?"

Tobias rolled across the ground, clutching his sides with laughter. Even Astrid's shoulders shook as she tried to maintain her composure.

"Oh, what's this?" Red snatched up a wooden spoon from the cooking pot, brandishing it like a sceptre. "A *peasant* dares to smile in my presence? Guards! Off with their head!" He swished the spoon through the air with dramatic flair.

"Does she really say that?" Tobias gasped between giggles.

"Oh, worse." Red draped himself across a log, one hand pressed to his forehead. "Last week she had the royal gardener flogged because his roses bloomed *pink* instead of red."

Wim lounged against the wall, watching Red's performance with a gleam in his eye that made Red's chest flutter. He pushed the feeling aside, focusing instead on Tobias's rapt expression.

"Tell us more about the palace!" The boy bounced in place, dark eyes wide with excitement.

Red adjusted his hood like a crown. "Well, there was the time she made all the maids crawl backwards for a week because one of them tripped over a bucket of water." He demonstrated, scuttling across the ground in an exaggerated crab-walk that sent Tobias into fresh peals of laughter.

"And then—" Red leapt to his feet, twirling. "She insisted every-one speak in rhyme during the winter solstice feast, just to entertain her. The poor cook nearly fainted trying to announce each course." He cleared his throat, adopting a trembling voice. "H-here comes the roasted pheasant fair, served with herbs and special care..."

Tobias clapped his hands in delight, and even Astrid couldn't contain her laughter now. Red couldn't help but bask in their at-tention, the decades of watching the Queen's ridiculous behaviour providing endless material for his mockery.

"Alright," said Astrid. "Time for bed. We leave at first light. You're going to have a lot of apologising to do when we round up your search party, Toby."

Tobias's face fell. "But I haven't even got to hear about the Queen's son, Makellos, yet! Is he truly the most beautiful man Fal-chovari has ever seen?"

"Oh, him? He's boring. No exciting tales about him." Red must have inserted some venom into his words, because Wim tilted his head.

Red had tried many a time in his childhood and adolescence to befriend the Queen's perfect son, and had been rejected more times than he cared to think about. The uptight man kept to himself, but had the whole palace under his spell. Red wasn't entirely sur-prised—the man was the very picture of beauty, with his skin as pure as white snow, and his silky, ebony-black hair. What Red would give for even a fraction of his allure...

Astrid climbed to her feet. She'd dressed properly once they got back, and Red's eye kept catching on her necklace—a cord with what looked like wolves' teeth threaded through. Were they the teeth of her enemies? The woman's presence was formidable even before the morbid accessory.

"You'll need your energy for tomorrow," Astrid told her son.

"But I'm not sorry for leaving!" Toby remained seated, folding his arms. "I need to help Wim!"

Red knelt beside Tobias, his heart twisting at the boy's fierce declaration. The child's devotion to Wim struck a chord inside Red, he couldn't deny it.

"Listen." Red took Tobias's hand in his. So much smaller. Red already felt a kinship with this little wolf pup, even though they'd spent but a handful of hours together. "I promise I'll help Wim in your place."

Tobias's eyes narrowed. "You swear?"

"Cross my heart." Red traced an X over his chest, careful to keep his gaze fixed on the boy rather than risk meeting Wim's eyes. His cheeks burned at making such a statement, but something in him couldn't bear to let this child down.

"No, no." Tobias shook his head. "You have to do a proper pack promise." He stuck out his little finger. "Hook your finger with mine and repeat after me. By the moon's silver light..."

"By the moon's silver light..." Red echoed, linking their fingers.

"And the forest's ancient might..."

"And the forest's ancient might..."

"I swear to help Wim find his cure, or may wolves chase me day and night!"

Red's lips twitched at the childish rhyme, but he repeated it solemnly.

Tobias beamed. "Now you have to howl."

"I most certainly do not."

"You do! It's part of the promise!"

Red glanced at Astrid, who raised an eyebrow in confirmation. Swallowing his dignity, he tilted his head back and let out what he hoped was a passable howl.

Tobias dissolved into giggles. "That sounded like a dying cat!"

"Hey now!" Red ruffled the boy's hair. "I'd like to see you do better."

Tobias demonstrated with a surprisingly decent howl of his own, which Red refused to admit put his attempt to shame.

"And I'll come and visit you at some point." The bold words tumbled out before Red could stop them. But it was alright—this pup would forget all about Red in no time. "I'll tell you all about the rumours of Hallin's Plumed Menace."

"*The Plumed Menace?*" Toby's eyes were as wide as saucers. "The one who killed Hallin's crown prince?"

Red winked. "He leaves a single feather atop his victims."

"Alright, that's enough. He already has nightmares without adding to his list of monsters, thank you, Red."

Tobias rolled his eyes, muttering something under his breath, but allowed his mother to guide him away to where she'd set up her bedroll.

Red eyed his own, just as a chilly gust of wind blew through the camp. It would be cold again tonight, but there wouldn't be any chance of a repeat of last night's sleeping arrangements, not after Astrid's reaction this morning.

He said he couldn't stand the sound of your teeth chattering, that was all!

Using both hands, Red rubbed at his face. These confusing thoughts were doing his head in. He climbed into his bedroll, pulling the fabric tightly around him, and shut his eyes. Tomorrow, he'd go back to calling Wim an insufferable mangy mutt. No more distractions.

A soft thump beside Red made him freeze. He cracked open one eye to see Wim spreading his bedroll mere inches from Red's own.

"What do you think you're doing?" Red propped himself up on his elbows.

"Setting up camp." Wim didn't look up from smoothing out the fabric. "Unless you'd prefer I sleep in wolf form and shed all over you again?"

Red's heart performed a frenetic tap dance. "That's not—I meant why are you setting up *here*?"

Maybe Astrid had told Wim he needed to sleep closest to Red, so that he'd be the one eaten if Wim turned feral in the middle of the night.

"Astrid snores." Wim's lips quirked. "Like a bear with a cold. Trust me, you don't want to be anywhere near that."

"There's plenty of space by the fire."

"Ground's all bumpy over there." Wim stretched out on his bedroll, folding his arms behind his head. The movement pulled his shirt tight across his chest. "Besides, you're hopeless at keeping warm. Consider this a favour—I won't have to listen to your teeth chattering all night."

Red flopped onto his back, yanking his hood over his face. "Fine. But if *you* snore, I'm pushing you into the stream."

"Wouldn't dream of it, sweetheart."

That word was starting to do crazy things to Red every time he heard it, though he knew Wim only used it to annoy him. He squeezed his eyes shut, willing his racing pulse to slow.

The rustle of fabric indicated Wim settling in beside him. Red could feel the heat radiating from the other man's body, calling to him like a siren song in the chilly night air.

This is going to be a very long night.

"Has Astrid really killed enough wolves to make a necklace of their teeth?" Red whispered as quietly as he could. This shift in conversation would steer them towards safer ground.

He glanced at Wim, only to find the man struggling to suppress a chuckle, his shoulders shaking as he barely contained his amusement. With a grin, Wim finally let out a hearty laugh. "She looks scary, but Astrid's soft as butter, really. The teeth thing? That's just what we do. When our milk teeth fall out, we hang onto them if we can. Then when we find our mate, we give them the teeth instead of rings. Most of us make them into trinkets, like what Astrid's wearing."

"Those were milk teeth? They were huge!"

"Have a closer look at the size of mine next time."

Red would rather not get too close to those razor-sharp incisors.

"Most of us don't bother wearing them. They'd get lost too easily when we're shifting all the time. But Astrid lost her wife, so she likes keeping them close. Tobias wears them sometimes when he's missing his mum."

A heavy weight settled in Red's chest. Loss carved deeper wounds than any blade. Every morning he touched the red hood, wondering about the mother who'd left him, imagining what could have been. And here was little Tobias, clutching his mother's teeth, trying to hold on to memories before they faded like footprints in fresh snow.

Red's fingers brushed against the worn fabric at his neck. The hood held no answers, no whispered secrets of who he was or why he'd been abandoned. Just thread and cloth, as silent as the palace steps where they'd found him.

His throat tightened. At least the boy had known love, had memories to cherish. Had someone who'd wanted him enough to leave a piece of themselves behind.

Disgust flooded his system, overriding his jealousy. Was he truly going to be resentful of this kid's childhood memories?

Pull yourself together, Red.

"So, you wildlings mate for life, do you?" said Red, trying for a playful tone.

"What's so funny about that? Loving someone forever?"

"It's the stuff of tales. Not real life."

For a long moment, Wim shuffled about. "I hope someone proves you wrong someday, Red."

Something in Wim's tone made Red's stomach flutter, and he found himself wishing, just for a moment, that he could believe in such things.

A long silence stretched, and Red had almost drifted off when Wim's deep voice next rumbled through the darkness.

"By the way, loved your wolf howl back there, sweetheart. Sounded real... delicate."

"Oh, stop." Red yanked his hood lower, grateful for the darkness hiding his burning cheeks.

"I could show you how, you know." The bedroll rustled as Wim shifted closer. "Got to use your throat properly. You were doing it through your nose."

"I was not using my nose." Red rolled onto his side, facing away from Wim. "And I don't need howling lessons from a mangy mutt."

"Mangy? I'll have you know my coat is extremely well groomed."

"That's not something to brag about."

"Says the one who spends twenty minutes fussing with his hood to make it just so."

"I do not— How dare— It needs to sit properly!"

A low chuckle vibrated through the small space between them. "Keep it down, sweetheart. Some of us want to sleep."

"You started it, you prick," Red hissed, but he couldn't quite keep the smile from his voice.

Eight

R ed drifted awake. He stretched, muscles aching from where he'd strained them squeezing through the narrow crack. His heart sank as his uncomfortably full bladder demanded attention.

Something was restricting his movement, however.

The weight of Wim's arm draped across his chest pinned him in place, heavy and warm. Through half-closed eyes, he watched the rise and fall of Wim's chest, the way his lips had parted slightly in sleep.

Just five more minutes.

But his damned bladder wouldn't be ignored. Red shifted, trying to wiggle out from under Wim's arm without waking him. The arm tightened, pulling Red closer.

Bloody hell.

"Wim." Red poked him in the ribs. "Let go."

Wim's only response was a soft grunt as he buried his face in Red's hair.

"For heaven's sake." Red managed to extract himself, though not without considerable effort. The cold night air hit him like a slap, and he grabbed his cloak, wrapping it tightly around his shoulders.

Unlike Red, Wim had no modesty concerns and would relieve himself right at the edge of camp, marking his territory like the animal he was. Red refused to do his business where anyone might stumble across him. Body still tired from the events of yesterday, Red meandered through the darkness, stumbling a few times over thistle bushes, until he found a secluded tree to do the honours on.

Once finally finished, Red headed back towards the warm glow of the dying fire. He was almost at the camp's edge when voices caught his attention—Wim and Astrid, speaking in urgent whispers. Red froze, ears straining. They were so quiet, it was impossible to hear them clearly. He inched forwards, ensuring he was covered in the darkness of a large pine tree.

"Look, he's... sweet, I'll give you that. But this golden arrow? Turn to *dust*? Come on, Wim!" Astrid's tone was sharp, even in a whisper. "You can't seriously believe this bullshit!"

"Don't be ridiculous. Course I don't believe it! It's stupid nonsense."

Ouch. Red felt the blow as a punch to his chest. There wasn't a hint of doubt or hesitation in Wim's voice. He thought Red's mission a folly, and had been humouring him all along, like a child.

Perhaps Red should slink back into the forest, protect his fragile pride from any more harm. A braver soul would announce his presence, defend his quest, but Red wasn't feeling particularly brave.

"Just before you left, you told me that your sickness was getting worse and worse. That you thought you might have only weeks left before you lost yourself completely. And now you're wasting time with this random man? You need to stick to your plan and get back to our pack! We need you, Wilhelm!"

"Nothing has changed, Astrid!"

"So what's going to happen when—"

"Shh!" Wim audibly sniffed the air. "I can smell him."

Fuck.

Red strode forwards with casual confidence, making a show of blinking in surprise at finding the two wolves awake and hovering near the fire. He yawned convincingly. "Just needed to piss."

Without another glance at them, Red slipped straight back into his bedroll, burying himself in it to hide his face. Red's throat con-

stricted as he lay rigid, paralysed with pure humiliation. The conversation replayed in his mind, each word a fresh wound.

Stupid nonsense.

Of course Wim hadn't believed him—who would? He was just
some pathetic nobody on a ridiculous quest, prancing about the
forest with delusions of importance.

His fingers curled into the fabric of his red cloak. The familiar
texture brought no comfort tonight. Instead, it felt like another lie
wrapped around his shoulders. A gift from a mother who'd abandoned him.

Stupid, stupid, *stupid*. He should have known better than to trust
a wolf. To think Wim actually cared about his mission, about *him*.
The warmth they'd shared, the playful banter, the way Wim's eyes
crinkled when he smiled—was it all an act?

Through the thin material, he heard Astrid and Wim return to
their bedrolls. Red tensed as he waited to see if Wim would move
close, put his arm over Red again.

He didn't.

A hot tear slid down Red's cheek. He brushed it away furiously,
but another followed. The thought of Wim laughing at him behind
his back was simply unbearable.

So was the thought of facing him tomorrow. He'd have to announce that they'd go their separate ways. Insist that he was only
slowing Wim down—the truth, after all.

*And face this place all alone? Would you even make it to the Dark
Forest?*

And say he *did* make it to the Dark Forest. What then? Everyone
knew the tales—massive spiders that drained men dry, horrors that
slithered in the darkness, waiting to feast on lost souls. Auntie Anne
had terrified him with bedtime stories of the Dark Forest's hungry
shadows, of men who entered and were never seen again—at least
not with their minds intact.

Red sighed. No, his very real and important quest to stop the
Great Famine was too critical not to utilise this wolf's help, despite

his betrayal. A wolf—especially one like Wim—might be the only thing standing between him and the Dark Forest's countless terrors.

Red would have to keep travelling with him. He'd use him for his cooking, his navigation, and possibly his warmth, in emergencies. Use his keen senses and predator's instincts to navigate the forest's deadly paths.

But he wouldn't trust him.

Red was excellent at divining people's intentions—never fell for a feint during training, could often read the tiniest flicker of emotion in someone's eyes.

He ran over every interaction he'd had with Wim since they met, scrutinising each moment. It had always bothered him why Wim had agreed to help him. The wolf's vague answers had niggled at him. Usually, Red could tell someone's true motivation within moments of meeting them, but with Wim... there was something different. Something hidden.

His resolve galvanised. He had a choice here—attempt to run away from this wolf, or stay and uncover whatever it was that Wim was keeping from him.

Life is full of choices, Red.

Red knew his present one.

No matter what games Wim was playing, Red would discover the truth.

Tomorrow, he'd watch more carefully. Listen more intently. The wolf might think him a naïve child who'd swallow any tale, but Red had survived the Queen's court. He knew how to play people's games.

Nine

True to their word, their guests left at daybreak. Red awoke to Astrid shushing Tobias as they gathered their belongings. Red sat up to wave goodbye to the little wolf, and his heart squeezed a little when Toby said, "See you soon, Red!" with such conviction Red almost believed that they'd meet again.

Astrid gave Wim a long, meaningful look as she said her goodbyes, before the pair of them disappeared into the forest.

Then, it was just the two of them again.

They went about their usual business, falling into the easy rhythm they'd developed. Wim rolled up both their blankets to stuff them into packs. Red gathered the cooking pot, wiping it clean with wet leaves, the morning air nipping at his fingers as he did so.

Wim made no sign of being suspicious that Red had overheard him last night, and so Red made a performance of humming a merry tune, pretending everything was fine.

Everything *was* fine. He was *fine*.

He just needed to get to the Dark Forest and say goodbye to this pesky wolf who was causing him grief.

"Here." Wim tossed him a carrot from their stolen stash. Red caught it with one hand, his other busy coiling rope.

"Ta." Red bit into the crunchy flesh as he watched Wim kick dirt over the remains of their fire. "Which way?"

Wim pointed southeast, where the trees grew closer together. "Five days' walk that direction, if the weather holds."

Still five days. They'd lost an entire day on finding and rescuing Tobias.

They set off through the undergrowth, the forest quickly swallowing them up.

Red lasted ten minutes before he couldn't resist starting his very subtle investigation.

"You never said how exactly you developed this... disease of yours," Red said.

Wim looked at him sharply. "No, I didn't."

Going well so far, then.

"Well... do you mind telling me?"

Wim was quiet for a moment, then sighed. "Dark magic got me." Wim's tone dropped low, and Red found himself leaning in to catch the words. "Was hunting way past our lands, right up near Hallin. Far away, but game was getting scarce..." He trailed off, seemingly lost in dark thoughts before he continued. "Heard crying. Little girl, all alone in the woods." His jaw clenched. "Least, thought it was a little girl. When I went to help, she changed."

"Changed?" Red's feet caught on a root, but he barely noticed.

"Turned into a soulstealer. Huge black beast, bigger than me in wolf form, alight with purple flames. My pack hears whispers about it now and then—The Black Beast. People found dead, not a mark on them. Turns out the stories were true."

Red's breath caught. "A... soulstealer? Those aren't real!" But even as he said it, his skin prickled with gooseflesh. Everyone knew the stories—creatures that fed on the essence of living beings, leaving behind empty husks.

"They're real enough." Wim's fingers brushed against his left biceps. "Shifted quick as I could when it came at me—saved my life—but not before it got its teeth in."

He stopped walking and pulled up his sleeve. Red's eyes widened at the mark beneath the dark hair. He'd noticed it before, but looking at it up close, the bite appeared fresh, as if it had happened yesterday. An angry circle of puncture wounds, a curious bright purple colour, slightly raised and painful looking.

"That's impossible." Red reached out to touch it without thinking, then snatched his hand back. "How is it still...?"

"Still raw? Part of the disease." Wim tugged his sleeve back down. "The bite never heals. And neither does what it did to me inside."

"I've just realised you haven't told me yet about where exactly you're going, to cure it."

"Hmm? The Dark Forest, same as you." Wim's voice remained even, but his left hand drifted to his neck, scratching at the short hairs there.

"Yes, but where exactly *in* the Dark Forest?" Red kept his tone light, even as a chill ran through him at the mention of that accursed place. Tales of travellers being devoured by monstrous trees flashed through his mind—childhood stories meant to frighten, but which now seemed all too plausible.

Wim glanced towards him again. "Do you know it well?" His hand dropped from his neck, but immediately returned to scratch again.

Red clucked his tongue, hopping over a fallen log, and impressing himself with the grace with which he landed. "No. I only know Oma's house is right in the middle of it. So, what exactly do you need the Dark Forest for? Is there like... a magical herb that will cure your illness?"

Wim paused for too long before he answered. "Perhaps."

Wim said nothing else, though his fingers continued their nervous dance against his neck. Red itched to slap his hand away.

"*Perhaps*? What do you mean?"

Wim appeared to trip, then steadied himself on a tree trunk. He remained there, facing the bark, hands pressed against it.

"Wim?"

The wolf did not turn around. Red's hand hovered in the air, then fell back to his side. His heart rate sky-rocketed. Just what was Wim playing at?

"Wim?" Red repeated. "What did you mean?"

"I *mean* for you to stop asking questions that don't concern you." Wim whirled around, teeth bared.

Holy shit. Red stumbled backwards, heart leaping into his throat. His hand flew to his bow before he could stop himself. Wim's entire demeanour had transformed—shoulders hunched, muscles coiled tight.

A growl rumbled deep in Wim's chest. "I don't owe you any information." He advanced, his words rough like gravel. "I owe you *nothing.*"

Red's back hit a tree trunk. He lifted his chin. Refusing to show how his hands trembled, he clutched his bow to his chest like a shield. "I'm sorry. I thought—"

"You thought what? That we were friends?" Wim's laugh held no warmth.

What the fuck?! What had Red done to deserve this?

"*No,*" said Red with all the conviction he could muster, but his voice cracked. He straightened his spine, forcing steel into his words. "I thought you were a man of some honour. Clearly I was wrong."

Wim's face flickered, the aggression dropping away, replaced by a grim frown. He stepped back, running both hands through his hair. "I... forgive me. That was—" He winced, pressing his palm against his temple.

Wim's pupils dilated, black swallowing the warm gold of his irises as his breathing grew ragged and uneven. Red's stomach twisted at the sight, and his fingers clamped around the wood of his bow. Then the wolf's fingers twitched, nails lengthening into vicious black claws before retracting again, the transformation rippling beneath his skin like a wave. Red knew all too well what those claws could do to human flesh.

"Something's—" Wim doubled over, a shudder racking his frame. When he looked up, his eyes had taken on an amber glow. "Got to go. Right now." Wim gasped, already backing away, his movements jerky and uncontrolled. "Need to get far away from you." He staggered backwards, pressing his palm against his temple. "Map," he growled, gesturing frantically. "Quick!"

Red fumbled with his pack, yanking out the crinkled parchment with trembling fingers. The map fluttered in the chill breeze as he spread it against the rough bark.

"Here—" Red's voice wavered as Wim lurched forward, jabbing a trembling finger at the map.

"Follow this stream—" Wim's words came in pained gasps. "Silver birches—then south. Two days' walk." Another violent tremor caused him to stagger backwards.

Two days? Red would be alone for two whole days? It took a shocking amount of energy not to protest, not to beg Wim not to leave him.

"Promise me—" Wim demanded, eyes flashing. "You'll stay on the path."

Something warm bloomed in Red's chest, despite everything. Even now, with whatever affliction gripped him, Wim worried about Red losing his way. Maybe even seeing Red again.

"I promise," Red whispered, but Wim had already staggered into the shadows between the trees, leaving nothing but the fading sound of laboured breathing and pine needles crushed beneath boots.

Alone again. Possibly for good this time.

How terribly convenient this happened just when you started asking difficult questions.

Though a sudden thought struck Red—had he somehow *caused* this? Had he put Wim under too much stress, triggering one of his episodes?

Or, alternatively, perhaps Wim had even been faking that whole thing, just to get away from Red. After all, Red barely knew this strange wild wolf.

You'll be fine by yourself. Get a grip!

It was time to leave—Red had stood still for far too long. He had golden arrows to shoot, quests to complete.

And so, he set off.

Red's feet dragged through the undergrowth, each step heavier than the last. He couldn't stop the map from trembling in his hands as he traced their planned route with his finger. *Their* route. But Wim wasn't here anymore.

The forest stretched endlessly ahead, a maze of thick trunks and gnarled branches that blocked most of the weak autumn sunlight. Red pulled his crimson hood tighter around his shoulders, fighting against the growing shadows that pressed in from all sides.

Left foot. Right foot. Keep moving.

A jay shrieked overhead, causing him to stumble. His heart pounded as he steadied himself against a tree trunk. The rough bark bit into his palm, grounding him in reality.

The path ahead curved sharply around a massive oak. Red forced himself forward, focusing on the crunch of leaves beneath his boots, but every snap of a twig, every rustle in the bushes made him whirl around, searching for grey fur, for familiar orange eyes.

Why does being alone feel so different now?

A branch snagged Red's cloak, yanking him backwards with brutal force. The clasp dug into his throat, choking off his air, and his fingers scrabbled at his neck to release the catch. He finally freed himself and dropped to his knees, gulping down precious air.

The cloak pooled around him on the forest floor. His heart stopped. Had it torn? He gathered the fabric in his hands, running his fingers over every inch, searching for snags or holes. Nothing. The rich red wool remained pristine, unmarred by the forest's assault.

Twenty-four winters of wear, and still the cloak endured. Through childhood scrapes and teenage adventures, palace corridors and forest paths—not a single tear. The fabric slipped like water through his fingers, soft yet impossibly strong. Just like his mysterious mother must have been, to brave leaving her baby on those cold palace steps.

Did she know how precious the cloak would be to me, throughout all these winters?

Red froze mid-step. Movement flickered between the branches—a flash of grey? His pulse quickened. His wolf had come back to him! "Wim?" The name escaped his lips before he could stop it.

But no, the sounds drifted down from *above*, musical and lilting. Someone—or something—lurked in the uppermost branches, where shadows tangled thick and dark. Laughter trickled down like poisoned honey.

Red's fingers found his bow, nocking an arrow in one swift motion. The muscles in his arms tensed as he drew back, scanning the canopy. His eyes darted from branch to branch, searching for any sign of movement.

More laughter, closer now. The sound skittered across his skin like spider legs. Red's arrow tracked the noise, but the dense leaves revealed nothing. Whatever creature haunted these heights knew how to stay hidden.

Hold on... That laugh. Red knew that laugh!

A voice rang out, high and clear as a bell: "Having fun on the Queen's time, little archer?"

The Queen's Shadow.

Red's stomach soured. What was this prat doing here?

Most knew him as The Royal Shadow, though Red liked to think of him as The Royal Pain in the Ass—always causing trouble where it wasn't needed, usually for his own amusement.

He was a malevolent spirit enslaved by the Queen. She had stripped the geist of his name, knowing that anyone who uttered it aloud would take control of him for themselves. He was one of 'The Collection'—magical beings Queen Schön possessed for her personal use.

The geist quickly flipped his dark hood up, laughing as his body fully materialised. In this human form, he could be mistaken for a nobleman of military standing in his late forties. Red had often been jealous of his black brocade coat and its beautiful ornate gold detailing. The garment commanded authority and respect—not that Red had any intention of bowing down to the aggravating entity.

"Come down from there, geist!" Red snapped at the spirit.

Still cackling, the Queen's Shadow slowly floated down to the ground ostentatiously, waving one leather-gloved hand in a performative circle. Hitting the forest floor, black leather boots solidified.

Red's bow remained trained on him. "What are you doing here?"

"What do you think I'm doing here? The Queen has sent me to check up on you."

"Check up? But I'm not even there yet!"

"Evidently." The man flashed Red a thin-lipped and cold smile. "But then, she did send a child to do a man's job." He rotated his hand in an impatient gesture. "Out with it—what excuses would you like me to pass on to explain your failure?"

Red swallowed, buying time. The last thing he wanted to do was to anger the Queen. "There's been a few... mishaps."

The Queen's Shadow's eyes darkened until they were impossibly black. He leaned uncomfortably close, sniffed at Red and then frowned. "Why do you smell like... wolf?" His mouth curved upwards into a wicked smirk. "Have you been lying with wolves?"

Red's heart sank faster than a stone dropped into a deep well. "Your insults have always been atrocious, but that one is simply pathetic."

The spirit's eyes swirled with shadows when his gaze roamed up and down Red's body. "Don't play coy. You reek."

Red couldn't help but flinch as he felt his face colour. "Just... fuck off back to the palace, and tell the Queen I'm almost there!"

The Shadow's form wavered, melting into pure darkness. The shadows around Red's feet writhed and twisted, reaching for his ankles with ghostly fingers.

Red jerked backwards. "Stop that!" he snapped, more high-pitched than intended.

The spirit reformed, closer than he had been before. "What's wrong, little archer? Scared of the dark?"

"I'm not scared of anything, especially not an overgrown shadow puppet." Red lowered his bow, forcing his racing heart to slow. "How does it feel, by the way? Being Her Majesty's pet?"

The smile vanished. "Watch your tongue."

"Or what? You'll go crying to your mistress?" Red's words dripped with venom. "That's all you can do, isn't it? Run back to her like a good little pet."

Darkness exploded outward from the spirit's form. The forest dimmed as if night had fallen in an instant. Shadows danced across tree trunks, taking the shapes of writhing serpents and snarling wolves.

Red's hands trembled, but he pressed on. "Does she at least pat you on the head when you fetch her slippers?"

"You little—"

"Or does she just snap her fingers and point?" Red clicked his fingers. "Here, boy! Heel!"

The Shadow's face contorted with rage. With a rush, shadows surged forward, attaching to Red's cloak and tightening the fabric around his throat. Though the geist's shadows slithered across his skin like frozen serpents, Red lifted his chin and held the spirit's gaze steady.

"You're an unwanted, foolish child, and I don't have time for your insolence. No wonder the Queen sent you to the *Schwarz Wald* in little more than a red cloak. You're entirely expendable—as you always have been, from the moment you were abandoned on the palace steps," the Queen's Shadow spat.

Red's chest tightened, but he forced out a laugh. "Better abandoned than enslaved. I may not have family, but at least I'm not spending eternity as someone's trained dog."

The shadows constricted around Red's throat, leaving him suddenly gasping for air, spots dancing in his vision.

"You dare—"

"What's wrong?" Red taunted. "Does the truth hurt? Go on then, run back to your kennel. Tell the Queen how mean I was to you. I'm sure she'll give you a treat for being such a good boy."

The geist let out an inhuman screech that pierced through Red's skull. The shadows around Red's throat dissolved as the spirit's form exploded outward, fragments of darkness scattering like shards of black glass.

Red's crimson cloak whipped upwards in a violent gust, the fabric snapping like a banner in a storm. The force knocked him backwards, and he stumbled against a tree trunk. His hood flew off his head, exposing his face to the sudden, bone-chilling cold that radiated from the dispersing spirit.

In moments, the forest returned to its natural state. Weak sunlight filtered through the canopy once more, and Red's cloak settled back around his shoulders. He adjusted the clasp at his throat, fingers trembling despite his best efforts to steady them.

He's gone, Red assured himself, smoothing down his hair while his breathing steadied. But for how long? Red had royally pissed him off. Goodness knows what the foul spirit would say to the Queen. She'd made her expectations extremely clear to Red, including what failure would result in.

After allowing himself one mighty sigh, Red trudged onward.

The sun crept across the sky like a timid child, ducking behind clouds whenever Red glanced up. His shadow stretched and shrank as hours trickled past, marking time's passage across the forest floor.

His legs burned. One foot in front of the other, again and again, until walking became a mindless rhythm. The forest blurred into an endless sea of brown and green, broken only by patches of weak sunlight that dappled the ground. His crimson cloak caught on brambles, tugged free, caught again.

More than anything, Red was bored. He hadn't fully appreciated having Wim permanently by his side, to chat to—or complain at—over the last few days. Now, it was just him and his thoughts. His anxious, turbulent thoughts. His brain churning over Wim, his quest, and what exactly the Queen's Shadow would tell her when the snitch reported back.

When Red next lifted his gaze, the sun had shifted from yellow to orange, painting long shadows across the leaf-strewn path. How many hours had passed? His muscles screamed the answer: too many.

A distant buzz caught his attention... voices carrying through the trees. Red froze, hand flying to his bow. The sound grew clearer: excited chatter, multiple people talking at once. His first instinct screamed to slip away into the undergrowth, to avoid any chance of confrontation.

But... there was something about the tone. A festive, enthusiastic energy. Something exciting was afoot.

Red's curiosity won out. He crept closer, keeping to the shadows of the larger trees. The voices grew louder, clearer—definitely commoners, by their accents. The clink of metal tools accompanied their chatter.

He peered around a thick oak trunk. About twenty people had gathered in a small clearing, clutching farming implements: scythes, pitchforks, even a few rusty spades. Their clothes marked them as farmers—rough homespun wool and leather, patched and worn. Despite their weapons, their faces shone with excitement and glee.

What could have drawn such a crowd so deep into these woods?

Red crept forward through the underbrush, careful to keep his movements slow and deliberate. His boots found purchase on patches of moss, avoiding the crunch of dead leaves. The excited chatter grew louder as he approached the edge of the gathered commoners.

A woman stood at the fringe of the group, her hollow cheeks and sharp collarbones visible above her threadbare shawl. Despite her gaunt appearance, her eyes sparkled with an almost manic energy as she gestured with a pitchfork.

"Pardon me," Red whispered. "What's all this about?"

The woman whirled around, her face lighting up at the prospect of sharing news. "Wolf sighting! Just this morning, near the stream." She clutched her pitchfork closer, knuckles white against the wooden handle. "Biggest one anyone's ever seen, they say. Grey as storm clouds."

Red's heart plummeted. *Wim.*

"We've not had meat in months," she continued, practically bouncing on her feet. "Think of it—enough wolf meat to feed the whole village! The pelt alone would fetch a fine price at market." She peered at Red's cloak with undisguised hunger. "You look like you know quality furs. Care to join the hunt?"

The crowd surged with renewed enthusiasm as someone shouted about fresh tracks. Red's fingers tightened around his bow, bile rising in his throat as the commoners brandished their farming tools like weapons.

But surely Wim should be miles upon miles away, in the opposite direction?

"I highly doubt you lot are capable of bringing down a wolf," Red said, not caring about his rude tone. It was true—this ragtag group of merry men likely couldn't bring down a sleepy kitten.

The woman scoffed, jabbing her pitchfork towards Red's chest. "We've got more than just tools, pretty boy. Jed and his lot laid out poisoned rats near the stream." Her grin stretched wide, revealing several missing teeth. "Once that beast's slowed down, we'll finish it off proper."

Ice flooded Red's veins. *Poisoned rats!* His mind flashed to Wim, hunting alone in the forest, stomach growling after days of sharing his food with Red. Would he be desperate enough to eat dead rats?

"Smart plan." Red forced the words past numb lips. His fingers found the smooth wood of his bow. "Actually, I'd love to help. Been tracking wolves for many winters now." The lie tasted bitter on his tongue. "This bow's brought down plenty."

The woman's eyes lit up as she took in his weapon—far superior to their silly farming implements. She turned to the crowd. "Oi! This one's a proper hunter!"

Faces turned towards Red, hungry eyes fixing on his bow. A burly man with a pitchfork stepped forward. "You know how to use that thing, boy?"

Red drew himself up to his full height. "I killed several slave traders with it just days ago."

Murmurs of approval rippled through the group. The burly man nodded, though he eyed Red warily. "Welcome aboard then. We're heading to the stream first—check on them rats."

Red's heart lurched wildly. He had to somehow find Wim first. Had to warn him. But how to slip away without raising suspicion?

"Excellent." Red kept his voice steady and light. "I'll scout ahead, see if I can pick up any tracks. I'm sure you know this, but wolves have keen noses—better if we spread out rather than moving as one big group."

The commoners nodded eagerly, already breaking into smaller clusters. They buzzed with a sense of purpose, of strategy, that made Red feel even sicker. They didn't notice his hands trembling as he checked his quiver.

Red was being foolish. Even if he did succeed in finding Wim, the wolf would likely bite his head off before Red could open his mouth. He'd certainly been close to doing just that, earlier. Really, Red should ignore this and press on to the Dark Forest—there had already been enough delays.

The path before Red split like a forked tongue, neither direction promising comfort. For someone who'd spent his life following orders, choosing his own path felt dangerous—yet thrilling.

Teetering on the edge of his decision, Red's mind suddenly conjured up the soft wolfish whimper of pain Tobias had made, trapped in that snare. His chest tightened at the memory. Whatever Wim was hiding, whatever game he was playing... Red couldn't bear the thought of the wolf meeting a similar fate, alone in these woods.

You're going soft in your old age, Red. That, or he had a soft spot for this damn wolf.

His stomach lurched as he turned away from the commoners, forcing his steps to remain measured and calm as he headed towards the treeline. The moment he passed the first row of trees, he picked up speed, all earlier weariness and hunger forgotten.

Then, Red ran, praying that he found his wolf before they did.

His wolf.

Shaking his head dismally, Red chastised himself. But it was no use—he couldn't deny it. Red had much more than 'a soft spot' for the insufferable mangy mutt.

That was dangerous. Caring, the Queen often said, made you weak, made you vulnerable.

The real question was: which would kill him first—the wolf, his secrets, or Red's own foolish heart?

Ten

R ed sprinted, his boots pounding against the forest floor as he followed the commoners' directions to the riverside trap. His heart raced with every step, every rustle of leaves, and every snap of a twig. His world narrowed to a point as finding Wim became his sole purpose.

The trees blurred together as he pushed himself to run faster, his legs burning with each stride. Sweat trickled down his face, and his breath came in ragged gasps. A sharp jolt followed by a hollow thud behind him told him the sack of carrots and potatoes—their hard-won bounty from the slavers—had fallen from his pack. He couldn't stop. Not now. Every time he slowed down, he pictured Wim eating one of the poisoned rats, his body convulsing, froth foaming at his mouth, pouring down his grey muzzle.

Finally, after what felt like an eternity, the foliage became less dense, and water gurgled nearby. Red burst into a small clearing, the stream on the far side of it. His eyes scanned the area, and his stomach dropped. Three dead rats lay in a neat row, their bodies stiff and lifeless. But it was the sound that followed that made his blood run cold: a scream.

Red's gaze whipped to the left, and his heart stopped. Wim stood close to two mangled, lifeless bodies, their clothes shredded and bloodied. Red let out a small cry before slapping his hand over his mouth. *Holy shit.* Ragged holes had been torn through their abdomens, revealing wet crimson cavities where flesh had been savagely ripped away, and he was fairly sure that the glistening, rope-like masses he could see were intestines.

"Jed and his lot," the woman had said, and it looked like Red had found them. His mind stuttered, unable to process what he was seeing. Wim had done this. Wim had ripped those two poor souls to shreds.

And now, Wim's massive paws pinned down a third man. The commoner's eyes bulged as Wim's jaws hovered inches from his face, ready to strike.

Red's mind froze, paralyzed by the horror of the scene. Wim's fur was matted with dirt, twigs, and blood, his eyes blazing with an unnatural hunger. The air reeked of death and bodily fluids, and Red's stomach churned with the stench.

The man's screams grew louder, more desperate, as Wim's breath washed over his face. Red's hand instinctively went to his bow, but he hesitated. What was he supposed to do? Kill Wim to save this random peasant? His mind spun with the impossible choice. He knew Wim, knew the man beneath the wolf, but in this moment, he was faced with a monster.

Wim's muscles tensed, his jaws opening wider, ready to deliver the killing blow. Time seemed to slow as Red watched, transfixed, as Wim's fangs hovered above the man's throat. Red's voice was stuck in his throat, unable to call out, unable to do anything but stand there and witness the carnage.

"Stop!" Red eventually managed. "Wim, stop!"

The massive wolf's head swung towards Red, and his heart clenched. Though the creature wore Wim's form—the same grey fur, the same muscular build—the eyes that fixed on him blazed with feral hunger. No trace remained of the warmth, the intelligence, the *humanity* Red had come to know.

A growl rumbled through the clearing, deep enough to vibrate through Red's boots and up his spine. The wolf's muzzle pulled back, revealing crimson-stained teeth in a grotesque parody of a smile.

"Ahhh," the beast's voice scraped like claws across stone. "It's *you*, the delicious one."

The pinned commoner seized his chance. He scrambled backwards on his hands and feet, then bolted into the forest, crashing through the undergrowth in blind panic.

Red's fingers tightened on his bow, but before he could raise it, the wolf lunged. The world spun as Red's back slammed into the ground, knocking the air from his lungs. His bow clattered away, far beyond reach. Massive paws pressed into his shoulders, and the stench of blood and death washed over him as hot breath ghosted across his face.

Rising panic consumed Red as the wolf's weight crushed him into the earth, leaves and twigs digging into his back. This close, he could see chunks of flesh caught between the beast's teeth, could hear the wet sound of saliva dripping onto the ground beside his head.

Those weren't Wim's eyes staring down at him. They held no recognition, no warmth—just raw, primal hunger.

"I can't wait to see if you taste as delicious as you smell." The wolf leaned towards Red's neck.

Think, think, think!

Could anything pierce through the feral haze clouding Wim's eyes? The weight of the massive wolf pressed him further into the ground, and sharp claws pricked through his shirt.

"What would Tobias say if he saw you now?" Red spat. "His brave, strong Wim, reduced to this savage beast? Is this the wolf who protected a scared child from a storm?"

The wolf's growl faltered for a fraction of a second.

"He adores you." Red twisted the knife deeper. "Called you his hero. But look at you—nothing but a rabid dog who can't control himself. He'd be *disgusted*."

Wim's jaws snapped inches from Red's face, but Red caught a flicker of something in those wild eyes—pain.

"You don't deserve his trust. Or his love." Red's words dripped with venom. "What kind of monster murders innocent people?

You're worse than the slave traders. At least they kept their victims alive."

The wolf's grip loosened slightly, a whimper escaping his throat.

"You promised to protect him. To teach him. But you can't even protect yourself from your own savage nature." Red made his lip curl in disgust. "You're nothing but a disappointment. A failure. Tobias deserves better than a beast who'd rip apart humans like they were prey."

Red was making himself sick with the words, hurled at Wim like poisoned arrows.

The massive wolf's body began to tremble, violent shudders racking his frame. His head dropped, ears flattening against his skull as whimpers escaped his throat. The sound pierced Red's heart—raw, wounded noises that spoke of deep pain.

Guilt crashed over Red. His cruel words had cut through the feral haze, yes, but at what cost? Each tremor that passed through Wim's body felt like an accusation. Red had weaponised Wim's love for Tobias, turned it against him in the most vicious way possible.

The pressure on Red's chest eased as Wim lifted his paw, backing away with his tail tucked between his legs. Blood still matted his fur, but the wild hunger had vanished from his eyes, replaced by something worse—shame.

Red didn't think. He surged forward and threw his arms around Wim's neck, burying his face in the thick grey fur. The wolf stiffened at the contact, but Red held on tighter, fingers curling into the soft strands.

"I'm sorry," Red whispered into Wim's fur. "Come back to me, Wim. I just need you to come back to me," he rasped. "I need you with me, Wim. I won't make it to the Dark Forest alone. I'll be walking in circles, starving half to death by nightfall. And who will keep me warm at night?"

"Get off me," Wim said. And it was Wim now, Red knew it for sure... somehow. "Red, get off me," he growled, though he made no attempt to shake him away.

"No."

Red's face was buried in Wim's fur, his cheek pressing against a bloody mat. He couldn't face the fully gut-wrenching display he was sure he'd see in Wim's eyes.

"Get off me." Wim's words were strained. "I'm covered in their blood. Their *flesh*. I can still taste it in my mouth." A shudder ran through his massive form. "You were right. I'm nothing but a savage beast."

Red's arms tightened around Wim's neck, even as the wolf tried to pull away. The copper tang of blood filled his nostrils, but he refused to let go.

"I should have ended this months ago." Wim's words came out in a broken whisper. "Before I killed anyone else. Astrid..." His voice caught. "She found me with the rope. Stopped me. Said there had to be another way." A bitter laugh rumbled through his chest. "But look what I've become. Those men—"

"Stop." Red pulled back just enough to meet Wim's gaze. The feral hunger had vanished completely, replaced by a deep well of self-loathing that made Red's chest ache. *You did this, you stupid fool.* "I shouldn't have said those cruel things. I only wanted to break through to you."

"Every word was true." Wim's ears flattened against his skull. "What kind of creature rips men apart like that? You were right about Tobias. That boy thinks I'm some kind of hero. I'm not." He jerked his head towards the mangled bodies. "I'm a fucking monster. Only thing left is to remove myself completely, make it so I can't kill again."

"No!" Red cried. "*You* didn't kill these men, Wim! It's just a bit further to the Dark Forest. You're going to cure your illness, and all will be well again. You'll go back to your pack, and cook for everyone again, and hunt and play with Toby." *And never see me again.* "Please, Wim, let's finish our journey. I can't do this without you!"

A distant shout pierced the air. Wim's ears shot up, his massive head turning towards the sound. More voices joined the first, growing closer with each passing moment.

"That man must have found his friends." Red's heart raced. "We need to leave. Now."

"Maybe I should stay here. Let them finish it." His eyes were fixed on the mangled corpses. "Their families deserve that much."

"Like hell you will." Red grabbed a fistful of Wim's fur, yanking the wolf's head around to face him. "You think dying will solve anything? Those men chose to lay poison for you. They weren't innocent victims—they tried to murder you first!"

"That doesn't excuse—"

"Shut up and listen to me." Red pressed his forehead against Wim's muzzle, ignoring the blood. His fingers tightened in Wim's fur. "I won't let you give up. Not when you're so close."

The voices grew even louder. Someone shouted about following a blood trail.

Wim's ears flattened. "Red—"

"No." Red cut him off. "Either we both leave right now, or I'm staying here to face that mob with you. My Auntie Anne once said life is full of careful choices. And now you have to choose, Wim. Choose to live. Choose to come with me. Choose Tobias, and Astrid, and your pack."

A growl rumbled through Wim's chest. "You're a menace."

"So I've been told." Red tugged at Wim's fur. "Now move your furry ass before they catch us both."

With a resigned huff, Wim surged to his feet. Red took the opportunity to quickly reclaim his bow.

"Climb on my back," Wim growled, crouching low to the ground. "We'll move faster this way."

Red's heart skipped as he stumbled back in shock. *Ride the wolf like a horse?! Madness!* The massive wolf's back stretched before him like a grey mountain, muscles rippling beneath thick fur. His mouth went dry. One wrong move and he'd tumble straight off.

"For fuck's sake, hurry up!" Wim's tail lashed in agitation as another shout echoed through the trees, closer now.

Red's fingers fumbled with the straps of his pack, cinching them tight across his chest. His bow jumped against his spine as he took a hesitant step forward. What if he lost his weapon?

Wim's fur felt coarse under Red's palms as he gripped two handfuls, the texture different from the soft downiness of his scruff. Red swung his leg over, thighs pressing against Wim's sides. Heat radiated through his breeches from the wolf's body, and Red's stomach lurched as he settled his weight.

Red never was the biggest fan of horse riding.

He'd just have to close his eyes and cling on for dear life.

The scent of pine needles and blood filled his nose as he pressed his chest against Wim's back, trying to find his balance. His fingers twisted deeper into the thick fur, heart hammering against his ribs.

"Hold tight," Wim rumbled beneath him. "And try not to pull my fur out by the roots."

Before Red could brace himself, Wim shot forward like an arrow loosed from a bow. The world blurred into streaks of green and brown as they tore through the forest. Red's stomach dropped, but instead of the nauseating bounce of a horse's gallop, Wim's movements flowed like water. His massive paws struck the earth in a rhythm that felt as natural as breathing.

"Got to find my pack," Wim said. "The beast always shakes it off when he takes control. Right pain in the ass."

Red nodded against Wim's fur, unable to form words as they wove between ancient oaks and leapt over fallen logs. The wind whipped his hair back, and his heart soared with each bound. This was nothing like the jarring, awkward motion of riding a horse. Wim moved with the grace of a predator, each muscle working in perfect harmony.

They reached a hollow beneath a lightning-struck tree. Wim snatched up his pack with his teeth, tossing it behind to Red with a quick jerk of his head. The leather straps settled against Red's back, and then they were off again.

The forest quickly became a blur again. Red's thighs gripped Wim's sides as they navigated the terrain, ducking under low-hanging branches and skirting around thorny bushes. The pack bounced against Red's spine in time with Wim's strides. Sunlight dappled through the canopy above, creating patterns that danced across Wim's grey fur that Red traced with one hand.

Once they'd put several leagues between themselves and the commoners, Red found himself grinning, then *laughing* as they bounded over a small stream. Water sprayed up around them, catching the light like scattered diamonds, soaking Red's side.

When was the last time Red had experienced such *fun?*

Was this what flying felt like?

No, not flying.

Freedom.

This was freedom.

And Red was terrified by how much he craved more.

After what felt like hours, Wim's pace began to slow. His sides heaved beneath Red's legs, and his breaths came in heavy pants. Red slid from his back, his own legs shaky as they touched the ground. His cheeks hurt from smiling, and his hair was a wild mess from the wind.

"Shift back," Red said softly, pressing his hand between Wim's two furry ears. "Please."

Wim shifted beneath his palm, and soon Red's fingers were tangled in Wim's thick chestnut locks. Bones cracked and reformed until a man knelt before him, head bowed, chest heaving. Wim tilted his face into Red's touch, and Red's hand slipped to cup his cheek.

Dark circles haunted Wim's eyes, carved deep like valleys in weathered stone. His shoulders drooped with invisible weight, and sweat gleamed on his bare skin despite the cool air. Something raw and wounded lived in his gaze as he looked up at Red—something that spoke of endless nights running from his demons, of carrying burdens too heavy for any man to bear alone.

Red's thumb brushed across Wim's cheekbone, catching on day-old stubble. The gesture felt achingly tender, far too intimate for near-strangers. Yet he couldn't bring himself to pull away, not when Wim leaned into his touch like a man starved for it.

"No one's ever..." Wim swallowed hard. "The feral state always takes over. Hours or days of violence, of hunting, of..." He caught Red's hand, pressed it further into his cheek. "But you broke through. Somehow, you got through to me when I was lost."

Rising to his feet, Wim strode a few paces away from him, stretching out his shoulder muscles. He towered over Red, his broad shoulders blocking out the filtered sunlight. A shadow crossed his features as his gaze drifted to the horizon.

"So many dead." The words fell like stones into still water. "So many lives I've taken. Fathers, sisters, sons—all dead because of what I am." Wim's hands clenched into fists at his sides. "Would've been more, if not for you."

Red's breath caught in his throat as Wim's large bare form stepped towards him. Red moved backwards on instinct, an automatic response to the predator approaching him. But Wim's hand shot out, fingers wrapping around Red's forearm with surprising gentleness.

"Thank you," Wim murmured, drawing Red closer until barely a handspan separated them. The warmth of his skin radiated through Red's sleeve where he gripped him. "For stopping me. For staying when you could've run."

"Of course." Red searched for more words, and came up short, distracted by the expanses of Wim's skin currently on display, and how much his fingers ached to touch him. One hand fought the edge of his riding hood, to dance across the worn hem.

Red's breath hitched as Wim pulled him into a crushing embrace. The wildling's massive frame dwarfed him completely, surrounding him in a cocoon of heat and strength. Though Red was clothed, every point of contact burned—chest to chest, Wim's arms locked around his waist, their legs tangled together. Red's face pressed against Wim's collarbone, his hands trapped between their bodies.

Red stretched his fingers to splay them across Wim's chest, mapping the ridges of muscle beneath warm skin. He barely reached Wim's shoulder, forcing him to tilt his head back to look up at him. The position left Red feeling vulnerable, exposed, yet somehow safer than he'd ever felt before.

A soft rumble vibrated through Wim's chest as he nuzzled the top of Red's head, his nose buried in strawberry-blond waves. The gentle gesture contrasted sharply with the raw strength in his arms as he walked Red backwards until rough bark pressed against his spine.

What is happening? Red's thoughts scattered like autumn leaves in a storm. A flurry of butterflies exploded in his stomach as Wim's face dropped to the crook of his neck, inhaling deeply. Hot breath fanned across Red's skin, raising gooseflesh in its wake.

"God above," Wim growled, the words muffled against Red's throat. "You smell absolutely fucking delicious."

The words echoed what the feral wolf had said earlier, and at their first meeting. But this felt different—charged with something that made Red's knees weak and his mouth fall dry. The hunger in Wim's tone held none of the feral savagery from before. This was something else entirely, something that made heat pool in Red's belly and his fingers curl against Wim's chest.

"Your scent's been driving me wild since I first caught it."

Every muscle in Red's body trembled. Like a fever dream, reality blurred at the edges. People didn't look at Red this way. People didn't want Red this way. Especially not someone like Wim. And yet here he stood, pinned between rough bark and Wim's burning heat.

"I can still taste them," Wim whispered. "Those men. I can still taste their blood. Still feel their flesh between my teeth, hear their bones breaking apart."

"Wim," Red said, his voice cracking, just like his heart.

"Give me something else to taste." Wim pressed his mouth to Red's ear. "Just for a moment, help me forget what I am."

A tiny part of Red urged himself to pause, to *think*. He was certain Wim was withholding something from him—some hidden reason that drove him towards the Dark Forest. The same Dark Forest where Red was supposed to be completing the Queen's quest. Their secrets and lies twisted around each other like thorny vines, threatening to strangle them both.

And yet...

His body was already moving of its own accord, drawn to Wim like a moth to flame. What were choices, really, when faced with a wildling like this? Had he ever truly stood a chance against those burning orange eyes, that primal strength, that dangerous tenderness that made his knees weak? No, resistance had never been an option.

Ever so slowly, Red raised himself up on to his tiptoes, slipping his arms around Wim's neck. He held his breath in anticipation, his pulse threading in such an unsteady rhythm he thought he might faint.

This seemed enough of an answer for Wim—he pressed his tongue against the base of Red's collarbone, and a shiver ran down Red's spine. The sensation was warm and wet, like a raindrop on a hot summer's day. Red's breath hitched as Wim's tongue traced a slow, deliberate path up the side of his neck, leaving a trail of heat in its wake. The rough texture of Wim's tongue sent sparks dancing across Red's skin, making him gasp.

Red's hands tangled in Wim's hair, the strands coarse and thick between his fingers. His heart raced as he pulled Wim closer, desperate for more of that intoxicating touch. But as his fingers explored the wild mane, they caught on a mat of dried blood. The coppery scent filled Red's nostrils, twisting his stomach, but he didn't pull away. Instead, he tightened his grip on Wim's hair, holding him there as if he could somehow erase the past with sheer force of will. Wim gasped, and for a moment, Red thought he might pull back. But then Wim's tongue found his neck again, more insistent this time, and all thoughts of blood and death were swept away.

Wim's hands slid down Red's sides, coming to rest on his hips. With a sudden jerk, he pulled Red forward, pressing their bodies together. The hard planes of Wim's chest were now flush against his own, the scorching heat of the wolf seeping through the thin fabric of Red's shirt. Wim's fingers dug into Red's hips, holding him there as if he might float away.

And then, without warning, Wim's hands were slipping around Red's ass, pulling him even closer. Red swallowed as his cock twitched in happy surprise, its length firming, seeking escape from the drawers that constrained it.

Red should stop this before it went too far.

He should—

Wim was no longer licking at his neck, but instead was alternating between soft little nips with his teeth, and light, feathery butterfly kisses.

"Wim," Red murmured shakily, closing his eyes and resting his head against the tree.

His hands roamed over Wim's broad shoulders, feeling the taut muscles beneath his skin. He could feel the strength in Wim's body, the raw power that had allowed him to take down those men with such ease. And yet, as Wim's hands trailed up and down the side of his thighs, Red felt anything but afraid.

Instead, he felt alive. More alive than he had ever felt. And as Wim's lips trailed down his neck, leaving a trail of fire in their wake, Red wished more than anything for this moment never to end.

"Red," Wim answered.

Red wasn't stupid. He knew Wim was only touching him like this because Wim needed a distraction and he was the nearest available body. But *holy fuck*, did it feel good to be wanted.

Please, Red almost begged.

Touch me.

Lick me.

Have me.
Kiss me.
Love me.

The last thought stabbed at his heart, and he squeezed his eyes closed to combat the hot prickle of tears that threatened to spoil the moment Red already knew would be so precious to him for the rest of his life.

"There are no words for how fucking delicious you are, sweetheart." Wim slid one of his hands around from cupping Red's ass to land it on his aching cock, tracing the outline of it with his fingers. He gave Red's neck another long, hot lick, then brought his mouth to Red's ear to whisper, "Let me taste you."

"You are... tasting me..." Red gasped, because despite everything, he couldn't bring himself to make presumptions about Wim's words.

"Let me taste you *properly*. I already know your spend will be the sweetest I've ever had in my mouth."

Red almost choked on his own saliva, his eyes flying open. Wim looked at him with a hungry smile. How was this happening? A few days ago, he and the wolf were trading insults, and now Wim was almost begging to suck his cock?

"But... I don't understand. You told me you didn't want me that way."

"I lied."

A gasp of shock left Red's lips.

"You're this gorgeous, young little thing, and I didn't want to give myself any temptations."

Gorgeous?! Had Wim hit his head on the run through the forest?

"I'm not—"

Wim silenced him by pressing the pad of his thumb to Red's lips. "You *are* young. And I know I shouldn't. But lord help me..."

Red parted his lips, and Wim's thumb slipped inside his mouth. Wim groaned as if Red's tongue was pressed against a much more sensitive part of him.

"I can't pretend I haven't dreamed of sucking your sweet cock for the last three nights."

In the reflection of Wim's large eyes, Red saw his own shocked face. "You... have?"

"Will you let me?" It was as if he were begging for water, not Red's cock. "Please?"

"Yes," Red said, because there was zero chance he was saying no. Though Red had often found himself on his knees, he'd never been on the receiving end of such a favour. The thought of Wim's mouth being the first to touch him there made his aching prick leak a little in excitement.

Wim started to fall to the ground.

"Wait!" Red said, and Wim stopped, eyes widening. "Kiss me first." The desperate words tumbled out before Red could stop them, and he immediately wished he could swallow them back down.

Kiss me first so I can pretend this is more than what it is. Let me live in a fleeting fantasy, where we're real lovers, not just two broken souls seeking comfort in the wild.

Wim flashed him a wolfish grin. "With pleasure, sweetheart."

Red's heart raced as Wim leaned in, his calloused fingers tenderly cupping Red's face. Time slowed each breath, stretching into eternity as their eyes locked. In Wim's gaze, a whirlwind of emotions—longing, vulnerability, a raw hunger—were unashamedly on display.

When their lips finally met, Red's heart stuttered in his chest, because nothing in his life had prepared him for how tender a wolf's kiss could be.

Red hadn't had many kisses. The few he'd had involved whichever partner gripping his chin with some force and shoving their tongue in his mouth with violent lashes.

It had never been like this—like Wim was savouring the taste of him. His lips moved with urgency yet profound gentleness, as if

Red were something precious to be cherished. And so, Red happily melted into the embrace, his fingers tangling in Wim's thick mane.

Wim nudged Red's mouth open with his tongue, and slipped its wet warmth inside, sliding it against Red's own in a soft tango.

Red prepared himself to taste the blood of the men Wim had killed within his mouth.

But there wasn't a single hint of death.

Instead, he tasted the wildness of the forest on Wim's hot tongue—the earthy musk of damp soil, the crisp tang of pine needles. Yet underlying it all was an essence that was uniquely, unmistakably Wim. Rugged and strong, yet infinitely gentle.

Then Wim kissed him with a ferocity that would have stolen Red's breath away, if he had any breath left to steal.

As their bodies pressed closer, Red lost himself in the solid warmth of Wim's powerful frame. The roughness of his calloused palms cradling Red's face contrasted with the exquisite softness of his kiss, overwhelming Red's senses to the point his knees began to shake and he had to squeeze them together.

When they finally broke apart, gasping for air, Red gazed up at Wim through half-lidded eyes, his swollen lips quirking into a dazed smile.

In that moment, the world around Red faded into insignificance. His royal quest, the whispering trees, the dappled sunlight filtering through the canopy, the very air they breathed—all of it paled against the blazing intensity of kissing Wim. Red's universe had contracted to this single point, centered on the man before him. The *wolf* before him.

Wim's thumb traced the line of Red's kiss-swollen bottom lip with a tenderness that made his heart clench. "Little Red..." he rumbled, his deep voice made husky with emotion.

This intimacy was the thing he'd been starving for his entire life without ever realizing it—and now that he'd tasted it, he feared he might never get enough.

Gathering his courage, Red surged up onto his toes to reclaim Wim's lips one last time. His fingers traced the line of Wim's jaw, revelling in the rough rasp of his stubble. If Red never had another kiss in his life, at least he'd had this one.

Red pulled back to study Wim. His cheeks were ruddy, and the smile that blossomed across Wim's face in response was blinding in its radiance, warming Red clear through to his soul. Then, the smile widened, became more wolfish.

"I think, for a kiss like that, you deserve a prize." Wim undid the clasp on Red's belt before he had time to blink, yanking on it until he'd completely removed it. It landed on the forest floor with a soft thud. "If you'll let me have the honour."

The way Wim kept acting like sucking Red's cock was a great gift to him was doing funny things to Red's stomach. Funny, terrible things.

So Red nodded, lest his voice betray him.

Wim dropped to his knees.

As Wim carefully pulled down his breeches, Red bit down on his lip, the burst of pain failing to calm his nerves. Was this really happening, or had he slipped into a fever dream?

Through the thin material of his drawers, his cock strained against the fabric, creating a visible outline. Wim pressed his open mouth against the cloth-covered length, his hot breath seeping through the material. Red's knees nearly buckled as Wim's mouth traced the shape of him, leaving a dark, wet patch on the fabric. The sensation was maddening—too much and not enough all at once. Only when Red let out a desperate whimper did Wim finally hook his fingers into the waistband of his drawers and slowly drag them down.

Red suppressed a laugh, the absurd turn of events sending him almost hysterical. Should he really be putting his cock into a wolf's mouth? It wasn't like Wim didn't bite.

When his member finally sprang free of the material that was entrapping it, it stood to attention, firm and desperate for Wim's promise. But when a whisper of wind caressed his bare skin, Red's fingers twitched with the instinct to shield himself from view.

"I know it's not..." Red trailed off, fumbling for words. *Much? A monster cock like your own?*

Wim's eyebrows drew together, and his head tilted to one side. "What?" Then he glanced between Red's face and his sorry length, bellowing a hearty laugh. "Red, your cock is as lovely as you are. And very... proportionate."

As lovely as you are.

Red stored the words deep within his heart.

Grinning, Wim gave the side of Red's cockhead a tiny kiss while his hand squeezed Red's ass, pulling Red towards him. The other hand buried itself in the patch of hair above his slender length, petting the strands.

Then, while still gazing up at Red with his gorgeous amber eyes, Wim licked the glistening wetness that awaited him at the tip of Red's rock-solid member.

Red yelped in a most unbecoming way, and would have flinched away if it weren't for Wim's steady hand.

Wim laughed. "Not quite the reaction I was hoping for. Let me try this."

Wim's tongue traced a slow, deliberate path from the base of Red's cock to its tip, making every inch of him quiver with a be-witching thrill. The sensation was so intense that Red had to press his palm against the rough bark of the tree to steady himself. He'd often wondered what it would feel like to have a man's tongue on his cock, but this was beyond his wildest dreams, and all Wim had done so far was lick him.

Wim repeated his efforts, though this time his tongue felt even wetter. Red's fingers curled into the uneven surface of the tree, find-ing purchase in the cracks and grooves as though they were lifelines. He leaned his head back, eyes fluttering closed as waves of pleasure coursed through him.

"I love this cock of yours," Wim whispered, the warmth of his breath fanning over Red's sensitive skin. The words sounded like they had been spoken in a secret language, one meant only for Red to understand. Wim kissed the shaft again, tenderly, reverently, as if it were a sacred jewel. "Besides, the size of it makes it all the easier to do this."

Red swayed on his feet, the anticipation twisting his insides into knots. Wim's hand, firm and gentle, found the back of Red's thigh, steadying him.

With a slow, deliberate motion, Wim took the head of Red's cock into his mouth. The heat and wetness were overwhelming, enveloping him completely. Red gasped, his breath hitching as Wim's tongue swirled around the tip, exploring every contour, every ridge. Wim's lips slid down the shaft, taking more of him in, inch by glistening inch.

Red's world narrowed down to the exquisite sensation of Wim's mouth enveloping him. Every touch, every movement, was a revelation. Wim's hands gripped Red's hips, holding him steady as he slid down further, taking the entire length of Red's cock into his throat. Wim swallowed repeatedly, and Red felt every constriction, and it was more than he could bear.

His eyes flew open, and he stared down at Wim. The sight of the wolf on his knees, his mouth full of Red's cock, was the most erotic thing he had ever seen. Wim's eyes met his, and there was a raw, primal hunger in them that made Red's blood boil.

Wim's mouth came off Red's length with a loud *pop*. The wolf took a moment to catch his breath. He continued his intense eye contact. "Stroke my head," he said, with such soft neediness that a small gasp left Red's lips.

Red's hands immediately found purchase in Wim's chestnut mane. Did he mean for Red to pull his hair? Red himself liked that a great deal. But no, Wim had said *stroke,* so Red ran his fingers through the thick strands with reverent tenderness. He traced gentle patterns against Wim's scalp, marvelling at how such a powerful creature could melt beneath such a soft touch. When his fingernails lightly scraped against Wim's scalp, the wolf let out a sound somewhere between a growl and a purr, his eyes half-closing in pleasure.

Fingers still entangled in his hair, Red guided Wim's mouth back to his waiting cock. Wim wasted no time, plunging Red's length straight down his throat again.

When the muscles of Wim's throat constricted once again around the head of Red's cock, he screamed. These jolts of pleasure were unlike any he'd ever experienced.

So this is what all the fuss is about.

Red's fingers threaded quickly through Wim's hair, pulling him closer, urging him on. He could feel every pulse, every contraction of Wim's throat as he swallowed around him, taking him deeper.

The intensity was almost too much, yet Red craved more. He needed more. Wim seemed to sense this, his hands moving from Red's hips to cup his ass, pulling him in impossibly tighter. The feeling of being completely consumed, of being taken in so deeply, was indescribable.

Red's breath came in ragged gasps, his entire body tense with the building pleasure. Wim's tongue worked magic, swirling and sucking, driving him to the brink of madness. Every nerve ending in his body seemed to converge at the point where Wim's mouth met his flesh, every sensation heightened, every touch amplified.

Wim's head bobbed, the rhythm steady and sure. Red could feel his own heartbeat pounding in his ears, could feel the sweep of Wim's tongue against the underside of his shaft as he withdrew, only to plunge back down again. The sensation of being taken in so deeply, of being enveloped in that heat, was unlike anything he had ever experienced.

Red's hips were soon bucking involuntarily in response to the building pleasure. The pressure built, a swelling tide within him that threatened to overwhelm him. *Not yet!* This was far too good to release so soon. Red bit deep into his lip again as he instinctively tightened his fingers in Wim's hair, then chastised himself. *Stroke him*. He relaxed his grip, smoothing down Wim's soft curls as if he were a puppy.

As Wim continued his punishing rhythm—showing no signs of tiredness—Red's mind chanted the wolf's name like a prayer, but his lips couldn't quite muster the courage to scream it aloud.

Instead, Red showed Wim how amazing he was making him feel by giving him small gasps and moans, his body trembling with the sheer intensity of the sensations coursing through him. "I'm—" he managed to choke out.

Wim's eyes met his, filled with the deepest depths of desire.

Nobody had ever looked at Red like this.

Like he was perfect exactly as he was.

It was exhilarating.

It was *intoxicating*.

The edge approached too quickly, the precipice looming before him. Red's body tensed, every muscle coiled, every nerve taut. And then with a final, desperate thrust, he plunged over, his release pulsing through him in wave after wave of ecstasy. Red removed a hand from gripping Wim's head to press it against his mouth, to muffle his uncontrollable cries.

Wim swallowed every drop, his throat working around Red's cock, the sensation drawing out his orgasm until he was left gasping, trembling, utterly spent. Red's fingers, still tangled in Wim's hair, relaxed their grip, sliding through the strands as the wolf slowly withdrew, his tongue giving one last languid swipe along the length of Red's shaft.

Red sagged against the tree, his breath coming in ragged gasps, his body quaking with the aftershocks of the most intense release of his life. Wim stood, his hands still on Red's hips, steadying him. The wolf's eyes were soft, his expression tender as he gazed down at Red.

"Sweeter even than I dreamed," Wim murmured, a low rumble that vibrated through Red's body.

Red managed a shaky smile, his breath still uneven, his heart still pounding. He pressed up against Wim's large frame, his solid presence the only thing grounding him. Wim's thumb brushed lightly over Red's cheek. He leaned into the touch, his eyes fluttering closed.

This was what it felt like to be cared for, to be cherished. Red needed to savour every last second of it, bury the feeling deep inside him, where perhaps he could bring it out again to marvel at when Wim and this wild adventure were but a memory.

The solid length pressing against Red's hip drew him from his reverie. Heat flooded his cheeks as he realized how selfish he'd been, lost in his own pleasure while Wim's arousal went unattended. Red's fingertips tentatively brushed across its impressive length, drawing a sharp intake of breath from the wolf.

"I should... I mean, would you like me to... ?" Red cursed his fumbling words, but Wim's gentle smile made his heart flutter.

"Only if you want to," Wim murmured, pressing a soft kiss to Red's temple. "This is more than enough."

"I do want to," Red said firmly, despite his burning cheeks. "Very much." He stroked Wim's cock again from root to tip, relishing in its velvety feel, and Wim growled deeply.

"Won't take much," Wim rumbled, pressing his forehead against Red's. "Those pretty sounds of yours have me very close already."

Red made a small, indignant noise at being teased, but his protest died in his throat as he sank to his knees. The forest floor was hard beneath him, twigs and leaves crunching as he settled into position. His heart stumbled over itself as he reached for Wim's hips, trying to steady his trembling fingers. He'd done this before, of course, but never with someone so... imposing. The stable master had been average at best, and Wim was...

Red stared at the almighty cock in front of him, his mouth going dry at the sight of it filling his vision. It was beautiful in its own way—thick and proud, rising from a nest of dark, wild curls that trailed up Wim's stomach like a shadowy path through a forest. The sheer size of it made Red's previous experiences seem laughably inadequate.

Red took a steadying breath, squaring his shoulders. After what Wim had just done for him—after making him feel more pleasure than he'd ever known possible—Red was determined to return even a fraction of that bliss. He might not have much experience with anything this... impressive, but by god, he was going to try his very best.

He tentatively took the cock in hand, its rigidity startling against his fingers. It pulsed in his grasp, a living beast yearning for release. Red's eyes widened, and he swallowed hard as he leaned forward, lips parting in trepidation.

The tip of Wim's cock pressed against Red's mouth, its girth stretching his lips to their limits. He paused at the initial contact, feeling the weight of it against his tongue. Summoning all his courage, Red attempted to accommodate the monstrous instrument, bringing it into his throat—but he only managed what felt like an inch before he met insurmountable resistance. Gagging, he quickly pulled away, a hint of shame warming his cheeks.

His thoughts swirled like a tempestuous storm. What was he going to do? He'd been fairly proud of his previous efforts in this domain—the stable master certainly had no complaints about Red's skill. But this was a whole other challenge. Impossible, even. A familiar, self-deprecating voice whispered through the chaos... *Of course you can't please him, Red, you pathetic, worthless fool.*

A sigh escaped Red's mouth as he gazed up at Wim, a pleading look in his eyes. "I'm... I'm sorry," he stammered, internally bracing himself for the derision that was sure to follow.

Wim's eyes softened, a frown playing at the corners of his lips. "What's wrong, sweetheart?"

The endearment only worsened Red's pain, the dagger in his heart twisting.

"I can't..." Red flapped his hand wildly around Wim's cock. "It's too big!" he snapped angrily. "Why the fuck is it so big?!"

Wim laughed so loudly, a flock of birds burst into flight. "Never had anyone complain about that before."

Red scowled, his cheeks now burning hotter than hell. Clearly, Wim's previous lovers must possess stupidly large mouths to go with their stupid faces.

"Ah, don't worry yourself, sweetheart," Wim said, gently cupping Red's face. His calloused thumb traced Red's furrowed brow. "Whatever you can offer, it's more than enough for me." His words resonated with sincerity.

Red huffed, trying to suppress his frustration. He allowed himself to take a deep breath, leaning into Wim's touch as he worked to regain his composure.

"Just relax," Wim whispered, soothing Red's racing thoughts. "Even the sight of your pretty little mouth an inch away from my cock has it twitching, eager to spend itself all over your face."

Red choked in shock. *What words!*

Red's gaze locked onto Wim's eyes, now twinkling with mischief, and his resolve slowly returned. With a renewed sense of determination, Red leaned in once more, his lips parting...

The taste of salt and musk hit Red's tongue as he wrapped his lips around the wolf's cockhead and sucked hard. Wim let out a low moan and a surge of satisfaction bubbled up within Red. He paused to savour the moment. *He* was doing that, bringing pleasure to this wild wolf.

"Fucking hell, sweetheart!" Wim growled, his hands gently kneading Red's shoulders. "That's perfect. You're perfect."

Perfect.

Tears prickled Red's eyes. Wim wouldn't know, of course, but that word meant everything to him.

Red returned to his task with renewed fervour, and quickly lost himself. He danced his tongue around the head of Wim's cock, drenching it in saliva. His hands joined the frenzy, and slid up and down the now slick length, spreading the wetness.

Oh, yes. Red was doing a very good job indeed, if Wim's grunts were anything to go by.

Then Wim abruptly threw his head back, and let out a guttural howl that echoed through the forest. The vibrations rippled through Red, and fuelled him onward.

Raw groans and guttural growls filled the forest. Red relished every single one—affirmation that he was doing something right... something *perfect* in fact.

With slow, tender movements, Wim's hand stroked Red's cheek, mapping the shape of it where it bulged with his cock.

Heart stuttering, Red tentatively placed his hand over Wim's. He gathered his courage, then guided Wim's hand towards his hair, giving it the smallest experimental tug, hoping Wim would understand without him having to voice his desire. When their eyes met, Wim's lips curved into a knowing smile that made Red's pulse race.

Wim's large hand tangled in Red's curls, grip tightening with delicious slowness until Red thought he might combust from anticipation. The sudden pull that followed walked the perfect line between pleasure and pain, forcing a broken moan from Red's throat as his head tilted back, exposing his throat to the wolf above him.

"You like this?" Wim asked, low and husky.

Red could only softly moan his affirmation, nodding as best he could.

It was what the stable master had done to him, the few times he'd fucked Red. Though their rough couplings had been performed with cold detachment—emotionless fumbles in the dark, with Red pressed up against the wooden wall of the stable, splinters of wood biting into his hands.

But this, with Wim, was different. Here, in this wild refuge of the forest, Red found himself stripped bare of more than just his clothes. Every touch, every growl, every heated glance made Red feel like he mattered—like he wasn't just some imperfect thing to be hidden away in the shadows of the palace. Every moment stripped Red of the shame he'd carried since childhood.

Wim tugged on Red's hair once more, forcing Red to moan around Wim's prick. His body shivered with pleasure, his own length twitching although it had just spent. Red's thoughts swirled as he found himself drowning in the sheer intensity of the moment.

Wim's growl deepened, vibrating through Red's core, as he warned, "Sweetheart, I'm close."

Red wrapped his lips tight around him, then with a final thrust, Wim released inside Red's mouth. The warm torrent of seed was more than he anticipated. He tried his best to swallow it all, but some spilled out, dribbling down his chin.

Red gasped for breath, the taste of Wim lingering on his tongue as he wiped his mouth with the back of his hand. His eyes fluttered upwards, meeting Wim's heated gaze with a mixture of defiance and newfound vulnerability.

Once Wim was fully spent, he collapsed onto the forest floor, pulling Red onto his lap in one fluid motion. The wolf's chest heaved against Red's back, his breaths coming in hot pants against Red's ear. With an almost tender ferocity, Wim nuzzled into the crook of Red's neck, inhaling deeply as if trying to memorise his scent. Then his tongue—rough and hot—dragged slowly up the column of Red's throat, cleaning away the remnants of their passion that had spilled there. The gesture was pure animal instinct, primal and possessive, yet somehow intensely intimate. His heart raced as Wim continued his meticulous attention, each lap of his tongue causing small gasps to escape Red's lips.

Red melted against Wim's broad chest, tilting his head to give the wolf better access. Red felt claimed, marked, cherished in a way that made his chest ache with an emotion he could not name. The heat of Wim's body enveloped him completely, as if the wolf was trying to shield him from the world itself.

In that moment, Red felt invincible, like he could conquer the world if he wanted to.

Wim, seemingly finally satisfied that Red was thoroughly covered in his saliva, stopped. Red leaned into his embrace, and as he rested his head against Wim's chest, listening to the steady rhythm of his heartbeat, he couldn't help but fear. Was he falling *in love* with this wild wolf?

The notion was terrifying. Not only were they merely temporary allies sharing a journey, but Wim was still keeping his secrets from Red... still thought Red's quest was stupid, even if he wouldn't say it to his face.

The wind picked up, carrying the scent of pine and earth through the air, and Red nestled closer to Wim, savouring the warmth and security his body offered.

Red would not spoil this magical moment with such thoughts.

"Like having your hair pulled, do you?" Wim ran his large hand through Red's hair, which must've resembled a bird's nest by now. "What else do you like?"

What did Red *like?* He was pretty sure Wim could do almost anything to him and he'd like it very much. But he forced himself to think back to what else the stable master had done to him. "I've been slapped before."

Wim's fingers stilled. "But did you like it?"

Had Red liked it? His encounters with the stable master had always been about the other man's pleasure—Red had never stopped to consider his own.

"I think so? I think I especially would if you were the one slapping me."

Wim made a thoughtful, disgruntled sound, but his fingers thankfully resumed their blissful strokes. Red fought very hard not to purr like a kitten.

Wim pressed a kiss to the top of Red's head. "I loved carrying you on my back earlier. I'll carry you for some of the journey from now on. It'll be quicker."

Quicker? Though he'd adored riding Wim, Red wanted to protest. He'd rather slow the journey down, spend more time together before they inevitably parted ways.

The memory of the evil, calculating look in the Queen's Shadow's eyes resurfaced. How long until the geist popped back up to check on Red? What would happen if he saw his furry travelling companion?

Alas, it did seem like the sooner they reached the Dark Forest, the better.

As Wim continued to cradle him in his arms, Red remembered the wolf hadn't answered his question from so many hours ago now—about how exactly the Dark Forest was going to help him find his cure—but there was no way Red was going to ask it again.

Not when they only had a handful of days left together.

Not when Wim made him feel so good.

So needed.

So *perfect*.

No, Red wanted to stay trapped in the bubble they'd formed for themselves for as long as possible. He'd treasure every single second until reality shattered their fragile dream.

Eleven

The rhythmic sway of Wim's gait lulled Red into a peaceful trance as the wolf carried him through the forest. Cradled against Wim's broad back, the warmth of his thick fur enveloped Red like the world's cosiest blanket. He buried his face into the soft scruff, inhaling the comforting scent of pine and earth that clung to Wim.

They'd been travelling this way for hours. After spending too long wrapped up in each other's embrace, Wim had announced they'd need to move quickly to make up for lost time.

With each of Wim's large strides, Red's thoughts drifted back to their intimate moments from earlier. The memory of Wim's rough tongue dragging across his skin sent delicious shivers down his spine. He savoured the lingering taste of the wolf on his lips—a heady musk that made his head spin with desire.

Red's fingers idly stroked through Wim's fur, relishing the opportunity to simply be with him without the burden of words.

When dusk began to settle over the forest, painting the sky in hues of burnt orange and dusky purple, Wim slowed to a stop beside a small bubbling brook. Red reluctantly slid from his back, his limbs grumbling from the effort of supporting his weight once more.

As the wolf shifted back into his human form, Red couldn't help but admire the play of muscles rippling beneath Wim's tanned skin. Surely they would share a bedroll again tonight? Red would be free to explore every inch of him.

But an uncomfortable silence stretched between them as they set up camp. Wim moved with an uncharacteristic broodiness, his brow furrowed in a perpetual frown.

Red found himself sneaking furtive glances at the wolf. Had he done something wrong?

Perhaps Wim regretted their earlier intimacy? Yes, that was likely it. The wolf had experienced a moment of madness, had simply used Red for cathartic release, and now was wondering how on earth he could get rid of him.

Panic clawed at Red's throat, making it difficult to breathe.

Finally, unable to bear the tension any longer, Red blurted, "If you're regretting what happened earlier, you might as well just say it."

Wim paused mid-motion, his eyes finding Red's. For a heartbeat, he simply stared, an unreadable expression on his face. Then, shaking his head, he moved to sit beside Red.

"Never that, sweetheart. Don't let your mind run away with you." Wim's deep voice was laced with a weariness that tugged at Red's heart. Reaching out, the wolf cupped Red's cheek with a calloused palm. "Nothing would ever make me regret that."

Red leaned into the gentle touch, some of the tension easing from his shoulders. "Then what is it?"

Wim's thumb stroked across Red's cheekbone as he seemed to consider his words. "I feel... fucking disgusted with myself," he said at last, his gaze dropping. "Those commoners... they were just trying to protect themselves. And I slaughtered them like animals."

Red's stomach twisted, the weight of Wim's words crashing over him like a tidal wave. He'd witnessed the carnage, seen the mangled remains of the two men torn to pieces by Wim's claws and fangs. At the time, he'd felt mainly relief that Wim hadn't been hurt.

But now, faced with the raw anguish etched into the wolf's features, Red couldn't help but empathize with his remorse. "You were defending yourself," he murmured, hating the way his voice shook. "They would have killed you without a second thought."

Wim shook his head, expression haunted. "That doesn't excuse what I did. Two people are dead because of me... and then I rewarded myself, taking pleasure from you." His hand fell away, leaving Red's cheek chilled by the loss of contact.

Red's throat tightened, robbing him of words. He wanted to protest, to assure Wim that he hadn't seen it that way at all. Wim hadn't been rewarding himself, he'd been seeking comfort and connection in a moment of pure darkness.

Instead, he reached for Wim's hand, entwining their fingers together. He held on tightly, hoping his presence would be enough of a tether to stop Wim from sinking into melancholy.

That night, Wim dragged their bedrolls together without discussion, combining them to make a larger one to share. Then, pulling Red's back flush against his chest, he whispered, "Little Red," into his ear, then promptly fell straight to sleep, his arms locked around Red's waist like iron bands.

The occasional tremor rippled through Wim's massive frame, his breathing uneven and ragged. Then a soft whimper broke the silence, and Red's chest ached at the sound. Was this Wim's recurring nightmare? Was he currently lost in an endless forest, calling out for his pack until his throat bled raw, but receiving no answer? Always searching, never finding his way home?

With great effort, Red twisted in Wim's grip, facing him in the darkness. His fingers traced the worried creases between Wim's brows, smoothing them with gentle strokes. He pressed his lips to Wim's beard, tasting salt, earth, and something uniquely *him*.

Pulling at his red cloak, he stretched it so that it covered both himself and part of Wim. God, how Red yearned to shelter him, to wrap Wim in the same fierce protection the wolf had shown him. To be his sanctuary, his home. He'd never be *pack*, but perhaps he could be something akin to it.

Though what right did he have to dream of forever when their paths would soon diverge?

The morning broke crisp and clear as they continued their journey on foot. After hours of trudging through the forest, Red had taken to filling the silence with stories from the palace—partly to distract himself from his rumbling stomach and aching feet, partly to see how often he could make Wim's lips twitch into a smile.

"And then, wouldn't you know it, Makellos tripped over his own feet and landed headfirst in the trifle. Cream everywhere. The Queen—"

A sharp shush sliced through Red's anecdote. Wim's hand clamped over his mouth, muffling the rest of the story. Annoyance at his hilarious tale being interrupted was quickly replaced by icy dread. What could Wim hear? Had the angry mob of commoners found them? But Wim's eyes—wide and gleaming—held not fear, but an almost childlike excitement.

"Deer," Wim breathed, lips barely moving. He inhaled deeply through his nose, a low growl rumbling in his chest. "A big one." A flicker of his tongue, tasting the air.

"How big?"

Wim looked at him and winked. "*Very* big."

Red rolled his eyes. "Well, we're going to hunt it, right?" After the loss of their vegetables, the prospect of fresh venison set his mouth watering. Wim would surely make short work of any deer—his powerful jaws could crunch through bone like kindling.

"Only if you're up for the challenge, sweetheart." Wim's smile twisted mischievously.

"Alright, wolf," Red declared, pulling an arrow from his quiver. "Let's hunt."

Wim grinned, teeth glinting in the dappled light. With a subtle nod, he slipped into the shadows of the forest, disappearing behind a trunk as thick as one of the palace walls. Red nocked his arrow, scanning the underbrush for movement.

A low growl drifted through the trees—Wim had the scent. Red followed the sound, and found Wim crouching low to the ground. Together, they carefully traversed the forest, Wim taking the lead.

Fallen leaves crunched in the distance, the sound rapidly drawing nearer. Wim cocked his head. "It's coming this way."

Then Red's breath caught in his throat as an enormous stag burst out of the leafy foliage.

He gasped, arm falling slack. The buck was massive, towering over six feet at the shoulder, its antlers spreading like a crown of branches against the sky. Its reddish-brown coat gleamed in the sunlight as muscles rippled beneath. It turned its noble head, leveling one great liquid eye at Red. For an endless moment, they simply... *looked* at each other.

It was a thing of pure beauty—not even the Queen could find fault in it.

For a moment, Red almost lowered his bow—did this splendid creature of the forest actually deserve to die today?

In a flurry of movement, a blur of grey exploded from the bushes, fangs bared. The stag snorted, pivoting on its haunches as Wim slammed against its flank.

Red's paralysis broke.

Sorry, beautiful thing. I really wish we didn't need to eat you.

He lifted his bow, drew back the fletching until it kissed his cheek, then sighted along the shaft. The huntsman's wisdom floated through his mind—*a clean kill is a merciful kill.*

The stag reared, hooves slashing the air as Wim danced just out of reach, taunting it with diving snaps of his powerful jaw. Red tracked their frantic movements.

Inhale.

Exhale.

His arrow flashed across the clearing in a blur, and punched through the stag's eye with a meaty *thunk*. The beast collapsed like a felled tree, antlers crashing against the mossy ground.

Silence fell. Even the birds had hushed, perhaps as awed as Red was by the magnificence they'd just witnessed. Wim padded over to the fallen stag, snout outstretched in curiosity. After a moment's inspection, he tossed his head back and unleashed a victorious howl that sent shivers racing up Red's spine.

Despite the exhilaration of the hunt's climax, Red felt a pang of sadness at the loss of such a majestic creature. But then his stomach gave a demanding rumble.

Wim shifted back to his human form, broad shoulders rippling as bones reshaped. "I'd say you and I make a great team, sweetheart."

Red's chest tightened. When was the last time anyone had treated him as an equal, rather than an unwanted nuisance or a servant to be ordered about? The way Wim looked at him now—eyes bright with shared triumph—made him feel seen in a way that both thrilled and terrified him.

They set to work cutting the carcass, Red slicing away thick slabs of haunch while Wim tackled the rest. By the time they'd finished, they had enough meat to provide the entire palace with an evening meal. Maybe two.

"That's... rather more than we can carry," Red said slowly, wiping sweat from his brow. What were they going to do? Auntie Anne's stern face appeared in his mind, lecturing him on waste.

Wim grunted, slinging an entire hindquarter over his shoulder. He considered the impressive pile. "Most of this will go bad before we can get through it."

"You don't say."

Wim was quiet for a moment. Then he turned to Red, eyes gleaming with an idea. "There's a market town half a day's walk from here. If we hurry, we can make it before nightfall. Trade this meat for things we need.

A market? Red's mind raced with possibilities—new boots, a fur cloak to ward off the chill nights, maybe even a new quiver. His stomach clenched with anticipation, then sank.

"Would that not… delay us even further?"

Though would Red truly mind extra time with the wolf?

He studied Wim's handsome face.

Of course he wouldn't.

And if he was being honest with himself, the thought of finally reaching Old Oma's cottage filled him with a quiet dread.

Wim seemed to read the conflict in his expression. He stepped closer, the scent of earth and musk surrounding Red. "Maybe a bit. But we can't let all this go to waste. That stag deserves better than to rot in the forest." His eyes held an intensity that made Red's pulse flutter. "What do you say, sweetheart? Fancy a little side adventure?"

Red swallowed hard, feeling the heat of Wim's closeness. The Queen's Shadow could return any second, expecting to see significant progress. He was days and days behind by now.

But this opportunity was too good to pass up. "I… I suppose a short detour won't hurt. My boots *do* have holes in them, after all. I can't possibly complete my royal quest if I lose a toe to frostbite."

They grinned at each other, the unspoken understanding passing between them.

"Right, then." Wim clapped his hands together. "Now comes the tricky part—carrying it all."

Dragging his gaze from Wim's lips, Red scanned their surroundings. His eyes landed on an enormous slab of bark, dislodged from a fallen tree. "There. We can use that as a sledge."

Red beamed at Wim victoriously, rather proud of his ingenuity.

They quickly piled the meat onto the makeshift sled, then Wim rummaged through his pack, producing a long coil of sturdy rope. Within minutes, they'd lashed the bark securely.

Wim tested the weight, giving the sledge an experimental tug. He grunted with effort but kept his feet. "Who knew there was such a large brain in that pretty little head of yours?" He took a few more large strides, and the bark slid across the floor.

"Wouldn't it be easier in your wolf form? I'm sure that big strong body could pull it with much less effort."

Wim narrowed his eyes. "And have you take the reins, treating me like an obedient dog? I don't think so, sweetheart." His smile turned wolfish. "Unless that's a fantasy of yours?"

Red opened his mouth, an indignant retort ready, but Wim cut him off with a low chuckle.

"I'll shift later perhaps, but for now... let me enjoy your company in this form, if that's alright with you."

That was more than alright with Red. He fell into step beside him, happily sneaking sidelong glances at Wim, admiring the flex of powerful muscles beneath sun-kissed skin.

Red's gaze traced the strong lines of Wim's jaw, the breadth of his shoulders, down to where his shirt stretched tight across his chest. Sometimes, even when Wim was simply walking, his loveliness stole Red's breath away.

Yet... even with his rugged handsomeness, his scars and that nasty bite mark would likely mean he wouldn't be *perfect* enough for Queen Schön.

Red's stomach churned. Even now, hundreds of miles away from the palace, the Queen's voice still whispered in his head, categorising beauty and ugliness as if people were objects to sort. He'd absorbed her poison deep into his bones, letting her shape how he saw the world.

His hand passed through his strawberry-blond hair.

How he saw *himself*.

If only Red could scrub himself raw, to tear out every remnant of her teaching that still lingered in his mind.

Though... here he was, marching through the woods for the same woman he despised, on a quest of her making.

A quest that would hopefully prevent thousands of people starving to death.

A quest you keep delaying.

"You're awfully quiet," Wim said, cutting through Red's spiralling thoughts.

"Just thinking about all the things I'm going to buy at the market," Red replied, a little too brightly.

Wim hummed, shooting him a disbelieving look.

It was terrifying, really, how easily Wim could see past his defences, as if Red were made of glass instead of the carefully crafted armour he'd spent a lifetime building.

Terrifying, and exhilarating.

Twelve

The sun hung low in the sky by the time they reached the market town, casting long shadows across the worn dirt path. Though Red had offered multiple times to take a turn hauling their load, Wim had simply laughed at him. Now, Wim's chest heaved with exertion, sweat darkening his shirt despite the cool autumn air. At least the meat wouldn't spoil in this weather.

The market occupied a natural clearing at the town's edge, though 'market' seemed a generous term for what remained. Skeletal wooden stalls formed uneven rows, many abandoned, their surfaces mostly bare. A few cracked straw baskets lay forgotten, and Red grabbed one, his nose twitching at the sour scent of desperation that permeated the air.

Tattered fabrics hung limply between wooden posts, faded reminders of more prosperous times. The few traders present hawked their wares in hoarse voices, while hollow-eyed children darted between the legs of weary-looking customers. What little food was on display looked pitiful—undersized turnips, withered cabbages, and gnarled carrots commanding eye-watering prices.

"Looks like we made it just in time." Red gestured to the sparse gathering. "Before everything's gone."

Wim grunted, adjusting his grip on the makeshift sledge. "Thank god for that. My arms are about ready to fall off."

Red instinctively recoiled from a gaunt woman shuffling by, her collarbones jutting sharply beneath her worn dress. *So many des-*

perate faces! After spending so long in the solitude of the forest, civilisation was both jarring and sobering.

As they made their way down the main thoroughfare, heads turned, conversations ceased entirely, and eyes widened at the sight of their impressive haul of venison being dragged behind them.

Red's skin prickled. He was never one for mass attention at the best of times, and fought the urge to shrink under their scrutiny.

"Meat," someone whispered, the word spreading like wildfire through the thin crowd. "Real meat."

"That's quite the catch you've got there," a gruff voice called out. Others gathered closer, sizing up both the game and the strange pair pulling it. "How much for a leg?"

And so began a trading frenzy unlike anything Red had ever seen. People emerged from shadows and alleyways as word rippled throughout the town that there was fresh venison on offer. While most could only look on with naked hunger in their eyes, the few with coin quickly approached.

A weathered man with a missing ear offered them the use of his butcher's cleaver—a wicked, heavy blade with a worn wooden handle. "For the liver," he proposed, eyes gleaming with fierce ambition. Wim agreed with a nod.

The butchering itself was a grim spectacle. Wim worked methodically on their makeshift sled, the cleaver rising and falling with practiced precision. Blood pooled in the hollows of the wooden slats, trickling between them to stain the dirt beneath. People pressed closer, watching with an intensity that made Red's skin crawl—the naked desperation of the starving. Even the children stared without blinking, their protruding collarbones testament to how long it had been since they'd seen real meat.

Red deferred to Wim to decide the prices of each cut of meat. The price of their product seemed to change very inconsistently, depending on the look of the customer.

When a merchant approached, his belly shockingly straining against an embroidered waistcoat, rings glinting on each pudgy finger, Wim's price for the prime cuts suddenly tripled. "Times are hard," Wim had drawled, watching the merchant's eyes bulge at the quoted amount. "Though I expect a gentleman such as yourself knows what fine meat is worth these days." The merchant paid, though not without much huffing.

Yet when a gaunt-faced woman shuffled forward, two hollow-cheeked children clinging to her patched skirts, Wim's entire demeanour transformed. He quoted her such a low price for a generous portion that Red let out a spluttered cough of shock. Then, while wrapping the meat in cloth, Wim somehow managed to slip in extra cuts when she wasn't looking, waving away her tearful thanks with a gruff, "Feed those little ones well."

Red was very glad they'd stashed their own supply of venison in his pack, lest Wim get too carried away with his generosity, as heart-warming as it was.

Pockets lined with gold and silver, it was time to see what meagre offerings the market still had. Red's feet ached in his worn boots as they weaved through the thinning crowd, but the weight of coins in his pocket made his steps lighter.

"These first." Wim steered him towards a leatherworker's stall, nodding at Red's boots. "Can't have you hobbling through the forest with your toes sticking out."

Red bristled, but couldn't argue. The bootmaker presented several options, and Red found himself drawn to a pair crafted from supple brown leather, lined with rabbit fur.

"They'll last you five winters," the bootmaker promised as Red tried them on. The comfort was immediate, like walking on clouds. Red wiggled his toes against the soft, fluffy interior, beaming up at Wim.

Next to the shoemaker stood a stool that looked empty at first glance. Five large, brightly coloured feathers lay on a tattered cloth, each one different from the others. The stall owner set down the half-eaten crust of bread he was carefully nibbling on. A distinctive scar across his lip pulled his mouth into a sneer. "Good sirs!" he said.

"These are genuinely authentic feathers from the Plumed Menace! The crown prince killer! Each was found left on one of his victims after he brutally slaughtered them."

Red stared at the man. "These are just random feathers you've probably dyed." He'd heard from some of the Queen's more influential guests that the Plumed Menace strictly used pigeon feathers, for some mysterious reason.

While the merchant spluttered indignantly at Red's accusation, a blur of movement caught Red's eye. A small boy, a touch smaller than Toby but far thinner, darted forward and snatched the half-eaten crust from the counter. His ragged clothes hung loose on his skeletal frame as he spun to flee.

The merchant's hand shot out like a viper, fingers closing around the child's throat. "You little thief!" He lifted the boy clear off his feet, shaking him violently. The bread crust tumbled from the child's hand as he clawed desperately at the man's iron grip.

With a snarl, the merchant hurled the boy to the ground. The child landed hard, crying out as he curled into himself. Tears already streaked down his dirt-smudged face. "Please, sir! I haven't eaten in three days!"

The merchant raised his fist, face purple with rage. "I haven't either, you little rat! I'll teach you to—"

In a flash, Wim's massive hand clamped around the merchant's wrist. His other hand seized the front of the man's shirt, lifting him until his toes barely scraped the ground.

"Lay another finger on that child," Wim growled, "and I'll tear you apart piece by piece." His tone had dropped to that dangerous timbre, more wolf than man, that made the hair on Red's neck stand up.

The merchant struggled, face reddening. "Unhand me! Guards! This brute is assaulting me!"

A crowd gathered, drawn by the commotion. Whispers and gasps shot through the onlookers as Wim held the merchant aloft with terrifying ease.

"That man attacked a child!" someone called out.

"The boy was stealing!" another countered. "Stealing *bread*!"

The crowd pressed closer, their faces a mix of horror and morbid fascination. Red's chest tightened at their growing numbers. This could turn ugly fast. This foul man likely had foul friends in the crowd.

Red stepped forward, his heart racing. His gaze darted between the merchant, still dangling from Wim's grip, and the terrified child huddled on the ground.

"Here." Red pulled out a silver coin, pressing it into the merchant's palm. "For the bread and your... inconvenience." He fixed the man with a cold stare, channelling every ounce of the haughty palace attitude he'd learned from dealing with nobility. "I trust that will suffice?"

The merchant's fingers closed around the coin, greed overtaking anger in his eyes. "Y-yes, I suppose it will."

"Excellent." Red's voice dripped with disdain. "Now, I believe my friend would appreciate it if you apologised to the boy."

The merchant's face twisted, but he muttered a grudging apology. Wim released him with a warning growl, and the man stumbled back, straightening his rumpled clothes.

Red turned to the gathered crowd, raising an eyebrow. "Nothing more to see here, unless you're interested in purchasing some extortionately priced feathers?"

A few nervous murmurs broke the tension. The crowd began to disperse, their attention already drawn back to their own desperate situations.

Red helped the boy to his feet, pressing another coin into his small hand. "Get yourself something proper to eat, you hear? If you can find it."

The child's eyes widened at the coin. He nodded vigorously before darting away into the crowd.

Wim's jaw clenched as they walked away from the market stalls. His shoulders were rigid, tension radiating off him in waves that made Red's heart thump.

"That silver could have fed three families," Wim said, dangerously quiet.

Red lifted his chin. "I prevented a riot."

"You rewarded that bastard for abusing a child!" Wim spun to face him, eyes flashing. "Is that how your nobles handle everything? Throw money at problems until they disappear?"

"Don't speak of me as if I'm one of them." Red jabbed a finger at Wim's chest. "Do you think I *wanted* to give that vile man coin? But what was your plan exactly? Shift into a wolf in the middle of the market? Rip his throat out in front of everyone?"

"He deserved far worse than to walk away with coin in his pocket!"

"And what about that boy? What happens to him after we leave?" Red's different-coloured eyes blazed. "That merchant would have taken his revenge on every street child he could find. Instead, I made him look foolish in front of his customers. Hit him where it actually hurts—his pride and his profits."

Wim's nostrils flared. "There are other ways—"

"No. Sometimes you have to play their game to win." Red's words softened. "You think I don't know what it's like? To be small and helpless while someone bigger decides your fate?" He swallowed hard. "That boy needs to survive in this town long after we're gone. I bought him a chance to do that."

Wim stared at him for a long moment, the anger slowly draining from his face. His massive shoulders slumped.

"You did what you had to." Wim ran a hand through his shaggy hair. "I just... seeing that man hurt the kid..."

"I know." Red softened his tone. "But there's always a choice to make, you know? I chose to feed the snake to stop it from biting the child."

Desperate to recapture the lightness they'd shared earlier, Red grabbed Wim's sleeve and tugged him towards a textile merchant's stall. Unlike the others, this one still had wares worth considering—two wool blankets that, while patched in places, appeared thick enough to ward off the autumn chill. The elderly woman behind the stall named a steep price, her gnarled fingers smoothing over the rough wool. Wim haggled briefly before counting out the coins. "Winter's coming," he murmured, tucking the rolled blankets under his arm. "Nights are only getting colder."

Next, they headed to what remained of the food stalls. The pickings were slim—a few wrinkled apples, some withered mushrooms, and root vegetables that had seen better days. The prices were heart-stopping, but with their newfound wealth, they could afford what most couldn't.

"How are people surviving on this?" Red murmured, examining a stunted carrot that cost more than a servant's daily wage at the palace.

"They're not," Wim replied grimly. "Not well, anyway."

Wim selected the best of what was available—a handful of wild mushrooms, some wizened garlic, and herbs that were more stem than leaf. A few small potatoes and carrots joined their haul, along with a tiny jar of honey whose cost seemed particularly unreasonable.

Red peered into their basket. "What exactly are you planning with... this?"

"Venison with forest mushrooms. Not exactly the feast I'd hoped for, but..." He shrugged. "I'll make it work. I'm going to cook you the best meal you've ever had... cooked in a single pot in the middle of the woods, that is."

Red laughed softly. He squeezed Wim's forearm, then caught himself about to reach up to press a kiss to his cheek.

Don't get carried away, Red. That's a dangerous game.

As the sun dipped lower, the few remaining merchants began packing up. Red spotted a wine seller preparing to close shop, his wares mostly untouched. In these times, wine was a luxury few could afford.

Indeed, the wine seller looked desperate for a sale. "Interested in something to drink, gentlemen?"

They ended up with two bottles of rich red wine, criminally expensive. When was the last time Red had tasted proper wine? At the palace, he mainly drank ale with the servants.

"This is mad." Red cradled one bottle, giddy with their extravagance. "We're in the middle of a famine, buying wine like water!"

Wim, tucking the second bottle into his pack alongside their other meagre treasures, winked at him. "A little madness makes life worth living, don't you think? Especially in times like these."

The setting sun painted Wim's skin in amber and gold, softening his rough edges and catching his chestnut hair, turning the strands into liquid copper. Wim caught Red's eye, his broad smile splitting his face in two, and Red's chest tightened with an ache so sweet it bordered on painful.

Madness. This was madness, indeed.

What are you doing to me, wolf?

The sun hung low on the horizon as they searched for a suitable camping spot. Really, they should've pressed on, made up for lost time at the market, but Red's feet refused to cooperate. Even with his new boots, the day of walking had taken its toll. Besides, they had market spoils to indulge in.

So when they reached a clearing with mossy ground, Red slung down their market basket with glee. Wim built a fire while Red sorted their purchases, laying out the ingredients like precious gems. The flames caught quickly, and soon Wim was chopping vegetables and tossing them into their pot with flourishes.

Every few moments, Wim's gaze flickered to Red, dark and intense. Heat crept up Red's neck each time their eyes met. The way Wim watched him made Red feel like prey about to be pounced upon—the kind to be savoured. His insides twisted with a delicious sort of anxiety, so he busied himself sneaking sips from one of the bottles of wine. Red knew little about wine, but it tasted sweet enough, and it quickly warmed him throughout.

The aroma of searing venison filled the air, followed by the earthy scent of mushrooms and garlic. Wim ladled the steaming stew into wooden bowls. "Done."

Red took a bite and closed his eyes. The venison melted on his tongue, perfectly cooked and seasoned. "This is... incredible. I've never tasted anything like it, even from the palace kitchen." Even if it had tasted of dirt, Red would have lied, but he didn't need to.

With an air of triumph, Wim uncorked the second of their wine bottles and took a long drink before passing it to Red. They passed the bottle back and forth, trading sips between bites.

"Where did you learn to cook like this?" Red asked, scraping his bowl clean.

"Had plenty of practice, feeding the pack." Wim's eyes caught the firelight. "Though I must say, I've never had someone practically purr over my cooking before."

A cough spluttered out of Red, and he grabbed the wine bottle, taking another deep drink. He poured too quickly, and the cool liquid spilt down his neck.

Wim's laugh rumbled through the clearing as he reached across, thumb brushing against Red's neck to wipe away the spilled wine. The touch lingered, and Red's breath caught in his throat.

"Such a pretty little mess you are," Wim's said, so low it was almost a growl.

There was that word again that Wim was so fond of, *pretty*. Red had enjoyed hearing it before, enjoyed the fantasy of it. This time, though, it twisted in his chest, sharp and unexpected, like thorns catching on silk.

Red jerked back, wine sloshing in the bottle. It had already gone to his head, and so his words were slightly slurred when he said, "You don't need to lie to me, you know."

Wim's hand froze mid-air, brow furrowing. "What?"

"About…" Red gestured vaguely at his face, heat creeping up his cheeks that had nothing to do with the wine. "*This.* You don't need to keep pretending I'm pretty. I know I'm anything but, and I've made my peace with that now."

The playful atmosphere vanished. Wim's expression darkened, and he shifted closer. Capturing Red's small chin with one hand, he forced him to look at him. "Who told you that?"

Red's fingers tightened around the bottle. "What do you mean? I own a mirror." His voice came out brittle, and he hated it. "But the Queen made sure I knew exactly what she thought about my… *imperfections.*"

"Your eyes?" Wim's tone held a dangerous edge.

"Yes. She likes this one." He pointed to his blue eye—the ocean on a bright summer's day. "But this one, she says, is the colour of a dirty puddle."

"She's the monster, not you." Wim growled—a sound that made Red flinch despite the gentleness of the fingers still cradling his face. "A creature like that has no right to wear a crown."

The wine loosened Red's lips even further, and he found himself saying, "My earliest memory of the Queen is of her ordering me to close my eyes whenever I was in her presence."

A harsh breath hissed through Wim's teeth, his eyes blazing with such intensity that the reflected firelight seemed to dance with his rage.

"It was mortifying. Then at last, I grew my hair long, and with my hood up as well, I was able to hide my eyes when needed." Almost instinctively, Red went to tilt his head down, but Wim held his chin firm.

The intensity of the wolf's gaze pierced Red. His warm hand slid from Red's chin to cup his cheek, thumb brushing beneath the brown eye that the Queen despised. "Listen carefully, sweetheart. I promise you, if I ever have the chance to rip out that woman's throat, I will. I swear it on my life."

Wim's raw fury was so palpable, Red shuddered. The wine-soaked part of Red's mind latched onto the words. This surely wasn't merely the righteous anger of a decent man—there was something else there, something fiercely protective in a way that made Red's heart swell and throb.

The moment grew so intense, he was forced to look away with a nervous laugh. "Oh? Shall we do the pack swear? Like little Toby made me do?" He lifted his hand, pinky extended, desperate to lighten the heavy moment.

Wim's lips twitched, but the dangerous gleam remained in his eyes. He wrapped his much larger pinky around Red's. "On my honour as a wolf. Those eyes are a gift from God himself. That witch doesn't deserve to even look at them."

Something dangerous and tender wrestled in Wim's expression as his thumb traced endless patterns beneath Red's eye. The wine must be affecting them both, Red thought, for Wim to speak like that.

"I've seen her treat her own son, Makellos, with the same cruel scrutiny."

"Are the two of you close?"

Red snorted through another gulp of wine. "*Pah*! He made it very clear when we were young children that I was beneath him. I tried again and again to talk to him, but he wasn't interested." Red took another swig, and almost went for another, but Wim snatched the bottle from him. "Though, I have to admit, it's true what they say. Makellos *is* the most beautiful person in the whole kingdom."

A loud rumble came from Wim's throat.

Red laughed. "It's not like that. I do not desire Makellos, I'm only envious of his beauty." Red tugged on his hair. He'd spent his childhood yanking on the straw, praying it would transform into black silk. His hand was quickly caught by Wim's larger one, completely enclosing it. Then, with his other arm, Wim reached around to grab Red's waist.

Before he knew it, Red was flying through the air—Wim lifted him as easily as a doll, to place him on his lap. A small sound of shock escaped Red's lips. Wim pulled him even closer, and Red's heart began to beat impossibly fast.

"This perfect beauty you envy sounds dull as dishwater. Soft white skin can't compare to an archer's hands." Wim traced the palm of Red's hand, circling the small calluses from his bow. "And hair as black as night is nothing special next to sunshine caught in copper."

"Oh please, you can't possibly pretend to like my hair!"

"Like? Sweetheart, I *love* your hair," Wim breathed into his ear, entwining his fingers in Red's tangled mop. "Though it does often stick up in random directions."

"Hey!"

"But luckily for you, I like the wild look."

Wim threaded his fingers through Red's apparently wild hair. He cradled Red's face again, and Red leaned into the touch.

"Want to know what I love even more than your hair?"

"Okay," Red whispered, then swallowed.

Wim's thumb brushed beneath Red's right eye. He pulled back to stare into it. "This eye of yours. Like... rich brandy in candlelight. Or fresh honey straight from the hive." He tilted his head. "And... well... like those autumn leaves I run through as a wolf."

Red snorted, though his throat tightened. If his tongue wasn't tied, he'd have teased Wim for fancying himself a poet.

Wim's tone softened to silk. "And this one..." His thumb shifted to Red's left eye. "Like winter frost on a clear night. The two of them together... most beautiful sight I've ever seen."

The words knocked the air from Red's lungs. His chest constricted. Without thinking, he surged forward, pressing his lips to Wim's. A sound of surprise rumbled through Wim's chest, but then large hands gripped Red's waist, pulling him closer. The kiss deepened, grew hungrier. Red's fingers tangled in Wim's hair as Wim's tongue swept into his mouth, tasting of wine and want. Heat blazed between them, and Red had the mad urge to rip off all of his clothes. He shifted in Wim's lap, desperate to get closer, to feel more of him.

"Sweetheart," Wim growled against his lips, "you're going to be the death of me."

Red's head spun, a delicious, intoxicating desire coursing through his veins. Every touch of Wim's hands sent sparks across his skin, and he found himself pressing closer, chasing that heat. Wim kissed him again, and Red's bravery grew with every press of his lips.

"You know." Red traced a finger down Wim's chest. "You put ideas in my head earlier, wolf."

"Oh?" Wim's voice rumbled through Red's entire body.

"When you described me treating you like an obedient dog at my command." The words came out bolder than Red would normally dare, wine loosening his tongue.

"Is that what you want, sweetheart?" A deep growl vibrated from Wim's chest. His grip tightened on Red's waist. "To have a big bad wolf at your mercy? And what would you order me to do?"

Red leaned in close to Wim's ear, the wolf's beard scraping against his cheek. "I'd have you on your knees, and then I'd make you use that wicked tongue of yours until I'm screaming so loud the whole forest—" The world tilted suddenly, and Red swayed in Wim's lap, his words cutting off as he lost his balance.

Strong arms caught him instantly. A hiccup burst from Red's lips, followed by another. He pressed his hand to his mouth, trying to stifle the giggles that bubbled up uncontrollably.

Wim pulled back, surveying Red's face with concern. "Just how much wine have you had? I forget you're just a little thing."

"I might have had the first bottle all to myself, while you were cooking dinner." Another hiccup escaped between Red's fingers, and he dissolved into more giggles, falling forward to rest his forehead against Wim's shoulder.

Wine was so much fun. Red should drink it more often.

He spied the bottle next to Wim on the log, and stretched his arm out to grab it.

"I don't think so." Wim blocked his efforts.

Red huffed, crossing his arms. "You're so *bossy*. Why do you always have to tell me what to do?" His lower lip jutted out in a pout. "I'm not a child."

"Could've fooled me, with that face you're pulling." Wim's tone held both amusement and exasperation. "Come on, you need some water."

"*No*." The word came out as a needy whine. Red's body moved of its own accord, hips rolling forward to grind against Wim. The friction sent sparks of pleasure shooting through him, and he gasped at the sensation of his hardness pressing against Wim's.

Wim's head fell back, eyes squeezed shut. "*Fuck*." He drew in a ragged breath. "You're making this fucking difficult, sweetheart."

Before Red could protest, strong hands gripped his waist and lifted him up. The world spun briefly before he found himself deposited onto the log. The sudden loss of contact left him cold and a pathetic sound came from his lips.

Wim stood, running a hand through his dishevelled hair as he stalked over to their packs. Red watched Wim through wine-hazed eyes, admiring the way his muscles flexed with each movement as he searched through their belongings.

"*Damn*." Wim held up both empty waterskins, shaking his head. "They're both dry."

"I don't need water." Red resisted stamping his foot, though it was a challenge. "I need *you*."

And god, how that was true! Red's rock-hard cock begged to be touched, and Red slipped his hand underneath his ass, in case it got carried away of its own accord.

Wim fell to the ground in front of Red and squeezed his leg. "Right, pay attention, sweetheart. I'm going to fetch some fresh water from the stream. When I get back, if you've cleared your head and drink enough to satisfy me..." He paused. "Then I'll happily do anything your wicked little heart desires."

Wim's mouth blazed a trail across Red's jaw, teeth grazing sensitive skin until he reached Red's ear. A gasp caught in Red's throat as Wim captured the lobe between sharp teeth, sending shivers down his spine.

Through heavy-lidded eyes, Red watched as Wim stepped back and stripped off his clothes. The firelight painted golden streaks across his muscled form, highlighting every curve and plane. Dark hair dusted his chest, trailing down his stomach to... Red's mouth went dry. Wim's proud prick was thick and hard, and Red's mind filled with possibilities of what it might feel like inside him. Would he dare ask? The wine still coursing through his veins whispered, *yes, yes, yes!*

Wim's form blurred and shifted, fur sprouting across his body as he transformed into the massive grey wolf. He shook himself once before managing to fling his pack onto his back.

"I'll be back before you know it," he said, voice deeper in wolf form.

Red's hand had wandered without his permission, palming himself through his breeches. A rumbling growl made him freeze, caught in the act.

"You better save that for me, Little Red." Wim's eyes glowed in the firelight. "Unless you want to find out what happens to naughty little things who don't follow instructions."

Red's lips curved into a deliberate smirk which he hoped was vaguely sultry. "Well then, you better be quick, wolf."

A blink of an eye later, Wim was gone, disappeared into the dark abyss.

Red was alone. Alone, again.

He stared into the fire, enjoying the show the shadows offered as they danced around the edges. They twisted into strange shapes that Red's wine-addled mind couldn't quite make sense of. He'd never noticed how *loud* the forest was at night—every crack of a branch or rustle of leaves made him jump. His heart refused to settle into a steady rhythm.

Back at the palace, he'd spent countless nights alone in the attic, perfectly content with only his own company. Now the solitude pressed in around him like a physical weight. The fire crackled, sending sparks into the darkness, and Red found himself counting the seconds until Wim's return.

A twig snapped somewhere in the darkness, and Red was abruptly reminded of the night he met Wim, when the wolf was stalking him in the shadows.

But he was safe here, wasn't he? Wim wouldn't have left him if he wasn't safe. Then again, where the fuck was he? Why wasn't he back yet? How long had it even been? Minutes? Hours?

What if something had happened to him?

Or perhaps after you threw yourself at him, he's run a mile.

Another noise.

Red's head whipped around, scanning the treeline. Nothing. Just shadows and more shadows, writhing like living things. The wine made everything blur at the edges, reality becoming soft and uncertain.

Was that movement? There—just beyond the fire's reach? Red squinted, trying to focus his vision. The darkness seemed to pulse, to breathe. His fingers clutched at his red cloak, pulling it tighter around his shoulders.

Another sound—closer this time. A whisper of movement, like fabric dragging across leaves.

Was this a cruel trick of the Queen's Shadow? To scare him into wetting his breeches before he laughed in Red's face?

"Hello?" The word escaped before he could stop it, small and afraid in the vast darkness.

The forest swallowed his voice whole.

Red's skin prickled. Even the familiar weight of his bow offered little comfort. His fingers trembled as he drew the cloak closer still, as if the fabric could shield him from whatever lurked in the darkness.

Pop!

Red nearly leapt out of his skin as the fire crackled. A laugh bubbled up in his throat—high and nervous—at his own jumpiness. But the sound died as quickly as it began when something *definitely* moved in the shadows to his left.

Red's breath caught. The darkness seemed to stretch, to reach for him with grasping fingers. His head spun, the wine making it impossible to tell what was real and what was imagination. He pressed himself back against the log, heart thundering in his chest.

Hurry back, Wim. Please hurry back.

A shape emerged from the shadows, moving towards the firelight. Red's shoulders sagged with relief.

"Oh, thank—"

The words died in his throat. It wasn't Wim.

Before Red could scream, a rough hand clamped over his mouth from behind. His arms were yanked backwards, twisted painfully as someone bound them with coarse rope. He thrashed against the iron grip, but the wine had dulled his reflexes, made his limbs clumsy and uncoordinated.

The figure stepped into the firelight. *No!* Red's blood turned to ice as he recognised the scarred lip, the cold eyes of the merchant from the market—the one who'd struck that child before Wim intervened.

The merchant's lips curved into an ugly smile. "You didn't go far, did you?" He crouched down, bringing his face level with Red's. "Now then, where's that brute of yours?"

Red couldn't answer, could barely breathe through the crushing pressure of the hand across his mouth. His chest heaved as panic clawed at his throat. The merchant's belt housed a row of sharp knives that glinted as he moved.

The ropes bit into his wrists as Red struggled, the knots only tightening for his efforts.

Red's teeth sank into the flesh of the man restraining him. The hand jerked away with a curse, and Red gasped in air.

"He'll be back any second," Red spat out. His words wavered more than he'd like, the wine still clouding his thoughts. "He'll tear you to pieces."

The merchant's cruel smile never left his face as he said, "That's why I brought friends." He pressed two fingers to his lips and let out a piercing whistle.

Shadows detached themselves from the darkness. Numerous figures emerged into the firelight. Their clothes hung in tatters, faces dirty and weather-beaten. *Bandits*. Red's stomach dropped.

"Found them just like I promised," the merchant said to a burly man with an eyepatch who seemed to be the leader. "Your turn now."

"Take everything!" The one-eyed bandit bellowed. The others descended like vultures upon their camp, ripping through their packs and supplies.

Red's heart stopped as one of them snatched up his bow and quiver. The golden arrow—the Queen's arrow meant for Old Oma—was hidden among the others. If they took it... his mission would be ruined. The Queen would have his head.

"Two gold pieces, as agreed," the one-eyed leader said, pressing coins into the merchant's palm. "For the tip-off about rich travellers."

"Wasn't easy tracking them through the forest," the merchant mumbled, pocketing the money. "And that big one could snap a man's neck without trying. I'd say all this was worth three, looking at it now."

The bandit leader spat. "You get what we agreed. You wanted revenge on the big one, we wanted their valuables. Fair trade."

Red's chest constricted. They'd been followed. All because Wim had stood up for that child at the market. And now their belongings were being ransacked, the golden arrow about to be stolen, Red's throat likely about to be cut, and Wim was going to walk right into an ambush when he returned.

If he returns at all, a small voice whispered. *Maybe he's already abandoned you.*

Red watched helplessly as the bandits gathered their belongings: their cooking pot, the sacks of fresh vegetables, their new blankets and the bedrolls, the clothes Wim had just shed, the remaining wine, their coin purses, and even the herbs they'd collected.

"What's this?" One of the bandits held up the golden arrow, its shaft gleaming in the firelight. "This ain't normal metal."

The merchant's eyes widened. "That should be worth at least another gold piece for me!"

Eyepatch barked out a laugh. "You got your payment. Be grateful for what you've got."

"Wait!" Red screeched. "Please, take everything else, but leave that arrow."

"And why would we do that?" Eyepatch's good eye narrowed.

"It's... cursed." Red's wine-addled mind scrambled for a convincing lie. "Anyone who touches it will die a horrible death within three days. Their insides will rot and—"

The bandits erupted in laughter. Red didn't blame them.

"I'll... trade anything for it." The words tumbled from Red's mouth before he could stop them.

Eyepatch's lip curled. "Trade what exactly? We've taken everything you own."

Red's heart plummeted to his stomach. His gaze fell to the red cloak around his shoulders—his most precious item. But not more precious than his own life. "This cloak. It's magical. It keeps you warm in winter and cool in summer. Never tears, never wears out. It's a royal enchantment, very rare."

"Is that so?" Eyepatch stepped closer, running the fabric between his fingers. A cruel smile spread across his face. "Well, if it's that valuable, we'll be taking that too."

"*No—*"

Rough hands seized the cloak, yanking it from Red's shoulders. The clasp at his throat snapped, the silver pieces falling into the darkness as they wrenched it away. A choked sob escaped his lips before he could swallow it back—the only thing he had left of his mother, ripped away like everything else. The last thread connecting him to any sort of belonging, any hint of being wanted, severed.

The night air bit into his exposed skin, but the cold was nothing compared to the hollow ache spreading through his chest. *Stupid, stupid, stupid.* If he hadn't drunk so much wine, if he hadn't let his guard down, if he hadn't been so desperate for Wim's touch that the wolf left to fetch him water...

And now he'd lost the one thing he'd sworn to keep safe, the one treasure he'd managed to hold onto through all these winters.

He watched, helpless and shivering, as his cloak was tossed carelessly into their pile of stolen goods. The rich red fabric seemed to mock him, a reminder of every foolish decision that had led to this moment.

"These boots look nice and new too," one of the bandits said, grabbing Red's ankle.

"No!" Red cried. He hadn't even realised he had one thing still left to lose.

They ignored his pleas and stripped the boots from his feet, leaving him bound and shivering in just his shirt and breeches.

Eyepatch's boot connected with Red's ribs, sending him sprawling face first into the dirt. His teeth sliced into his bottom lip, and copper flooded his mouth. Pain bloomed across his side as he struggled to draw breath against the dirty ground.

"Not so mouthy now, are you?" Eyepatch sneered.

The merchant's boots crunched through the leaves as he approached. "Look at him. Pathetic." He crouched down beside Red, fingers gripping Red's chin and forcing his head up. "Your brute's abandoned you, boy. Can't say I blame him. Who'd want a freak with ugly eyes?" His thumb brushed Red's cheekbone. "Though I suppose some might pay good coin for something... unusual."

Red jerked his face away, spitting blood onto the merchant's boots. The merchant recoiled with a curse, wiping his boots on Red's shirt.

"That beast of yours probably realised what an ugly little thing you are and ran for the hills." The merchant's lips curled into a cruel smile.

The merchant's words burrowed deep. It was as if he somehow knew Red's deepest insecurity, knew the very thing that had made the Queen despise him, and that had kept him from finding friendship or acceptance within the palace walls. And the man was right, Wim had clearly left him, repulsed by Red's advances. Maybe he'd sobered up enough to realise what Red truly was—damaged, broken, unworthy—just like everyone else eventually did.

You're nothing but an ugly, unwanted orphan. Unlovable.

The voice in his head sounded like the Queen's, cold and cutting. She'd been right all along. He'd never belonged anywhere. Not in the palace, not by Wim's side.

The Queen had seen it, Makellos had seen it, and now Wim had finally seen it too.

"Right!" Eyepatch cut through Red's spiral of self-loathing. "Pack it up, we're moving out."

Footsteps crunched through leaves, growing fainter. No one spared him a backwards glance as they melted back into the shadows, leaving him bound and alone by the dying fire. The noises faded into the night.

And then the silence pressed in, suffocating.

He'd failed. Failed the Queen's mission. Failed to save Falchovari from its famine. Failed himself.

Red lay still, tasting blood and dirt, waiting until the last footstep disappeared.

Then his shoulders shook as the first sob tore from his throat. Another followed, then another, until he was crying properly. The sobs tore free from his throat, harsh and ugly in the empty night.

The tears carved hot trails down his cheeks as he curled into himself on the frozen ground.

He'd just lay down here, bound, until he starved to death, then the birds could pick at his flesh.

At least he'd be of some use then.

Thirteen

WIM

Wim's blood sang with one purpose: return to Red.

His paw hit the ground wrong yet again, sending fresh waves of pain shooting up his leg. He ignored it, pushing through the undergrowth as fast as his injured limb would allow. The wine had dulled his senses earlier, making him careless, and he'd tripped, spraining his ankle.

The forest spoke to him differently in this form. Every rustle, every scent, every movement held meaning that his human mind would miss, whereas his wolf-self understood the language of the woods with ancient clarity.

But Wim wasn't presently paying any attention to the forest.

Mine-protect-return.

The thoughts pulsed through him with each stride. Like a hook beneath his ribs, Red's scent drew him forward. His pack was heavy with the waterskins he'd filled, a reminder of his promise to return quickly.

The alcohol had quickly left his system, thankfully. He cursed the foolish market purchase, for not only had it caused Red to become intoxicated, but it stupidly allowed him to leave his Red alone in this dangerous forest. The thought of Little Red alone in the darkness made his chest tight. Strange, this pull. In his thirty-two winters, he'd never felt such an urge to return to anyone's side.

His nose twitched, seeking that now-familiar scent—wild berries, woodsmoke from all their fires, and something uniquely *his*.

The smell of blood hit him first.

Fear flooded his veins, the beast inside him snarling to life. He quickened his pace, dried leaves crunching beneath his paws. Other scents layered over Red's—unfamiliar men, steel, sweat. The market trader's stench.

Through the trees, he caught sight of their camp. Or what remained of it.

His Red sat hunched on the ground, wrists bound behind him, tear tracks cutting through the dirt on his face. A split lip leaked blood down his chin.

The beast roared for blood, for revenge, but Wim forced it down. Red needed him calm. Needed him here.

A whine escaped his throat. "Red! What happened?!"

"Where the fuck have you been?" Red's voice cracked raw, and the sound pierced Wim's heart. His Red twisted against the ropes, sitting up with blazing eyes full of hurt and fury. "What do you think happened? Look around! We were robbed!"

Wim shifted back to human form, ignoring the ache of transformation. His hands trembled as they found the ropes binding Red's wrists—his clever, skilled Little Red who should never be bound like this. He worked quickly to loosen the knots, breathing in Red's scent to calm the rising beast inside him. Every mark on Red's skin made his blood boil.

"God, I'm so sorry. I shouldn't have left you." The words felt inadequate. "The stream was further than I thought and the wine... it slowed me down more than I realised." His fingers ghosted over Red's ribs, checking for injuries, marking each hurt done to what was *his*. "Like a fool, I caught my leg in a rabbit hole. It took a while to mend."

After rummaging through his pack, Wim quickly slipped on a large, loose shirt that covered most of him. Wim cupped Red's face, thumb brushing away a smear of blood from the split lip. The beast howled for vengeance, but he pushed it down. Unlike the feral kills of his past, these men would face something worse—his controlled rage.

"Who did this?"

Red jerked away from his touch, and the rejection stung. "That awful man from the market led bandits to us. I was *attacked*!" The accusation in Red's scream pierced Wim deeper than any arrow could, and he deserved it. He'd failed to protect what was *his*. "They're long gone now. Along with everything we had." Red's voice broke. "The golden arrow... my *cloak*..."

That red cloak—the damned thing his Little Red treasured above all else. Wim had thought the man's obsession with it too much at first, but now he couldn't imagine him without it, the fabric as much a part of Red as his sly smile or sharp tongue. Even when they slept, Red kept it close, fingers curled in the worn material like a child with a comfort blanket. To have it ripped away by those bastards... Wim's jaw clenched. He'd track down every last one of them just for that alone.

Fresh tears spilled from those unique eyes he'd grown to adore, and Wim couldn't bear it. He pulled Red onto his lap, relief flooding through him when his Little Red's rigid body finally melted against his chest. He encircled Red with his arms, one hand stroking up and down Red's arm while the other smoothed his tangled hair, breathing in their mingled scents.

"Shh, sweetheart. I've got you now."

And I'm never letting you go again, he thought, even knowing he must. Even knowing that what waited ahead in the Dark Forest might change everything. *Would* change everything.

Red's tears slowed as Wim worked through the knots in his hair, letting his heartbeat steady against his chest. The warmth between them chased away the chill of the night air. Wim's nose caught the copper tang of blood from Red's split lip.

"Your lip..." He brushed his thumb near the split, careful not to hurt Red further. "May I kiss it better? Wolf saliva has healing properties."

Red blinked, tilting his head back to look up at him, and Wim's breath caught at the trust in those eyes. "Are you making that up?"

"No tricks. I promise."

Red gave him a small smile, and Wim couldn't help but smile back, even as his heart ached. How many more moments like this could they share before his secret destroyed everything? Then Red nodded once, and the simple gesture of trust made Wim's chest tight.

He pressed his lips to Red's, feather-light, letting his tongue dart out to heal the wound. The metallic taste of blood mixed with lingering wine, and beneath it all, Red's unique flavour. The beast inside him purred with satisfaction as the split began to heal.

Red pulled back, touching his healed lip in wonder. "I'm so sorry. I was just vile to you, when you're hurt yourself."

"You were scared and by yourself, sweetheart. Anyone would lash out." Wim tightened his arms around Red, fighting the urge to shift and wrap him in fur instead. "God, I should never have gone. Should've been here to protect you." He exhaled a large breath, ghosting across Red's cheek. "Makes me want to tear something apart, thinking of you alone like that."

His keen ears picked up the quickening of Red's pulse as fingers traced the healed lip. "The golden arrow... without it, I can't save the kingdom. The famine will continue, more people will starve." Red's voice trembled. "I've failed everyone."

Guilt churned in Wim's gut. But he couldn't think about that right now. It wouldn't help.

"Tell me something, sweetheart. Do you really believe all that?" Wim kept his tone gentle, curious. "That some fancy arrow's going to turn the old witch to ash and fix everything?"

The conviction in Red's tone as he wrenched himself from Wim's lap gouged at something tender in his chest. "Of course I do!" Red spun away, and Wim's arms felt empty without him. "You think I'd be out here marching through this bloody forest, freezing my ass off and battling bandits for the fun of it?" Those delicate hands shook as Red gestured wildly. "Children are dying! The crops won't grow, the animals are sick—"

Frustration burned in Wim's chest. How could someone so brilliant, so perceptive, be so thoroughly deceived by that viper of a queen? His Little Red, who was remarkably quick-witted, claimed to hate Queen Schön as much as Wim did, yet here he was, believing every poisoned word that woman had fed him.

But... then... what if it was all true? Wim's certainty wavered. After all, he was following his own desperate quest, chasing a cure that seemed just as fantastical. Who was he to judge?

"Shh, sweetheart." He caught Red's flailing hands in his own, thumbs rubbing circles on those palms that wielded a bow with such deadly grace. "I didn't mean to upset you."

Red tried to pull away, but Wim held firm, tugging him closer until their foreheads touched. He breathed in their mingled scents, trying to ground himself.

"I know why you doubt it," Red said bitterly. "It's because you can't believe the Queen would send someone so incompetent on such an important mission."

"No!" The word burst from Wim's chest. "*Christ,* how can you think that of me?" He cupped Red's face between his palms. "Listen here, sweetheart. That queen of yours is poison through and through. I wouldn't trust a single word from her mouth." His wolf bristled at the mere thought of that woman's influence over his Red. "But you? You're something else entirely. Those slavers you put down with that bow of yours—fine, clean shots, barely wasting an arrow. And when you squeezed yourself through that cliff face, to save some stranger's child from a snare? Nothing incompetent about that."

He stared at Red, stunned by his own torrent of praise. But now that he'd started, he couldn't stop. His hands cupped Red's face, forcing those mismatched eyes to meet his. His wolf surged forward, demanding Red understand his worth.

"Look at me now. In all my thirty-two winters, all the lands I've walked, all the people I've known…" His thumbs traced Red's cheekbones, mapping every feature. "Never met anyone who comes close to you. Brave and fierce and brilliant—and entirely your own person."

The rapid flutter of Red's pulse beneath his fingers, the widening of those beautiful eyes… Wim could smell the disbelief rolling off him in waves. Before Red could protest, before Wim could reveal too much of his own heart, he jumped to his feet, hauling Red up with him.

Right, enough of that. His Little Red needed his cloak back.

"Right then, sweetheart. If this arrow's meant to save the kingdom, we'll get it back." His grip tightened on Red's fingers, unwilling to let go. "Those thieves won't have made it far, not with all that loot weighing them down."

Red gaped at him. "You can't be serious. We're just going to… what… chase them down and take everything back?" Those delicate hands fluttered dramatically. "There were loads of them! And they all had *weapons*."

A predatory smile spread across Wim's face, his wolf rising to the surface. Unlike his feral episodes, this hunt would be calculated, controlled. These men had hurt what was his. They would learn their mistake. "So do I."

"But we don't even know which direction they went!" Red's voice pitched higher, sending a protective surge through Wim's chest.

He tapped his nose with one finger. Their scent trail lay clear as daylight to his wolf senses, fear-sweat and greed leading away through the trees. "That shouldn't be difficult."

"But…" Red wrapped his arms around himself, and Wim caught the sour scent of fear. "It might be dangerous!"

Wim's broad shoulders lifted in a casual shrug. "Didn't we make short work of those slavers together? This lot won't know what hit them."

He watched as the words died in Red's throat, scenting the shift in his emotions—concern, worry, something deeper that made Wim's chest tighten. His Little Red cared for him now, far more than he had when they'd first met. The knowledge both thrilled and terrified him, considering their time together had an inevitable end.

While Red wrestled with his thoughts, Wim rooted through the ruined camp, trying to focus on the immediate problem to calm his spiralling mind.

"Well, what do we have here?" He held up Red's old, hole-ridden boots triumphantly. "They left you with these. At least something's going right."

"Oh, what joy!" Red's retort carried that familiar bite, but his smile—god, that smile—made Wim's heart stutter. He threw the boots to Red, watching as he pulled them on with a grimace.

"Ready?" Wim let his eyes gleam in the darkness, already feeling the pull of his wolf form.

"Ugh." Red kicked at a clump of grass. "Fine. But if we die, I'm going to kill you."

Wim's laugh echoed through the trees, even as his chest ached with things unsaid. How could he tell Red that he'd tear apart anyone who tried to harm him? That the thought of Red's death made his wolf howl in agony? *That his own mission would destroy whatever was growing between them?*

"That's the spirit, sweetheart. Now, hop on."

He slipped off his shirt, stuffing it into his pack before he let his shift take him, bones cracking and reforming, fur rippling across his skin, tail swishing once against the forest floor. Then his wolf form stood before Red, massive and grey, easily as tall as Red's chest. He kept his eyes fixed on him.

Blood rushed through Wim's veins, almost dizzying him.

Mine-protect-mine.

"Show-off," Red muttered, but Wim's keen ears caught the smile in his voice as Red climbed onto his broad back. Those lovely fingers tangled in his thick grey fur, and Wim suppressed a shiver of pleasure. "Right, then. Let's go catch some bandits."

I'll keep you safe this time, Little Red, Wim promised silently as he caught the bandits' scent. *No matter the cost.*

Fourteen

The wind whipped through Red's hair as Wim bounded through the forest following an invisible trail. Without his cloak, the night air bit into Red's skin, raising gooseflesh across his arms. He pressed closer to Wim's warmth, burying his face in the thick grey fur.

Wim's pace slowed, his massive paws silent against the earth. Red strained his ears but heard nothing beyond the rustle of leaves.

A low growl vibrated through Wim's chest. Red leaned down, pressing his lips close to Wim's ear. "What is it?"

Wim shook his head once, continuing forward at a creep. After several more minutes, Red caught the sound of rough laughter floating through the trees—Eyepatch's distinctive cackle made his stomach clench.

Wim stopped, lowering himself so Red could slide off. The wolf shifted back to human form, crouching close. "Stay here," he whispered. "I need to get closer, see what we're dealing with."

Red's fingers shot out, grabbing Wim's wrist. The thought of being alone, even for moments, sent ice through his veins. But he forced himself to nod, releasing his grip.

Wim disappeared into the shadows. Red counted his breaths, fighting the urge to call out. When Wim returned, Red nearly sagged with relief.

"They're settling down for the night," Wim murmured. "Two keeping watch, but they're nearly asleep on their feet. One's nodding off by that large oak, the other's perched on a stump near their supplies. The rest are already out cold. At least some of our belongings are piled near the centre of camp."

"So what's the plan?" Red whispered.

"Simple enough. Wait for them to sleep, then I'll slip in and take back what's ours."

"Absolutely not. I'll do it. Unlike *some* people, I can move without sounding like a lumbering bear!"

Wim rumbled in disagreement. "Might want to remember who's the predator here, sweetheart. We know how to sneak up on our prey."

"It's mainly *my* items we need. I'll find them quicker than you will," Red insisted. "Plus, they're less likely to immediately kill me upon sight—they'll recognise me, at least."

Wim's jaw clenched, but after a long moment he growled out, "If that's how you want it. But I'll be right here in the shadows. One wrong move from them..."

"Look," Red started, accidentally biting into his still slightly sore lip. "If they *do* grab me, do the sensible thing and run, would you?"

Wim's eyes flashed dangerously in the dark. "After all the trouble I've gone through keeping you alive?" His tone was light, but his expression was deadly serious. "I'm not going anywhere without you, sweetheart."

"Well... at least promise me you'll *try* not to kill them. I don't want you to harbour any more guilt, especially on my account."

The wolf scoffed. "Not making any promises about that, sweetheart," he said softly, yet there was steel beneath the words. "They touch you, they die."

Red couldn't help the butterflies that exploded in his stomach, despite the fact they were induced by threats of violence.

When they could hear no more voices, Red crept forward, keeping his footsteps as light as a cat's. The bandits' camp sprawled before him, their bodies scattered around dying embers. The first lookout's chin rested against his chest, soft snores escaping his lips.

Red froze as the man stirred, muttering something unintelligible before settling back into slumber.

Holding his breath, Red slipped past the dozing guard. The second watchman sat slumped against a tree stump, a half-empty bottle of cheap spirits dangling from his fingertips.

And there, in the centre, lay a jumbled heap of belongings, including Red's pack and new boots. His fingers trembled as he reached for his bow, relief flooding through him as he lifted it from the pile. His quiver sat beneath, and he checked inside—the golden arrow glinted in the dim firelight, its shaft unmarred. Their basket from the market lay on its side, and Red snatched it up.

A few feet away, Eyepatch snored beneath their new blankets, the ones Wim had bartered for at market. Red's jaw clenched. The brute had wrapped himself in both, leaving his companions to shiver in their threadbare coverings.

Where was his cloak? Red scanned the camp, searching for that familiar flash of crimson. Nothing.

A small cart sat at the edge of camp, its wooden sides weathered and cracked. Red crept towards it, careful to avoid the sleeping forms between him and his target. Inside, sacks of grain competed for space with leather pouches and what looked like stolen trinkets. He rifled through them as quietly as possible, stomach sinking with each empty container. A crate beside the cart yielded nothing but mouldy vegetables and a nest of mice.

His chest tightened—the thought of losing his only connection to his mother made him want to tear the camp apart.

One of the bandits rolled over, muttering in his sleep. Red froze, muscles rigid, barely daring to breathe. The man's hand flopped out, inches from Red's foot. After what felt like ages, the bandit's breathing evened out again.

Red retreated, step by careful step, until he reached the treeline where Wim waited. He clutched the bow and quiver to his chest, along with a small sack of supplies he'd managed to reclaim.

"My cloak," he whispered, a lump forming in his throat. "I couldn't find it. It's nowhere to be seen!"

"You searched everywhere?" Wim asked gently. "At least we got your bow back, sweetheart. And that arrow you need so badly."

Red's fingers tightened around the bow. "But... my cloak..." He swallowed around a lump in his throat. "I can't shoot properly without it." He fought hard to keep the wobble from his voice. "It helps steady my aim in the wind and..." A deep breath in. "It's all I have left of her."

The wolf cocked his head to one side, amber eyes searching Red's face, understanding dawning in their depths. "Stay right here, Red," he murmured, already scenting the air. "If it's got your smell on it, I'll find it."

Before Red could protest, the massive grey wolf padded silently into the camp, nose low to the ground. Red pressed against a tree trunk, heart hammering as Wim weaved between the sleeping bodies.

The wolf paused near Eyepatch, sniffing the air. Red followed his gaze and spotted a flash of crimson peeking out from beneath the stolen blankets. That greedy bastard had wrapped himself in both thick blankets they'd bought at market *and* taken Red's cloak as an extra layer.

Red expected Wim to retreat, to return with the news of its location. Instead, the wolf crouched low, assessing the situation. The idiot was going to try something.

Don't, Red wanted to shout. *It's not worth the risk*. If Eyepatch woke up while Wim was that close... Red's stomach churned at the thought of the bandit's blade finding Wim's throat. All because of a stupid cloak.

Wim crept closer, careful paw steps bringing him within inches of the sleeping bandit. His teeth closed around the visible edge of red fabric. Ever so slowly, he began to pull.

Heart lodged in his throat, Red readied and raised his bow as Wim tugged at the cloak. The fabric refused to budge, caught beneath

Eyepatch's bulk. Wim's muscles tensed with each careful pull, yet the cloak remained trapped.

The sight of the wolf so close to the cruel bandit proved too much. Red crept forward, one hand fluttering in frantic gestures as he approached.

"Leave it!" he mouthed, waving in sharp, desperate movements.

The cloak remained in Wim's strong jaw. "You can hardly be Little Red without your fucking red riding hood, can you, sweetheart?" he hissed.

Before Red could stop him, Wim gave one final determined yank. The cloak slipped free with a sharp snap of fabric—

Eyepatch jerked upright, blade already in hand. His good eye fixed on them, widening with recognition at the sight of Red.

Fuck. Red's blood turned to ice. *We're dead.*

"INTRUDERS! MEN! TO ARMS!" Eyepatch's bellow shattered the night's quiet. His blade slashed through the air where Wim had crouched moments before.

Shapes burst from blankets across the camp, metal glinting as weapons emerged from sheaths. Curses and shouts filled the air as bandits stumbled over each other, some still half-asleep and confused. Red clutched his bow, frozen still for a precious moment.

The ropes cutting into his wrists, the taste of blood in his mouth, their cruel laughter as they'd bound him and left him sobbing in the dirt. The memory crashed over him like icy water, threatening to drown him in panic. *No. Not this time.* He wouldn't be helpless again—this time he had his bow, and this time he had Wim.

The camp transformed into a nightmare of moving shadows and steel. Three bandits charged towards them while others searched blindly in the wrong direction, their eyes not yet adjusted to the darkness. Red's fingers trembled as he nocked an arrow—the close quarters made his stomach twist. He'd trained for distance shots, not this frenzied mess of bodies mere feet away.

A snarl ripped through the air as Wim pounced—his massive form bowled into the nearest bandit, sending the man flying backwards into a tree trunk with a sickening crack. Before anyone could react, Wim's jaws closed around another man's arm. The bandit screamed as Wim shook him like a rag doll, tossing him aside where he lay still.

Well, at least Red had *tried* to get Wim to promise no more murder.

Red drew back his bowstring as a third bandit lunged at him with a rusted sword. At this distance, Red could see every detail of the man's face—the crooked teeth, the week-old stubble, the whites of his eyes. The arrow felt wrong in his fingers, too close, too personal. But there was no time for doubt. Red released the string. The arrow struck true, burying itself in the bandit's throat. Blood sprayed across Red's face as the man crumpled, gurgling his last breath mere inches from Red's feet.

Red stumbled backwards, tripping over the dead bandit at his feet. His bow clattered to the ground as rough hands seized him from behind. Instinctively, he knew who'd caught him—Eyepatch.

Terror clawed up Red's throat, threatening to choke him. His body remembered those same hands pinning him down before, remembered the helplessness, the violation of being touched against his will. The world narrowed to pinpricks of sensation—the blade's cold bite, the nauseating press of Eyepatch's body against his back, the stench of his foul breath. *No! Not again.* Heart stuttering, Red's legs turned to water beneath him, and only Eyepatch's bruising grip kept him upright.

Across the clearing, Wim had one of the remaining bandits trapped in his jaws. The man thrashed and screamed, blood seeping from puncture wounds in his shoulder.

Red's eyes locked onto Wim's. The wolf paused, his ears flattened against his skull, a deep growl rumbling through his chest.

"Well, well." Eyepatch's gravelly voice sent shivers down Red's spine. "You're this one's friend, aren't you? The brute the merchant described? A real life wildling! I bet your pelt would fetch me a pretty penny."

Wim's growl grew louder, his teeth sinking deeper into his captive's flesh. The bandit's screams reached a fever pitch.

"Drop him," Eyepatch commanded, pressing the blade harder against Red's skin. A warm trickle of blood rolled down Red's neck. "Or I'll paint the ground with your friend's blood."

Red's breath came in sharp gasps. His legs trembled as Eyepatch's free hand slid up his thigh, squeezing painfully.

"Once I'm done skinning you," Eyepatch purred. "I'll take my time with this odd little thing..."

Something shifted in Wim's eyes. The warm amber Red had grown familiar with disappeared, replaced by something savage. The wolf's hackles rose, his muscles bunching beneath his fur. Blood dripped from his muzzle as he released his victim, who crawled away whimpering.

His already massive form seemed to grow larger, his teeth longer, his claws sharper. The air around him crackled with violent energy.

This wasn't Wim anymore—that feral creature that lurked beneath his skin was back.

The monster that had torn those villagers apart.

It was as if Eyepatch could sense it as well—his grip loosened, the blade trembling against Red's throat. The bandit's swagger evaporated as Wim stalked forward, each step deliberate and predatory. Saliva dripped from the wolf's jaws, mixing with blood on the forest floor.

"Stay back!" Eyepatch growled out. His fingers dug painfully into Red's arm as he dragged them both backwards. "I'll kill him! I swear I'll—"

The wolf's muscles coiled. In the split second before he launched, Red caught a glimpse of those large, fearsome eyes—no trace remained of the man who'd held him through the cold night, who'd cooked him countless meals and teased him about his howl.

Red dropped his weight, twisting free as Wim struck. The knife sliced a shallow line across his collarbone as he fell, but he barely noticed the sting. Eyepatch's scream pierced the night as Wim's teeth found his throat. The sound cut off in a wet gurgle, replaced by the crack of bone and tear of flesh.

Blood sprayed in an arc, coating the ground, the trees, Red's face. Eyepatch's body convulsed, his good eye wide with terror as he choked on his own blood.

"You... monster..." The words bubbled from his ruined throat, barely intelligible.

Wim's jaws clenched. One sharp twist, and Eyepatch went limp.

The remaining bandits broke, scattered into the darkness, crashing through undergrowth in their desperation to escape. Their panicked cries faded into the distance, leaving only the sound of Red's ragged breathing and the wet drip of blood from Wim's muzzle.

"Wim?" Red's voice quivered as the blood-soaked wolf prowled towards him. Those savage eyes fixed on him, muscles bunching beneath matted fur.

The wolf pounced, knocking Red onto his back. The air rushed out of his lungs as sharp teeth hovered inches from his throat, hot breath washing over his skin.

"It's me." Red forced himself to meet that feral gaze. "Your Red. Your Little Red. You saved me, now please... come back to me."

The wolf froze. Recognition flickered in those golden depths. "*Mine,*" he growled, then the massive form shuddered, and suddenly Wim was there, human and naked, crushing Red beneath his weight.

"God, Red." Wim's hands roamed frantically over Red's body, checking for injuries. His fingers found the shallow cut across Red's collarbone, and his expression darkened. Without hesitation, he lowered his head and ran his tongue along the wound. The sting immediately lessened.

"It's only a scratch," Red whispered. "Thanks to you."

Wim continued to lap at the wound, slow and deliberate. Each stroke sent shivers down Red's spine that had nothing to do with healing. The wet heat of his mouth lingered longer than necessary, trailing past the cut and down Red's neck. Red's fingers tangled in

Wim's hair before he remembered where they were—surrounded by corpses in a blood-soaked clearing. He pushed gently at Wim's shoulders. "We need to go. The others might return."

Wim pushed himself up, retrieving the blankets and Red's cloak from where they'd fallen. His hands trembled as he wrapped the crimson fabric around Red's shoulders.

Red clutched the familiar material, breathing in its scent. The weight of it settled something inside him, like finding a missing piece of himself.

"Wait." Wim's hand stilled on the cloak's clasp, and his brow furrowed. "This catch is damaged."

Red glanced down to see the ornate silver fastening hanging askew, its delicate hinge bent at an odd angle, broken during the earlier scuffle.

"Here, let me see."

Before Red could object, Wim reached up and unfastened the cloak,

"Damn," he muttered, fingers tracing the intricate floral design. "I don't know how to fix something so fine." Wim studied the clasp intently, running his thumb along the delicate metalwork. His brow creased in concentration as he prodded the hinge with a calloused fingertip. "I think I can bend it back into place," he murmured. "Just need to get the angle right..."

Red watched, mesmerized, as Wim set to work. The wolf's massive hands seemed too large and rough for such a delicate task, yet they moved with deft precision. Wim's tongue poked out between his lips as he carefully manipulated the clasp. A few strands of chestnut hair had fallen across Wim's forehead, dampened by sweat and streaked with drying blood. Red's fingers twitched with the urge to brush them aside, to map the sharp angles of Wim's face and commit every detail to memory.

When had this wild, feral creature become so captivating? Just minutes ago, Red had witnessed the brutal, animalistic violence

Wim was capable of. He'd seen the way Wim tore into Eye-patch, all semblance of humanity stripped away as the wolf claimed his prey.

And yet, here he knelt in the aftermath, tenderly repairing Red's most treasured possession with those same deadly hands.

Wim exhaled a soft grunt of satisfaction as the clasp finally clicked back into place. "There. Good as new."

A large lopsided grin formed on Wim's face, and Red went to his tiptoes to kiss Wim's cheek. "My hero," he said, not quite as teasingly as he intended.

As they prepared to leave, Red couldn't help but smirk.

"Good thing you wouldn't make that promise about not killing anyone, isn't it?"

Wim's lips quirked. "Next time someone puts a blade to you, I'll be sure to mind my manners." His fingers ghosted over the cut on Red's neck, touch feather-light yet possessive. "Rather live with the guilt than without you, sweetheart."

Those words shouldn't have made Red's heart stutter—not here, surrounded by death, with blood cooling on his skin—but they did. And that terrified him more than any blade at his throat.

Fifteen

"Wim, stop!" Red exclaimed, laughing to the point of hysteria.

He lay flat on his back, the wolf having deposited him on the forest floor a few moments ago, after the long ride away from the bandits.

Now Wim was nuzzling his furry snout into the crook of his neck, tickling him with his whiskers.

"Stop!" Red screamed again, through peals of laughter. Wim was laughing too—a deep, rumbling sound that vibrated through his chest and against Red's body.

Perhaps the night's events had sent them both slightly mad—the fear, the fighting, the frantic escape—but here they were, giggling like children, alive and *together*. The relief of it all bubbled up inside Red's chest like sparkling wine.

"Get off me, you mangy mutt!" Red shrieked, hitting the wolf as hard as he could.

Wim responded by flopping his entire weight onto Red, crushing him beneath thick grey fur, and proceeded to lick a wet stripe up his cheek. Red squirmed and cursed, but his protests were undermined by the laughter he couldn't quite contain.

Tears were leaking out of Red's eyes, and he couldn't breathe, and they'd just slaughtered countless bandits, but somehow, it was possibly the happiest moment of Red's life.

"Right, then!" Red twisted like an eel, managing to squirm just enough space between them to grab a fistful of Wim's tail and give it a sharp tug. The wolf yelped in indignant surprise, leaping sideways, which gave Red the perfect opportunity to scramble away on all fours, cackling with triumph.

Jumping to his feet, Red reached out to catch the tail again. "Oh wolf, what a big tail you have," he teased.

Wim growled. He pulled his tail free, then snapped it towards Red. "All the better to swat irritating little brats with, sweetheart."

Red reached out again, eyes sparkling with mischief. "Oh wolf, what big *paws* you have!"

Before he could dart away, Wim pounced. The world spun as Red tumbled backwards, finding himself suddenly pinned to the forest floor beneath those massive paws. His heart performed acrobatics as Wim loomed over him, a dangerous glint in his amber eyes.

"All the better to pin you down with, sweetheart," he snarled, his voice rough with promise.

Red gazed up at him, breath catching. Those large eyes burned into his own, making his chest fill with honeyed warmth. They might have been the eyes of a dangerous predator, but Red had never felt safer than when they were fixed upon him. "Oh wolf, what big *eyes* you have!"

The air shimmered around them as Wim's form shifted, and suddenly it was warm human hands stroking down Red's sides, human fingers trailing across his collarbone, his chest, his ribs. Wim leaned down, pressing a feather-light kiss against Red's lips.

"All the better to see your beautiful face with, sweetheart," he murmured against Red's mouth, husky with desire.

Wim's tongue slipped past Red's lips, exploring his mouth with a slow, deep kiss that made Red's toes curl. When they finally broke apart, Red was breathless. "Oh wolf, what a big *tongue* you have."

"All the better to lick you with, sweetheart," Wim growled against his skin, before dragging his tongue along Red's collarbone, a hot, wet stripe that made Red shiver.

Then Wim's mouth trailed hot kisses down Red's throat as his calloused hands slipped beneath his shirt, mapping every inch of skin they found. Red arched into the touch, gasping when teeth grazed over his pulse point. Their bodies pressed together, desperate for more contact, and that's when Red became acutely aware of Wim's hard length pressing against his thigh. Heart racing, he slid a tentative hand down between them, tangling his fingers in Wim's nest of thick hair before wrapping his hand around Wim's cock and squeezing it gently. Wim's appreciative hum made his heart beat even faster, his own manhood swelling against the fabric constraining it.

"Oh wolf," Red whispered against Wim's ear, voice trembling with a mix of desire and shyness he couldn't quite hide, "what a big *cock* you have."

Wim's answering growl vibrated through Red's entire body. "All the better to fuck you with, sweetheart."

Each beat of Red's heart sent him free-falling. Heat coiled low in his stomach, and he swallowed thickly. Wim pulled back, his scrutinising, heated gaze burning into Red, making his skin tingle with anticipation.

Red forced himself to perform an elaborate gasp of shock. "What makes you think I'd let a mangy mutt like you fuck *me*?" he declared, in his most haughty tone.

"Careful now, little rabbit," Wim growled, dangerously low. "Might want to remember which of us is the hunter here." His teeth grazed Red's chin, a deliberate reminder of their sharpness.

Red found his face splitting into a wide smile. He deliberately wiggled his hips against Wim in a way that was pure provocation, then suddenly twisted his body, sliding out from beneath him with a serpentine grace that left the larger man grasping at air.

"You know," Wim said, voice pure warning, "if you're going to be naughty, I'll have to put you over my knee and spank you."

A wicked thrill shot through Red, all the way to his firm prick.

"Spank me?" Red echoed, arching one delicate eyebrow. He pulled his face into a wide grin as he took a deliberate step backwards, throwing Wim his best saucy wink. "Only if you're able to catch me, wolf," he declared, before spinning on his heel, ready to bolt into the darkness.

"Don't you dare." The words rumbled from Wim's chest, a dangerous growl that made Red's heart skip. "Or I'll have to hunt you down and teach you what happens to disobedient little things that try to run from wolves."

For a moment, Red froze, his body trembling with a delicious mix of fear and anticipation. His breath caught as Wim's eyes raked over him like physical touch, burning with predatory hunger. Then, adrenaline surged through his veins, and he bolted. His new boots pounded against the forest floor as he fled, ducking between trees, his red cloak streaming behind him like blood in water.

"Run if you want, Little Red." Wim's words echoed through the trees. "You'll only make it better for me."

The sound of pursuit sent a thrill down his spine—heavy footfalls, the snap of branches, then deadly silence. Red's breath came in sharp gasps as he weaved through the shadows, trying to lose the wolf in the darkness. But with each step, he could feel Wim's presence getting closer, stalking him, toying with him. Playing with his food.

"I can smell you, Little Red," Wim purred from the shadows, in the deep voice of his wolf form. "The fear rolling off your skin... and something else. Something *sweeter*. You're leaking for me already, aren't you?"

Red whimpered at the words, his cock straining in his briefs. His pulse thundered in his ears as he changed direction, diving between thick trunks. Moonlight dappled the forest floor, creating a dizzying maze of silver and shadow. His feet barely touched the earth as he sprinted onwards, each step carrying him deeper into the darkness.

"You're getting slow in your old age!" Red threw over his shoulder, as boldly as he dared.

A growl rumbled through the darkness, so close Red could almost feel it vibrate through his bones. A branch snapped to his left. Red spun, catching a glimpse of glowing eyes watching him from the darkness. His breath hitched as heat pooled low in his belly. He could see Wim's massive form now, stalking him through the shadows, muscles rippling beneath his fur.

"Such pretty prey." Wim's voice caressed him from the shadows. "Running so beautifully for me. Your heart's beating so fast, little one. Are you scared? Or excited for what I'm going to do to you when I catch you?"

Red's cock throbbed, begging him to stop and submit, beg for mercy.

But Red pushed himself faster, harder. "You'll never catch me, wolf!"

A dark chuckle answered him, seeming to come from everywhere at once. "But I already have you, little one. I can hear your heart racing. Smell how desperate you are. How badly you want me to pin you down and take what's mine."

Red gasped, stumbling slightly at the words. He caught himself against a tree, chest heaving as he tried to catch his breath. The rough bark bit into his palms as he listened intently for any sign of pursuit.

Nothing.

The forest had gone deathly quiet.

Red's skin prickled with awareness. He was being watched. Hunted. Wim was out there, somewhere in the darkness, deciding exactly how he wanted to claim his prize. The thought sent another wave of heat through his core.

He pushed off from the tree, ready to run again—but strong human arms suddenly wrapped around him from behind, pulling him back against a broad chest. Wim's extensive erection pressed against him, making him moan despite himself. It wouldn't be long now until it was finally inside him, and the thought had Red's heart leaping out of his chest.

"Found you," Wim growled against his neck, teeth grazing the sensitive skin. One large hand splayed across Red's stomach, holding him still, while the other traced dangerous patterns along his hip. "Did you really think you could escape me? That I wouldn't track down such sweet prey?"

Red writhed in the iron grip, his body betraying him as he pressed back against Wim's hardness. "Let go of me, you mangy mutt! I almost—"

"Hush now," Wim growled against Red's ear. "You were always meant to be mine, little rabbit. And now I'm going to take you apart, piece by piece."

Red tried to twist away, but Wim spun him around, pinning his back against the tree trunk. The wolf's eyes burned with hunger as he pressed their bodies together, leaving Red trapped between bark and beast. Their cocks aligned, offering delicious friction through Red's breeches, and drawing desperate sounds from both of them.

"Please," Red gasped, though he wasn't sure if he was begging Wim to stop or demanding more.

"Please what, Little Red?" Wim rolled his hips, grinding against him as his hands gripped Red's ass. "Tell me what happens to pretty little things who run from wolves."

"They get eaten up," Red whispered, his entire body trembling with need.

"That's right," Wim purred, before claiming Red's mouth in a bruising kiss, smashing his lip against his teeth. "And I'm going to eat you alive."

In one fluid movement, Wim threw Red face down onto the forest floor, following him down to straddle his thighs. His large hand pressed between Red's shoulder blades, pinning him against the earth. The scent of crushed leaves and moss filled Red's nostrils as Wim's weight settled over him.

"Now then." Wim's voice was all pure, dark promise. "What was that about outrunning a wolf, little prey?"

Red twisted his head to the side, meeting Wim's burning amber eyes with false defiance. "I almost got away. I stand by every word!"

"Stand?" Wim's hand tightened on his hip. "I don't think you'll be doing much standing for a while, sweetheart."

Delicious anticipation had Red's breath catching in his throat.

"You never had a chance." Wim's hand fisted in Red's hair, pulling his head back to expose his throat. "I was toying with you the whole time, sweetheart. You should know how much I like to play."

"Liar," Red said on a wavering exhale.

"Still doubting me?" Wim growled. Fingers tore at Red's breeches, yanking them down to expose his butt cheeks to the frigid air. Then Wim's palm landed softly against Red's ass, more of a pat than a slap. He paused, clearly eyeing Red to gauge his reaction. "Should I show you exactly how helpless you are?"

Red's sharp intake of breath and the way he pressed back against Wim's hand answered for him. A second gentle slap followed, testing, waiting. Red moaned into the dirt, loud and clear.

Another slap followed, harder this time, then another, each one stealing the breath from his lungs. His fingers clawed at the earth beneath him as pleasure bloomed across his skin.

"How many strikes do you think you deserve for making me chase you through my forest, Little Red?" Wim's words dripped with dark desire as he kneaded the stinging flesh. "For thinking you could escape a wolf?"

"I—" Red's reply cut off with a desperate moan as Wim's hand came down again, harder still. His hips bucked against the ground, seeking any friction against his aching cock. Each impact sent lightning through his body, leaving him trembling and desperate.

"Look at you," Wim purred, his free hand sliding beneath Red to give his cock just one torturous, teasing squeeze. "Getting so hard from being punished. Such a naughty little thing you are."

"Shut up," Red managed, though his voice was wrecked with need, betraying how much he was enjoying being at the wolf's mercy.

He swallowed hard, heart pounding in his ears, as Wim's hand came down against his ass once more. The strikes grew in intensity, each one stoking the blazing fire that flared within him. He writhed against the forest floor, gasping as the enormous wolf leaned in close, his hot breath ghosting over Red's exposed neck.

"Is this what happens to prey that runs from wolves?" The words rolled like thunder in his chest. "They get caught and claimed?"

Red could only whimper in reply, his body now completely surrendered to the delicious onslaught of Wim's dominance.

Wim's hand finally slid beneath him again. "Or perhaps this is what you were running towards all along, sweetheart?" He rubbed gently at Red's straining cock, and Red couldn't contain the broken cry that tore from his throat. "Tell me what you need, Little Red."

Red opened his mouth to speak, but only desperate, needy sounds escaped—unintelligible gasps. He pressed back against Wim's bulk, his body trembling with want, tears threatening to erupt.

Wim's dark chuckle reverberated through Red's very soul. "Such good little prey you are," he murmured, just before his teeth found the sensitive flesh where Red's neck met his shoulder.

A blissful rasp tore from Red's throat as a shiver shot through him. Oh, how he wished for Wim to sink those canines into him again, deeper.

Instead, with effortless agility, Wim flipped Red onto his back, looming over him with predatory intensity. Red's heart skittered beneath his ribs as those burning amber eyes devoured him.

"And now that I've caught you…" he said. "I think I'll have a taste."

Before Red could process the words, Wim was sliding down his body, large hands gripping his thighs and pushing them apart. The wolf's hot breath ghosted over Red's exposed skin, making him shiver with anticipation.

"W-what are you doing?" Red managed to stammer, though the answer was becoming rapidly apparent.

Wim's grin was pure wickedness in the moonlight. "Eating my prey, of course."

Without further warning, Wim's large hands gripped Red's thighs, lifting them to rest over his broad shoulders. The spongy moss beneath Red's head felt cool and damp, a stark contrast to the heat flooding through him.

"The spoils of the hunt," Wim growled, his voice deeper than Red had ever heard it. His massive hands kneaded the flesh of Red's buttocks, the skin still tingling and sensitive from the earlier punishment.

Red's breath caught as Wim's thumbs spread him open to the cool night air. He should have felt embarrassed—exposed and vulnerable in the middle of the forest, positioned like an offering—but all he felt was desperate, burning need.

Wim's rough tongue continued its exquisite torture, tracing paths along Red's skin, then applied the perfect amount of pressure at Red's entrance.

A thrill shivered through him, seizing every muscle.

When Wim pressed his tongue inside him, Red's hips bucked wildly, his entire body trembling with need. The sensation was unlike anything he had ever experienced, and he couldn't help but let out a high-pitched cry of pleasure. His fingers clawed at the earth beneath him, tearing up fistfuls of moss and soil as pleasure sparked through his entire body.

"Wim," Red gasped, attempting to lift his head from the ground. Moonlight filtered through the canopy above, casting dappled shadows across Wim's form as his tongue worked its magic.

The wolf growled against him, the vibration sending shivers up Red's spine. Strong hands gripped his thighs tighter, keeping him exactly where Wim wanted him. The message was clear—Red was caught, claimed, *devoured.*

"Wim, please," Red whimpered, though he couldn't articulate what he was begging for. More? Mercy? The forest floor felt unsteady beneath him as pleasure threatened to overwhelm him completely.

Wim's response was to intensify his movements, his tongue thrusting deeper into Red's hole, sending almighty shivers to rack through him, to wreck him. Red's vision blurred, and he was soon lost in the overwhelming sensations. The wolf was relentless, eating him with the single-minded focus of a predator savouring its prize. Each swipe of that wicked tongue sent waves of ecstasy crashing through Red's body.

Red's cock lay hard against his stomach, leaking and untouched. He desperately wanted to reach for it, to stroke himself in time with Wim's ministrations, but he couldn't seem to coordinate his limbs. All he could do was take what Wim gave him, moaning shamelessly into the night.

And Wim, merciful and merciless in equal measure, showed no signs of relenting, his tongue thrusting deeper, harder, claiming Red's body as his own. Wim was getting him so wet, saliva streamed down his buttocks in rivulets.

The sounds of the forest faded away until all Red could hear was his own ragged breathing and the obscene, wet noises of Wim's mouth against him. Leaves and twigs dug into his flesh, but the discomfort only heightened his awareness of the pleasure Wim was giving him.

Red's thighs trembled against Wim's shoulders as the wolf's tongue pushed impossibly deep, and a particularly clever twist of Wim's tongue had Red screaming into the night, hips bucking wildly upwards.

"Mine," Wim pulled back to growl, the word vibrating through Red's entire being. "My prey. My Red."

Suddenly, Wim released his grip, allowing Red's legs to fall before climbing on top of him, breathing hard, eyes wild with barely contained desire. "If I don't stop now, I'll take you right here on the forest floor. And for what I want to do to you next, we need more than just my tongue."

Large hands gripped Red's hips, pressing him into the earth. The ground was hard beneath him, rocks digging into his back, but Red barely noticed—his entire world had narrowed to Wim's burning gaze, the massive form caging him in.

Yes, yes, yes!

The ache between his legs was maddening. Red didn't care about the discomfort, or the dirt, or anything else. He needed Wim's hands on him, needed that dangerous mouth, needed that magnificent cock splitting him open.

Red's body trembled with need, every nerve ending screaming for more, right now. "I don't care, just—"

"I do." Wim's tone left no room for argument as he scooped Red into his arms. "When I claim you fully, it will be somewhere worthy of you. Not on dirt and rocks that will bruise your beautiful skin." He nuzzled against Red's throat. "I'm going to drag you back to our camp and take you properly on our new blankets. Get our scent all over them. Mark you as mine until neither of us can move."

Red forced his face into an expression of mock gratitude. "Oh, thank you, most gracious wolf. How *considerate* of you to think of my delicate sensibilities." He batted his eyelashes dramatically. "Whatever would I do without such a gentleman to look after me?"

Wim leapt up with startling speed. In one deft sweep, he grabbed Red and tossed him over his broad shoulder like a sack of flour.

Red yelped in surprise, the world spinning as his feet left the ground. His indignant protest was cut short by another sharp slap against his now-aching bottom, making him yelp again.

"Put me down this instant!" Red demanded, though his command held little authority from his current upside-down position.

Wim's only response was to charge through the forest at an impossible pace, his long strides eating up the distance back to their camp. The trees blurred past as Red bounced against Wim's shoulder, his red cloak fluttering behind.

With a triumphant growl, Wim reached their campsite and deposited Red onto their gloriously soft blankets. Red chose to ignore the dark splatter on the edge of one—likely a smidge of bandit blood—and nestled into them, clutching the fabric.

Red looked up at Wim, ready for him to smother him with his weight—but to his absolute horror, the wolf turned away and began gathering wood.

"What the fuck are you doing?!" Red propped himself up on his elbows, watching in disbelief as Wim arranged kindling.

"Making a fire for you," Wim replied simply, as if it wasn't the most ridiculous thing he could be doing right now.

"I don't need a *fire*!" Red's voice came out embarrassingly close to a whine. "Wim, please... I can't wait any longer!"

"You'll catch a cold," Wim said matter-of-factly, though Red caught the hint of a smirk playing at his lips.

"It's not cold at all," Red insisted, fighting to keep the desperation from his tone. "Just come here. Please?"

Wim glanced over his shoulder, his eyes gleaming with mischief. "Patience, sweetheart. I plan to be on those blankets with you for a very long time. We'll need the fire's warmth before the night is through."

"It must be almost dawn by now!" Red practically shrieked, before giving up and lying back on the blankets. "I'll fall asleep if you're not careful!"

Wim only laughed in a way that told Red he knew there was no way in hell Red would be sleeping before Wim fucked him senseless.

Heat bloomed across Red's skin as the fire roared to life, its orange glow casting dancing shadows across their blankets. Despite his earlier protests, the warmth did feel divine against his exposed skin... not that he'd admit it in a hurry.

The blankets shifted as Wim's weight settled over him like a living furnace. Wim's face pressed against his own, and Red couldn't help but gasp at the rough scratch of his beard. The texture sent tingles across his skin, somehow both gentle and overwhelming at once. Wim's hot breath tickled his ear, and Red melted into the touch like snow in sunlight.

Red's hands found Wim's arms, exploring the solid muscle beneath his fingertips. His touch wandered up towards Wim's biceps, where his fingers discovered the raised edges of the bite mark from the soulstealer. The puckered flesh felt wrong beneath his fingertips, and Red's chest tightened as he imagined the monster's teeth clamping down around Wim's arm.

A moment of pure selfishness struck Red—because he was ever so glad that the soulstealer had bitten Wim, forcing him away from his pack and into Red's path. A horrible misfortune for Wim, yet a precious gift for Red—for the time with this wildling would be something he treasured forever. He was as sure of that as he was of the moon being in the sky.

Wim's hips rolled against his own, that impressively large length of him pressing into Red's own. Wim leaned in close to Red's ear to whisper, "I can't wait to be inside you."

Suddenly the reality of what they were about to do crashed over Red like ice water. His breath caught in his throat as nervousness fluttered in his stomach. This wasn't like his fumbled encounters in the stable—this was Wim, and he didn't want to look the fool.

And *fuck*, he must already not be acting appropriately, because Wim stiffened, pressing his hands on either side of Red's head to push himself up.

Concern danced in Wim's narrowed eyes. "You... You have done this before, yes?"

Oh ground, please swallow me up.

"Yes!" Red bit back, the mortification flooding through every inch of him. "Of course I have!" What did Wim take him for, an inexperienced virgin? Though that wasn't far from the truth, was it? Red sighed, and dropped to a mumble to add, "A few times, with one other."

Tensing, Red turned his head to one side so he didn't have to see the look of horror or pity in his eyes. But Wim cupped his face with his large palm, bringing it gently back to face him.

"Just one other? The... The one who slapped you?"

"Yes. The palace's stable master." Red's stomach turned at the memory of those piggy eyes following the younger stable boys before they finally landed on him one day. When the stable master showed interest, Red had known exactly what he was doing to himself—seeking validation in all the wrong places—but that didn't make the memory of the stable master's hot breath on his neck any less uncomfortable now.

"Tell me," Wim demanded, fingers firm but careful on Red's jaw. "Did he show you the respect you deserve?"

Red thought of rough hands that had never quite hurt but never quite cherished either, of being bent over stable gates and taken quickly, of how the stable master wouldn't look at him afterwards, wouldn't acknowledge him in daylight. It hadn't been cruel, just empty, leaving Red feeling hollow and somehow smaller each time.

"I'm... not sure," Red said, biting into his lip. The words hung between them, heavy with meaning. A frown split Wim's forehead in two, and his grip on Red's jaw gentled into something that made Red's chest ache.

"Well," Wim said softly, pressing his forehead against Red's. "At least now I get to be the one to show you how good it can feel."

Red's breath hitched at the promise in that sentence. He tried to summon his usual haughtiness, but it crumbled under the intensity of Wim's words, Wim's touch. "Is that so?" he managed, his embarrassing breathlessness betraying how much he wanted exactly that.

The firelight danced across their skin as Wim attacked Red's clothing with eager hands. Red cursed his leather vest, its tight laces teasingly stubborn as Wim wrestled with them, each tug met with a frustrating resistance.

"I will tear these laces with my teeth," Wim threatened, sighing in relief when they eventually yielded. Wim launched the vest far from the blankets as if it had personally slighted him before his hands found Red's exposed skin. The talk of the stable master had caused his cock to soften somewhat, but now his body responded eagerly to Wim's touch, as if thirsting to make new memories. Soon his length ached almost painfully—his need evident and urgent after the relentless teasing in the forest.

Red's eyes fixed on Wim's face, studying the sharp angles of his jaw, the fullness of his lower lip, remembering the skill of that beautiful, wicked mouth against his most intimate places just moments ago in the forest.

Wim's hands traced Red's thighs, his touch gentler now than it had been during their wild chase. His fingers grazed over Red's bottom, still sensitive from the spanking.

"Did I hurt you too much earlier, sweetheart?" Wim asked softly, all traces of the predatory wolf momentarily subdued.

Red shook his head, butterflies spinning dizzy circles in his stomach. "No, it... it felt good. Really good."

"Mm, you took your punishment so beautifully." Wim's palms kneaded the tender flesh, soothing away the lingering sting. "Such a perfect little thing you are."

Wim's lips brushed against Red's inner thigh, sending shivers up his spine. Red wanted to say something, but all he could manage was breathy little pants as he clutched the blanket, twisting it in knots. Then he remembered how Wim had reacted when he'd run his fingers through his hair before, how the wolf had practically purred at his touch.

Red's trembling fingers found Wim's thick hair, threading through the dark strands and scratching gently at his scalp. A deep, rumbling groan vibrated against his thigh, and Wim pressed his face closer, clearly as affected by the touch as Red remembered.

"Your *stable master*," Wim murmured against Red's skin. "He never cherished you like this, did he?" he asked, followed by a growl that could only be described as possessive. Red enjoyed it very much.

"He's not *my* stable master," Red replied, his voice catching as Wim's beard scratched deliciously against his sensitive skin.

"Good," Wim snarled. "He better not be."

Red almost wanted to laugh at Wim's absurd envy towards this man he'd never met, and would never meet. A man who meant so little to Red—nothing compared to what Red felt now towards the wildling presently between his thighs.

Then again, hadn't Red been just as ridiculous, burning with jealousy at the mere thought of Wim's past lovers, with their stupidly large mouths?

Wim pressed his lips to the inside of Red's knee, then slowly worked his way higher, leaving a trail of kisses along his inner thigh. Red shivered with anticipation, his body still tingling from Wim's earlier attentions in the forest.

"But you never answered me. Did he taste you? Did he make you scream like I did?" Red's mind struggled to respond, his brain muddled by tingles coursing through his body from Wim's touch.

"No," he managed to rasp. "No, Wim. You're the first."

Wim's response was to pause, his hot breath on Red's skin making him shiver further. "The *only* one," he growled, words dripping with that dangerous possessiveness again. "No one else will ever touch you like I do," Wim growled. "No one else will ever make you feel what I make you feel."

"No," Red agreed breathlessly. "No one but you, Wim."

As if in answer, Wim's tongue found Red's hole again, pressing inside, claiming him once more. Yet a mere moment later, it was gone again, and there was something much firmer at his entrance. A finger, gently circling, easing its way in.

Yes! Red almost shouted aloud. But then the blessed pressure vanished, and Wim's heavy form twisted, reaching beyond their nest of blankets to reach for his pack. A moment later, a small glass bottle of perfumed oil was being wiggled in Red's face, Wim's smug face behind it.

"I got it from a market stall while you were trying to convince that poor merchant you knew something about wine."

"Hmph. I know I like it, at least."

"Aye, we certainly learned that the hard way, didn't we?"

"Oh, stop. Get on with it before I perish with need!" Red exclaimed, his hand reaching towards his prick, only for Wim to bat it away with violent force and a growl.

Red's breath hitched as Wim's fingers slid over his entrance ever so gently, the oil making the touch slick and smooth. The sensation was different from Wim's tongue... warmer, more deliberate. He'd never felt anything quite like this tenderness before—it was almost too much—and he bit his lip, lest he embarrass himself by crying out before Wim had even breached him.

Wim's heavy weight suddenly pressed against him as the wolf crawled up his body, claiming Red's mouth in a searing kiss that swallowed his whimpers of pleasure. Wim's fingers circled his hole, teasing and probing, before finally slipping inside. Red's body tensed at the intrusion, but Wim's gentle touch soon had him relaxing into it. He'd touched himself there before, of course, but it had never felt like this.

Maybe it was the gentle tenderness in this wild wolf's touch, or the way he seemed to know exactly what Red needed. The trust between them now, or how safe Red felt beneath Wim's protective frame. How their bodies seemed to fit together as if made for each other.

When Red had left the palace, he'd never in a million winters imagined this—had never dared to hope for someone who would touch him with such care. Even in his wildest dreams, he couldn't have conjured up this feeling of rightness, of belonging. And wasn't it strange that he'd found it here, beneath a wolf who should have been his enemy, but instead had become his—

Red gasped.

Wim's fingers had curled inside him, pressing *just there*, and the sudden burst of intense pleasure made his body shudder.

"Did I hurt you?" Wim asked, tensing with concern.

"No," Red managed to say, rendered breathless. "It just... felt good."

Wim's fingers moved again, and Red felt that same burst of pleasure. He moaned again, hoping Wim would get the hint. Pressing his lips to Red's once more, Wim gently coaxed his mouth open, sliding a warm hand across the expanse of his chest.

Red arched up, rubbing his prick against Wim's solid mass. When that didn't bring him any relief, he reached between them to grasp himself—he couldn't bear the torture any longer.

Wim caught his hand with his own before it could reach its destination, and Red didn't suppress his noise of exasperation.

"Patience, sweetheart. You're going to release with me inside you."

The command-cum-threat warmed Red's insides, his heart beating impossibly faster. "Well, bloody well get inside me, then!"

The wolf laughed, showing no sign of removing the gentle finger that still worked Red open, stretching him slowly, as if they had all the time in the world. As if the task was giving Wim all the pleasure he needed.

"I'm going to fuck you so good, you'll forget he ever existed."

What? Who?

Was Wim *still* going on about the bloody stable master?!

"I'm going to ruin you for anyone else." Wim picked up his pace, and then, without warning, slipped a second finger inside him, forcing a cry from Red's throat. "I'm going to mark you from the inside. Make you *mine.*"

That word—*mine*—sent a shiver through Red's entire body. How many times had Wim said that now? And each time, it felt more real, more possible.

Red's chest tightened with a bittersweet ache. He wanted desperately to believe Wim meant it beyond this moment, beyond their journey. Wanted to believe that whatever this was between them wouldn't end.

Heat prickled the corners of his eyes, and he rapidly blinked back the tears.

Red, this gorgeous beast of a man wants to fuck you until you forget your own name, so pull yourself together and enjoy it, for fuck's sake.

"Please, Wim," Red whispered, his throat so constricted he could barely breathe. "*Please.*"

Wim stilled his fingers, the heat of their combined bodies forming a sticky sweat between them. He leaned in and gently pressed his lips to Red's, the kiss soft and tender.

"You're so beautiful," Wim murmured against Red's mouth, prompting a fresh crop of tears threatening to spill. "And I can't wait to have you."

He pressed his sharp teeth to Red's neck, grazing his pointed canines over his pulse point.

Red's breath caught in his throat—was Wim about to *bite* him? But no, the pressure against his flesh gentled, then Wim quickly replaced his teeth with that hot, wet tongue of his, licking where he'd just grazed him.

"Forgive me. You just taste so delicious."

Red rasped an appreciative purr to let Wim know he could eat him any day of the week and that would be quite alright with him.

Pulling back, Wim poured more oil over his length, the glossy liquid making the size of his cock even more apparent. Red swallowed hard, trying not to show his apprehension at taking such a monstrous thing inside him.

"You ready?" Wim asked, those chestnut eyes boring into him.

Red nodded, words failing him again. He shuffled on the blankets, making to flip over onto his hands and knees.

Yet Wim blocked him, gripping his shoulders. "Where are you going?"

"Shouldn't I..." Red trailed off, the heat in his cheeks nothing to do with the roaring fire. Here he was again, embarrassing himself.

"I may be a wolf, but I do not always mount like an animal. Especially when I find the face of my lover so pleasing."

Wim gently pushed him back onto the blankets before grabbing his thighs again, lifting them onto his shoulders, then positioned his very sizable length at Red's entrance. Red couldn't help but suck in a large breath. Then, feeling the pressure nudge against him, he closed his eyes tightly. Wim began to push inside him, and Red braced himself for the inevitable pain, biting his lip to stifle any sounds of discomfort that threatened to escape.

As the initial bite eased, Red breathed out a shaky sigh of relief. The pain was more than manageable, nothing he couldn't handle. He opened his eyes to see Wim watching him with concern.

"Are you okay?" Wim asked, voice strained.

"Very okay," Red replied, reaching to entwine the fingers of one hand with Wim's own, and squeezing tightly.

Wim nodded, leaning down to brush a kiss across Red's lips before he slowly continued inching inside him. The sensation of being filled by him soon sent an intense wave of pleasure coursing through Red that overshadowed any lingering sting.

Red ran his fingers through Wim's hair, holding on to him as if it were the only thing anchoring him in this world right now.

Then he felt it—Wim had reached all the way inside him, the man groaning in pleasure before he captured Red's lips in another searing kiss.

Wim began to move, his thrusts gentle but insistent. Each one sent waves of pleasure more sensational than the last down Red's spine, and he could feel himself becoming more and more sensitive with each stroke. He closed his eyes for a moment, trying to absorb the sensations without letting them overwhelm him completely.

When he opened his eyes again, it was to see the starry sky above them. The stars seemed so close they might reach out and touch him, their distant light filtering into his eyes like ethereal teardrops. The sight took his breath away; he felt as though he was floating outside of himself, carried aloft on waves of devotion and desire.

He arched up into Wim, revelling in the weight of his lover's body on top of him. He could feel every muscle in Wim's chest pressing into his own skin, every heartbeat thudding against his rib cage. It was a feeling both intimate and terrifying—to be so close to someone else that you could feel their very essence mingling with your own.

And yet... it was also incredibly comforting.

Red reached up to run his fingers through Wim's hair, savoring the softness of it between his fingertips. He wanted nothing more than to stay like this forever—just the two of them under the vast expanse of stars, in this forest that had become their home.

Red's prick had deflated just a smidge, but a few moments of Wim's firm, slick strokes along it had it fully erect again, the coiled heat in Red's stomach threatening to erupt.

They soon moved together in sync, their bodies becoming one entity lost in passionate bliss under the starlit sky.

"Does it feel good?" Wim asked, voice dropping to a gravelly whisper.

Couldn't Wim tell from the noises Red was making? He violently nodded, continuing to thread his fingers through Wim's hair, smoothing the strands down again and again.

Wim let out a whine. "Tell me. Tell me how good I'm making you feel."

Oh, fuck.

A strangled sound left Red's throat before he forced himself to form the words that Wim evidently needed to hear.

"Fuck, Wim, you're fucking incredible," Red gasped, his back arching as the other man's hand worked him into a frenzy. "So good, so... fucking... good."

Red cringed at himself, but Wim chuckled darkly, the sound dangerously low and feral. He was close to release—Red could feel it in the way his body moved, in the way his fingers dug into Red's hips. "You like that, sweetheart? You like it when I make you feel so good?"

"Fuck yes," Red moaned, his voice barely recognizable as his own. His body was a burst of firelight, every touch and caress sending sparks flying. "Don't stop, please don't stop." He gasped, drawing a large breath in before continuing. "God, Wim, you feel so, so good—I never knew it could be like this. I'm so close. Don't hold back."

"You want more?" Wim asked, his words like dark velvet as he pulled back from Red.

"Yes," Red replied without hesitation. His entire body was on fire, every nerve ending screaming for more, more, more. Impossibly, he felt himself growing harder than ever before, as if Wim alone was able to take him to new levels.

Wim let out a growl, the sound sending a shiver down Red's spine. He could feel the wolf at the surface now, its presence both thrilling and terrifying. Wim thrust inside him, hard, with fresh intensity. His movements became more frantic, his touch more urgent. Again those sharp canines of his scraped across his neck, coming dangerously close to biting him before Wim dragged his mouth away.

When a hand found a fistful of Red's hair, to tug it hard, holding back became impossible.

"Oh fuck, I can't... I'm going to..." Red gasped, his body trembling on the edge of release. "Wim, I'm going to..."

With one final slick stroke, Red was sent spiraling over the edge, his vision blurring as waves of bliss washed over him, the world exploding around them in a haze of sensation.

He screamed like never before, the sound tearing at his throat. He screamed until some part of his brain still left activated brought his hand to his mouth to muffle the sound.

Scream silenced, guttural grunts and soft moans filled the night air instead. Then the sounds coming from Wim became simply feral as he picked up his punishing pace, fucking Red all the way through his release. Again and again he hit that magic spot inside Red, impossibly drawing out more and more bursts of pleasure from him.

Distantly, he became aware of Wim's voice echoing in his ear, murmuring words and praises, things like, "That's it, sweetheart," and, "You're so perfect to me."

Red whimpered. His body couldn't take any more—every nerve ending was alight, every muscle strained. "Please, Wim. I want to feel you come apart inside me. Mark me. Make me yours." He said the last sentence in a whisper, more a plea than a demand.

Wim's movements became erratic, desperate, and the way he called Red's name reverberated around them like a prayer. Finally, with a primal roar, Wim shattered, his release flooding Red's body in the most beautiful way.

In that moment, Red knew, as sure as daybreak, that he would never experience anything like this again. It was more than just sex, more than just pleasure. Red couldn't explain it, not properly, but he'd never felt so alive. So real. So tangible.

Minutes passed, or perhaps it was hours, or moments. He wanted to say *something* to Wim, but couldn't find the right words to express how he was feeling, so he stayed silent, listening intently to the wolf's heavy breaths, and enjoying the feeling of Wim's fingertips trailing up and down his arm.

Red would have happily never moved again, but finally, Wim gently pulled out. He sat up and reached for his leather bag, rummaging around until he found a soft rag. With a tender touch, he wet the cloth with fresh dew from the grass before returning to Red's side.

Wim's movements were slow and careful as he cleaned Red, taking his time to make sure every inch was attended to. Red kept very still, trying to savour every second.

As Wim finished, he tossed the rag aside and pulled Red into his arms again, holding him close. Despite being sweat-soaked, their lovely new blankets still felt wonderful as Wim wrapped them both in a tight cocoon. The tired-looking wildling smiled at him, an expression filled with such tenderness that it made something inside of Red swell.

Red's body felt pleasantly heavy, his limbs languid as he snuggled deeper into Wim's embrace, the wolf's warmth surrounding him.

"You were quite vocal there, sweetheart," Wim murmured against Red's ear. "I believe the entire forest knows exactly how much you enjoyed yourself."

Red's cheeks flushed."Oh, do shut up." He jabbed an elbow into Wim's ribs, earning a low chuckle. "As if you weren't practically begging me to tell you how good you were."

"Mm, can't blame me for wanting to hear those words from your pretty mouth." Wim's fingers traced lazy patterns across Red's skin. "Tell me again how 'fucking incredible' I am?"

"You're insufferable is what you are." Red twisted in Wim's arms to face him, finding a smug grin plastered across the wolf's face. "I didn't hear you complaining when I was stroking your ego. In fact, you seemed rather desperate for my praise."

"Perhaps." Wim pressed a kiss to Red's forehead. "But I wasn't the one screaming my pleasure to the stars."

"I did not scream!" Red protested, though he had to admit his memory of those moments was rather hazy. "And anyway, you were practically purring every time I said something nice about you. Like a great big pussy cat rather than a fearsome wolf."

"Come on, sweetheart." Wim's voice was playfully coaxing, eyes sparkling with mischief. "Give me something sweet to hear now."

"Absolutely not." Red turned his nose up. "Your head is quite big enough already."

"Please?" Wim nuzzled against Red's neck. "Just one little compliment?"

"You're impossible," Red laughed, pushing at Wim's chest. "And entirely too pleased with yourself."

"Those weren't very nice compliments at all," Wim pouted, though his eyes still danced with amusement.

"Fine." Red rolled his eyes. "You're rather good at..." He gestured vaguely between them. "That."

"*Rather good?*" Wim raised an eyebrow. "That's not what you were screaming earlier, is it?"

Red grabbed one of their smaller blankets and attempted to smother Wim with it, both of them dissolving into laughter as they wrestled playfully, their bodies still slick with sweat as they rolled across their makeshift bed, neither willing to admit defeat.

Wim's fingers danced along Red's sides, finding every ticklish spot with uncanny accuracy. Red squirmed and thrashed, trying to escape the merciless assault.

"Stop! This isn't—" A burst of undignified laughter escaped him. "This isn't fair! You're playing dirty!"

"All's fair in love and tickle fights, sweetheart." Wim's grin turned wolfish as he redoubled his efforts, his strong hands pinning Red in place.

Red's shrieks echoed through the forest clearing as he twisted beneath Wim's relentless attack. "I yield! I yield!"

Finally, Wim released him, and Red collapsed back onto their nest of blankets, chest heaving as he caught his breath. They settled into a comfortable position, Wim's arm draped across Red's middle.

The playful mood shifted as Wim's fingers traced along Red's ribs, following each pronounced ridge with gentle concern. "You need to eat more when you get back to the palace. I can't believe even the palace doesn't get enough food."

Back to the palace.

Four tiny words that hit Red like a punch to the gut, shattering their peaceful moment. Reality crashed back in—their inevitable parting looming large.

"I've been giving Auntie Anne extra food," Red admitted quietly, staring up at the fading stars peeking through the canopy above. The first signs of dawn had arrived, painting the horizon in shades of cheerful pink and gold that seemed to mock the heaviness settling in his chest. He shifted closer to Wim, seeking warmth against the morning chill, or perhaps against the cold reality that their time together was finite.

"This Auntie Anne," Wim's tone softened. "She's been good to you, hasn't she? Like a proper mother should." His grip suddenly tightened on Red's arm, urgent. "Listen to me, sweetheart. I need you to promise me something."

Red's heart immediately started an unpleasant tap dance. "What is it?" he asked, hardly daring to breathe.

"Don't let him touch you again, when you return. This *stable master* of yours." Wim said the name like it was burning acid on his tongue. "The thought of you with anyone who treats you like less than a prince..."

The words should be making Red feel good about himself—Wim was clearly jealous of this random stranger. So why did Red feel even worse all of a sudden?

He's not asking you not to return to the palace.

It was true that the notion was entirely impossible. But did Wim even know that? He could at least ask, surely!

Why would he? This is all just a bit of forest fun to him. A warm body to entertain him on the long journey. Comfort from another person after being isolated in his cottage, then banished from his pack.

Red's heart grew heavy as something bitter and angry crystallised inside him, sharp as icicles. Something that demanded to wound in return.

"Hmm? Him? No, I'm quite done with him. But the head chef has tried his luck a few times. I could finally take him up on his offer. His hands are always so warm from the ovens."

Wim recoiled as if Red had slapped him across the face. His shoulders hunched inward, and the playful light in his eyes extinguished. A low, wounded sound escaped his throat—somewhere between a whine and a growl.

Is this the reaction you hoped to achieve, Red?

Wim's entire body went rigid. "Why would you say such a thing?" He shifted away from Red, leaving a cold space between them.

The pain in his words cut deeper than any blade. Red's chest constricted. He'd meant to wound Wim, to make him feel a fraction of the hurt bubbling inside himself. But watching the wolf curl in on himself, seeing the rigid set of his jaw and the way his fingers trembled against his thigh... it was unbearable.

But Red had started down this thorny path now, and despite the way it would cut at him, he needed to see it through to its bitter end.

"Why not? You're the one who brought up the stable master. What do you expect me to do exactly, go back to the palace and pine for you for the rest of my life?"

Because that was exactly what Red would end up doing. He already knew it.

"Sounds like you'll forget all about me as soon as you see that palace chef!"

Red rolled his head against the hard ground, exhaling slowly. "As if you'll be thinking about *me* once you're reunited with your precious pack. I know this is all just a bit of fun for you. A distraction from your loneliness."

Wim jerked upright, his entire body going rigid. "*What?!* What makes you say that?"

Red let out a bitter laugh, propping himself up on his elbows. "Is it not true? What is this, then, Wim? Enlighten me."

"I don't understand—"

"Oh, don't you?" Red hated the tremble in his words. "You call me 'yours' when you're inside me, practically bite my neck, and then the moment it's over, you pull away." He gestured to the space between them. "You won't even look at me properly. And—" His voice betrayed him, and he had to swallow down a thick lump. "You haven't once asked me to stay with you instead of returning to the palace!"

Wim's mouth opened and closed, his face contorting through several expressions before settling on something between confusion and hurt. "Red—"

"No." Red sat up fully now, wrapping one of their blankets around his shoulders. "Don't 'Red' me. You mark me with your teeth, leave bruises on my hips, whisper how I belong to you... but as soon as we're done, you act like... like..."

The words stuck in his throat, choking him. Like this was temporary. Like Red was just convenient. Like he wasn't worth keeping.

"Red, it isn't that way at all!" Wim pleaded, orange eyes wide. "I promise."

"Well, how the fuck am I supposed to know that if you don't tell me?!"

"Oh, Red," Wim's words were infuriatingly soft, his hand covering most of his face. "There's... things I haven't told you."

No shit.

Red's heart squeezed painfully as he asked, "There's someone else, isn't there? Back home, for you?"

"No!" Wim exclaimed violently. "No one else, Red. I promise."

"Tell me, then!"

"Right now, we should get some sleep. It's already dawn, and we need to make up for lost time when we wake."

Red's jaw clenched so tight his teeth ached. How dare Wim dismiss his feelings like that? Like they were nothing more than an inconvenient topic to be swept under the rug?

Coward.

He twisted away from the wolf, curling into himself. His arms wrapped around his torso—a pitiful attempt at self-comfort that only made him feel more foolish.

Look at you, throwing yourself at him like some lovesick maiden from one of Auntie Anne's romance novels. Begging him to ask you to stay. As if you even could.

His cheeks burned with shame. He'd known Wim for what... a handful of days? Yet here he was, practically demanding declarations of forever from a man who'd made it clear their arrangement was temporary.

Pathetic.

The night air seemed to pierce straight through his skin, settling deep in his bones. Without Wim's supernatural warmth pressed against him, the forest's chill was brutal. Red pulled his knees closer to his chest, trying to preserve what little heat remained.

He felt rather than saw Wim's movements behind him—the careful way he draped another blanket over Red's shoulders, then another moments later. The gestures only twisted the knife deeper.

Don't pretend to care now. Not when you won't even discuss what this means.

Despite the added layers, Red's teeth began to chatter. His body, spoiled by nights spent pressed against Wim's furnace-like warmth, refused to generate enough heat on its own. Each tremor felt like a betrayal—his own flesh revealing just how much he'd come to rely on the wolf's presence.

The cold seeped deeper, making his muscles ache. Still, Red remained stubbornly curled away from Wim, refusing to give in to the temptation. He wouldn't crawl back like some desperate creature seeking scraps of affection.

"Red?" Wim's voice cracked with vulnerability, a sound Red had never heard from the powerful wolf before. "Can I please hold you? Please?"

The tears Red had been fighting burst forth, streaming down his cheeks in hot trails. His breath hitched as he tried to speak, mortification burning through him at this display of weakness. "If you must," he managed, the words coming out thick and watery.

Wim's arm snaked around his waist, hesitant at first, before suddenly yanking Red against his chest in an iron grip. The wolf released a deep sigh of relief, his breath tickling the back of Red's neck.

Red squeezed his eyes shut, but the tears continued to fall, soaking into the blankets beneath them. His shoulders shook with silent sobs as Wim's warmth enveloped him completely.

The wolf's grip didn't loosen, as if he feared Red might slip away like morning mist between his fingers. In that moment, wrapped in Wim's desperate embrace, Red had one final thought before sleep finally claimed him—how was it possible to feel simultaneously so secure and so utterly terrified?

Sixteen

WIM

Wim couldn't sleep.

Red's slight form curled against his chest, their naked bodies still sticky with dried sweat. His Little Red's breathing had finally evened out, the occasional hitched breath the only remnant of earlier tears.

Wim's arms tightened around Red, guilt churning in his gut like acid. The memory of those tears... god, *he'd* done that—made Red cry. His fingers traced where bruises surely bloomed across Red's hips, marks left by his own desperate hands. He'd claimed Red so thoroughly, marked him inside and out—and *fuck*, he'd been so close to biting his neck and declaring him his mate.

A soft whimper escaped Red's throat. Wim pressed his lips to Red's temple, breathing in their mingled scents. Wild berries and woodsmoke, mixed with the musk of their coupling. The beast in his chest purred with satisfaction at how thoroughly their scents had merged.

But that satisfaction twisted into shame as Red shifted closer, seeking Wim's warmth even in sleep. Such trust. Such vulnerability. And here he was, holding Red close, all the while—

No. He couldn't think about that. Not with Red's heartbeat steady against his chest. Not with the memory of Red's breathless cries still echoing in his mind. Not when his own heart felt ready to burst from the tenderness of it all.

God, but he'd been beautiful. The way Red had come apart beneath him, all that fierce pride melting into raw need. The sounds he'd made when Wim had finally pushed inside him. How he'd trusted Wim completely, letting him take control.

"Oh wolf, what big eyes you have!"

The playful words haunted him now. Red had looked up at him with such open affection, such joy. No fear. No hesitation. Just pure, devastating trust.

And Wim had taken everything Red offered... gorged himself on it like the beast he was.

His eyes fixed on the golden arrow, sticking slightly out of his quiver. Moonlight caught its surface, making it gleam like a taunt. That fucking arrow. The Queen's vile manipulation wrapped in gold, sent with her little soldier who'd do anything for a scrap of praise after her cruel treatment of him.

Wim's jaw clenched. The Queen. Of course she'd chosen Red for this task. Who better than the orphan desperate for her approval, in some sort of strange, twisted way? Wildlings knew well the pain she could inflict—how many of their kind had she had hunted? How many packs destroyed because they didn't fit her idea of perfection?

And now she'd sent his Red on this suicidal mission with a pretty golden arrow and pretty golden lies.

Red mumbled something in his sleep, pressing closer. A possessive surge went through Wim as Red's fingers curled against his chest. How many times had Red done this as a child, reaching for comfort that never came? The thought of Red alone in that castle, surrounded by the Queen's poison...

"I've got you," Wim whispered, though Red couldn't hear. His thumb brushed Red's split lip—now healed by his wolf's lick. Just hours ago, he'd kissed that mouth, swallowed Red's moans, whispered promises he had no right to make.

"Make me yours."

Red's desperate plea echoed in his mind. And oh, how Wim had wanted to. Still wanted to. The beast inside Wim howled at him to wake Red up, offer him those promises of forever, mark him as his mate, to—

The arrow caught the fading moonlight again. Wim's chest tightened until he could barely breathe.

Carefully, so carefully, Wim extracted himself from Red's embrace. His Little Red made a soft sound of protest that nearly broke Wim's resolve, but he managed to slip free without waking him. He pulled one of their blankets over Red's bare form, trying not to let his gaze linger on the marks he'd left across that pale skin.

The arrow seemed to mock him as he approached the quiver. His fingers trembled as he drew it out, its weight somehow both lighter and heavier than he'd expected. The metal was cool against his palm, but something about it made his wolf bristle with unease.

He had to know. Had to be certain.

Wim grabbed his breeches and shirt, pulling them on with trembling hands. A final glance at Red—still curled on his side, looking so young in sleep—then he stalked into the forest, the golden arrow clutched in his fist.

When he was far enough that his movements wouldn't wake Red, Wim held the arrow up to the first light of dawn. His enhanced vision caught every detail of its craftsmanship, every delicate etching in the gold. But beyond that surface beauty, his senses detected... nothing. No magical signature. No enchantment. Nothing that would mark it as special beyond its precious metal.

Wildlings could often sense enchantments, could taste them in the air like approaching storms. Yet this arrow gave off nothing—which was strange in itself. Red had said the Queen had spoken of its power with such conviction.

Just another of the Queen's lies, then?

Rage burst through him like wildfire. He slammed the arrow against a nearby boulder, again and again, trying to snap the shaft, to bend its perfect shape. But the metal held firm, unmarked by his assault.

Of course it wouldn't break. Of course the Queen would make her pretty lies unbreakable.

Wim stared at the unblemished gold, suspicion growing. Gold was one of the softest metals—it should have bent or dented easily under his strength. The Queen must have done something to it, some magic so subtle even his wildling senses couldn't detect it.

His fist clenched around the arrow until his knuckles went white. The memory of Red's conviction burned in his mind: *"Children are dying! The crops won't grow, the animals are sick—"*

And here was Wim—no better, really—desperate to believe his own pretty lies about magical cures.

A wave of nausea rolled through him, replaced by pure, molten rage. His feral sickness began to rear its head, and it took all of Wim's strength to push it back down, channelling his anger into the arrow. He struck it against the rock once more, with every inch of his might. The clang echoed through the trees, but the gold remained pristine, untarnished. Like the Queen herself—beautiful and untouchable while everything around her rotted.

His chest heaved as he stared at the arrow. Such a small thing, to cause so much pain. To make Red's eyes light up with purpose, to give him hope.

Wim's stomach lurched. He doubled over, bile rising in his throat. *"What is this, then, Wim? Enlighten me?"*

What was it? Everything. Nothing. A dream he couldn't keep.

His wolf whined, remembering how perfectly Red had fit in his arms, how right it had felt to finally have him. But the memory of Red's tears afterward, of his broken voice asking why Wim wouldn't ask him to stay with him...

The arrow slipped from his grip, landing in the dirt. Wim stared at it, at its perfect golden surface still gleaming in the moonlight. He could leave it here. Let the forest swallow it. Take Red far away from the Queen's machinations, from Old Oma, from everything.

But Red would never forgive him.

His Little Red, with his fierce heart and unwavering loyalty. Who'd rather freeze than admit weakness. Who'd kill to protect strangers. Who'd given himself to Wim so completely, trusting him with everything...

Mine-claim-mark-mate.

The beast howled inside him, fighting against the inevitable truth: no matter how great the pull towards each other, he and Red were doomed.

The sun crept higher in the sky, every inch of its movement taking them towards their inevitable ending.

Because... for how long could they possibly continue to journey together? With Red so smart, it was only a matter of time before he realised that they were both heading to Old Oma's. And when he did, Wim would see the same gut-wrenching look of betrayal on Red's face as he saw last night.

Wim picked up the arrow. Its weight settled in his palm like a death sentence.

He struck it against the boulder again, and again, and again.

Seventeen

"**E**njoying a nice lie-in this morning, are we?"

Red shot upright, his heart lurching into his throat. The Queen's Shadow's face filled his vision—those impossibly dark eyes boring into him, framed by straight black hair that hung like a funeral shroud. A cruel smile played across the spirit's lips, sharp as a blade's edge.

Fuck.

Instinctively, he reached out to where Wim should have been, just to his side, but his hands closed around thin air.

Where was Wim?

Red's eyes darted around their camp, searching desperately for any sign of the wolf. The bedroll beside him was cold and empty. His gaze landed on their gear, relief flooding through him at the sight of Wim's worn leather pack propped against a tree—if that was still here, then he hadn't abandoned him after their argument.

"Looking for your pet wolf?" The Shadow's smile widened, revealing teeth too white, too perfect to be human. "Don't worry, he hasn't gone far. But there's something *else* you've lost that you should be worried about."

Red stared at the spirit. What new game was this twisted creature playing? The Shadow's words scratched at the edges of his mind like thorns seeking purchase.

The golden arrow.

Ice crystallised in his veins as his hand flew to his quiver. His fingers trembled as they brushed past ordinary arrows, searching, desperate. Steel tips, wooden shafts, falcon feather fletching—but no trace of gilt. No magic golden arrow.

"Where is it?" Red's voice quavered, his fingers clenching around the quiver. "This isn't funny!"

The Shadow's form rippled like ink in water, that terrible smile never wavering. "Don't ask me! You'll have to ask the wolf. He's the one who ran off with it."

"*What?* Why the fuck would he do that?" Red cried. "He doesn't even..." The words died in his throat. He wouldn't give this creature the satisfaction of seeing him unravel, of watching him piece together whatever cruel plot was unfolding.

Cackling, the Shadow rose, pulling his brocade coat tight around him.

"Are you off to tell the Queen?" Red shouted it in a tone to suggest he didn't care, when in fact, he did very much. He quite liked his head on his neck.

Instead of answering, the Queen's Shadow's form twisted, stretching like ink dropped in water, before dissolving into wisps of black smoke that curled into nothingness. An acrid scent lingered in the air.

Red's fingers trembled as he dressed and gathered his belongings. His breath came in short, sharp gasps, and sweat beaded across his brow despite the morning chill. What the fuck was Wim doing with that arrow? He needed to find him, immediately.

"Wim?" he called out, though barely above a whisper. No response, only the rustling of leaves in the breeze and the distant call of a dove.

Which way would he have gone? Red spun in place, scanning the forest floor. The dense canopy above cast dappled shadows that played tricks with his vision, making every root and hollow look like a possible trail.

Wait—*there*. A broken branch lay across a patch of disturbed earth, its fresh splinters catching the weak morning light. Red traced the direction with his eyes, noting more subtle signs: a displaced stone, bent grass, the faintest impression of what could be a large footprint.

He picked his way through the undergrowth, following these tentative clues. The forest grew denser, branches snagging at his cloak, roots threatening to trip him with every step.

Clang.

Red froze. The sound rang out again—metal striking something, like a hammer on an anvil. But that was impossible. They were miles from any settlement.

Clang. Clang. Clang.

The rhythm was steady, methodical. Red crept forward, ducking under a low-hanging branch. The sound grew louder with each step, more aggressive, as if the striker were getting angrier.

Then he saw it.

Wim crouched beside a massive, flat boulder, muscles rippling beneath his shirt as he gripped the golden arrow in white-knuck-led hands. His face contorted with desperation, jaw clenched. The arrow's shaft glinted as it struck stone again and again, each impact sending shards of light dancing across the forest floor.

Clang. Clang. Clang.

Red's fingers moved of their own accord, nocking an arrow to his bow. The string drew taut with a familiar creak.

"Stop!"

Wim's head snapped up, eyes wild and feral. The golden arrow hung suspended in his grasp, caught mid-strike.

"You fucking traitor." While Red's arms shook with rage, his aim remained steady. "This was your plan all along, wasn't it? Get close to me, make me trust you, then destroy the Queen's arrow?"

"Red—"

"Shut up! I trusted you." The words tasted like ash in his mouth. "I let you in, I..." His throat closed around the rest of that sentence. "And the whole time you were working against me."

Wim's expression shifted from shock to something darker, more dangerous. His fingers tightened around the golden arrow.

"Put it down." Red pulled the bowstring back further, arrow tip aimed at Wim's chest. "Or I'll shoot you."

Wim let out a guttural shout that echoed through the trees, hurling the golden arrow at the ground. It struck the earth with such force that it bounced, rolling to a stop between them. Red's fingers remained locked on his bowstring, arrow still trained on Wim.

"I should shoot you anyway," Red spat, vision blurring with unshed tears. His chest constricted, making each breath a battle. "For treason. Don't you—" He swallowed hard, fighting to steady himself. "Don't you *want* the famine to end?" The betrayal crashed over him in waves, each one threatening to drag him under. His next words came out as a broken whisper. "Why would you do this to me?"

"Easy now, sweetheart," Wim's tone was gentle, hands lifting slowly. "Put the bow down and let me tell you everything."

"No!" The word tore from Red's throat, raw and desperate. "Answer me, goddamn you!"

"Use that clever head of yours!" Wim's hands clenched into fists at his sides. "If all I wanted was to destroy your precious arrow, don't you think I'd have done it already? Could have taken it that first night and vanished into the woods, couldn't I?"

Red's arms trembled from holding the bow taut, but he refused to lower it. His eyes narrowed. "You told me that you like to play with your food. Clearly, you decided to take that to a whole new level."

Red's arms shook as Wim advanced, each step bringing him closer. The bow wobbled, his grip slipping with sweat. "Stay back!" The words ripped from his throat, desperate and raw.

Tears blurred his vision, turning Wim into a dark smudge against the forest. Red blinked hard, trying to clear his sight, but the tears kept coming.

"I just wanted to take a closer look at that fucking golden arrow you're putting your life on the line for. To see if I could prove you wrong somehow." Wim's voice grew closer, steadier. "Goddamn her for twisting you up like this! For someone so clever, you've swallowed her lies without question. Just think it through properly, sweetheart. Does it really add up?"

The words struck deeper than any arrow could. Red's chest tightened, crushing the air from his lungs. His fingers burned from holding the bowstring so tightly.

"We've already been through this!" Red inhaled a stuttering breath. "It doesn't make sense that she sent someone so pathetic, so unskilled, to do such an important job, am I right?" The truth poured out of him like poison from a wound. "Because there's no way I could possibly succeed. You're right, Wim, I *am* a nobody. I'm expendable. That's why she sent me. In case I fail, in case Oma kills me first—then it's no great loss to her. I know that, alright?"

"Red—" Wim's voice dropped to a whisper, soft as velvet against Red's frayed nerves.

"I heard you and Astrid that night," Red spat. "You called my quest stupid nonsense."

Any remaining colour dropped from Wim's face as his expression contorted to one of pure horror. "I'm... sorry," he said. "You weren't supposed to hear that."

"Well, I did! And it cut me deeply!" More than he'd care to admit. "But—"

"That still doesn't explain why I found you striking the arrow as if you wished to break it!" Red's hands trembled on his bow, but he kept it high.

Silence stretched between them, thick and heavy as winter fog. Wim's hand crept up to scratch at his neck—that familiar gesture that betrayed his discomfort. Red's stomach twisted at the sight.

"If I managed to destroy it, I hoped you'd see that it wasn't a magic arrow after all, just some game the Queen is playing." Wim's words fell like stones into still water, each one sending ripples of doubt through Red's mind.

"But why do you care if it's real or not? It's worth a *try*, isn't it? To stop the famine?" The bow wavered in his grip as exhaustion crept through his muscles.

Wim opened his mouth, then closed it again. His shoulders tensed, jaw working as if chewing on words he couldn't quite spit out.

Red's fingers tightened even further. "I know you're hiding something. Have been hiding something this whole time. I'm not stupid! I've trusted you with every tiny piece of me—"

The raw anguish in his words must have been enough for Wim to risk injury, because he lurched towards Red, swiftly knocking the bow to one side to scoop Red into his arms.

Wim's arms locked around Red like iron bands, crushing him against that broad chest. Red thrashed, but Wim's grip only tightened as he sank to the ground, pulling Red down with him. The rough bark of the tree pressed into Red's back through his cloak as Wim arranged them both, settling Red between his legs.

"Let me go!" Red slammed his fist into Wim's shoulder, but it was like hitting stone. His legs kicked out, seeking purchase, trying to break free. "I hate you! I fucking hate you!"

"No you don't." Wim's voice rumbled through his chest, vibrating against Red's cheek. One large hand slid up to cradle the back of Red's head, fingers threading through his hair.

How dare he! This fucking monster had manipulated Red from the start, had tricked him with sweet words and even sweeter kisses, had made him feel all sorts of crazy things for him.

Red writhed harder, twisting and bucking against Wim's grip. His elbow caught Wim in the ribs—a blow that would have winded most men, but Wim didn't even flinch. Frustrated tears spilled down

Red's cheeks as he fought, each movement more desperate than the last.

"Shhh," Wim murmured, his fingers working gentle circles against Red's scalp. "I've got you."

This was too much. Red's heart gave up and broke in two. Who knew that heartbreak could be so physically, viscerally painful? Not Red, until now.

"Stop it!" Red swallowed against the rising lump in his throat, and he pressed his palms flat against Wim's chest, trying to push away, but Wim held firm. "Haven't you done enough? Just stop—"

"Never." Wim's other hand stroked down Red's spine, steady and rhythmic. "I'm not letting you go."

Red's struggles gradually weakened, his movements becoming less coordinated as exhaustion crept in. Still, Wim's hands never ceased their soothing motions—one in his hair, one on his back, as constant as the tide.

"I hate it," Red whispered, his forehead pressed against Wim's collarbone. His fingers curled into Wim's shirt, no longer pushing away but clinging close. "I hate that you've done this to me."

"Shhh." Wim's thumb brushed away a tear from Red's cheek. "I'm going to explain everything to you, I promise. Just breathe with me for a moment."

Red's chest heaved with ragged breaths that slowly, gradually, fell into sync with Wim's steady rhythm. The forest around them grew quiet, as if holding its breath, waiting.

Red's mind spun with possibilities, each more absurd than the last. Perhaps Wim was actually the Queen's long-lost secret second son, sent to test Red's loyalty. Or maybe he was some sort of forest spirit bound to play tricks on passers-through. Could he be Old Oma's grandson, sworn to defend her from assassins? Or what if he was actually three squirrels in a man costume who needed the arrow for their acorn-based religion?

Red squeezed his eyes shut, pressing his face into Wim's chest. "Please, Wim, I can't take it anymore. Just say whatever it is!"

Wim's fingers stilled in Red's hair. The silence stretched between them, thick as mud.

"The truth is, Red, we're both going to the same place."

Red pulled back just enough to glare up at him. "I know that! That's why we're bloody travelling together, isn't it?!"

"No, Red," Wim said quietly. "The *exact* same place."

"Oh..." Red's brow furrowed as understanding dawned. "Old Oma's? But... what? Why?"

"This bloody kills me to say, but I have to say it. I can't let you shoot that witch through the heart with that arrow, Red."

Like a complex puzzle box finally clicking into its solution, each piece of their journey slotted into place in Red's mind. Every lingering glance, every hesitation, every time Wim had changed the subject when discussing their destination, Wim's dismissal of his quest... it all formed a complete picture that Red hadn't been able to see until now.

"Your... cure." The words felt strange on Red's tongue, as if speaking them might make this new reality more concrete.

Wim nodded, drawing Red closer to him, in case he might try to escape. His warmth seeped through Red's clothes, a stark contrast to the cold revelation washing over him.

"Whether she turns to dust, or simply falls to the ground dead, it matters not. I can't let you shoot her, because *I* need that heart. I need to claim her beating heart."

Red's stomach lurched. The image of Wim, wolf-formed, tearing his teeth into a still-pulsing heart made his non-existent breakfast threaten to make a reappearance.

The realisation hit him like a punch to the gut—they were both assassins. Both on their way to murder the old witch in her home. The only difference was their method and their reasoning.

Red pressed his forehead against Wim's chest, breathing in his familiar scent of pine and leather. How had he not seen it before? All those times Wim had questioned the Queen's motives, tried to make Red doubt his mission—had he been protecting his own agenda?

But then, why share this now? Why not continue the deception until they reached Old Oma's cottage? Why risk everything by confessing?

"I did wonder, you know." Red traced patterns on Wim's chest with his fingertip. Really, he should have been untangling himself from the wildling, forcing himself to sit an arm's reach from him. But he couldn't resist. "I was confused as to why you didn't tell me the exact nature of your cure. But can't you find another witch's heart to have? Why does it have to be *my* witch?"

Wim's arms tightened around him. "Has to be Old Oma's heart. Her soulstealer's the one that did this to me."

Red's finger stilled. "You know that for sure? What even was it, exactly? This soulstealer?"

"A creature she created. A dark thing that feeds on people's essence—probably what powers her magic." Wim's volume was barely above a whisper. "The healer who examined my wound found her magical imprint. Said there was no mistaking it."

Red shifted in Wim's lap to look up at his face. The morning light caught the stubble along his jaw, the shadows under his eyes seeming deeper than before.

"So..." Red's throat felt tight. "If I do succeed in turning her to dust with the arrow... what will happen to you? Is there another way you can cure yourself?"

Wim's gaze dropped to where his fingers were tangled in Red's cloak. "I don't know."

The simple words sliced through Red with the precision of a huntsman's blade. His chest constricted as the implications sank in. If he succeeded in his mission—if he killed Old Oma with the golden arrow—he might condemn Wim to a life of slowly losing control, of becoming more feral until... until what? Until his pack had no choice but to put him down? Until he hurt someone he cared about?

The image of Wim's wolf form, eyes glazed and savage, tearing through human flesh, flashed through Red's mind. But worse was the memory of Wim afterwards—broken, guilty, horrified by his own actions. How many more times would that scene repeat if Red took away his only chance at a cure?

Red cleared his throat. "So why now? Why attack the arrow this morning?"

"I just... couldn't bear it anymore. After you were angry with me, I hated myself for it. Wasn't thinking clear. Thought if I could just make that cursed arrow disappear, I could take Old Oma's heart, get cured, and then..."

"And then?" Red held his breath, every muscle tensing.

"And then..." Wim inhaled one ragged breath. "Then I'd finally be free. No more beast taking control. No more fear of hurting innocent people in the forest. I could live a proper life again. Could go home to my pack."

"Right, yes, of course. Your pack." Red couldn't quite hide his disdain. *Don't be stupid. He's a wolf. Of course he's primarily concerned with his pack!*

"And perhaps..." Wim whispered, arms tightening around Red. "Perhaps free to properly court a particular mouthy little thing in a red cloak. If he'd want me."

Red's breath caught in his throat. He pulled back just enough to search Wim's face, looking for any sign of mockery or deceit. But Wim's expression held nothing but raw vulnerability, his eyes dark with an emotion Red couldn't quite name.

"You'd want that?" Red's voice came out very, very small. "With... *me*?"

"Aye, with you." Wim's thumb traced Red's cheekbone. "I'd be a fool not to. You're beautiful. And infuriating. And brave. And absolutely maddening."

Heat bloomed across Red's face. He ducked his head, but Wim caught his chin, tilting it back up.

"I mean every word, sweetheart. Once I'm cured, once I'm myself again... nothing would make me happier than to be with you. I know it's been mere days together, but... don't you feel it too? This thread pulling us together. My pack always said you know your mate the moment you find them—like the stars themselves align to tell you they're yours."

What was Wim saying? Red hardly dared to blink, his heart pounding with such velocity it dizzied him.

The wolf took a deep breath, his gaze holding Red's with an air-crackling intensity. "I should have known the moment I smelled you, that night when I tracked your path for hours while the beast had control. I know this all probably sounds mad to you, but... a little madness makes life worth living, don't you think?"

Wim's words settled in Red's chest like warm honey, sweet and golden. But beneath that sweetness lurked the bitter truth that soon bubbled to the surface.

"But it can't be," Red said, though his soul screamed at him to stop, stop, *stop*. "The Queen will never let me leave the palace. She'd sooner see me dead, just to prove a point. And..." Red reached for the golden arrow, still on the ground. He forced himself to speak with conviction. "I *will* be shooting Oma with this golden arrow. If there's even a small chance of curing the famine, I have to take it. It's my duty. Not to the Queen, but to Falchovari."

Red stared at the golden arrow in his palm, its surface catching the filtered sunlight through the leaves. His chest ached with a familiar emptiness—the same void he'd felt his entire life. But that day in the throne room... that had changed everything.

He'd knelt before Queen Schön, heart racing as her cold gaze had swept over him. The marble floor had bitten into his knees, but he'd barely noticed the pain. Her voice, soft as silk but sharp as a blade, had laid out his task with precise clarity. Each word had filled that hollow space inside him with purpose, with meaning.

"You alone can save us," she'd said, and for the first time in his life, Red had felt *chosen*. Not cast aside, not overlooked, not whispered about behind raised hands. She'd selected him for this vital mission. *Him!* The orphan boy with the strange eyes who'd spent his childhood dreaming of belonging.

Now, with Wim's warmth still lingering on his skin, Red closed his fingers around the arrow's shaft. This was his chance—perhaps his only chance—to prove his worth. To show everyone who'd ever doubted him that he could be more than just the foundling left on the palace steps. If he succeeded, children wouldn't go to bed hungry anymore. The fields would flourish again. His kingdom would thrive.

The memory of the Queen's smile—that rare thing she'd bestowed upon him—burned in his mind. For the first time, she'd looked at him as if he mattered, as if he was worth something.

Red traced the arrow's delicate engravings with his thumb. Everything he'd ever wanted lay within his grasp: recognition, purpose, belonging. All he had to do was complete his mission.

But...

Oh, if only it didn't mean losing Wim in the process!

Red stared at the mountain of a man in front of him, Wim's form blurring as his eyes leaked with furious tears. Wim had crashed into his life like a storm, destroying every careful wall Red had built around himself. Where Red had expected a monster, he'd found gentleness. Where he'd feared mockery, he'd discovered unwavering understanding. Wim's rough hands had shown him more kindness than any silk-clad noble. His deep laugh had filled empty spaces Red hadn't known existed within himself.

Even now, trapped between duty and desire, Red couldn't deny how Wim made him feel whole. Complete. As if all his jagged edges finally had somewhere to fit. The wolf had seen past his different-coloured eyes, past his sharp tongue and prickly defences, straight through to the lonely soul beneath. And instead of recoiling, Wim had reached out and pulled him closer, wrapping Red in warmth and acceptance he'd never known he craved.

Oh, why had fate done this to him?

It would have been so much easier if they'd never met.

Wim slumped against the tree, his broad shoulders curved inward. His eyes fixed on some distant point beyond the trees, glazed with a sheen that made Red's chest ache.

"I sort of wish I still hadn't told you the truth, as much as the lie was burdening me." Pain threaded through each of Wim's quiet words. "These past days... they've been..." He trailed off, dragging a hand down his face.

Red's fingers itched to reach out, to smooth away the creases of pain etched across Wim's features. Instead, he wrapped his arms around himself, clutching his red cloak closer.

"They've been perfect," Red finished for him. The words escaped before he could stop them, honest and raw. "Well, except for the bandits. And the slavers. And that time you tried to eat me."

A ghost of a smile flickered across Wim's face. "You're never going to let me forget that, are you?"

"Not bloody likely." Red bumped his shoulder against Wim's, drawing another weak smile from him.

Silence settled between them, heavy with unspoken words. To distract himself from the agonising fist squeezing his heart, Red traced his fingers over the golden arrow's shaft, feeling its smoothness beneath his touch. He'd never detected magical energy thrumming through it, but what did he know?

This was it then. The moment they parted. Maybe if Red begged Wim, the wolf would give him a half day's head start.

"What if..." Wim cleared his throat. "What if we just... pretend? For now?"

Red looked up, catching the desperate hope in Wim's eyes. "Pretend?"

"That we're still just two travellers, sharing a path." Wim's hand found Red's, his thumb brushing over Red's knuckles. "Until we reach Old Oma's cottage. Then... then we'll deal with what must be done."

Red should say no. Should walk away now, before their inevitable clash which would tear him apart. But the thought of continuing alone, of losing these potential precious moments with Wim…

"Alright." Red squeezed Wim's hand. "Until we reach the cottage."

"And then?"

Red met Wim's gaze. "And then… we'll see what happens."

It wasn't a solution. Not really. But what was the harm in a little make believe? A few more memories to be made, to be stored in the deep crevices of Red's mind, to be brought out once he was back at the palace, alone in the attic once more.

Red knew better than most how dangerous hope could be. Yet as Wim's fingers traced patterns on his skin, he decided that perhaps some poisons were worth tasting.

Eighteen

The following days blurred together like watercolours bleeding across parchment. Each morning, Red woke tangled in Wim's arms, savouring the warmth before they packed up camp. They walked for hours through dappled sunlight, sharing more stories of their lives—Wim's tales of pack gatherings around bonfires, Red's memories of sneaking extra tarts from the palace kitchens. Their laughter echoed through the trees, masking the growing weight in Red's stomach.

Nights brought Wim's cooking, the aromas of herbs and roasted meat drawing them close around the fire. Red found himself mesmerised by Wim's hands as they chopped vegetables or stirred stews, imagining those same fingers trailing across his skin. But neither of them pushed for more than gentle touches and shared warmth as they lay beneath the stars. Perhaps they both knew that crossing that line again would make their inevitable parting even more unbearable.

Wim's feral sickness continued to threaten to emerge, and Red couldn't help but notice the gap between his episodes seemed to be shortening. Red tried not to show his fear when Wim leaned his arm against a tree, breathing deeply while his body trembled. He'd always try to order Red to move away from him, but Red refused, and would grab Wim's knuckle-white fist, unfurl it, and slip his hand into his.

Often, holding Red's hand for a short period would be enough to keep the monster at bay, but on one occasion, Wim left him for an entire day, returning with haunted eyes and blood-soaked hair.

As the forest grew darker and older around them, Red caught Wim inventing reasons to pause their journey. "Look at these mushrooms—perfect for tonight's soup." Or, "The light's hitting those leaves just right, let's rest here a moment." Red played along, pointing out interesting birds or claiming his boots needed adjusting. Collecting flowers for their basket, which he swung as they walked.

Each delay was precious, each moment stored away like treasure.

On their final morning, they came across an absurdly tall tower, stretching into the sky like a giant's needle piercing the clouds. Dark stone, weathered and ancient, wrapped in thick thorny vines. The tower was surrounded by a circular stone wall, moss-covered and crumbling in places.

They walked the perimeter, searching for an entrance that was not there. On the far side, partially hidden by long grass, a body lay crumpled on the ground. Red rushed forward before Wim could stop him.

"Don't—" Wim growled, but Red was already kneeling beside the corpse.

It was a drained husk, skin grey and paper-thin, stretched over hollow bones like old parchment. The victim's mouth gaped in a silent scream, eyes sunken so deep they were barely visible.

"Dark sorcery," Wim muttered.

As they hurried away, Red stared at the tower's highest window, but saw no flicker of movement in the darkness.

With the ancient trees of the Dark Forest looming ahead, they moved at a snail's pace. Red spotted a blue-winged butterfly and insisted on following it, while Wim discovered three different types of berries that simply had to be sampled. Neither mentioned how their five-minute breaks stretched into half hours, or how their usual chatter had dwindled to weighted silence.

The trees changed without warning. One moment, Red walked through familiar forest—oak and birch with their welcoming branches. The next, ancient pines towered overhead, their trunks wider than the palace's pillars. Thick, dark moss draped every surface like an infection. The air grew heavy, tasting of decay and secrets.

Red's steps faltered. "This is it, then."

Wim's fingers brushed against Red's wrist, a ghost of contact that sent shivers down his spine. "The Dark Forest."

They stood at the threshold, where vibrant greens faded to muted greys and browns. Even the sunlight seemed hesitant to pierce the canopy overhead, creating a stark line between light and shadow. The border between their journey and its end.

Red's throat tightened. He reached for his mother's cloak, clutching the fabric between trembling fingers. All those nights spent imagining this moment, planning his triumphant march into these feared woods—none of it had prepared him for the reality. Not just of the forest's oppressive presence, but of the man beside him. The way Wim's warmth called to him like a beacon, even as duty pulled him forward into the darkness.

"We could—" Wim's voice grew raw. He cleared his throat. "We could rest here. Just one more night."

Red shook his head, though every part of him screamed to agree. "I couldn't bear it."

Together, they stepped across that invisible line. The forest swallowed them whole, ancient branches creaking overhead like old bones. Their footsteps fell silent on the thick carpet of needles. Even the birds ceased their songs, as if recognising intruders in their midst.

Red pressed closer to Wim, their shoulders touching. Neither spoke. What words could capture the finality of this moment? The knowledge that every step forward brought them closer to choices neither wanted to make.

The darkness wrapped around them, suffocating. Red's chest ached with each breath, heavy with unspoken confessions and promises he couldn't keep. Beside him, Wim's jaw clenched, his eyes fixed ahead with desperate determination.

They were no longer travellers sharing a path, but star-crossed souls bound by fate's cruel design. The Dark Forest had claimed them, sealing their separate destinies with each step deeper into its shadows.

"I have a second map," Red said, his voice very small.

He brought out the crumpled, aged parchment with the map of the Dark Forest inked on it, and unfurled it, the crackling of the yellowed map joining the eerie chorus of the forest. Wim leaned closer, his breath warm against Red's cheek as they studied the inked trails snaking across the page.

There, nestled between twisting pathways, was a tiny sketch of a cottage. Red's fingers traced the delicate cursive beneath it—*The Witch's Abode*. Despite the miniscule rendering, he couldn't shake the sense of foreboding that simple drawing inspired.

"Doesn't look too far," Wim murmured, but the furrow in his brow betrayed his doubt. This forest could easily play tricks on one's perception—the massive trunks and endless canopy dwarfing any distance marked on paper.

Red's gaze followed the primary route highlighted in faded red ink. "We head southeast for half a mile, then veer west at... this marking." He squinted at the strange symbol, a series of slashes that could have indicated anything from a creek to a landslide. "After that, it's just over a ridge, and we should be able to see Oma's cottage."

"Ready?" Wim's voice was low, the roughness in it betraying his own trepidation.

Red swallowed hard and gave a tight nod. Tucking the map back into his cloak's inner pocket, he forced his feet to move forward, following the barely visible trail stretching before them.

The simplicity of the directions belied the arduous journey lying ahead. They soon found themselves in an atmosphere so steeped in darkness, it seemed to cling to their skin. Red found himself clutching the map tighter, as if the fragile parchment could somehow shield him from the oppressive force surrounding them.

With each step, the world shifted continuously. The towering pines sharpened into twisted silhouettes, their branches gnarled claws scratching at the shadowed sky. Underneath the thick blanket of needles, Red's boots crunched over fallen twigs and scattered bones—whether animal or otherwise, he couldn't tell, and didn't want to know. The forest seemed to breathe around them, inhaling and exhaling with sinister purpose.

Red's fingers found Wim's sleeve, gripping the fabric in a white-knuckled hold. He stared resolutely ahead, fighting the urge to glance over his shoulder at whatever terrors lurked behind. Only the solid warmth of Wim's presence kept his feet moving, one faltering stride after another, into the heart of this cursed wood.

The deeper they ventured, the more Red felt the weight of unseen eyes upon them. The sensation crept up his spine like icy fingers, every hair on his neck standing on end.

"Do you feel that?" Red whispered, his voice barely audible.

Wim's nostrils flared, his posture stiffening. "We're being watched."

A rustling sound came from somewhere to their left, too deliberate to be the wind. Red's hand instinctively moved to his bow, but before he could nock an arrow, something darted between the trees—a flash of movement in the shadows.

"What was that?" Red hissed.

Wim's hand shot out, pulling Red behind him. "Stay close."

The forest floor seemed to writhe under their feet as thick, ropey vines slithered from beneath the carpet of needles. One snaked around Red's ankle, its grip surprisingly strong for something so seemingly innocuous.

"Wim!" Red gasped, stumbling as the vine tightened.

With a snarl, Wim drew his knife and slashed at the offending tendril, which recoiled with an unnatural hiss. More vines emerged from the shadows, reaching with questing fingers toward them.

"Move!" Wim commanded, slicing through another vine that had wound its way up Red's calf.

Red's heart lodged in his throat as they sprinted forward, dodging the grasping vegetation that seemed intent on ensnaring them. The vines retreated after several yards, but the sense of being stalked only intensified.

As they pressed onward, the canopy thickened, steadily choking away the meager light that filtered through.

"Look," Red whispered, pointing upwards.

Silken strands glistened in the dim, murky twilight that somehow penetrated the dense canopy, stretching from branch to branch in intricate patterns. Not the delicate webs of ordinary spiders, but massive, rope-thick tapestries that hung like ghostly curtains across their path.

"Don't touch them," Wim warned, voice low and tense.

The darkness above them shifted, and as Red's eyes adjusted, he saw them—dozens of tiny pinpricks reflecting what little light remained, like malignant stars scattered across a black velvet sky. Not celestial bodies, but spiders the size of dinner plates, their segmented legs twitching with anticipation. One descended on a silken thread, dangling just above their heads, mandibles clicking wetly.

Red stifled a cry, pressing himself against Wim's side as they carefully navigated beneath the arachnid sentinels. The creatures tracked their movement, rotating in unison like macabre puppets on invisible strings.

"They're herding us," Wim muttered, his free hand resting on his knife. "Driving us deeper."

"Deeper toward what?" Red's voice trembled despite his efforts to steady it.

The answer came in the form of a low, wet squelching sound from the path ahead. The forest floor undulated, not with vines this time, but with pale, bloated forms—maggots the length of Red's forearm, their translucent bodies pulsing as they feasted on something large and recently deceased.

The stench hit them a moment later—the unmistakable reek of putrefaction. Red gagged, pressing his sleeve against his mouth as they skirted the writhing mass. On the ground lay what had once been some sort of animal, now unrecognizable beneath the undulating carpet of scavengers.

"The forest is feeding," Wim observed grimly. "And we're trespassing at dinner time."

A particularly massive maggot raised its blind head toward them, sensing their warmth. It lurched in their direction with surprising speed, leaving a glistening trail of slime in its wake. Wim's boot came down hard, crushing it with a horrible wet sound. The rest of the brood stirred, disturbed by the death of their kin.

"We need to move," Wim urged, pulling Red away from the increasingly agitated swarm. "Now."

They quickened their pace, weaving between the trees as more vines attempted to snare their ankles. The forest was alive with malevolence, each element working in concert to impede their progress or drive them into greater danger.

A low moan echoed through the trees—not wind, but something that mimicked human suffering with chilling accuracy. It was joined by another, then another, until a chorus of phantom wails surrounded them from all sides.

"Ignore it," Wim growled, his grip on Red's hand tightening. "This forest plays tricks on the mind. It feeds on fear."

But Red couldn't help glancing over his shoulder, half expecting to see ghostly figures pursuing them through the gloom. Instead, he spotted movement at ground level—more of the bloated maggots, following their trail in a grotesque procession.

Red poured all his energy into staying close to Wim, matching each of his quick strides with a wide step of his own. Thank goodness Wim was here with him, that he wasn't going through this alone.

But with each unsteady breath, with each sidelong glance at Wim, anticipation built within Red.

At what point was their game of 'pretend' supposed to end? Was Red going to *finally* get to the house after all this time, only for Wim to push him to the ground then tie him to a tree?

If he made to attack, Red would have to shoot him.

As if you could really do that, you fool.

Red swallowed, clutching Wim's sleeve even tighter.

Only moments left until you lose him.

Wim must have been thinking the same thing—he tugged Red's hand off his shirt sleeve to interlace their fingers, squeezing their hands tightly together.

Red squeezed back so hard his joints ached, pouring every unspoken word into that desperate grip. Their fingers remained locked together as they navigated deeper into the Dark Forest's belly, speaking only in hushed murmurs when absolutely necessary. The forest pressed closer, darker, colder with each step.

They followed the winding path marked on Red's map, occasionally forced to detour around massive spider webs or pulsating colonies of maggots. Twice more, the sentient vines attempted to ensnare them, Red having to dive and duck out of their reach while Wim slashed at the more persistent tendrils.

The forest constricted around them, the trees growing closer together until they had to turn sideways to slip between the massive trunks. The air grew thick with spores that drifted like snow, coating their clothing in a fine, ashen powder that smelled of grave dirt.

What felt like hours passed in that horrible silent march through the darkness, until a rough, cobblestone path emerged before them—a narrow strip of dead earth winding between rows of black-spotted toadstools. The mushrooms oozed a viscous purple fluid that pooled in the divots of exposed tree roots.

They pressed onward, trusting the path to lead them. The vines grew thicker here, pulsing with a life of their own, retreating just enough to allow passage before closing ranks behind them.

And then, suddenly, the path widened. The oppressive canopy parted just enough to allow a single shaft of sickly green light to illuminate what lay ahead. Bones and trinkets hung from branches on tattered ribbons, clicking together in the stale air like macabre wind chimes.

And at the end of this grotesque gallery...

There it was.

Old Oma's house: *The Witch's Abode.*

The cottage was a hunched, twisted thing with moss-covered walls and a chimney belching dark smoke into the perpetual twilight. Windows like hollow eyes stared back at them, and Red's stomach lurched at the sight of what looked like bloodstains where a doorstep should have been.

"Well..." Red cleared his throat. "No sign of any light. Doesn't look like anyone's home. Let's try again later."

Wim did not respond to his humour.

"What's your plan, then?" Wim dropped Red's hand, causing a surge of anxiety to assault his stomach. "To get inside, I mean?"

"Oh... umm..."

Red had imagined climbing a tree and shooting her when she hung up her laundry or something, but the witch didn't seem like the sort. He looked down at the basket he'd somehow managed to keep hold of through their harrowing journey. It was a miracle it had survived—the handle was frayed where a vine had nearly snatched it away, and several of the blooms were crushed. Still, some of the chrysanthemums and pansies remained, their vibrant colours a stark contrast to the gloom surrounding them.

Red had clutched that basket like a talisman through the forest's horrors, refusing to let go even when the spiders descended or the maggots surged toward them. Something about abandoning it felt like surrendering completely to the darkness.

"I'll knock on the door and pretend to be selling flowers!"

Wim's laughter cut through the eerie silence. "Selling flowers? To a witch? That's your grand scheme?"

Red's cheeks burned. The basket suddenly felt childish in his hands, the bright petals garish against the forest's gloom. "Well, I don't see you coming up with anything better."

Wim's tone took on an edge. "Because I actually planned for this moment."

The words stung more than they should have. Red's fingers tightened around the basket handle, his other hand inching towards his bow. Every movement Wim made now seemed threatening—the way he shifted his weight, how his shoulders tensed, the gleam in his eyes.

This is it. He's going to attack. He's going to transform and tear you apart right here.

Wim's arm shot out suddenly and Red stumbled backwards, heart racing, bow half drawn before he could think.

The hurt that flashed across Wim's face made Red's chest ache. Wim had only been reaching for his pack, movements slow and deliberate now as he withdrew something that caught the dim light.

"Just grabbing this," Wim said softly, holding up a leather cord strung with tiny, pearl-white teeth. "My milk teeth. Saved them all this time." His thumb traced one of the small fangs. "Waiting for..."

My mate.

Red's bow lowered, shame flooding through him. The delicate, precious necklace hung from Wim's finger.

"Why are you showing me them?" Red asked, hardly daring to breathe, his heart pounding rabbit-fast. Was Wim...? Did this mean...?

"I'm going to use it to bait Oma into opening the door. Wildling teeth have magical properties."

Red's heart plummeted so fast a wave of nausea punched through his gut. Of course. Of course Wim hadn't meant... More heat flooded his cheeks as mortification crashed into him. How could he have been so stupid? To think that Wim would choose *this* moment, standing before a vile witch's house, to make some grand romantic gesture?

His throat closed up, chest tight with humiliation. He'd nearly reached for the necklace, like some lovestruck fool. Thank god he hadn't actually stretched out his hand—that would have been unbearable.

Red turned away, pretending to adjust his cloak while he blinked back the sting in his eyes. When he trusted his voice wouldn't crack, he managed, "No, you can't risk those. They're too precious."

"They're just teeth," Wim said, as gentle as a whisper.

"But they're not, are they?" Red's fingers twisted in his cloak. "You'll need them one day." *Once you're back with your pack, free from your beast, and free to find your true love.*

"Only plan we've got." Wim tucked the necklace into his palm. "Better than peddling flowers to a witch, at least."

Red couldn't even muster the energy to be properly offended. His gaze fixed on the cottage door, that bloodstained step. This was where their pretending must end, wasn't it? This moment. This choice. The culmination of their careful dance of 'just travelling companions' rather than enemies turned lovers turned rival witch assassins.

The cottage loomed before them, patient as a spider in its web. Red's chest ached with words he couldn't say, promises he couldn't make. They both had their missions. No amount of wishing could change that.

Wim moved toward the door, necklace dangling from his fingers, and Red followed, diving ahead so he was in front.

A rumbled chuckle burst out from Wim. "Always rushing headfirst into danger, aren't you, sweetheart?"

Red shot him a look over his shoulder. "Well, one of us has to be brave."

"Is that what you call it?" Wim's voice held that dangerous edge that always made Red's stomach flip. "I'd call it being an impossible brat."

They reached the door. Lightheadedness struck Red like a thunderbolt.

They were out of time.

Clearly, their unspoken plan was to knock on the door and... see what happened. See if Red could nock an arrow and shoot her through the heart before Wim had time to shift and lunge for her chest.

Wim looked down at the necklace in his palm. Looked at Red with the saddest puppy dog eyes. Looked at the weathered, dark oak door.

Then Wim's large hand—that same hand that had stroked Red's, traced every part of his skin, held him clutched tight against him at night—reached for the black metal doorknocker.

No.

"Wait!"

The word escaped before Red could stop it. His chest squeezed tight as Wim paused, those dark eyes fixed on him with an intensity that made breathing difficult.

"You should be the one to kill her." The words tumbled out in a rush, shocking Red even as he spoke them. But as soon as they left his lips, he knew they were true. "Take her heart. Take your cure."

Wim's expression shifted, something raw and vulnerable crossing his features. "Red—"

"No, listen." Red's hands found Wim's chest, pressing against the solid warmth there. "The Queen sent me because she thinks this witch is causing the famine. But... we don't know that for certain, do we?" It pained him to admit it, after all these miles. "It's just her suspicion. But your illness—that's real. I've seen what it does to you."

"The famine is killing people," Wim said softly. "Children are starving."

"And if we're wrong about the witch? If killing her changes nothing?" Red's fingers curled into Wim's shirt. "But we know her heart could cure you. You could go home, be with your pack again. With Tobias and Astrid."

Wim caught Red's hands in his own, thumb tracing circles on Red's palm. He looked deeply at Red, his gaze the most sincere thing. "No."

"What do you mean, no?"

"You had the right of it, before." Wim spoke hoarsely, as if every word cost him. "If killing the witch might end the famine, even the smallest chance... you've got to take that shot. Can't put my needs first. Not with so many folk starving."

"But—"

"My pack can manage without me." Wim pressed their foreheads together. "Those little ones in Falchovari might not last the winter."

Red wanted to argue, to shake sense into him. But Wim's logic pierced through his desperate need to protect him. How many times had Red walked through the Royal City, seeing hollow-cheeked children begging in the streets? How many graves had been dug in the past month alone?

Still, the thought of Wim living with his curse, slowly losing himself to the beast within... "There has to be another—"

A sharp crack split the air. Red and Wim sprang apart as the door creaked open on its own, revealing only darkness beyond.

"My, my..." A voice like splintering ice slithered from the shadows. "What an interesting pair you two make."

Red's blood froze. His fingers found Wim's sleeve again, gripping tight as that ancient voice continued:

"Do come in, dears. I've been expecting you."

Nineteen

Red stepped through the doorway, every muscle coiled tight. The interior struck him as impossibly vast for such a small cottage, stretching back into darkness that his eyes couldn't penetrate. He fumbled for Wim's hand, gripping it tight.

"Get that bow ready," Wim hissed in his ear. "You know, that fancy golden arrow of yours?"

Ah.

With hands that were only *slightly* trembling, Red rooted through his quiver to load the golden arrow. After so long waiting to use it, the act felt surreal, as if he had stepped into a dream.

A massive stone hearth dominated the left wall, its flames casting wild shadows across rough-hewn wooden beams. The air held an odd sweetness—like rotting fruit mixed with burning herbs—and Red fought the urge to cover his nose. Dried plants hung from the ceiling in dense clusters, their shapes unfamiliar and twisted. Scattered around the room stood wooden tables laden with glass jars containing things that made Red's stomach turn: eyeballs floating in murky liquid, what looked like human teeth, and writhing shadows that seemed alive.

Wim leaned in to whisper, "Stay close," his breath warm against Red's ear.

A creaking sound drew their attention to the far corner. There, barely visible in the flickering firelight, a rocking chair swayed back and forth. Red could make out a figure seated in it, but darkness clung to them like a second skin, refusing to reveal more than a vague outline.

He couldn't shoot that—he had no idea of where the heart lay.

The floorboards beneath their feet gave soft groans of protest with each step. As they drew closer, the sweet-rot smell grew stronger.

The figure in the chair continued its gentle rocking, paying them no mind. Yet Red felt watched—studied—as if countless invisible eyes tracked their every movement.

"Come closer, my dears." The voice slithered through the air like oil on water.

Red's fingers tightened on his bow as he took another step forward, the golden arrow trained steady. His palms felt slick with sweat, but the countless hours of practice would keep his aim true.

A cackle burst from the rocking chair—a sound that raised every hair on Red's body. It pierced his ears like broken glass, echoing off the cottage walls until it seemed to come from everywhere at once.

The figure sprang up with unnatural speed, and Red's breath caught in his throat. She stood before them, a woman whose age seemed to shift with each blink. Her grey hair writhed like living smoke around a face that appeared both ancient and ageless. Her skin reminded Red of old parchment—thin and yellowed—with strange symbols that seemed to move beneath its surface. But it was her eyes that made his blood run cold. One was completely white, like fresh snow, yet somehow fixed directly on him.

Those unseeing eyes studied him with an intensity that made his skin crawl. Her head tilted at an impossible angle, a predatory bird examining its prey.

This is it. The moment he'd travelled so far for. The Queen's words echoed in his mind... *"Straight through the heart."*

Red drew back his bowstring. No hesitation. No doubt. The golden arrow gleamed in the firelight as he aimed directly at her heart.

Now, Red!

Old Oma threw back her head and erupted into hysterical laughter. The sound bounced off the walls, not the malicious cackle of an evil witch, but the sound of someone who'd found something very, very funny.

But Red steadied his aim, finger tensing on the bowstring. The golden arrow yearned to fly, its metal surface catching the firelight in mesmerising patterns.

"Wait!" Wim's hand shot out, pushing Red's bow toward the ground.

Red spun to face him, rage bubbling up. "What are you doing?" Had Wim changed his mind? Did he want to eat her heart after all?

"Wait!" Wim's eyes were wide, darting between Red and the witch. "Look at her eyes."

"What?" Red blinked, confusion replacing his anger. "What do you mean, her eyes?"

But even as he protested, Red found himself taking a step closer to Old Oma.

He saw it, then—her mismatched eyes.

One as white as snow, the pupil bleached to nothing, like looking into a frozen lake.

The other, a deep, hazelnut brown, flecked with the smallest hints of amber.

The pair of them fixed on him with an intensity that made his breath catch. The longer he stared, the more familiar that brown eye seemed, like looking into a mirror that showed only half his face.

Old Oma's laughter grew more hysterical, her entire body shaking with it. She wheezed, clutching her sides, tears streaming down her weathered cheeks. The sound filled every corner of the cottage, bouncing off walls and echoing in Red's skull until he could barely think.

Without warning, she lunged forward. Red's bow slipped from his grasp, clattering to the floor as her bony fingers clamped around both his arms. She shook him hard enough to make his teeth rattle, her face inches from his own.

A deep growl ripped through the cottage. "Take your filthy hands off him!" Wim thundered, the words echoing off the walls.

But Old Oma paid him no mind. She released Red's arms only to grasp the edges of his cloak, running the fabric between her fingers with a reverence that made his stomach twist. Her weathered face transformed as wonder bloomed in her eyes.

"My son! My son!" She pressed the red fabric to her face, inhaling deeply. "My baby!"

Her expression shifted again, joy crumbling into something raw and wounded. Tears spilled down her wrinkled cheeks as grief crashed over her features. Her hands trembled against the fabric.

"All this time..." she whispered, her voice breaking between elation and accusation. "My son!"

Red's legs gave out. The rough floorboards rushed up to meet him as his knees buckled. The cottage walls spun, and black spots danced at the edges of his vision.

This wasn't real.

This must be the fault of the spores of those poisonous toadstools they'd seen earlier in the Dark Forest. This was nothing but a fever dream—some twisted hallucination where a witch claimed to be his mother.

His mother.

The same mother who'd abandoned him on the palace steps. The same mother... he'd been sent to kill?

Red's chest constricted. Each breath came shorter than the last, his lungs refusing to expand properly. His vision tunnelled until all he could see was Old Oma's face, those mismatched eyes—*his* hazelnut eye—staring down at him.

Strong hands gripped his shoulders. Wim's face swam into view as he kneeled in front of Red, blocking out the witch.

"Red, eyes on me. Listen to my voice." Wim's hands moved to cup Red's face. "Match my breaths. In through your nose, out through your mouth."

Red tried to follow Wim's exaggerated breathing, but his body wouldn't cooperate. His heart hammered against his ribs as if trying to escape.

"That's it. One more." Wim pressed their foreheads together. "Just like that. Keep going."

"Let's go, Wim. Now!" Red cried. "Get me out of here!"

Because he'd waited all his life to meet his mother, and he refused to let it be this mad old witch.

He'd prefer to stay orphaned.

Red's vision continued to swim as his brain fought to process what was happening. Wim's solid presence beside him was the only thing keeping him from completely losing his grip on reality.

"Explain, now!" Wim barked.

Old Oma backed away, her earlier manic energy fading into something softer as she gazed at Red. "*Red*. Is that your name? I can't believe you've come back to me!"

"He was sent to kill you," Wim's voice cut through the air. "By the Queen. With that arrow. The Queen said you were the one causing the famine, and that if Red killed you, he'd fix everything."

A bitter laugh escaped Old Oma's lips, sharp and cold as winter frost. "What a brilliant tale. All lies, I'm afraid." Her eyes—one white, one creepily familiar—narrowed. "She always did enjoy her games. But this one... keeping my son alive for twenty-four winters, just so she could send him to kill me?"

Red's mouth went dry. The words scraped past his lips: "You... know Queen Schön?"

"*Know* her?" Old Oma's face twisted into something ugly. "She's my sister!"

Red tried to breathe, he really did, but his efforts were futile. The sweet-rot smell of the cottage pressed in around him, and the firelight from the massive hearth seemed to spin, casting wild shadows.

"No." The word came out small, his usual cutting tone failing him. "You're lying."

"My son!" She reached towards him with one bony hand.

"Don't!" Red's hand flew up, warding her off. His fingers caught the edge of his red riding hood—his mother's hood, the one thing she'd supposedly left him with—and he yanked it closer, as if it could shield him from this truth. "She sent me to... She wanted me to..."

Old Oma took another step towards him. "My boy—"

"I'm not your boy!" The words tore from his throat, raw and ragged. They echoed off the cottage walls, bouncing back at him from between the hanging dried herbs and grotesque jars. "I was abandoned. Left on the palace steps like—like rubbish!" But even as he said it, twenty-four winters of confusion started sliding into horrible clarity. The Queen's particular brand of cruelty. The way she'd always looked at him with such calculating eyes. How she'd nurtured his hatred of imperfection, of his own eyes, while keeping him close enough to use.

My whole quest was a lie. My whole life was a lie.

"She knew," he whispered, his voice barely audible over the crackling hearth. "This whole time, she knew."

The Queen was his aunt. She was his fucking *aunt*.

She'd known exactly who he was all along.

A soft cry escaped Red's lips, and he pressed his fist to his mouth.

He'd lived with the Queen for twenty-four winters, thinking he had no family in the world. Every night, he'd curled up in the attic, sleeping above his own flesh and blood. The same woman who'd sneered at his different-coloured eyes, who'd made him feel worthless for something he'd inherited from her own sister.

Queen Schön had known. She'd known every time she'd cast those icy glares his way. Known every time she'd compared him unfavourably to Makellos—his cousin. Known when she'd handed him that golden arrow and sent him to murder his own mother.

Wim's hand swept across his back in slow, steady strokes. The touch anchored Red to the present, kept him from drowning in the tide of betrayal threatening to pull him under.

"Why did you do it?" Red's voice betrayed him by breaking. "Why did you leave me on the palace steps?"

Old Oma's laugh pierced the air, sharp and brittle. "Leave you? Oh, my darling boy." She shook her head, wisps of grey hair dancing like smoke. "You were stolen from me before I could even give you a name. The Queen's Shadow appeared to collect you—quite apologetic about the whole thing. Said he couldn't disobey a direct order. He'd been told to return with the babe before sunrise, and return with the babe he would." Her tone softened. "But he lingered there, looking at me with expectant eyes. He gave me time to work out how to protect you from the dark magic Schön wields."

His mother hadn't left him. Hadn't abandoned him on the cool palace steps, to be picked at by vultures, should they please.

He'd been wanted, after all.

A tear slid down Red's face, and his chest tightened as Old Oma moved forward, crouching before him. Her weathered hands cupped his face, and he fought the urge to pull away. The touch felt foreign, wrong—yet somehow familiar, like a half-remembered dream.

"You were born with your father's beautiful blue eyes." Her thumb traced his eyebrow, her touch feather-light. "Those eyes made me fall in love with him the day I met him, chopping wood just by my cottage."

Red's breath caught. His father—where was he?

But Old Oma's fingers trailed down to brush against his red cloak, then she said quietly, "I had to give you three things for the spell to work. I chose an eye..." Her finger traced beneath his brown eye. "This cloak..." She tugged gently at the worn fabric. "And my heart."

Something cracked inside Red's chest. His hand flew to his chest, where his own heart thundered against his ribs. Three sacrifices. Three pieces of herself, given to protect him from the Queen's magic.

He peeled his throat open to croak, "You have no heart?" while glancing at Wim, who kept his face impassive.

Old Oma's fingers wrapped around Red's wrist, yanking his hand forward to press against her chest. Red waited for the familiar thud of a heartbeat, the rhythm that marked life itself.

Nothing.

His palm met only stillness beneath her skin. No flutter, no pulse, not even the faintest tremor of life.

"How are you still alive?" The words scraped past his lips in a horrified whisper.

A bone-chilling howl split the air, closer than comfort would allow. Red's spine stiffened at the sound—different from Wim's howls, darker somehow, as if it carried death within its notes.

"He's coming!" Oma's eyes widened with terror. "He's smelt you!"

Red's head spun with confusion. "Who?"

But Wim's growl held recognition. "Your soulstealing beast." His lips curled back from his teeth. "That's how you're still alive." In one fluid motion, he yanked up his sleeve, revealing his ugly scar that pulsed with an unnatural purple light. "Caught me mid-shift."

Oma's fingers traced the air above the mark, her face twisting with understanding. "You're a wildling."

"A healer told me that to cure myself, I had to come here and claim your heart." Wim's voice held a note of desperation that made Red's chest ache.

His mother reached for Red, but he jerked away, disgust churning in his gut. "You're stealing people's souls? Killing innocent travellers?"

"You don't understand—"

"What's there to *understand*?" Red spat out. "You're using some beast to murder people so you can live without a heart!"

Wim's hand settled on Red's shoulder, but he shrugged it off. The cottage walls seemed to press closer, that sweet-rot smell growing stronger until he could taste it on his tongue.

Old Oma's eyes filled with tears, and for a moment, she looked almost childlike. "But I must live! I must find a way to free myself from this place and finally destroy *her*!" Oma screamed the last word, balling her bony fists.

Red blinked, his rage momentarily derailed by confusion. "What do you mean, 'free?'"

"Your dear aunt"—Oma spat the word like poison—"bound me to the Dark Forest with blood magic. I cannot leave its borders." She gestured at the cottage windows, where twisted branches pressed against the glass. "She meant it as a death sentence, but I found... other ways to survive."

"By feeding innocent people to your pet monster?"

"By doing what I must!" Oma's voice rang through the cottage. "And if I never find a way to escape... Well, when Schön finally dies, her magic will die with her. The binding will break, and I can leave. Do you know how many winters I've been locked in this cursed place?" Her shoulders slumped. "I never wanted this. But what choice did she leave me?"

Red's hands clenched into fists.

"There's always a choice," Red snarled. "You chose to become a murderer."

Old Oma flinched as if he'd struck her. "You can't imagine what it's been like, being trapped here, year after year, watching my sister bring the kingdom to its knees. The power she has..."

"I know," said Red. "I've seen it. Where did she get it from?"

"The dark sorcerer Ulrich took us in when we were orphaned at five." Oma's voice trembled. "He raised us to serve him, turned us against each other—our own flesh and blood. His methods..." She drew a shaky breath, eyes haunted by memories. "They were more brutal than you could possibly imagine. He manipulated us into despising each other. Before we knew it, we'd fallen straight into his trap, hurling words and spells at each other, each more deadly than the last. When Schön declared her intentions to take the throne by force, there was nothing I could do. Though we were both taught by Ulrich, Schön was always more... ambitious with what she learned. But she wasn't content with just imprisoning me here," Oma spat.

"She had to destroy every sliver of happiness I somehow managed to build for myself. First, it was my lover—your father. Then, I watched her servant whisk my baby boy away."

"My father." The words felt strange on Red's tongue. "What happened to him?"

"He fell victim to her dark magic, like so many others," Oma said, her voice hollow. "The same magic that has kept Schön looking young and beautiful while she's ruled for over two hundred winters."

Red stared at her, struggling to process this information. "But that would make you—"

"Ancient?" Oma laughed bitterly, gesturing at her withered form. "Yes. I haven't always looked like this. My birds tell me your dear aunt uses her powers to maintain her youth and beauty, but I've had to focus my magic elsewhere as of late. Time has taken its toll on my appearance, but I endure."

Another howl pierced the air, closer this time—so close the sound vibrated through Red's bones. A deep, guttural growl followed, raising every hair on his body.

Old Oma's face drained of colour. She stumbled backwards, hands trembling as she pressed them against her chest where her heart should have been.

Wim moved like lightning, positioning himself between Red and the cottage door. His shoulders bunched, muscles tensing as if preparing to shift.

The door exploded inward with a thunderous crack. Splinters flew through the air as an enormous black hound prowled into the cottage. Its fur absorbed the firelight like a void, creating an outline of pure darkness. Yellowed fangs gleamed from a mouth that hung open, strings of black saliva dripping onto the floor where they sizzled and burned the wood. The creature's eyes blazed with an unholy purple fire—the same shade as the mark on Wim's arm.

The stench of decay rolled off the beast in waves, filling the cottage with the smell of open graves and rotting flesh. Red gagged, pressing his sleeve against his nose.

Old Oma's voice quavered. "Here he is." She gestured towards the monstrous creature. "Your father."

Twenty

Red jumped to his feet before staggering backwards, blinking rapidly as his gaze darted between Old Oma and the monstrous creature. The hellhound's purple flames cast dancing shadows across the cottage walls, each flicker making the beast appear larger, more grotesque.

This... *thing* was his father?

The same creature that had tried to take Wim's soul, biting him and leaving him diseased?

A burst of hysterical laughter escaped Red's lips before he could stop it, high-pitched and unnatural.

"You must be joking," Red said, no louder than a whisper. "That's not—he can't be—" The words tangled in his throat as another wave of that putrid stench washed over him.

The hellhound's massive head swung towards him. Those burning purple eyes fixed on Red's face with an intensity that made his skin crawl. One massive paw stepped forward, claws scraping against the wooden floor with a screech.

A growl rumbled through the cottage, deep enough to rattle Red's bones. Black drool splattered onto the floorboards, eating through the wood like acid.

"Stay back, my love," Oma said, with a note of tenderness that made Red's stomach turn. She stretched her hands towards the beast, palms up in a placating gesture. "We don't want to harm these two. They've come to pay us a visit!"

The hellhound's ears flattened against its skull, though it stilled at her words, eyes never leaving Red.

"I think we should leave," Wim said quietly into Red's ear. "Now."

But Red was solely focused on Oma. "How is this... beast my father?!"

The hellhound's jaws parted, revealing rows of obsidian teeth dripping with that same acidic saliva. It lunged forward, muscles bunching beneath its midnight fur.

"No!" Oma flung herself between Red and the beast, arms spread wide. "My love, please. Control yourself."

The creature's chest heaved, purple flames flickering brighter around its form. A keening sound, like metal scraping metal, tore from its throat. Did any part of the beast recognise Red as its kin?

Oma's voice softened as she kept her eyes locked on the hellhound. "Your father was a woodchopper, seeking rare darkwood that only grows here. He stumbled upon my cottage, half frozen and lost." Her lips curved into a wistful smile. "We fell in love over steaming cups of nettle tea and shared stories by the hearth."

The hellhound's growls quieted, reducing to a rumble.

"For seven blissful winters, we lived in peace. Then I fell pregnant with you." Oma's face darkened. "But my sister... that spiteful witch... Her network of spies discovered our happiness. She couldn't bear to see me content within my prison, while she remained bitter and alone." Oma's fingers curled into fists. "She cursed your father, twisted him into this form. And when you were born..." Her voice cracked. "She stole you away."

Red studied Oma's face, noting the lines of grief etched around her mouth, the shadows beneath her eyes. For the first time, he saw beyond the mad old witch's exterior. Here stood a woman who'd lost everything—her lover, her child, her chance at happiness—all because of her sister's spite.

The realisation settled like lead in his stomach. How many winters had she spent in this cottage, watching over her lover—a monstrous beast—all the while pondering the fate of her stolen child?

"And then, for her final trick, she was going to get me to kill you with this arrow." Red scooped up his bow, examining the golden arrow. "Is this even magical in any way? You were supposed to turn to dust…"

Oma's stare fixed on the arrow as if seeing it for the first time, her lips moving in silent words. The hellhound's purple flames intensified, casting a horrible glow across the cottage walls.

A low, guttural sound rumbled from the beast's throat as its burning gaze shifted between Red and the golden arrow. Its massive head lowered, shoulders hunching as if preparing to spring. The acidic drool fell faster now, eating holes into the floorboards with violent hisses.

Red took an instinctive step back, his fingers tightening around the arrow. The hellhound's eyes tracked the movement, pupils narrowing to slits within those eerie purple orbs.

"Mother?" Red whispered, the word unfamiliar on his tongue. He dared not look away from the creature. "What's happening?"

But Oma seemed transfixed, her own gaze locked on the golden arrow with dawning horror. "Put that arrow down," she snapped. "Before he—"

In a blur of midnight fur and violet fire, the beast launched itself at Red.

Time seemed to slow. Red could see every detail with horrifying clarity—the hellhound's body suspended in mid-air, jaws stretched impossibly wide, violet flames trailing like ribbons behind it, heat radiating from them. His heartbeat thundered in his ears, one singular thought crystallising in his mind: *this is how I die.*

A mass of grey fur burst between them. Buttons scattered across the floor, shreds of Wim's clothing floating through the air as his massive wolf form materialised. His grey coat bristled, hackles raised along his spine as he faced down the hellhound.

The two beasts circled each other, fangs bared. The hellhound towered over Wim, its shoulders twice as broad, its head level with the cottage's low-hanging beams. Black drool splattered onto the floorboards, eating through the wood with a hiss.

"Control him!" Red screeched, icy terror coursing through his veins. "Make him stop!"

She shook her head, eyes glazed. "I cannot. The curse has taken him too far."

The beasts clashed in a fury of teeth and claws. Wim's jaws snapped at the hellhound's throat while the monster's flames scorched the air around them. Their snarls filled the cottage, a symphony of rage that made Red's ears ring.

The hellhound's massive paw swept out. Its obsidian claws caught Wim's flank, ripping through flesh and muscle. Blood matted Wim's grey fur as he stumbled, a pained yelp escaping his throat. Three deep gashes stretched from his ribs to his belly, the wounds already starting to bubble and smoke where the hellhound's acidic touch had burned him.

Red's fingers trembled on his bow as the hellhound's claws tore through Wim's flesh again. With a wounded cry, the grey wolf crumpled, blood pooling beneath his massive form. His golden eyes found Red's, clouded with pain but filled with a fierce protectiveness that made Red's chest ache.

The golden arrow sat heavy in Red's hand. His gaze darted to Oma—his mother—who stood frozen against the wall, her face a mask of anguish. She'd lost him once. Could he make her watch as he destroyed the only thing she had left?

The hellhound loomed over Wim, purple flames casting shadows across its fur. Somewhere beneath that monstrous form lay Red's father. A woodcutter who'd fallen in love over cups of nettle tea. A man who'd never had the chance to hold his son.

But Wim...

Wim, who'd gone without to feed Red when he was but a stranger to him. Who'd made him laugh until his sides hurt. Who'd held him through frozen nights and kissed away his insecurities. Who'd looked at his different-coloured eyes and called them beautiful.

The hellhound's jaws parted, acidic drool burning holes in the floorboards beside Wim's head. Its muscles bunched, preparing for the killing blow.

Red's heart squeezed. He'd spent his whole life wondering about his parents, dreaming of the day he'd find them. But as he watched Wim's blood seep across the cottage floor, he realised something with startling clarity—he couldn't lose him. Not for anything.

Red nocked the golden arrow, drew back the bowstring until it kissed his cheek. Tears blurred his vision as he aimed at the hellhound's chest.

"I'm sorry," he whispered, voice breaking. "Father."

A piercing scream tore through the cottage as Red released the arrow. The sound ripped at his eardrums, his mother's anguish filling every corner of the room.

The golden arrow struck true, burying itself in the hellhound's massive chest. The beast staggered backwards, purple flames flickering around its form. The dying embers of its gaze fixed on Red, and for a heartbeat, he saw something shift in those otherworldly eyes—recognition, perhaps. Or accusation.

Red's stomach dropped. The arrow jutted from the creature's chest, but nothing happened. The beast took another step forward, acid dripping from its jaws onto Wim's prone form.

"It will turn her to dust," the Queen had declared.

Yet Wim had laughed with Astrid at the idea, calling it utter nonsense.

All Red could do was pray that the man who'd captured his heart wasn't about to be ripped to shreds by his own flesh and blood in front of his very eyes.

Red held his breath—

The hellhound's next step faltered.

Its purple flames sputtered, sparks fizzing. A strange crackling sound filled the air as cracks appeared across the beast's fur, spreading outward from where the arrow pierced its chest. Golden light spilled from the fissures, growing brighter with each passing second.

The creature threw back its head and *howled*—a sound of pure agony that shook dust from the rafters. Its form began to crumble, chunks of fur and flesh dissolving into glittering ash that hung suspended in the air before dispersing like smoke.

Within moments, all that remained of the hellhound was a pile of shimmering dust on the cottage floor. The golden arrow clattered against the wooden boards, its tip still gleaming as if freshly forged.

Red scrambled across the wood, his knees skidding through the hellhound's glittering remains as he reached Wim's side. The grey wolf's massive form shuddered with each laboured breath, blood seeping from the deep gashes across his flank.

Oma's wails echoed through the cottage, but Red blocked out the sound. His hands trembled as they hovered over Wim's wounds, unsure where to touch without causing more pain.

"Wim?" Red said around a sob. "Stay with me. Oh, please don't leave me."

If Wim died in his arms, right here, right now, Red wasn't sure what he'd do.

The wolf's form rippled, bones cracking and fur receding until Wim lay naked and bleeding on the floor. His skin had taken on an ashen pallor, sweat beading across his brow.

"Did good, didn't I?" Wim's words slurred together, his eyes unfocused. "Protected... my Little Red..."

"Shut up, you fool." Red yanked off his cloak, pressing it against the worst of the wounds. The red fabric darkened quickly with blood. "Save your strength."

Wim's hand fumbled for Red's, his grip weak and clammy. "Should've seen... your face when you... shot that arrow." His chest heaved with shallow breaths. "Beautiful... so fierce..."

"I said be quiet!" Red's vision blurred with tears as Wim's eyes fluttered closed. He tapped Wim's cheek roughly. "No, no, no. Look at me."

Wim's eyes cracked open, but his gaze wandered past Red's face. "It's so cold..."

"Don't you dare." Red pressed harder against the wounds, ignoring the way the acidic burns bubbled beneath his hands. "Don't you fucking dare!"

A weak laugh escaped Wim's lips, ending in a wet cough. "Always... so demanding..."

His eyes slipped closed again, head lolling to the side. Blood continued to pool beneath him, spreading across the wooden floorboards in a crimson stain.

"Wim?" Red's voice came out small, broken. He shook Wim's shoulder, panic clawing at his chest when there was no response. "Wim!"

Red's tears splashed onto Wim's bare chest, mixing with the blood that seeped between his fingers. His hands shook as he pressed the cloak harder against the wounds, but the bleeding wouldn't stop. The acidic burns spread across Wim's skin like poison, eating away at flesh beneath Red's palms.

A keening sound filled the cottage. Red lifted his head to see Oma crawling through the hellhound's ashes, gathering handfuls of the glittering dust and pressing it to her chest. Her wild hair hung in tangles around her face as she rocked back and forth, mumbling nonsense under her breath.

"My love, my love, my love..." She scattered the ashes into the air, watching them float down like twisted snow. Her fingers scraped against the floorboards, desperate to collect every speck. "Gone, gone, gone..."

Wim's skin grew colder beneath Red's touch. His chest barely moved with each shallow breath, the rise and fall becoming weaker by the second.

"Do something!" The scream tore from Red's throat, raw and desperate as he watched his mother's manic movements. "I know you're hurting, but he's gone now! My father is dead, but Wim might yet be saved! Please! He's all I have."

The words echoed in the cottage's silence. *All I have.* The truth of it struck Red like a physical blow. No family, no real home, no place to truly belong—except here, with this infuriating, protective, beautiful man who'd claimed his heart between stolen kisses and shared laughter.

Wim was his anchor in a world that had never wanted him. His safe harbour in a lifetime of storms.

And now he was slipping away, taking Red's heart with him.

Oma continued to scrape at the ashes, her nails leaving marks in the floorboards. Her mumbling grew louder, more frantic, a stream of nonsense punctuated by broken sobs. She crawled through the glittering remains of the hellhound, her skirts dragging trails through the dust.

"My love, my love..." She pressed her face into the ashes, inhaling deeply. "Your scent still lingers, even now. Do you remember how we danced beneath the blood moon? How you'd bring me darkwood flowers that only bloomed at midnight?"

If his mother had an ounce of sanity before, there was nothing left now.

Red's hands trembled as he held pressure on Wim's wounds. "Please," he begged. "Please, *mother*. Help him."

But Oma seemed lost in her memories, swaying back and forth as she clutched handfuls of dust to her chest. "We were going to raise our child together. Watch him grow strong and beautiful. But she took it all away. Everything, everything, everything..."

Suddenly, she stilled. Her head snapped up, eyes fixing on Red's face with an intensity that made him flinch. She crawled towards him, leaving smears of ash in her wake.

"My son." Her cold hands cupped his face, thumbs brushing away tears he hadn't realised were falling. "My baby boy." Her voice faltered as she studied his features, drinking in every detail. "From the moment I felt you kick inside me, you had me. All of me. My love, my soul, my heart. I swore I'd do anything to keep you safe. But it wasn't enough! She took you from me!"

Fresh tears spilled down her cheeks as she pressed her forehead against his. The scent of herbs and decay clung to her skin. Her gaze drifted to Wim's prone form, taking in the blood-soaked cloak pressed against his wounds.

"Will he take good care of you, this wolf of yours?"

"Yes!" Red clutched Wim's hand tighter, his voice infused with desperation. "The very best. He's protected me, cared for me, shown me what it means to be loved. Please, help him."

Oma's eyes softened as she gazed at their joined hands. A strange calm settled over her features, smoothing away the wild despair that had twisted them moments before. "Very well, my love." Her cold fingers pressed against Red's chest, right above his thundering heart. "Take good care of my heart."

Before Red could say anything else, she began to sing—an eerie melody that made the cottage's shadows dance. Green light spiralled from her fingertips, wrapping around her form like ethereal vines. The hellhound's ashes rose from the floor, swirling through the air in a glittering tornado that engulfed them all.

The magic pulsed through Red's chest where she touched him, spreading outward in waves of emerald fire. It flowed down his arms, through his hands, and into Wim's wounds. The acidic burns began to heal, flesh knitting back together as Oma's form grew increasingly translucent. Her song reached a crescendo, then abruptly halted.

Now shimmering like cobwebs in sunlight, Oma bent down. She pressed her fading lips against Wim's ear, whispering words in an ancient tongue that Red didn't understand before she straightened, her eyes meeting his one final time.

Then her body burst into thousands of tiny green fireflies that scattered across Wim's skin, each one sinking in and leaving healed flesh in its wake.

Red stared at the spot where his mother had vanished, her sacrifice burning behind his eyelids. A maelstrom of emotions churned in his chest—grief for the parents he'd barely known, gratitude for her final gift, and an overwhelming need to ensure it hadn't been in vain.

A gentle squeeze of his hand yanked him from his thoughts. Amber eyes fluttered open, still glazed with pain but unmistakably alive. Wim's chest rose and fell with steady breaths, his skin warm and whole beneath Red's trembling fingers.

"Wim!" Red traced the unmarked skin where deadly wounds had been moments before. "I thought—god, I thought you'd left me."

"Not a chance." Wim's large hand cupped Red's cheek, where tears still streamed. "*Never*. It would take more than a hellhound soulstealer to keep me from you, sweetheart."

Red surged forward, crushing their lips together. The kiss tasted of salt and copper, desperate and deep. He swung a leg over Wim's hips, straddling his lap as strong arms wrapped around his waist. Wim's mouth opened beneath his, a pleased rumble vibrating through his chest as Red's fingers tangled in his hair.

Their breaths mingled as Wim pressed their lips together, again and again. Red devoured each kiss hungrily, like they were the only sustenance he needed. He poured everything he couldn't quite say into the kiss—his fear, his relief, his overwhelming need to feel Wim alive beneath him. Wim responded with equal fervour, one hand sliding up Red's spine to cradle the back of his head, holding him close as if afraid he might disappear.

Eventually Red drew back, pressing his swollen lips together to smile shyly at Wim. His fingers slid up Wim's arm to land on his bite wound. Oma's magic had healed all of his other wounds—so why not that one too? But the raised, hot flesh still remained, and Wim hissed in pain at Red's touch.

"Is your beast still lurking within you?"

Wim's eyes squeezed shut, and a silence stretched.

"Aye," he eventually whispered, barely audible in the cottage's stillness. "Yes, it is."

Red's heart plummeted as his fingers trembled against Wim's skin. After everything they'd been through—the fighting, the revelations, his mother's sacrifice—the bloody curse *still* lingered? The beast still threatened to consume the man Red had grown to love?

"But..." Wim's eyes opened, and his hand found Red's chin, tilting his face up until their eyes met.

"But?" Red hardly dared to breathe.

"Old Oma told me something, right before she... disappeared." Wim's thumb traced Red's bottom lip. "Said I needed to claim *your* heart. That'd be my cure."

Red's pulse quickened, and he placed a hand on his chest. "What does that mean?"

"Reckon..." Wim's eyes glowed with sudden intensity. "No, I *know* it now. If you'd give me the gift of being my mate, trust me with that precious heart of yours... then this curse'll break."

Red's breath caught in his throat. The word 'mate' echoed in his mind, carrying with it the weight of forever. Of belonging. Of home.

"Yes." The word tumbled from Red's lips before he even knew what he was saying. "Yes, yes, *yes*, Wim. A thousand times, yes. *Please!*" Red's cheeks flushed as he caught himself. Here he was, practically throwing himself at Wim like some lovesick fool again. He straightened his spine, attempting to gather the shreds of his dignity. "I mean... that would be... acceptable, I suppose."

A grin spread across Wim's face, transforming his features from weary to radiant. His eyes crinkled at the corners as he gazed up at Red. "Acceptable, is it?" His large hands tightened on Red's hips. "That's quite the shift from 'a thousand times, yes.'"

"Oh, shut up." Red swatted at Wim's chest, but couldn't hide his own smile.

Wim surged up, capturing Red's lips in a searing kiss that stole the breath from his lungs. When they broke apart, Wim pressed their foreheads together, his voice rough with emotion. "My fierce, beautiful Little Red."

"So... are we mates now?" Red nervously laughed, eyes darting between Wim's very much unchanged bite mark and his face.

Wim scratched the back of his neck.

"Just say it!"

Wim's voice dropped to a low, rumbling growl that sent shivers down Red's spine. "I need to bite you."

"Bite me?!" Red's hand flew to his neck, eyes wide.

Wim shrugged apologetically, though his eyes gleamed with something primal. "Just a little bit."

Heat flooded Red's cheeks as his pulse quickened. The thought of Wim's teeth against his skin, marking him, claiming him... He tilted his head, exposing the pale column of his throat. "Do it! Do it now!"

Wim's gaze darkened as he stared at Red's offered neck. His nostrils flared, and a soft growl rumbled in his chest. But then he glanced around the cottage, taking in the hellhound's scattered ashes and the lingering scent of death. He shook his head, pressing a gentle kiss to Red's throat instead.

"Not in this old shack," Wim murmured against his skin. "I want to take you somewhere proper."

Wim slipped into his spare clothes, and then they were out of the house within the minute, Red throwing his stained cloak back on. He might never get Wim's blood out of it, but he didn't care one bit.

As they travelled back up the path towards the woods, Red turned to stare at the cottage. The chimney no longer puffed its thick grey smoke. Indeed, it was as if the house had died with Oma—it had none of its earlier presence. Now it looked sad, and alone.

As a child, he'd imagined his mother as a beautiful princess, swept away by tragedy. Or sometimes as a common woman who'd been forced to abandon him. In his darkest moments, he'd pictured her cold and cruel, leaving him on those palace steps without a backwards glance.

The reality had been... altogether something else. A witch driven mad by love and loss, twisted by isolation and grief. Her cottage had reeked of decay and desperate survival, her eyes wild with a darkness that spoke of too many winters alone with her memories.

And yet.

She'd loved him. Red could see that now, in the way she'd touched his face, studying every feature as if committing them to memory.

In how she'd protected him from the monster who would have destroyed him simply for his imperfect eyes. In her final sacrifice, giving up her very essence to save the man Red loved.

His throat tightened as he watched the cottage fade into the forest's gloom. She hadn't been the mother of his childhood dreams, but she'd given him something far more precious than those fantasies—she'd given him a future. With Wim.

Red glanced at the man walking silently beside him, his massive form a comforting presence in the growing darkness. Soon they would find somewhere private, somewhere safe, and Wim would claim him properly.

Red would have somewhere to belong.

His mother's final gift hadn't just been Wim's life, it had been the chance for them to build something real together. Something lasting.

"Thank you," Red whispered to the darkening forest, to his mother. "For everything."

Twenty-One

WIM

*M*ine-claim-mark-mate.

The burning need to claim Red clawed through Wim's chest as he walked behind him. Every step, every sway of those narrow hips, every swish of red cloak, drove him mad with *want*. He'd planned to lead them both far from this cursed place before claiming the one who belonged to him, but his control now stretched gossamer-thin.

The bond thrummed between them, raw and wild. Wim's teeth ached with the need to mark that pale throat. To pin Red against the nearest tree and—no. Not here. Not in this dark, gloomy place that reeked of death.

But soon. Very soon.

Red's scent filled his nostrils—wild berries mixed with lingering fear-sweat from their ordeal. But beneath it all lurked that intoxicating sweetness that made Wim's wolf surge forward, desperate to chase, to hunt, to claim.

Then another scent cut through the air—night-blooming jasmine. Pure. Clean. Perfect.

Wim lifted his head, nostrils flaring. The breeze carried promises of soft petals and secret places. He gripped Red's shoulder, steering them in a different direction.

"What are you—" Red started to protest.

"Trust me, sweetheart." The endearment rolled off his tongue like silk. "There's somewhere special nearby."

Red spun to face him, those gorgeously mismatched eyes so wide and so, so trusting. The sight knocked the breath from Wim's lungs. Gone was the haughty palace brat who'd stumbled into his forest. In his place stood someone raw and real—someone who'd sacrificed his own blood for Wim's life.

Wim crushed his mouth to Red's, drinking in his gasp of surprise. His hands found Red's waist, pulling him close enough to feel the thundering pulse beneath that milk-pale skin.

Memories of Oma's cottage flooded back—the sickening crunch as the hellhound's teeth had torn into his flesh, the copper tang of his own blood pooling beneath him. He'd known then that death approached on swift wings. The beast that was Red's father had meant to end him. Perhaps the hellhound only sought to protect its own mate—Old Oma—from a perceived threat.

Yet Red had chosen him, without hesitation. Had given up the chance to know his true parents, had watched his mother sacrifice herself to save Wim's life. The depth of that gift staggered him.

The witch's dying words rang in his ears: only by claiming Red's heart could he ever hope to be free of his feral sickness.

Red's fingers tangled in his hair, dragging him deeper into the kiss. Wim growled low in his throat, his wolf rising to meet that demanding touch. This beautiful, fierce creature had become everything to him.

He broke the kiss, pressing his forehead to Red's as they both caught their breath.

"It's not much further."

Wim grabbed Red's hand, half running through the Dark Forest, dragging Red along beside him.

The jasmine scent grew stronger as Wim pushed through a curtain of hanging vines. Seeing what lay beyond had his breath catching in his throat.

A hidden grotto.

Crystalline water tumbled down moss-covered rocks into a circular pool, its surface like polished obsidian in the dim light. Steam rose up from the water—a hot spring. The heat it generated filled the grotto with warmth, a pocket of bliss within the cold forest.

Along the water's edge, clusters of luminous fungi pulsed with blue-green light. The glow caught Red's face, painting his skin in mystical hues that made his eyes shimmer, and Wim's chest squeezed at the sight of it.

"It's beautiful here," Red whispered, releasing Wim's hand to crouch beside a patch of the glowing mushrooms. His hands hovered just above their delicate caps. The fungi's light rippled across the pool's surface, creating patterns that danced like starlight on the water. "I've never seen anything like them."

The awe in Red's words made Wim's wolf preen with satisfaction. Wim inhaled deeply, savouring how the jasmine mixed with Red's berry sweetness. Here, away from the oppressive darkness of the witch's territory, everything felt lighter. Purer.

Crossing his legs, Red stared into the pool.

It was breathtaking here. But something about the way Red held his back completely straight... a tightness to his jaw...

"What's wrong, sweetheart?" Wim ran his knuckles across Red's chin.

Red's shoulders tensed beneath Wim's touch. "I just can't stop thinking... that you have no choice in all this. Right?"

The words pierced Wim like an arrow. He dropped his hand, stomach churning over waves of panic at the fear threading through Red's voice. How could Red think that?

"You think I—" Wim couldn't finish the sentence. The mere suggestion tasted like ash in his mouth. *He's been through a lot,* he told himself. What with finding his long-lost parents and then the subsequent death of said parents not ten minutes later.

If Wim could take all the hurt away and give it to himself, he'd do it in a heartbeat.

"Well, it's true isn't it?" Red wrapped his arms around himself, shrinking away. "Old Oma said you needed my heart to break your curse. So now you have no choice. You'll never get to have a wolf-mate, because you were forced to mate with me, and then be stuck with me forev—"

"Stop." Wim's voice shook terribly. He shifted to face Red properly, fighting the urge to gather him close. "Look at me, sweetheart."

Those perfectly unique eyes met his, swimming with unshed tears.

"That first night in the forest, when I found you... I could hear your heart beating." Wim brushed away the tear that escaped down Red's cheek. "Didn't understand it then, but I do now—your heart was singing to mine all along. Everything we've got? It's real as anything. I promise. I wanted you since the first moment I caught your scent."

Wim hadn't known what the smell meant back then, but now he did perfectly: *mine, mine, mine.*

"When Old Oma said I needed your heart... well, it all fell into place. Makes perfect sense now, doesn't it? How you're the only one who could tame the beast in me, bring me back to myself when no one else could."

Red's lip trembled. "But still, now you're obligated to—"

"I'm not *obligated* to do anything." Wim caught Red's chin between his thumb and forefinger. "I wouldn't be asking to make you mine if I wasn't dead certain I want you by my side for all my days."

Red looked away from him. "But you can't be completely certain of that already," he mumbled. "Don't you want to wait a bit, at least?"

"No. I don't want to wait a day longer, because I already love you, you impossible fool." The words burst from him like a dam breaking. "Because watching you sleep makes my chest ache. Because your smile lights up the darkest parts of me. Because even when you're driving me mad with your stubbornness, I can't imagine wanting anyone else."

Red blinked rapidly, more tears spilling over. "But what if—"

"No what-ifs." Wim pressed their foreheads together. "I choose *you*. *You*, Red. Not because of any magic or illness. I wanted you *before* we found out you have Oma's heart. You know that in your bones, sweetheart. You've got to know it."

His voice was cracking more by the second. *Fuck*, what more could he say to get Red to believe him?

"And... after we are mates... I suppose we will go and live with your pack?"

Wim pressed another kiss to Red's forehead. "*Our* pack, sweetheart."

The thought made Wim giddy with joy. Everyone would love Red, he knew it already.

"But... I'm not a wolf," Red whispered. "Not a wildling."

"It doesn't matter," Wim replied forcefully. "You can still be pack."

"But I'll never be able to run beside you."

Wim shrugged. "I'll carry you on my back."

"Are... there any other humans there? Where your pack lives?"

Red's eyes lit up in hope and Wim's heart sank. "No... but don't you worry about that. And if any of them so much as looks at you wrong..." He rumbled a warning growl in his chest, and Red gave a weak laugh.

Red could have asked Wim not to return to his pack, but he didn't, and for that, Wim was overwhelmingly grateful. Wim would have agreed, of course, though it would have split his heart in two.

"What about the Queen? What if she comes looking for me? Sends her Shadow?"

Then I'll burn the world down to keep you safe.

Wim grabbed Red's hand, and squeezed it tightly. "We'll have to hope your mother's protection still stands."

"I suppose the Shadow helped my mother when the Queen sent him to steal me. Perhaps when he comes next, he can somehow be persuaded to form some trickery against her." Red's expression changed, eyebrows knitting together. "And... we will live in your cottage?"

Wim nodded through a pang of homesickness quickly replaced by images of Red kneeling by the fire, warming his hands while Wim cooked him the most delicious of meals.

Red's eyes widened. "Tell me about it."

"Built it myself, from the ground up. Three good-sized rooms, and a proper thatched roof that keeps the cold out. There's a large hearth in the main room—perfect for when you want to sprawl out on the rug with one of them adventure books you love so much. We could read them together."

Red hiccuped a laugh.

"And there's an enormous bed, all soft with feather pillows. Where I'll take my time making love to you before holding you all night, safe in my arms."

"Stop!" Tears were pouring down Red's cheeks, and his shoulders shook. The sight tore at Wim's heart—what did he say so wrong?

"I can't—" Red pressed his hand to his mouth. "You can't possibly want all that with *me!*"

"Course I do," Wim protested. "Come home with me, Red. I'll cook for you every day. You can spend your days keeping an eye on Toby, and your nights in my bed." Wim swiped at the torrent of tears flooding Red's face, as if he could permanently erase his sadness. "You'll never be alone again." He pressed their lips together, licking the salt from Red's lips. "I'll take such good care of you. Let me love you, Red."

But Wim must *still* be saying the wrong thing, because Red's tears weren't stopping. If anything, they were increasing by the second.

"Why are you still crying?" The words came out as almost a whine.

Red pulled back and scrubbed at his face with his sleeve. "It's just... I've spent twenty-four winters living in a dingy attic, with only spiders for friends, walking around the palace with my eyes on my feet in case I crossed paths with the Queen..." Red gave a watery laugh. "And now you're offering me a real home? With pillows and fires and—and—" He gestured wildly at Wim. "Everything I've ever dreamed about?"

Wim's chest constricted. He reached for Red, but he scrambled to his feet, pacing beside the shimmering pool.

"And you want to cook for me? And read adventure stories together?" Red asked, in almost a high-pitched squeak. He stopped abruptly, running both hands through his hair. "God, I sound mad."

"Not at all, sweetheart."

"I do! Because normal people don't get this excited about... about..." Red waved his arms again. "About cottages and cooking and—and someone actually wanting them!"

The raw vulnerability in Red's tone made Wim's wolf whine. He stood, catching Red's flailing hands in his own.

"Then we're both mad." Wim pressed a kiss to Red's knuckles. "Because I get excited thinking about cooking for you every day. About showing you our home. About watching you curl up by our fire."

Red's lower lip trembled. "Our home," he whispered, like he was testing how the words felt on his tongue.

Dropping to the mossy ground, Wim rummaged through his pack to find where he'd stowed away his necklace of milk teeth. He still remembered that day he'd threaded them onto the cord, one by one, imagining who he'd give it to.

Never in his wildest dreams would he have imagined it would be a loud, opinionated pipsqueak who was infatuated with a red riding hood, but there they were.

He wouldn't have it any other way.

Wim rose, pressing the cord of milk teeth into Red's palm. "May I?"

Red nodded, the bright glow of the fungi illuminating the smile on his face.

Wim's fingers found the clasp of Red's cloak first, releasing it with reverent care. The crimson fabric pooled at Red's feet like spilled wine. Next came the leather vest, its laces yielding one by one to Wim's patient touch.

The grotto was as warm as a summer's day, thanks to the hot spring, yet Red shook head to toe like a leaf under his touch.

"You're shaking," Wim murmured, brushing his lips against Red's collarbone.

"So are you." Red's voice wavered as Wim slipped the vest from his shoulders.

The cotton shirt beneath felt impossibly soft against Wim's calloused hands. Red lifted his arms, allowing Wim to pull the garment over his head.

He savoured each newly revealed inch of pale skin, mapping the smattering of freckles across Red's shoulders and down his arms. The blue-green light painted shadows across the planes of his chest. Alongside his wildly messy curls, he looked every bit a magical pixie. Beautiful. *Perfect.*

"You're so perfect to me," Wim whispered in Red's ear, as his trembling hands found Red's belt, working the leather free with deliberate slowness. Red's breath hitched as the last pieces of clothing fell away, leaving him bare beneath the star-scattered canopy.

It took moments for Wim to shed his own clothes, grateful for the warmth radiating from the pool. Then, gathering the necklace from Red's fisted palm, Wim lifted it high. The sharp teeth gleamed like pearls in the blue light as he lowered it over Red's head. The cord settled against Red's throat, a perfect fit, as though it had been crafted for this moment alone.

"My Red," Wim breathed, pressing his forehead to Red's sternum. The steady thrum of Red's heart beneath his skin sang of home, of belonging, of forever. "My mate."

Red's eyes were impossibly wide as he ran his fingertips over each of the teeth in turn, as if he were cherishing every one. "Thank you. I'll never take it off."

Red's hand travelled through the scruff of Wim's beard to cup his face, and Wim shut his eyes, leaning into the touch. Every gentle stroke felt like the first warm breeze after a long winter, thawing something deep within him.

Wim ran his hands over Red's ribs, still slightly protruding despite Wim's best efforts. When they got back home, Wim would hunt every hour of the day until he found Red enough food to eat.

Most importantly, he was going to love him so hard, it would become impossible for him not to love himself.

His Little Red was far from perfect, but those imperfections were what made him perfect to Wim.

"I knew it in my bones when I first caught your scent—you were meant to be *mine*." Wim dropped his tone to a seductive purr. "And now I get to have you."

Before Red had time to register what was happening, Wim brought the flat of his palm against his left buttock, giving him a very firm slap.

Red let out a yelp of surprise before his lips turned up into a challenging smirk. "Oh, will you now, wolf? You think you can tame me that easily?"

"Tame you?" Wim circled behind Red, trailing his fingers across bare skin. He ran a finger up and down Red's spine, then lightly squeezed his nape. "*Never*. I like you wild."

Pressed up against him, Red shivered into Wim's waiting arms. "Good, because—" His words cut off with another yelp as Wim landed another swat to his ass before kneading into the muscles, rubbing deep circles with his thumb.

"Because what, sweetheart?" Wim's arm pulled Red even closer to him, and he began nuzzling into his neck where the milk teeth rested. The scent of berries and arousal filled his nose, making his wolf growl with satisfaction.

"Because I bite." Red twisted in his arms, nipping at Wim's jaw through his beard.

The sharp sting of teeth sent heat coursing through Wim's body. He caught Red's wrists, pinning them behind his back with one hand. "Surprise, sweetheart. So do I."

Red's pupils dilated, eyes dark with desire. "Prove it," he said, on a heavy breath.

Wim dipped his head to Red's throat, grazing his teeth over the silky soft skin. "Last chance to run away, Little Red."

"I'm not going anywhere." Red pressed closer, defiant even in surrender. "You're stuck with me now."

Wim's heart raced with an intoxicating blend of primal hunger and a tender possessiveness he'd never known before. Red was his—all sharp wit and sweet surrender wrapped in soft, freckled skin that begged to be mapped with Wim's lips.

Wim ran his thumb over each of Red's nipples, teasing them into hard peaks. Red's sharp intake of breath sent a pleased hum through Wim's chest. Fiery blood flooded south as he savoured the feel of Red's responsive body.

"Fuck," Red gasped, arching into the touch. "God almighty!"

Wim chuckled, dropping to his knees like a devotee, drinking in the sight of him in the luminous glow. He pressed the flat of his tongue against first one taut bud, then the other. Red whimpered, then groaned as Wim nuzzled his face into the soft hair at the top of his prick, mouthing all the way to his hipbone.

"Please," Red panted, voice rough with longing.

Wim raised his head, eyes gleaming with desire. "I wish I could take my time with you," he murmured. "But I'm too impatient for you to be mine."

Red's glorious cock—so slender with its slight curve—was there waiting, fully erect for him without even the slightest of touches.

And as he pressed his lips to Red's shaft—that first touch deliberate and lingering—Wim's eyes never left Red's, two different stars shining in the dimness, making Wim's world entirely brighter.

With a hand on either side of Red's hips, he savoured the soft gasp that escaped Red, the way his body buckled ever so slightly. And then, in a single greedy swallow, Wim took Red fully into his mouth, taking him as far back into his throat as he could.

Red's reaction was instantaneous—a sharp, high cry, his fingers threading through Wim's hair. The pull against his scalp spurred Wim on, and he worked Red with relentless dedication, the wet suction of his mouth matched by the rhythmic squeeze of his hand around the base of Red's cock.

Every moan that tore from Red's throat, every shudder that racked his frame, every helpless jerk of his hips fed Wim's desire.

But it was when Red stopped pulling his hair, and started stroking it—in gentle, slow, rhythmic motions—that Wim became absolutely undone.

Between Red's thighs, Wim felt like a conquering hero. He owned every gasp and whimper, every stuttered curse and broken plea. Wim would not merely be Red's protector—he would strive to be his sanctuary, his solace in a world that had given him far too little kindness. He was determined to show Red just how cherished he truly was, to carve out a space within his own heart where Red would be safe and adored forevermore.

The hands stroking his hair became frantic, the only warning before Red's entire body went rigid. Red's cock throbbed against Wim's tongue before he tumbled headlong into his release with a choked sob, with Wim catching every tremor and wave, drinking him down as if his life depended on it.

How lucky Wim was that Red tasted as delicious as he smelled.

As the tremors subsided, Wim gently released Red from his mouth, planting tender kisses along his inner thighs before meeting his gaze once more. The sight of Red, disheveled and spent, cheeks flushed with the aftermath of his pleasure, sent a fierce surge of protectiveness coursing through Wim's veins. He would go to the ends of the earth to keep this magnificent creature safe. He would move mountains if it meant keeping that soft, contented look on Red's face.

Red's legs appeared to give way, and he half fell into Wim's lap, throwing his arms around his neck.

Wim gathered Red's pliant form into his arms, marvelling at his lightness. With utmost care, he laid Red on the soft moss, arranging his limbs with gentle touches. Red's eyes fluttered, heavy-lidded and content, as Wim positioned him like a precious treasure on display.

The ethereal glow transformed Red's pale skin, turning each freckle into a tiny star. His chest rose and fell with languid breaths, the necklace of milk teeth gleaming against his throat.

"Look at you, all laid out for me like this." Wim stared in awe at Red in all his glory. "How did I ever think you were a tasty snack? You're a whole fucking feast."

Starting at Red's navel, Wim dragged his tongue in one long, slow stroke up his torso, tasting salt and sweetness. Red arched beneath him with a soft gasp.

"Do it now," Red breathed. "Make me yours."

"Soon," Wim promised, resisting the alluring temptation of sinking his teeth into Red that very second. Because he was far from done with him.

A pout that could have melted stone appeared on Red's lips. Then his gaze flicked downwards, landing on Wim's straining arousal. With a growl of surrender, he leaned back on his heels, offering himself up to Red.

Red's eyes widened, and he quickly crawled closer, like a moth drawn to a flame. Delicate fingers wrapped around his sizable girth, and Red nuzzled into his groin for a moment. Then that perfectly small mouth widened as far as Red could stretch it.

Wet heat enveloped Wim's cockhead as Red devoured it in one fell swoop.

What a fucking sight.

What Red's mouth couldn't reach, his fingers took good care of—firm, wet strokes along his length in sync with his sucks.

Pleasure racked through Wim like lightning bolts, leaving him frenzied and breathless, fisting handfuls of moss.

Red looked up at him through hooded lashes before dipping a fraction lower, taking even more of Wim inside that sinful mouth of his. Wim's body gave a shallow thrust of its own accord, inching just a sliver more inside its magnificent tightness. He moaned around Wim's cock, delightful slurping sounds soon following.

Tiny licks from Red's small tongue teasing the hooded skin of his cockhead almost had Wim spending his seed right there and then—he could feel his balls threatening to draw up.

No. That wouldn't do. "Stop," Wim said weakly. "You're far too good at that, sweetheart."

Wim tugged gently at Red's hair, trying to guide him away. But Red only hummed in response, doubling down on his efforts with renewed enthusiasm.

"You little brat," Wim gasped, pushing at Red's shoulders, but Red only made a defiant noise, gripping Wim's thighs tighter, nails digging into the flesh. "You're going to get punished for this."

A wet bubble of laughter sounded from Red's stretched mouth, and Wim took his chance, pulling his cock out.

"Hey! I wasn't finished!"

"Oh yes you were." Wim lunged for Red, pushing him back onto the moss, pinning him with his body weight. "Someone's gotten rather bold," he hissed into his ear, then reached for his pack to find the oil in its tiny stoppered vial.

"Are you complaining?"

Wim slapped the side of Red's thigh. "Behave." Shifting to kneel before him, Wim gently hoisted his legs, resting them on his own. The position left Red exposed and vulnerable, but the trust within the depths of his eyes humbled Wim beyond words. It was a gift, and he planned to treasure it for all his days.

In a swift movement, Wim uncorked the vial and let the oil spill onto Red's entrance. The liquid glistened, inviting him in.

Slowly, Wim inserted his index finger, savouring the way Red's body clenched around it. He couldn't resist leaning in for a taste of Red's lips, stealing a kiss that left Red breathless and begging for more. Their tongues moved together, messy and fervent, as Wim added another finger, stretching him further.

"Kiss me," Red begged between panted breaths, his hips bucking against Wim's hand. The words sent a surge of desire through Wim, and he obliged, crushing their mouths together as he pushed deeper.

Within seconds, Red's breath turned into whimpers. "More," he demanded into Wim's mouth.

Wim laughed, teasing him with shallow thrusts before finally giving in, filling him completely with two long fingers. Red cried out, the sound echoing through the forest as he rocked against Wim's hand.

Overwhelmed by the intoxicating scent of their combined arousal, Wim could wait no longer—his neglected, untouched cock screamed at him for mercy, demanding Red.

As Wim withdrew his fingers, Red let out a wounded sound, desperate and lost. "Quickly!" he cried, panic etched in every trembling syllable.

Wim smirked, pouring more oil over his cock until it glistened in the dim light. Red cast a nervous glance towards Wim's shaft, biting his lip with something akin to uncertainty.

Leaning in, Wim captured Red's ear with his teeth. "Remember, you were made for my cock, sweetheart." His words barely a whisper against Red's ear, he added, "You were made to be *mine*."

He didn't give Red a chance to register what was happening before he lifted him up, light as a feather, cradling him against his chest as he stepped into the hot spring. The luminous toadstools cast shifting patterns across the water's surface, turning ordinary ripples into ribbons of celestial light. Steam curled around them as they descended the natural stone steps into the deeper water.

Wim settled them both into a smooth hollow in the rock, the warm water lapping at their shoulders. Red's head fell back against Wim's chest, his strawberry-blond curls darkening where they met the water.

The small waterfall tumbled over moss-covered rocks, its gentle song echoing off the grotto walls. Beneath its cascade, crystal formations caught the blue-green glow, scattering light like fallen stars across Red's pale skin.

"You're so damn beautiful." Wim traced the constellation of freckles across Red's shoulder with reverent fingers. The milk teeth necklace floated on the water's surface, each tooth catching the light like tiny moons. "If I tell you that every day for the rest of our lives, will you finally believe it?"

Red twisted in his arms, those brilliant eyes reflecting the surrounding glow. One blue like summer sky, one brown like autumn leaves—both equally precious to Wim.

"Maybe." Red's lips curved into that familiar half smile. "But you might have to prove it."

The waterfall's mist created halos around them, and drops of water clung to Red's eyelashes like diamonds. Here, in this magical grotto that seemed to exist outside of time itself, Wim could hardly believe his good fortune. That this fierce, beautiful creature had chosen him, had trusted him enough to bare not just his body but his heart.

For the first time, he was so incredibly grateful the soulstealer had bitten him that day.

Wim cupped Red's face in his hands, thumbs stroking over high cheekbones. "Just look at you," he breathed. "All lit up like this. Like you've got starlight under your skin."

Wim's cock, pressed against Red's thigh, gave an impatient throb, and Wim twisted Red so that he was positioned just above it.

"Lower yourself," he said, gripping the base of his length.

Red, arms wrapped around Wim's neck, did just that. Wim's cockhead soon nudged up against his tight ring, and couldn't help but *growl*.

The water lapped against Red as he continued to sink down in the tiniest of increments, biting his lip.

The primal beast within Wim demanded he thrust up into Red's deliciousness; it took a fair bit of self-control to restrain himself.

Red whimpered, his nails digging into Wim's shoulder blades.

"Shh, sweetheart," Wim soothed, his heart cracking at causing Red even the slightest bit of pain. "It'll feel good in just a moment. I promise. Kiss me."

He brought Red's lips to his, easing his tongue in softly, sliding it against Red's at the same slow pace he was inching his cock inside him. Wim glided his hand through the warm water to find Red's prick, stroking it gently, determined to feel it firm up once again.

When Wim was almost all the way in, he couldn't help but rumble appreciatively. "That's it," he breathed into Red's ear, pushing upwards just a tiny bit.

And when Wim was buried to the hilt, his beautiful lover heaved an almighty sigh of pleasure, and he claimed Red's mouth in a possessive, bruising kiss.

The kiss deepened—desperate, hungry—and Wim seized Red's hips, lifting him up, the feeling exquisite against his cock. Higher and higher he lifted him, until just his cockhead remained inside him.

"Ready?" Wim asked.

Red nodded.

Wim brought him down quickly, so that their bodies were flush together, and Red cried out, a sharp, blissful thing, tightening his arms around Wim's neck.

Wim lifted him up again, faster this time, and soon Wim was sliding in and out of Red quicker and quicker, intensifying the delicious friction. And as Red's body moulded to fit Wim's, Wim would have sworn their hearts beat in tandem, a primal drum that echoed through the night.

They kissed and kissed throughout it, and the air they shared was heavy with each other's breaths. Wim continued to stroke Red's cock in time with his own thrusts, delighted when it twitched and thickened.

Yes, he was making his Red feel very good indeed, and inside him, his wolf preened. Though his usually mouthy menace was yet to tell him such, and a small whine escaped his lips.

"Tell me how good I'm making you feel," he growled into Red's ear, before closing his teeth around his lobe, biting down hard.

Red gasped, a breathless prayer. "So, so good, Wim." His wet hands flew to Wim's hair, stroking back his tangled mane before scratching into his scalp all around his ears. "You're being so good for me."

A pleased little howl escaped Wim, and he fisted Red's hair, giving it a forceful tug as he fucked into him even harder.

The response from Red was instantaneous—he squeezed himself around Wim's cock, and he had to quickly bite his hand, lest he spend inside Red before he was ready.

He growled a warning at Red, who offered him a delightful laugh in reply.

Wim squeezed Red's hip even tighter, thrusting while subtly changing the angle just so—

Red screamed as he hit that special spot inside him.

Wim smiled smugly, not that Red saw it—his eyes were firmly closed, his face the very picture of euphoria.

"Who do you belong to?"

Red only whimpered in reply.

"*Who?!*" Wim surged into him with violent force, as Red clearly needed a reminder.

"You!" Red said on a groan. "You, Wim. Always you. Now. Forever. In our next lives."

There were no words for how good Red felt—he couldn't get enough. Wim was drowning and Red was air.

Wim brought his lips to Red's neck, and once he started, he felt like a man possessed. He licked and sucked and nipped around Red's neck, delighting in every whimper and gasp that escaped those perfect lips. He buried his face in Red's hair, inhaling the sweet scent that was uniquely his.

Red's hands were clutching at Wim's shoulders, his nails digging into his skin as he squirmed into him. Wim's lips found a particularly sensitive spot just above Red's collarbone, and he sucked hard, savouring the taste of his skin.

"I'm marking out where I will bite you," Wim murmured, his voice thick with delicious possessiveness as he tugged firmly on Red's curls. Red's whole body shivered in response, and it only made him more determined to leave his mark.

"Bite me!" Red begged, practically sobbing. "Do it now! Have me, Wim. Take me. Rip me apart. *Please!*"

Wim tugged Red's hair back, forcing him to look at him. "No," he said. "Not until you spend again with me inside you."

"*What?!*"

Wim continued to stroke Red's length, his touch firm and commanding. "You will," he insisted, his voice dripping with gravelly desire.

Red, panting and flushed, shook his head. "I can't," he gasped.

Abruptly, Wim decreased his thrusting, slowing his pace to an easy, torturous slide. "I can do this for as long as it takes," he growled, his eyes boring into Red's, then he continued to bathe Red's neck in kisses and nibbles, soft little nips, like they had all the time in the world.

As he stroked Red's cock in time with his slow, deliberate thrusts, Red whined as if pained, though his length grew harder and harder. Then Red's hips began to move involuntarily, his body writhing in the water, sending small waves crashing against the rocks.

"Fuck!" Red croaked, his eyes squeezed shut, his fingers digging into Wim's shoulders. "Wim!" His tone was panicked, his entire body trembling.

Red's prick pulsed and Wim quickly lunged for the back of his neck, grabbing a fistful of his hair. With a swift motion, he pulled Red's head back.

Time slowed as Red's eyes, wide with anticipation, met Wim's. In that moment, Wim could see the trust and desire that burned within Red. And so, he did what he had secretly been longing to do since the moment he first laid eyes on his bewitching red-cloaked menace.

Mine-claim-mark-mate.

A familiar burn rippled through his gums, his teeth shifting—not quite wolf, not quite human—as his canines stretched into something wild and wanting.

With a low, possessive growl, Wim leaned forward and sank his teeth into the tender skin of Red's neck, feeling the warm blood rush to the surface. Red cried out, his body bucking as his release exploded out of him, but he didn't pull away. Instead, he wrapped his legs tighter around Wim's waist, pulling him closer, deeper.

At the same moment, Wim felt a searing heat at the base of his cock, a pressure building that made his wolf howl with triumph beneath his skin. His body was claiming Red in the most primal way possible—the way reserved only for true mates.

The glowing toadstools seemed to suddenly pulse brightly around them, and in that moment, the invisible thread that had been tugging between them since they first met blazed golden-bright in Wim's mind, weaving itself into an unbreakable cord that bound them together.

That knowledge, combined with the pulsing of Red's body around his cock, was too much, forcing Wim's mouth to leave Red's neck. He threw his head back and *howled,* the sound filling the grotto, bouncing off the rocks to create a primal chorus that shook the stones.

Wim fully intended to fuck Red all the way through his orgasm and beyond, but then Red whispered those three little words...

"I love you."

Wim's control snapped.

With a final, guttural moan, Wim spent himself deep inside Red, his body shuddering with the force of his own climax. As his release flooded Red, the base of Wim's cock swelled rapidly, locking them together in the most ancient of ways. His throat tightened. Wim had often wondered if he'd ever experience the privilege of having a true mate. And here he was, his knot inside Red.

"God almighty!" Red gasped, his mismatched eyes flying wide. "What in the—are you getting bigger inside me?" His voice cracked, caught between a yelp and a moan. "Wim! I can't—it's—"

"Shh, sweetheart," Wim soothed, cradling Red closer as the knot reached its full size. "It's the wolf's way of claiming a true mate." He pressed tender kisses to Red's temple, relishing the exquisite pressure around his swollen base. "We're joined completely now."

Red's breath came in short pants. "You might have warned me," he said with a trembling laugh. "That your cock has... extra features."

A bead of blood dribbled down Red's neck, as red as his cloak. Wim pressed his tongue against it in an instant, licking up his neck all the way to his wound. The metallic tang mixed with Red's natural sweetness made his wolf howl beneath his skin. "Mine," he murmured against the sore skin, as he drenched the wound in saliva. It would heal within the hour, leaving just the lightest of marks—just enough to let the world know who Red belonged to.

Wim shifted slightly, causing Red to whimper as the knot tugged inside him. "We'll be locked like this for a while," Wim murmured against Red's ear, unable to keep the smug satisfaction from his voice. "My wolf making certain every drop stays deep within you."

Then, as the last waves of pleasure ebbed away, something felt... *different*.

The constant gnawing presence that had haunted Wim for so long—that primal beast beneath his skin—was no longer lurking in the shadows of Wim's mind. The persistent ache in his arm, a reminder of the soulstealer's bite, had ceased its endless throbbing.

Wim touched his biceps with trembling fingers, expecting to feel the familiar raised scar tissue. His breath caught. The skin was smooth, unblemished, as if he'd never been bitten at all.

"Red." His voice cracked on the word. He pulled back to stare at his mate with wonder-filled eyes. "My sickness—it's lifted. You've done it."

Red blinked up at him, eyes still hazy with satisfaction, their bodies still intimately joined by Wim's knot. "What?"

Ever so carefully, Wim lifted Red off him, easing out his spent cock, the knot now reducing.

"The beast inside me—it's completely gone." Wim pressed fervent kisses across Red's face. "You did this. You've given me back my life."

For many painful months the monster had bubbled just under the surface of Wim's skin. He felt strangely light without it—like he might float away.

He captured Red's mouth in a deep, reverent kiss that he hoped spoke of devotion and gratitude beyond his words.

When they finally broke apart, breathing heavily, Wim murmured against Red's lips, "You've given me everything. Given me back my freedom. Given me your trust. Your heart. I swear I'll spend every day earning all of it." His hand cupped Red's cheek, thumb stroking over the scattered freckles. "I'm going to spend the rest of my life making you smile, my fierce little mate. I swear it."

Red's eyes widened, a mix of joy and mischief dancing within them. "You swear it?" He lifted his pinkie finger, waggling it in front of Wim's face. "On a pack swear then, I hope?"

Wim couldn't contain his groan, the sound echoing off the grotto walls. Tobias was going to go absolutely nuts when he returned home with Red. "Come here, you menace."

Their pinkies linked together, water droplets sliding down their joined hands.

"I, Wilhelm Hoffmann, swear to dedicate my life to making you happy." Wim swallowed around a thick lump. "To protect you, cherish you, and love you with everything I have."

Red's cheeks flushed delightfully pink. "And I swear to be yours, always. To trust you, support you, and…" He paused, a smile tugging at his lips. "To stop being quite so dramatic about everything."

Wim snorted. "Now that might be a promise you can't keep."

"Oi!" Red splashed water at him.

"Time to seal it with a howl," Wim said, pulling Red closer. He tilted his head back and let out a long, melodious howl that reverberated through the cave.

Red attempted to join in, but what emerged was more of a strangled yelp than anything resembling a wolf's call. The sound bounced off the rocks, somehow managing to sound even worse with the echo.

Wim pressed his face into Red's wet curls, shoulders shaking with suppressed laughter.

"Oh, do shut up," Red grumbled. "We can't all be perfect at everything."

"Don't worry, sweetheart." Wim planted a kiss to Red's temple. "We have forever for me to teach you how to howl properly."

Epilogue

Two months later

R ed pressed his back against the rough-hewn logs of the city wall, his breath misting in the chill night air. The royal guards' boots scraped against the walkway above, their spears catching glints of amber lamplight as they patrolled between the watchtowers. Several handlers kept fierce dogs on thick leather leads, but none would match the raw power of his wolf, who crouched beside him in the shadows.

"Three more minutes until the shift change." Astrid's whisper carried on the breeze. Her dark eyes gleamed as she peered around the corner, tracking the guards' movements.

Red's fingers found the familiar worn fabric of his cloak, drawing it closer. The thought of seeing Auntie Anne again after these long months made his chest tight with longing. He'd promised Tobias a full performance of their rescue mission, complete with dramatic sword fights and daring escapes. The boy had sulked for days when told he couldn't join them, but even his fierce pout hadn't swayed his mother.

"Ready, sweetheart?" Wim's low voice sent a shiver down Red's spine as his mate's familiar scent wrapped around him like an embrace.

"You know me. I was born ready." Red tilted his chin up, meeting Wim's smirk and those amber-orange eyes that still made his breath hitch when they bored into his.

The guards above called out their positions, boots crunching as they began the changing of the watch. Red's pulse quickened as he counted down the precious seconds until their window of opportunity. The massive wall loomed above them, a fortress of timber that had kept him trapped for so many winters.

"Now." Wim's command galvanised them into action. He unwound the coiled rope from his stomach, the movement lifting his shirt to reveal a tantalising strip of skin...

Not the time, Red.

The grappling hook glinted dull bronze in the dim light as he tossed it to Astrid. She caught it with practiced grace, her movements fluid as she spun it in swift circles above her head. The hook sailed through the air in a perfect arc, catching on the wall's edge with a muffled clank that made Red's breath catch. His eyes darted to the guard posts, but no shouts of alarm rang out.

Wim tugged the rope, testing its hold. "Solid."

"Quickly now." Astrid's voice carried an edge of impatience.

But Wim's attention had already shifted. His dark eyes found Red's, that familiar cocky grin spreading across his face. "Kiss for luck?"

These past two months had brought countless kisses—lazy morning kisses tasting of herb tea, playful nips exchanged while hunting, desperate embraces in hidden forest corners, tender touches beneath starlight. Each one precious, each one stored away in Red's memory like treasured jewels.

"We don't have time for—" Astrid's hiss cut off as Wim reached for Red, strong hands gripping his waist.

The kiss blazed fierce and claiming, Wim's mouth hot against his. Red's fingers curled into the fabric of his shirt, drinking in the warmth of him, the solid strength. When they broke apart, it left Red's heart thundering against his ribs.

"For luck," Red whispered, straightening his cloak with trembling hands. Because what if Wim died tonight, during this crazy plan to rescue Auntie Anne—a selfishness on Red's part to not be without the woman who was the closest thing he had to a mother?

Red's mouth still tingled from the kiss as Wim gripped the rope. His wolf scaled the wall with impossible speed, muscles flexing beneath his shirt as he vanished over the top in the space of a heartbeat.

Red blinked at the empty rope, sharing a glance with Astrid in the shadows. The silence stretched between them, broken only by distant owl calls and the shuffle of guards' boots.

Beyond the wall, the palace rose like a gleaming beast against the night sky. Moonlight caught the silver-gilt window frames and alabaster towers that stabbed upwards into the stars. The grand architecture masked the cold reality within those walls—decades of isolation, of the Queen's cutting remarks about his eyes, of meals taken alone in his cramped attic room. His gaze drifted to that highest window, imagining dust gathering in the corners where he'd once curled up with borrowed books. By now, the spiders would have claimed his old bed, weaving their delicate webs across the wooden beams.

In the throne room below, the Queen would be holding court, perched on her gilded seat. Her perfect lips would curl with displeasure at some perceived flaw, her sharp words cutting deeper than any blade. How many times had Red stood before that throne, shoulders rigid as she dictated his future?

For twenty-four winters, others had carved his path—which clothes to wear, where he could go, how he would serve, when to speak, how to stand, who to be. But now... now he'd chosen Wim's rough hands and tender heart. Chosen pack bonds and forest paths, chosen love that saw past his imperfections to the fire burning beneath.

Freedom tasted sweeter than any palace feast, felt warmer than any velvet cloak. His chest expanded with the weight of it—this precious gift of choosing his own destiny. Of being chosen in return.

The rope jerked against the wall, swaying in tight movements. Red's fingers curled into fists, willing them to hurry.

"Thank Christ," Astrid muttered. "There's only twenty seconds left."

Two figures emerged from the darkness above—Wim's broad shoulders first, then Auntie Anne clinging to his back, her grey-streaked hair escaping its neat bun. Her maid's uniform caught the dim light, the starched apron a pale beacon. The sight of her made Red's chest squeeze. After tonight, she'd never don that uniform again. No more serving the Queen's cruel whims, no more sleeping in cramped servants' quarters. Astrid's spare room awaited, along with days spent minding young Tobias while his mother hunted.

They reached the ground with barely a whisper of sound. Before Red could move, Auntie Anne swept him into her arms, crushing him against her chest. The familiar scent of lavender soap and baking bread enveloped him—the same comforting smell that had soothed countless childhood hurts.

"My dear boy." Her voice wavered. "Your letter... when I read what you'd planned..." She pulled back, cupping his face between weathered palms. "And to think you found such happiness with your wolf. Though I nearly fainted dead when I read that part. And now I've seen him in real life..." The woman wolf-whistled, eyeing Wim up and down. "I have to say, you certainly weren't exaggerating, were you?"

Red felt his cheeks warm. The letter had taken hours to compose, explaining everything from meeting Wim to discovering his true parentage. Getting it to Auntie Anne had been another challenge entirely.

"Your messenger was quite resourceful," Auntie Anne whispered. "Slipped right past the guards dressed as a honey seller."

Red glanced at Astrid. "Your connection proved useful after all."

Astrid smirked. "My friend runs deliveries between villages. The palace guards know his face but not his allegiances. And he owes me several favours. But less chatting, more escaping," she demanded, already coiling the rope around her arm. "The next patrol starts in seconds."

They crept along the shadowed path, keeping close to the city's outer wall. Red's heart skipped at every snapping twig, every rustle of leaves. The familiar weight of his bow across his back offered little comfort—one wrong move could alert the entire guard rotation.

Wim's presence ahead carved a path through the darkness and Auntie Anne walked between them, her steps remarkably quiet. Perhaps all the avoiding the Queen's notice had taught her more than just which corridors to dodge.

Once they'd put enough distance between themselves and the wall, Red caught up to walk beside her. "What will the Queen think? How long until she notices your absence?"

Auntie Anne's laugh carried a sharp edge. "Oh, she won't notice for days, dear one. I've been preparing for weeks since your letter arrived. Called in every favour owed to arrange coverage for my duties." She patted his arm. "The kitchen girls will say I'm abed with fever, and Martha's agreed to bring meals to my empty room. By the time anyone realises, we'll be long gone."

"Clever." Red couldn't help but smile. He should have known she'd think of everything—she always had.

"The Queen's too wrapped up in her mirror these days to notice much else. The court whispers she hasn't left her chambers in days."

All the talk of the Queen—his aunt—sent an uncomfortable chill down Red's spine. He'd spent so much time desperate for her approval, never knowing the truth of their connection. Now that twisted bond felt like a rope around his neck, one he was finally cutting free.

"But have you even heard the news from the palace?"

Red's ears pricked up at Auntie Anne's question, though he'd spent the past two months trying to forget the palace existed.

"What news?"

"Both the Royal Shadow and the Queen's son have disappeared. Neither of them have been seen in months. Mind you, the Queen has been even more foul-tempered because of it."

Red's mind whirred. The Queen's Shadow, gone? Every evening Red had gone to sleep paralysed in fear, terrified he'd wake up to find Wim slaughtered by his hand.

Or he'd imagine himself waking up back in the palace, having been magically transported there by the geist, his cruel, sneering face laughing at him as he looked around in panic.

But to hear that he was somehow gone? Red's breath came easier, his chest expanding with a freedom he hadn't fully claimed until this moment. No more looking over his shoulder, expecting darkness to coalesce into that haunting figure.

"Where did Makellos go?" Red asked.

"Well, rumour is he's dead, but the Queen has been acting very strangely indeed recently. Nobody quite knows what's going on."

Makellos—dead? The perfect prince with his flawless skin and midnight hair. The boy who'd had everything Red had ever wanted: respect from the Queen's court, beauty beyond measure, a place of belonging, a name that meant something. Red had spent so many years envying him. How peculiar that Red now found himself holding his breath, silently bargaining with whatever deities might listen that the rumours weren't true.

Wim growled. "That woman's days are finally numbered. I can feel it in my bones."

The forest thinned as they approached the meeting point where Astrid had arranged a cart. Soon they'd be heading back to the pack lands—back *home*.

The thought caught him off guard. When had Wim's territory transformed from 'the pack lands' into 'home' in his mind?

Perhaps it was the moment they'd first returned there, after the long return journey. Tobias had launched himself at Red before even acknowledging his 'best friend,' tiny arms wrapping tight around

Red's neck as he babbled about how he'd told the whole pack about him. The pure acceptance in that gesture had stolen Red's breath.

Or maybe it was that first night in Wim's cottage, curled up in his enormous bed. The mattress was ever so soft, the pillows stuffed with countless feathers, and Red had been buried in soft furs that still carried Wim's scent. Red had never felt safer than when those strong arms pulled him close, Wim's chest warm against his back as they drifted to sleep.

Was it during those mornings learning to cook together, the little flour they had dusting their clothes as Wim taught him to knead what little bread they could muster? Or the evenings spent teaching Tobias to read by candlelight while Wim carved wooden animals nearby? Maybe it was the way Astrid and the other wolves included him in pack decisions now, valuing his opinion as if he'd always belonged.

The answer hit him as they crested a small rise. It was everything. Every shared meal, every casual touch, every burst of laughter. It was belonging without having to earn it, acceptance without conditions. Everything the palace had never been.

Red glanced at Auntie Anne, who'd gone quiet beside him. Her eyes were wide as she took in the stars above, no longer blocked by palace walls. She'd find that same acceptance among the pack, he knew. The same freedom to simply exist without judgment.

Wim caught his eye, that familiar warmth spreading through Red's chest at his mate's gentle smile. Yes, this was home—wherever Wim was.

Moonlight spilled across the dirt path as they approached the waiting cart. Red's legs ached from their rushed escape, but relief flooded through him at the sight of their getaway vehicle. The driver gave them a crooked grin and touched two fingers to his cap in greeting.

Wim moved first, his powerful frame easily climbing onto the wooden platform. He turned back, extending one large hand towards Red. His eyes glinted with warmth in the darkness. "Ready, sweetheart?"

The familiar endearment, once used to irritate him, still sent pleasant tingles down Red's spine, still caused butterflies in his stomach. He gazed at Wim's outstretched hand—those strong fingers that could shift into deadly claws, yet touched him with such tenderness. This hand had protected him, fought for him, loved him. And now it offered him another step towards their shared future.

"Yes," Red said, clasping Wim's hand and allowing himself to be pulled up. He settled beside his mate, heart full to bursting. "Let's go home."

The End

Thank you for reading Little Red Riding Hood! If you enjoyed the book, it would be tremendously appreciated if you could **take a moment to rate and/or review**. This really does make all the difference to indie authors!

Other books in the series:

Little Red Riding Hood by TJ Rose
Zel by Amanda Meuwissen
Hansel and Gerhardt by W.H. Lockwood
The Elves and the Shoemaker by Emory Winters
Cinder by D.N. Bryn
The Frog Prince by A.M. Rose
Rumpelstilzchen by Sam Northman
Snow White and the Seven Little Miners by Kit Barrie

A Bite for a Bite...

If you'd like even more Red and Wim, you might be interested in A Bite for a Bite: a GriMMMM bonus novelette. When Red and Wim are forced to take shelter from the snow at an inn, they bump into two people that look familiar. And that redhead has especially biteable thighs...

- The fairytale foursome of your dreams

- They all need a bite of Hansel's thighs

- Not even one bed... but they'll make do

- One night only vibes

- Red's small mouth is up to the challenge

- Hansel's dick is bigger, no, Wim's is

Follow the QR code at the end of the book to subscribe to my newsletter. You can find all bonus material in 'The Vault' section of my website.

Acknowledgements

Sam Northman – Thank you for being the first to read Red, and for supporting him through his small-mouth times. I'm excited for readers to get their hands on Rumpelstilzchen so they can learn all the sides of The Queen's Shadow!

WH Lockwood – Look, enough is enough. Maybe we should stop flirting in our acknowledgements sections and write a book together? Could be fun. Let me know your thoughts.

Thank you to the rest of my awesome beta team (Jordy, Arlene, T, Angela & Helen) for your excellent work helping whip Little Red Riding Hood into shape! Each of your inputs was tremendously helpful and I'm always so grateful for the amount of support I receive during my writing process.

Thank you to the other authors of the GriMM collaboration for being so fabulous to work with! Everyone's stories are excellent and I feel lucky to have found such an amazing line up of authors!

Thank you to my amazing proofreader, SJ Buckley, for polishing Red to perfection!

And finally, a massive thank you to Lina, our phenomenal cover artist. What a beautiful set of covers! I'm still over here drooling...

For links to my other books, newsletter, shop and social media accounts, scan the QR code: